Praise for RATTLE

"Amid the outpouring of crime novels centered on missing children, *Rattle* is up there with the best of them . . . A gem of a scary debut."—*The Times*

"Harrowing and horrifying, head and shoulders above most of the competition."—Val McDermid

"Vividly contrasts the apparent normality of suburbia with the awful truths it can conceal . . . A thriller that is capable of keeping you up all night—and then haunting your dreams. Creepy and accomplished, it is not quite as scary as Lecter, but close."—*Daily Mail*

"Serial killers don't come much scarier than the monstrous creation who haunts this astonishingly assured debut, which transforms London's leafy suburb of Blackheath into a realm of mythic horror . . . As the tension and urgency escalates, Cummins takes you on a macabre but riveting thrill ride."—*Sunday Mirror*

"Sharp, moving and wholly original."—Tammy Cohen

"*Rattle* isn't merely a creepy page-turner, it's also an affecting exploration of the inner lives of the female detective, the missing children, and their shattered families. Powered by a procedural element which builds towards a bold and chilling climax, this is as heartrending as it is gripping."—*Crime Scene*

RATTLE

FIONA
CUMMINS

PINNACLE BOOKS
Kensington Publishing Corp.
www.kensingtonbooks.com

PINNACLE BOOKS are published by

Kensington Publishing Corp.
119 West 40th Street
New York, NY 10018

This book was previously published in the United Kingdom by Macmillan.

ISBN-13: 978-0-7860-4258-6
ISBN-10: 0-7860-4258-3

First Pinnacle paperback printing: March 2018

10 9 8 7 6 5 4 3 2 1

Printed in the United States of America

First electronic edition: March 2018

ISBN-13: 978-0-7860-4259-3
ISBN-10: 0-7860-4259-1

PROLOGUE

On still nights, when the curve of a winter moon is smudged in the flow of the River Quaggy, the dead clamor for him.

He cocks his head and, through the whispering darkness, picks out the loosely formed sobs of the child.

The boy's mumbled distress pulls at him across the sweep of the city, and he fights the urge to leave at once. Even the passing of the years cannot quiet the shiver that swells through him as he contemplates a lifetime's work.

From every generation, a collection of its own. His father, his father's father, and the men who walked before them.

But now it is *his* time, his privilege and his duty.

He savors the way the moon seeps through the slats in the blinds at his father's house, and the wash of light on the bones.

Ribbons and sheets of ossified matter. Stalagmites and bridges. Twisted plates and bony nubs. A plaque engraved with the letter *C*.

The shadows in the house deepen. He stands alone

in the hallway, drinking in the glory of the skeleton in its glass case, mesmerized by its distortions, the incursion of bone into thoracic cavity, the calcified trimmings decorating his spine.

A young boy trapped in a prison of stone.

For years he has been seeking this rarest of specimens, searching amongst the dead and the living. Always looking, always hoping.

And now, after all this time, he has found another one.

FRIDAY

ONE

3.21 p.m.

If Erdman Frith had chosen pizza instead of roast beef, his son might have been spared.

If Jakey Frith had been a little more ordinary, the bogeyman that stalked the shadows of his life would have been nothing more than a childhood memory, to be dusted off and laughed at on family occasions.

If Clara Foyle's parents had been a little less self-absorbed and a little more focused on their five-year-old daughter, her disappearance might never have happened at all.

As for Detective Sergeant Etta Fitzroy, if she hadn't been haunted by thoughts of what might have been, of what *she* might have been, both children would have tumbled from the blaze of newspaper headlines into the darkest reaches of infamy.

But none of them suspected anything of this on that wet November afternoon, just hours before their lives collided and cracked open to reveal the truth of them all.

Especially not Erdman Frith, who was dithering in the freezer section: aisle three for pepperoni and a pension; aisle five and he might as well be as dead as the lump of sirloin he was lifting into his cart.

No, Erdman Frith wasn't thinking about death at all. He was more concerned with what Lilith would say when she saw . . . dum . . . dum . . . dummmmm . . . Red Meat.

Erdman pictured her, lips pursed tighter than a gnat's arse.

"What about the saturated fat content, Erdman?"

"Doesn't red meat contribute to bowel cancer, Erdman?"

The gnat's arse would pucker.

"Or mad cow disease, Erdman. They claim they've eradicated it, but who's to say they're telling the truth?"

Did she honestly expect him to answer that?

Once upon a time he'd have teased the worry lines from her face, firing silly jokes at her until they were both laughing, and she would lean into him, fingers tangling his hair, breathing him in, her fears forgotten.

"Why do they call it PMS, Lilith?"

"I don't know, Erdman, why do they call it PMS?"

"Because mad cow disease is already taken."

Bada bing.

But these days he couldn't even raise a smile.

These days, her eyes followed Jakey's every move, her fears not forgotten, but amplified a thousandfold by a cruel enemy that was reducing their son—and now their marriage—into paper butterflies, fragile and easily broken.

They told their boy, Lilith and Erdman, that he had a little problem with his bones. That was something of an understatement. Jakey's "little problem" would end up killing him.

The medical team who'd delivered him had suspected it immediately, thanks to the telltale malformation of his big toes. Fibrodysplasia ossificans progressiva. Thirty-five letters. A letter, give or take, for each year Jakey was expected to live. The average life expectancy. Any more would be a bonus.

By chance, a nurse in the maternity unit had spent the previous six months working in an Australian hospital where a teenager had reported with strange bony growths and increased loss of movement. They'd injected painkilling drugs into her muscles, she'd explained, surgically removed the extra ribbons of bone, and all they had done was make it a million times worse. By the time she was diagnosed, she was practically a statue, barely able to move at all, except to speak. She could still speak. The nurse had told them that as if it was some kind of blessing.

Six years on, even the specialists were shocked at the speed of the progression of his illness. Jakey's flare-ups were unusually severe for one so young. His body was following the characteristic path of the disease, but already it had reached his arms much earlier than they'd anticipated. A fall or a bump could trigger a life-threatening episode.

They were told to enjoy their time with their son.

Erdman's fingers grazed the cool, damp packaging in his cart. He should put it back. Lilith would kill him and he didn't want to upset her, not really. He longed for the joyous freedom of their love, before it was tangled up in hospital appointments and medications. But he was weary of always doing what she told him to do.

Anyhow, *he* didn't have BSE or CJD, or whatever the hell it was, and he was pushing forty. If that metaphorical cowpat was heading his way, it would have dumped on his life by now, which, let's be honest, was already shitty enough. Even if the worst did happen, he wouldn't notice the transition from middle-aged man to vegetable. A potato had more fun than he did.

Fuck it. Jakey loved roast dinners and he needed building up.

Had Erdman known that he was sealing his son's fate in that most glamorous of locations, Tesco on Lewisham Road, the whole family would have become vegetarian. But he didn't, and so he headed home, smug in the knowledge that, as he had done the shopping, it was his prerogative to decide what they had for tea.

TWO

3.23 p.m.

"*Ip dip doo. The cat's got the flu, the monkey's got the chicken pox, so out go you.*"

Poppy Smith was pointing straight at her, giggling through the gap in the top row of her teeth, but Clara Foyle wasn't smiling.

"Not playing," said Clara, and turned her back on the small knot of children and their game of tag.

She marched off in the direction of the gates at the far end of the playground, her hands buried deep into her pockets. It was almost empty, just a few stragglers waiting for the older boys to finish an impromptu game of football. Poppy called after her, making lobster claws with her fingers, and everybody laughed, but Clara pretended not to hear. Poppy's mother was supposed to be looking after Clara, but she was gossiping with another mother, her back to the little girl, and didn't notice her wandering off while Poppy was too busy whispering with the others to see.

That was his first stroke of luck.

Mrs. Foyle called them scavengers, those playground mothers who gathered in impregnable clusters at the school gates every afternoon. To Clara, they looked like birds, with their bobbing heads and pink lipstick and pretty clothes. She didn't know that some birds liked to pick clean the bones of other people's lives.

Five minutes earlier, she'd tugged on Poppy's mother's coat and whispered that she needed to go to the toilet. Mrs. Smith hadn't answered, but carried on talking, flapping her arms about like wings. Clara had squeezed her legs together and hopped about a bit, but now her tights were damp and chafed against her thighs when she walked.

"No, Mummy, I don't like Poppy anymore," she had whined to her mother that morning when Mrs. Foyle had explained who would be picking her up.

"I'm sorry, my darling, but it can't be helped. You'll have a lovely time. Anyway, it's Gina's afternoon off, and I've got an appointment."

Clara had sulked and cried, but it had done no good. Her mother would not be swayed. To Mrs. Foyle, perfectly coiffed hair was more essential than breathing.

The wind flexed its muscles, skittering leaves across the playground. Clara was cold, and her head ached, and she wanted her mum. She patted her backpack to make sure her purse was still there. The children were not supposed to take money into school, but Clara had slipped it into her bag after breakfast, when Gina wasn't looking. She liked the sound the coins made when they clanked together.

The chilly air pinched again. It made her think of her father, and the way he squeezed her cheeks between his fingers, leaving them reddened and sore.

Clara shivered and fumbled with the zipper of her coat. Mrs. Lewis, her homeroom teacher, caught her eye through the staff room window and waved. She lifted a shy hand in return, and shouldered her backpack, which was almost as big as she was.

The side gates stood open. Mr. Crofton, the caretaker, would lock them on his late-afternoon rounds, but for now the heavy metal bars were fixed in place against the green railings, the path to freedom unchallenged.

Between jackhammer thumps of her heartbeat, Clara slipped through the school gates and stood on the pavement outside. A shiver that had nothing to do with the wind tickled her insides. Quickly, she glanced back. Across the concrete expanse of the playground, Poppy was playing with Sasha, and Poppy's mother was still talking and flapping. Three more steps, and Clara would be around the corner and out of sight.

The little girl grinned nervously to herself.

Across the road, a man in a black pin-striped jacket unfolded his body from the car that had been parked there every afternoon for two weeks. He also began to walk. His strides were longer than hers and he soon overtook Clara, but she was too intent on her own escape to notice him.

A few streets on, a woman coming out of a convenience store thought it was strange to see the girl walking home by herself through the Friday afternoon dusk. She registered Clara's uniform hat, looked for an adult, and vaguely noted the man in the black pin-striped jacket. His eyes held hers, and in that frozen moment, she was reminded of her family's elderly dog. He had died that summer after being eaten from the inside by maggots, an awful, prolonged death by fly-strike. When she had found Buddy, still alive but in shock, his eyes had been empty. As empty as this man's. A powerful sense of revulsion overcame her, and the plastic bottle of milk she was carrying, slick with condensation from the cooler, began to slide from her fingers. The man looked away, and the woman remembered to tighten her grip before the milk hit the pavement and burst.

She forgot his face almost instantly.

The man turned into a shop next to the one the woman had just left. It was empty, save for the shopkeeper, who was talking on the phone in Punjabi, the hard line of his jawbone holding the receiver against his shoulder while he scribbled figures on a scrap of paper. He was calculating how much it would cost to install CCTV, and didn't look up at his customer.

The jars drew Clara in behind him. She loved sweets, and here were rows and rows of brightly colored gobstoppers and toffees in shiny wrappers and cola bottles and chocolate raisins and rainbow crystals of every flavor.

One-two-three-four-five different colors, counted Clara in her head. *Five. The same number as me.*

Her stomach growled. Lunch had been almost four hours ago, and she had wrapped her turkey pie in a napkin and dropped it in the trash while Mrs. Goddard was shouting at Saffron Harvey for spilling peas all over the dining hall floor.

The man wearing a black coat stood in front of her. Because Clara was so small she could not see his face, just a five-pence-sized patch of what looked like rust intersecting the fine white stripes of his pocket. Even though she was young, she knew about rust, because her father had been complaining about the gardener letting the tools go rusty, and had shown her the rake. It wasn't rust, though. It was dried blood. And she didn't know anything about blood. Not yet.

"A quarter of Raspberry Ruffles, please," he said.

When Clara left the shop a few moments later, clutching a paper bag of strawberry bonbons in one hand and her change in the other, the man was waiting outside, leaning against some railings.

"Whaddya get?" He was cheery, friendly, rifling through his own paper bag before selecting a sweet and removing its wrapper. He popped the chocolate into his mouth and grinned at the girl.

"Mmmm . . . delicious . . . do you want one?"

He shook the bag at her, and she took a step backwards. Her backpack bumped against the telegraph pole, making her stumble.

"S'okay, I won't bite."

The bag quivered again, and she leaned forward, suddenly entranced by the gleaming twists of pink. She reached out a hand to help herself, and the man's bony fingers closed around her wrist.

"Mummy asked me to walk you home. 'Cos you don't like the dark. Okay?"

With a shy nod, she allowed herself to be guided down the street, and towards a block with a row of crumbling garages. A late-afternoon mist was beginning to drift down, blurring the parked cars and the pavement ahead. Dusk was due at 4.09 p.m., and it was touching twenty to.

She sidled closer to the man, nervous of him, but more nervous still of the darkening day, the rapid leaching of color from sky. He turned to look at her, his eyes black clots.

The street was narrow with squat blocks of flats on either side. The buildings had no front gardens, just a concrete strip dotted with overflowing garbage cans. One or two of the upstairs flats were in darkness, but most of the downstairs ones had light blazing from their windows, and her eyes were drawn to the giant TV screens in more than one sitting room. Her tummy rumbled again, and she slid her left hand into her pocket and plucked out a bonbon. The pink dust left a trace on her fingertip. She sucked hard on its sweetness, which, for a moment, carried away the bitter, anxious taste in her mouth.

Clara lived on Pagoda Drive in Blackheath, an enclave of exclusive properties a world away from this neighbourhood, with its graffitied slide standing on a patch of scrubland. She had her own bedroom, painted in pink, and a matching wardrobe stuffed with Disney princess dresses. Sleeping Beauty was her favorite.

She tried to tell the man that she had changed her mind, that she would try to find her own way home, but he didn't hear her. He was striding along, still gripping her wrist in his hand. When she tried to wriggle it free, his nails dug into the pale strip of flesh protruding from the cuff of her coat.

At the end of the empty street was a disused factory with several broken windows and a DO NOT ENTER sign. Parked in front was a dented grey Ford van with no windows.

The man turned to the girl, and this time there were no friendly crinkles around his eyes. Still holding her wrist, he waved his keys, and the van made a bleeping sound. He jerked his head towards it.

"Get in." His voice was gruff.

Clara didn't want to get in his van, so she shook her head and tried to pull away, but her small frame was no match for him. As she opened her mouth to scream, he wedged his hand between her teeth. She bit down hard. He did not cry out, but the anger was there in the threat of his eyes, the bruising of his fingers into delicate skin.

She was struggling and tried to kick her legs, like she'd been taught in swimming, but it was no good. The man put his other arm around her waist and hoisted her in. He climbed in behind her and slammed the doors.

Poppy's mother, Mrs. Smith, noticed that Clara was gone about six minutes after she had left the playground. By the time she had scoured the school grounds, and used her mobile phone to call the police, the skies had darkened and the van was driving away.

THREE

5.56 p.m.

Two hours and seventeen minutes after Clara Foyle was abducted, Erdman sat down opposite his family. Lilith was cutting up Jakey's carrots, her mouth a seam of displeasure; Jakey was singing under his breath, his mind elsewhere.

Erdman ran his fingers through his hair, or what was left of it, as dull as the paintwork on Jakey's toy car. The one he'd left in the wading pool for two weeks, and was now next to useless.

Useless.

That was a word he was well acquainted with. He could never quite shake the feeling that he hadn't lived up to expectations: his mother's, Lilith's, his own. He'd always convinced himself there was plenty of time, but as his waistline thickened and his hair thinned, he was uncomfortably aware that his life was, in all probability, closer to its end than its beginning.

Glancing at his son, Erdman's heart gave a funny sort of jump. Jakey prompted in him a curious mixture of protectiveness and bafflement that, even after five years, he struggled to understand. Jakey's lips moved, but Erdman couldn't make out the words.

As he tried to find a way into the silence, Lilith grimaced at her plate. She'd worn the same expression in bed that morning when he'd accidentally stroked her thigh.

"Are you going to carve the meat or what?" The gnat's arse shriveled. "I mean, really, who has roast dinner on a Friday night?"

The words of conciliation on his lips congealed. Appetite dwindling, he gazed at the beef, marbled with fat and running pinkish juices, and switched on the carving knife. Its low buzz reminded him of the noise he sometimes heard from the locked bathroom door, when Lilith announced she was having a soak, so could she have half an hour's peace, please. He wished he hadn't bothered to sneak home early and had gone to the pub instead.

Lilith was staring through rain-blurred windows into the dark square of their garden. He wanted to drag her back into his life, but he didn't know how.

A memory surfaced, unexpectedly, of a pub lunch a couple of months after they'd met.

He'd always been wary of large groups, but she'd charmed his friends with funny stories from the school where she'd once worked. As they left, she'd slipped her hand into his, and he could still remember his absurd sense of pride.

God, he missed her.

Jakey's singing went up several notches. It often did at mealtimes. Erdman wondered if it was his son's way of drowning out the sound of a family's disintegration.

"What's that song?" said Lilith, her brow creasing.

"Shiiiiiiiiiiiiiiiiiiiiiit! I mean, ow, *ouch*."

A burn of pain lit Erdman's finger as the blade slipped and bit deep, its serrated teeth slicing through skin and subcutaneous tissue. Jakey stopped singing, saucer-eyed. The water in their glasses vibrated. Erdman's empty plate was spattered with ruby droplets, like a grisly version of the Jackson Pollock he'd seen at the Tate last month.

The knife spun in frantic circles until Lilith switched it off. As Erdman staggered against her, he was briefly aware, for the first time in several months, of the fullness of her breasts.

After a few seconds, the heady sensation lifted, and he looked down at his hand, which she'd wrapped in a napkin after lowering him into the chair. He could have sworn the fabric was white, but now it was a vivid scarlet.

"Get Daddy some water," said Lilith. The boy didn't move. "Go on."

With a six-year-old's reluctance to leave the bloodied scene of the action, Jakey limped into the kitchen. As he reached the archway, he turned to look at his father. Erdman managed a smile. And a little wave. With his left hand, obviously.

It was starting to sting, his finger. *Shit*. Erdman rested his injured hand on his thigh while Lilith lifted a corner of the damp linen. Fresh blood *plip-plipped* with purpose, speckling the pale laminate floorboards. He couldn't bring himself to look at the cut, that thick flap of ruined skin. Lilith's sharp intake of breath told him all he needed to know.

Outside, a car alarm went off.

Not a car alarm.

Jakey.

Lilith dropped his hand and sprinted towards the kitchen. When Erdman stood, the walls rippled like the inside of a swimming pool. As soon as they'd stopped moving, he stumbled after her. His heart filled his mouth at the scene before him.

Jakey was sprawled across the floor, one arm beneath his body, the other stretched out in front of him. His head was twisted on its side. A stool had been tipped over. Fragments of glass were strewn across the tiles, and water was pooling near the oven.

Lilith's face was stricken, guilt and fear and accusation rolling across her features. Jakey was struggling to sit up, gulping and crying.

"Nice and easy does it, sweetheart," said Lilith.

Pushing aside his own pain, Erdman held out his uninjured hand to his son.

"Where does it hurt, champ?"

Jakey didn't reach for his father as he usually would. Instead he drew in a shuddering breath, winced, and began to cry again. For the briefest of moments, Erdman's eyes met Lilith's.

"My arm, Daddy," he said, through a waterfall of tears. "I fell on my arm."

As Lilith helped Jakey to his feet, Erdman was assessing the damage. Jakey's working arm, the one he used to eat and drink and play and write, was now hanging by his side at an odd, awkward angle. Already, it was beginning to swell, and reminded Erdman of a fat pink sausage, about to burst its skin. The other arm, rigid and unyielding, was drawn in at the elbow, fixed in that position since Jakey was three.

"Anywhere else, Jakey?" he said. "Did you bump

your head? Fall on your knees? What about your ribs? You need to be careful when you're using your stool—we've told you that a hundred times before. Didn't you use the handrails? Why didn't you get the bottled water from the fridge?"

His son's bottom lip quivered, and he began to sob again, noisily and messily. From the way Lilith was glaring at him, Erdman knew he'd pushed it too far. Jakey still hadn't moved his arm, and now it was a strange, mottled purple.

"Sit down, sweetie," said Lilith. "I'll get you a drink. And one of those biscuits you like."

Lilith's whisper was hot in Erdman's ear as she reached into the cupboard behind him for a glass. For a moment, he remembered the feel of her mouth on him, but the pain in his hand and concern for Jakey pulled him back to the present.

"Listen, you need stitches. It's a deep cut. Nasty. And I don't want to scare Jakey, but we'd better get him down to the ER, too. I'll give him his steroids now, but he'll probably need an X-ray." Her own mouth trembled. "I think his arm is broken."

Erdman groaned, regretting the wasted meal, but truth be told, his appetite had deserted him.

Jakey swallowed down the anti-inflammatory. His tears had quieted, but now they tracked silently down his face. Using his good arm, Erdman hoisted his son onto his hip, careful not to knock him. After a few seconds, his bicep started to ache, but he ignored it and carried Jakey outside to the car. The security light flicked on, the blood from Erdman's hand leaving a trail of spots on the driveway. His son shifted in his arms to look at them.

"Are you going to die?" Jakey's face was a pale moon against the winter night sky.

"'Course not, champ," said Erdman. He buckled Jakey into his seat and kissed his hair. "Daddy just needs a couple of tiny stitches." He forced his voice to steady. "And we need to get you checked over. Can't have you with a bad arm."

As Lilith drove them to the hospital, Jakey began to sing again. His voice was quiet, but Erdman was sitting next to him in the back, and could make out his son's clear notes above the drone of traffic.

Unlike Lilith, he *did* recognize the song that Jakey was singing. He recognized it, because Carlton—Erdman's brother—had sung it with him when they were little.

And Carlton had been dead for thirty-six years.

At the Royal Southern, Jakey and Lilith were directed to the children's emergency room, while Erdman had to wait an hour for a harassed intern to inspect his wound. His name tag announced him as Dr. Hassan.

"It looks like you've nicked the bone, but I don't think you've damaged the tendon." He peeled off his latex gloves. "It'll probably ache for a few days, but you did the right thing by coming in. It'll heal faster with stitches."

The curtain swished and Lilith's head poked around. Erdman could see her knuckles were white with the effort of pushing Jakey in his hospital-issue wheelchair.

In summer, the merest hint of sun made his freckles pop like a dot-to-dot puzzle. That November night, the 16th, Jakey's skin was completely colorless, as if the network of veins and vessels just below the surface was filled with milk.

"Sorry," she mouthed at the doctor. "I just wanted to let my husband know what's happening with our son." She didn't wait for permission to speak, but she was smiling. "They don't think it's broken, but he's going for an X-ray, just to be sure."

The balled fist in the pit of Erdman's stomach unclenched.

"Seriously? But it looked so . . ." He was aware of Jakey's eyes on him. "That's really great."

"I was just telling your husband he needs some stitches," said Dr. Hassan.

There it was, that word again. Erdman concentrated on keeping down his lunch, and tried to ignore the thumping in his ears. Sweat beaded his upper lip. He shut his eyes. He knew he looked like shit.

"He's funny with needles," said Lilith. "And blood. He fainted when Jakey was born. They had to whisk him off in a wheelchair. Took him a good couple of hours to recover." She leaned over and squeezed Erdman's knee, to take the sting from her words.

Dr. Hassan chuckled and patted Erdman on the back. "Happens to the best of us, my friend. I fainted the first time I saw a postmortem."

"What's a postmortem?" asked Jakey, his eyes bright with interest.

"Well, young man, it's when—"

Lilith interrupted the doctor. "It's just a medical procedure, darling. Now, let's get you down to X-ray, and then we'll see about getting you something to eat."

FOUR

6.01 p.m.

Clara's mouth was pressed hard against something rough, and with every jolt, it rubbed the skin in the dip of her chin. Her wrists were tied behind her back with a length of surgical tape that crisscrossed the scant flesh. The binding cut deep between her thumb and her finger.

The van was flying over bumps, its tail end thumping down heavily after every descent, and the pain in her chin and the strangeness of the situation were making the muscles of her stomach tighten. Clara was usually a child who cried easily, but for once the tears did not come. A kind of numbness had set in.

The man had propped her against a box, and she was wedged between two rolls of carpet. There was a strong smell in the back, like butchered meat left to rot. It was cold and dark, and she couldn't see.

Something crawled over her cheek. She wanted to scream, but the man had said he would kill her mother if she did. Clara believed him. He had been smiling when he said it, just before he had shut the van doors, but she knew it wasn't a joke.

Her stomach rumbled again. During afternoon break, Poppy had told Clara they were having sausages and chips for tea. Clara's mother never let her eat food like that. The van juddered again. Her thoughts flitted back to her mother: pink nails and thick black eyeliner, and the way she pushed her glasses up the bridge of her nose whenever she scolded Clara, the way she pressed her cheek against Clara's in a facsimile of warmth, but always maintained a gap between their bodies. Mrs. Foyle didn't like sticky faces and hands.

The van stopped and then jolted, before the rumble of the engine died away. There was a *tick-tick*ing sound as it cooled. A loud, metallic *clunk* made her jump, and Clara realized it was the van doors sliding open. A bulb without a shade dangled from the ceiling, and it gave off just enough light for her to see she was inside a garage.

This garage belonged to a house, tall and thin like the man who had taken her. She couldn't see it, but the house had small, shuttered windows and a handrail flanking steps leading down to a basement. A path of cracked black-and-white tiles, woven with weeds, led to a front door, where blue paint had peeled off and left patches shaped like countries. A wrought-iron number 2, dulled from age or weather, had lost a screw, and hung upside down, an inverted cedilla. Spits of freezing rain landed on the pavement. Almost completely dark now.

The man lifted Clara from the van by hooking his arms around her legs. As her feet made contact with the garage's concrete floor, the light seemed to dim, and the bulb popped and went out.

The sudden change in temperature chilled her, and she blinked into the darkness. The man dug his fingers into her shoulders and propelled her towards an internal door.

She was concentrating so hard on trying to keep her balance in the disorienting blackness that she didn't notice the lip of the step, and she tripped, tearing her woolen tights and skinning both knees.

A few moments later, she found herself inside the hall of the house. When her eyes had grown used to the dull lighting, she saw the floor was bare, and there was no furniture to speak of, except a glass cabinet in the corner on top of a bureau. Then she noticed another. And another. As Clara struggled to process what she was seeing, the man stepped out of the shadows, drying his hands on a towel. He undid the binding around her wrists and offered her a glass of milk. Some instinct warned her not to drink it, but Clara was so thirsty that she gulped it down anyway. The man's pinched face seemed to collapse downwards, and for the second time that day, everything went fuzzy around the edges.

FIVE

7.52 p.m.

Amy Foyle sat perfectly still on her daughter's bed while everyone else was in motion.

Two police officers were searching Clara's bedroom, opening her wardrobe, her chest of drawers, even the wooden jewelry box that she'd gotten for her fourth birthday and painted herself. One picked up her hairbrush and placed it in a see-through evidence bag.

"For DNA purposes," he explained. "I might need her toothbrush, too."

Don't touch that, she wanted to scream. *It doesn't belong to you.*

They had arrived, the police, just as she was having the dye rinsed from her hair, her throat exposed and vulnerable. She hadn't picked up the frantic voice mails from Poppy Smith's mother; her phone was buried at the bottom of her Hermès bag.

They'd led her outside, still wearing the hairdressing cape, and it was only when they were nearly home that she realized she'd left behind her coat and forgotten to pay.

An hour later, when Miles had turned up, flanked by the officers who had driven through rush-hour traffic to collect him from his private practice in London Bridge, she was still wearing it. He had unfastened the Velcro, and it had dropped, silkily, to the floor. The gesture had felt inappropriate, like he was undressing her for bed.

"She better not be playing some kind of stupid game," was the first thing he'd said. And then, "She'll turn up."

"But it's dark," she said. "There's roads, the pond on the Heath—" She put a hand over her mouth, to stop the horror from spilling out.

He had taken the glass from her other hand, wrapped his arms around her, and she had pressed her face against the damp fabric of his suit. He smelled of soap and safety.

"What are they doing, the police?" He let her go, hung his jacket on the back of the chair, ran his fingers through silver-grey hair.

So, she told him the excruciating details—how they'd asked for a description of Clara, for some recent photographs, for the color of the coat and gloves she'd been wearing that day.

How they were knocking on doors, searching the streets close to her school, the Common, and up into Greenwich Park, how they'd taken all the telephone numbers of the parents of Clara's friends, how, because of her age, her vulnerability, if they didn't find her within the next few hours, they were planning to issue a nationwide Child Rescue Alert.

How most children who disappear are safely back home within twenty-four hours.

Most, but not all.

"She'll turn up," he said again, his voice calm. "Where's Eleanor?"

"At your mother's. I thought it would be better—"

"I want her here, with us. She needs to be with her family."

Amy didn't like to point out that his mother *was* their family. She watched him open his briefcase, take out his laptop.

"What are you doing?"

"I just need to finish this report."

Amy picked up her glass from the hall bureau and let it slide through her fingers. At the sound of it shattering on the tiled floor, an officer stuck his head around the door.

She saw her own anxiety reflected in the lines of Miles's face, knew that switching on his computer was another way of coping, of maintaining some control, but she couldn't help herself. Panic pinwheeled inside her. She threw words at him like stones.

"Our daughter is missing. Don't you think that's more important than a fucking report?" She picked up his jacket, thrust it at him. "Shouldn't you be out there looking for her?"

He peered at her over his glasses.

"Don't be hysterical, Amy. The police need space to do their job, and I want to be here when she gets home."

She couldn't look at him then, couldn't share his optimism. Always his fucking optimism. And that goddamn oh-so-reasonable tone. But there was a truth to his words that she couldn't ignore.

"You're right." She reached for his hand, briefly squeezed it. "Sorry. I'm just scared."

He patted her arm. "It'll be okay."

But even then, she didn't believe him.

Police moved through the house, their voices low and serious. They stood near the family computer, talking about online grooming, and multiplayer servers and social media sites, even though Amy had repeatedly told them that Clara was too young to use them. She watched them watch Miles, trying to assess his reactions, and guessed they were watching her, too. She heard them ask for a list of the patients he'd seen that afternoon. *To confirm his alibi.* That bizarre thought made her feel like she'd been cut adrift from her life. That the pattern of their Friday nights—wine, dinner, sex—had been redrawn in a way that was unrecognizable, ugly.

One officer—she couldn't remember his name, there were so many of them—stepped into the hall. His expression was bland, unreadable.

"Dr. Foyle, Mrs. Foyle, I'd like you both to come into the sitting room and take a seat."

Amy rested a palm against the wall to steady herself. She had a pain in her chest, like being scoured with a wire brush.

Have they found her?

They've found her.

If she's alive, he'd have told us by now.

So, she's dead.

Dead.

No.

Please, no.

The officer who had come to get them was standing by the fireplace, his colleague by the window. Both men swallowed at the same time, and the jerking of their Adam's apples reminded Amy of a hangman's noose.

"We wanted to let you know that a Child Rescue Alert has now been issued," said the first officer. "It's a fairly new but very high-profile way of sending a quick message to all national media outlets to tell them that Clara is missing. If someone has seen Clara, we'll know about it."

"Good," said Miles.

"Interpol is issuing a Yellow Notice in case anyone tries to leave the country with her, and there's a detective on her way who has a great deal of experience in missing persons cases."

"Good," said Miles again.

"Um, earlier, you said you were going to wait awhile before you issued the alert, that you had to be absolutely sure it was the right thing to do, and that Clara had probably just wandered off." Amy's heart quickened. "I was just wondering why you've decided to do it now."

The officers' eyes met for the briefest of moments, and Amy felt the breath of fear on her neck. She caught the flesh of her cheek between her teeth and bit down. A dart of pain reminded her this was real.

"I'm so sorry to have to tell you this, but a credible witness saw a little girl matching Clara's description outside a sweetshop in Blackheath Village this afternoon.

"She didn't see much, just the back of a head, but she was talking to a man." His face opened up to let pity slip in. "She left holding his hand."

SIX

8.13 p.m.

In the artificially lit hellhole that was the Royal Southern's ER department, Erdman was sitting with his head between his legs and taking deep breaths. A teenager with a broken leg sniggered. Erdman didn't blame him. It was a ridiculous sight, a grown man, knees poking up on either side of his head, a cardboard bowl in hand. To put it bluntly, he looked like a twat.

Lilith and Jakey were in the cafeteria, buying overpriced sandwiches. His son's arm wasn't broken. That knowledge brought with it a palpable sense of relief, but Erdman knew the next few days would be critical. Already, he was bracing himself for the possibility of a flare-up, the anguish on Jakey's face as he clawed at his inflamed skin, coupled with his own helplessness as he counted and recounted the lumps that preceded the invasion of bone. He hoped the steroids would do their job, although they came with their own set of problems. It killed him every time to watch his son pitch from a kind of manic wildness into a depressive slump.

Especially when there was only a fifty-fifty chance the medication would work.

Christ, how much longer? Dr. Hassan had promised there wouldn't be much of a wait, but he'd been there for hours. If a cut like his was left untreated for too long, the window for sutures would close along with the wound.

Cautiously, he lifted his head. The waiting room lurched sideways and he shut his eyes, the taste of vomit in his mouth. When he opened them again, the world was more or less steady. He wanted some water, but he didn't dare bend down to pick up his plastic cup. Instead he passed the time by watching the hospital's unfortunate inhabitants.

A man with a rumpled shirt and a face to match was holding a bag of melting sweet corn to his right eye. His other was trained on a television mounted on the wall next to a couple of faded posters urging new mothers to breast-feed and smokers to give it up. A young mother, no older than twenty, was trying to soothe a baby, who was wailing thinly. She, too, was glued to the screen.

Erdman swiveled his head a few degrees, trying not to move too quickly. *I look like bloody Bubo*, he thought. *That's where I should be, at home watching* Clash of the Titans, *not stuck in this shithole with the TV turned down.* On the screen, a blonde with a neat cap of hair and a too-wide mouth was mouthing something Erdman couldn't hear. Her makeup had settled into the cracks around her eyes. It made her look old, even though she must have intended the opposite. An image of a dimpled girl with pigtails filled his vision, followed by live footage of police officers, and clusters of people holding flashlights.

He strained to catch what the newscaster was saying, but the volume was too low. His eyes scanned the yellow news feed at the bottom of the screen.

> *Breaking news: Five-year-old Clara Foyle goes missing after leaving school playground on her own. Community joins officers to scour Greenwich Park and surrounding Heath.*

Another picture flashed: Clara Foyle giggling with someone who looked like an older sister. The sun lit her hair from behind, softening her freckles and creating a halo effect. More footage, this time of a shop cordoned off with police tape. The news feed continued.

> *Clara Foyle was last seen at a sweetshop in Blackheath, southeast London, around 3.30 p.m. She was wearing a yellow and black school uniform. Parents praying for "good news."*

Erdman rubbed his eyes with his good thumb and finger. Poor sods. How would he cope if Lilith rang him at work one Friday afternoon, just when he was thinking about sneaking off to the pub, and told him that Jakey was missing, that he hadn't made it home from school? He shook the thought from his mind, as if that simple act of imagining might somehow make it happen. The uncertainty would be the most terrible part. And the waiting. Waiting for that knock on the door. *I'm sorry, sir. We've found a body*. How could any marriage survive that? Erdman swallowed down the lump in his throat.

"God, are you *still* waiting?" Lilith appeared with Jakey trailing behind her, a limp triangle of cheese sandwich in hand.

"Yeah, shouldn't be long now."

Lilith plunked herself down on the chair next to him while Jakey inspected some drops of dried blood on the floor. "We were watching this in the canteen. I had to drag Jakey away in the end. He kept asking if someone had stolen her. Terrible, isn't it? Her poor parents. Mind you, what on earth was she doing on her own?"

They lapsed into silence, guiltily transfixed by the neatly packaged vignettes about a family just like them.

After a few minutes, Lilith touched her husband on the elbow.

"You haven't forgotten about Monday afternoon, Erd?"

"Um . . ."

Lilith sighed. "You have, haven't you?"

"It's Take Your Dad to School Day. Remember, Daddy? All the daddies are coming to my classroom. Miss Haines says it's going to be fun."

Erdman couldn't think of anything less fun. But he couldn't tell his son that.

"I'll be there," he said.

They sat for a long while. Two paramedics rushed in with a stretcher, but the excitement only lasted a couple of minutes before their grey-faced charge was whisked away. A whiteboard on the wall informed new arrivals that the average waiting time was four hours. The evening sky deepened into a violent blue. Behind them, a cleaner in a yellow top and trousers pushed a mop back and forth.

"God, what a dreadful uniform," muttered Lilith.

Erdman's stomach roiled, not helped by the shitty diaper smell from the baby a couple of rows back. Jakey lolled on the chair, his finger up his nose, Lilith's foot jigged up and down, and the news feed went 'round and 'round, one family's story of heartbreak stuck on repeat.

Erdman tried not to think about the needle's sharp point, the thread burrowing through the holes in his skin, the way his vision went white around the edges whenever he had an injection. He wondered if it might be linked to some half-buried memory.

Thank God he and Lilith had known enough to make sure Jakey's childhood immunizations were administered orally. He'd heard terrible stories about the effects of injections on children like Jakey. Doctors in Pennsylvania were breaking new ground with their research, but there was still no cure. He breathed out slowly, and tried to quell the panic that threatened to consume him whenever he thought about Jakey's future. He looked at his son, who was staring, oblivious, at the floor.

"I'm bored," whined Jakey.

"You and me both, champ," said Erdman. Wasting his Friday night in this depressing place was not his idea of fun, either.

Lilith was scrolling through news websites on her phone. She yawned without covering her mouth.

"Why don't you take Jakey home?" He hadn't known he was going to say that and regretted it as soon as he did.

"You sure?"

But Lilith's question was perfunctory. Already, she was on her feet, pulling on her coat, and helping Jakey with his.

"I'll take the car, shall I? You'll be all right on the bus . . ."

Yeah, 'course I will. " 'Cuz I really love getting the bus home with all the Friday-night drunks.

"I'll be fine."

As he watched Lilith and Jakey disappear through the hospital's automated doors, towards Car Park A and the drizzling darkness, he was still half-hoping she would stay.

He couldn't blame her. The hours she had spent here with Jakey. That both of them had. He hated this place almost as much as she did.

The minutes crawled by.

"Erdman Frith," called an exhausted-looking nurse.

At last. He followed her into the treatment room, stumbling into a CAUTION—WET FLOOR sign. He raised an apologetic hand at the cleaner, who nodded in return.

A doctor with a droopy moustache examined Erdman's hand, and let it drop. He had his back to his patient, but Erdman caught his exchange with the nurse all the same.

"Tell Kaleb to stop wasting my fucking time. We're busy enough as it is."

The nurse smiled her tired smile. "I'm sorry you've been waiting for such a long while, Mr. Frith, but Dr. Levison doesn't feel you need sutures. I'll dress it for you, but the cut isn't as deep as we first thought."

By the time he left the hospital, the rain was sheeting in his face. The wind had picked up, and it chilled his wet skin. What he wouldn't give to be sitting in front of the TV with the heating cranked up to block out the drafts, marital or otherwise.

He peered at the timetable. If he'd read it right, it promised a bus in twenty minutes, but he wasn't convinced he *had* read it right. He was still trying to decipher the fine black print when a single-decker rolled into view.

Erdman fumbled in his coat pocket for his Oyster card, dropped it on the rain-stamped floor, picked it up, and swiped it across the yellow reader, his cheeks pinkening. He found a seat by the window and stared, unseeing, through the condensation.

As the brake lights of the bus receded into the night, Erdman briefly shut his eyes and wondered who would notice if he didn't make it home.

But he should not have wasted time feeling sorry for himself.

His son was already in danger.

And Erdman had ten days left to save his life.

SEVEN

9.31 p.m.

Lilith tipped the last of the glass shards into the pedal trash can and turned her attention to the dining room floor. The blood from Erdman's hand had hardened into rusty pennies, and she scrubbed against the polished wood to clean them off.

She sat back on her haunches, surveyed her handiwork. God, she was tired. And she still had the remains of their spoiled dinner to clean up. Erdman was not back from the hospital yet, but at least Jakey was in bed. He had been so *difficult* since they had gotten home, moody and withdrawn, and although he'd apologized for the Car Incident, she'd been relieved to shut his door on him and come downstairs on her own.

Lilith didn't know what had got into her usually mild-mannered son, but whatever it was, she didn't like it. She made a mental note to book their crappy car in for a service.

As punishment, she had refused to read him a bedtime story. Not that Jakey had seemed to care. It was one of Erdman's books, some creepy folktale he'd had since he was a boy. The cover displayed a tall, thin man with a grinning skull for a head. A bogeyman who preyed on children. It gave her the heebie-jeebies. But Jakey had asked for it every night since he'd found it in a box of Erdman's old things. Not tonight, though. Instead he had thrown it across the room.

She sighed, and scraped congealed gravy and cold potatoes onto a plate. Perhaps it was his medication, or maybe he was just tired from the strain of being at the hospital for most of the evening. Perhaps she should give him the benefit of the doubt, but Jakey had been damn rude. It hadn't helped that she'd been trying to drive home in torrential rain when the car had beeped its first warning, flashing up this message on the dashboard.

Rear seat belt unbuckled.

"Jakey," she had snapped. "Don't mess around with your seat belt. Do it up now, please."

"I haven't undone it."

"Jakey." Her voice was steel.

"I haven't."

"Don't tell fibs."

"I'm not," he half-shouted. "I haven't touched it."

Lilith knew he was lying. That message only showed up when a backseat passenger undid the belt, or didn't do it up in the first place.

She tried a new tack. "Sweetheart, if we have an accident in this dreadful weather and you're not wearing your belt, you could be seriously hurt. Please do it up now. For Mummy."

"I haven't undone it," he insisted.

Lilith had slammed her hand against the steering wheel, and the car swerved into the oncoming lane.

Panicked, she'd overcorrected herself, causing the driver behind her to lean heavily on his horn.

"Shit."

"I haven't undone it," he said again, more softly this time.

She ignored him, her eyes scanning the dark roads for a place to pull over. She would damn well get out of the car and do it up herself. But the rain was making it difficult to see, and now the ribbon of red taillights ahead was forcing her to brake.

Stuck in a line of traffic, she had half-twisted to look at him. The pale smudge of his face stared back at her, illuminated in the headlamps of passing cars. "C'mon, Jakey. I just want you to be safe."

"I haven't undone my seat belt," he said, then burst into tears.

She had thought about explaining to him that the weight of a passenger's body triggered a sensor that alerted the driver when the belt was unbuckled, that there was no one else in the back so it *had* to be him, but she didn't think he'd understand.

Her eyes flicked down to Jakey's buckle.

It was done up, the metal clip securely in place.

But the message hadn't changed.

REAR SEAT BELT UNBUCKLED.

She checked to see if her handbag was on the backseat next to him. She carried enough crap for it to register about the weight of a small human being—but the seat was empty.

It was just a glitch in the system of a car that had seen better days.

She had started to apologize, to tell Jakey that adults

sometimes made mistakes, too, when she heard him mutter beneath the ceaseless drumming of the rain.

"Go away," he hissed. "Go away and leave me alone."

"Just because you say it quietly doesn't mean I can't hear you."

"Mummy, I—"

"I know it's been a tricky, tiring day, but that's no excuse. You don't speak to Mummy like that." Lilith's fingers tapped the gear stick.

"But I—"

"And you're still talking back to me. How about you say you're sorry instead?

"You never listen," he burst out. "Never, ever, ever. You're the meanest mummy in the world. I want my daddy."

The traffic began to move again, the rain easing off. She could see Jakey's face in the rearview mirror, pinched and miserable, and she regretted her sharpness, felt the itch of motherly guilt.

"Hey," she said. "I didn't mean to jump down your throat."

But he didn't reply, just stared out the window into the rain, his eyes filmy with tears and singing that strange little song.

She had left it at that, but as soon as they got home, he had asked to go to bed. When she had come up to tuck him in, he had turned his back on her and refused a good-night kiss.

Now that she was alone, she realized that he'd been right. She hadn't bothered to listen to him, or given him a chance to explain. Some children were compulsive liars, but Jakey, until now, had always been scrupulously honest.

It wasn't his fault they didn't have enough money to buy a better car.

She found she couldn't settle down. She finished clearing up and paced restlessly about their house, waiting for Erdman.

Thank God Jakey's arm was okay. She had been so sure it was broken, had already given him an extra dose of steroids to calm the inflammation. But when the doctors had ordered an X-ray, they found that it had only been badly bruised.

She thought about his arm's lumpy, swollen, misshapen appearance, and offered up a silent prayer.

Just a bruise, the doctor had said. Just a bruise. Please, God, let it stay that way.

EIGHT

2.57 a.m.

Detective Sergeant Etta Fitzroy could tell a lot about someone from the state of their front door.

She'd seen ones with peeling paint and broken doorbells, or with splintered wood where they'd been kicked in, or with four different locks to keep out unwanted visitors, but this was her favorite kind: freshly painted with a gleaming silver knocker and a hanging basket with foliage still dripping from the recent downpour.

Not tonight, though. Tonight she did not want to stand on this doorstep of privilege and wealth, and grind this family's hope into dust.

As she turned onto Pagoda Drive, Fitzroy took a tissue from her pocket and wiped the shine from her face. Parents expected a calm, professional presence. They deserved it.

The rain had stopped, but the pavements were blackly slick, the smoke-scented air cold against her skin. The Foyles' three-story Georgian home was the grandest on the street. Fitzroy guessed it must be worth three million, at least. Lights blazed in its windows, even though it was almost 3 a.m.

Walking up the garden path, Fitzroy drew in a damp, nervous breath. She never knew whether to expect angry, accusing voices or soft questions soaked in tears. Whatever the family's reaction, she understood it and forgave it, knowing it was rooted in despair.

Her hand hesitated above the knocker, but before she could bring it down against the varnished wood, a silver-haired woman of indeterminate age opened the door, buttoning up the jacket of her tailored suit. Her eyes were tired. For a moment or two, she stared at the detective. Fitzroy was used to it. With one eye a deep brown, the other a startling blue, she had learned to ignore the reaction. The woman remembered herself.

"Come in," she said. "You must be soaked through."

Fitzroy held out her right hand. "You must be Mrs. Foyle."

The woman laughed, an unexpected sound, displaying two rows of perfect white teeth.

"Goodness, no. Well, yes, actually, I *am* Mrs. Foyle, but not the one you've come to see. I'm Elisabeth, the mother-in-law."

"I'm sorry for your trouble."

Elisabeth Foyle's mouth rearranged itself into a somber line.

"Thank you," she said. "Follow me."

She led Fitzroy through a vast hallway with a checkerboard floor and a wide mahogany staircase. Several opulently furnished rooms later, they reached a closed door at the end of a corridor. Elisabeth knocked softly, but didn't wait for an answer. She held open the door and stood back to allow Fitzroy to pass.

The room was huge, with floor-to-ceiling windows that peered out onto what Fitzroy assumed were well-maintained lawns. A brick fireplace dominated the far wall, and on a pale green sofa in the corner sat a woman. Her glossy hair was caught up in a ponytail and it gave her an air of youthfulness, but Fitzroy noticed the deep grooves around her mouth and eyes, even from several feet away. The woman's shoulders were rounded, as if she'd already conceded defeat. Two uniforms were talking quietly in the corner.

This house would not sleep tonight.

"Can I get anyone a drink?" trilled Elisabeth, her mask slipping. It wasn't the first time Fitzroy had met a woman like Mrs. Foyle Senior. Excitement at discovering one's family at the center of a nationwide drama was more common than most people realized.

"Tea, thank you," she said.

Fitzroy glanced around the room, noticed a crutch leaning by the fireplace. Flames reflected in its alloy coating like dozens of tiny fireworks. Family photographs—those awkward, posed shots—lined the mantelpiece.

"My husband thinks she's coming home."

Amy Foyle's voice had a clipped, bitter edge, as if the only way to contain her anguish was to parcel it up so tightly that no emotion could leak out. In Fitzroy's experience, women as brittle as this were usually the first to break.

Without waiting for an invitation, Fitzroy sat on the sofa beside her.

"And what do you think, Mrs. Foyle?"

"You're the expert, Detective Fitzroy. Shouldn't you be telling me?" she said, her voice climbing in distress.

Fitzroy decided that no, she should not. She should not tell this worn-down wisp of a woman how she had spent twenty minutes hanging on the phone while the coroner's liaison officer checked to make sure Clara's body hadn't already been found; that a police search adviser was, at this very moment, arranging for the search to resume at first light; that as well as sightings of Clara, they would be scanning the landscape for scraps of her coat or her school bag. Her Peppa Pig underwear.

That they were still trying to eliminate Miles Foyle from their inquiries.

"I'm sorry it's so late," she said instead. "There are lots of calls coming in, and I was waiting for an update before I came to see you."

Mrs. Foyle sat up very straight. "You have news?"

Fitzroy cursed herself for her clumsy phrasing, and blamed the lateness of the hour. She clasped the woman's hand in her own. Her French manicure was chipped around the edges. That imperfection in Mrs Foyle's polished veneer tugged more powerfully at Fitzroy than any tears.

"Not at the moment. I'm sorry."

Mrs. Foyle bit her lip and stared at the television screen. Clara was running away from her older sister, Eleanor, who was chasing her with a hose. Although the volume was turned down, Fitzroy could just make out her shrieks of terrified pleasure.

"My husband filmed that in the summer." Her voice was flat. "He's upstairs, trying to settle Eleanor now. She's just had the most horrific nightmare."

"Mrs. Foyle, have you had a chance to think of anything else that might be helpful to this investigation? Anything at all? Any seemingly irrelevant detail about your daughter? Did she mention she was upset by anything? Had she ever spoken about being approached by a stranger?"

"I've already told your colleagues everything."

"Of course." Fitzroy was gentle. "But sometimes we can suddenly remember something, and even though it doesn't seem that important, it might be the piece of information that helps us to find Clara."

A single tear spilled down Mrs. Foyle's cheek. Fitzroy watched it fall from her chin.

"I know this is difficult. I know you've answered hundreds of questions about your daughter. I know you're frightened and worn down, and that it feels intrusive to have police in your house, checking your computers, touching Clara's things. But I've been asked to come here tonight because I have some experience in cases like this, and I might be able to help you."

Fitzroy angled her body so that their knees were almost touching.

"Is Clara a healthy, happy child, Mrs. Foyle?"

Mrs. Foyle was stopped from answering by the arrival of Elisabeth, who kept up a monologue as she poured milk and handed around biscuits.

"I wish she wouldn't do that," she said, as soon as her mother-in-law had gone.

"Do what?" Fitzroy kept her voice even.

"Act like nothing has happened. She keeps talking about the party we'll have when Clara comes home, when everyone knows that she's probably—"

She broke off, unable to articulate what most of the armchair commentators had already concluded. And then, as Fitzroy had known she would, Mrs. Foyle fell apart.

She didn't howl or scream or rail against the unfairness of it. She simply sat in her chair and cried, until her nose was blocked and her cheeks were blotchy, and she was unable to speak in coherent sentences.

Fitzroy felt an answering pulse of sympathy. In Mrs. Foyle's fractured sobs, she could hear the echoes of all the families of the missing and the dead.

Grace Rodríguez's mother, Conchita, had been standing at the sink.

Fitzroy had watched her, busy amongst the suds, cleaning the endless teacups and plates she hadn't eaten or drunk from.

Gifting her a final few seconds of hope.

Sensing a presence, Conchita had turned and seen the detective framed in the kitchen door. The saucer she was wiping had slipped from her fingers, and Fitzroy could still hear the sound it made as it struck the flagged flooring and cracked in half.

Conchita Rodríguez had not needed Fitzroy to speak. One glimpse of her face had told her everything.

Her knees had buckled, collapsing her onto cold, hard tiles. Fitzroy had sunk to the floor and wept with her.

A year later, while David slept, Fitzroy blinked into the darkness, raking over the evidence, looking for something she might have missed. She would bring a daughter home to her mother, just like she had promised. Finding Grace's body would allow Mrs. Rodríguez some kind of closure, if nothing else. But for now, Amy Foyle needed her.

Fitzroy put an arm around the younger woman's

shoulder. Through expensive silk, she felt the jut of her collarbone, the convulsions of shock and disbelief.

It was a cruel reminder of the daily horrors she witnessed in her police work. Could she bear to bring another child into this bleak landscape of the modern world, to expose herself again to the risk of loss?

Yes, thought Fitzroy. *Oh yes.*

Mrs. Foyle took a gulp from her glass and dabbed at her eyes with a tissue. Fitzroy smelled the alcohol fumes on her breath.

"Sorry about that," she said.

"No need to apologize."

Amy plucked at her skirt with trembling fingers. "Detective, you asked me if Clara is happy. I'm not so sure she is."

Fitzroy sat back, opened up her chest, inviting confidences, fixing all her attention on the young mother next to her. This was important, but she would not speak. She wanted Mrs. Foyle to fill the space between them with all the reasons why Clara was unhappy.

Fresh tears spilled onto Amy's cheeks. She didn't bother to wipe them away.

"It's my fault, you see. I wanted to have my hair colored, so I asked a friend to pick her up, but Clara didn't want to go and I made her." She covered her face with her hands and started to weep again. "I *made* her."

"Why didn't Clara want to go?"

"Poppy Smith, the girls in her class, they—"

Fitzroy waited.

"They behave with the natural cruelty of children."

"Why would they do that?"

Amy picked at the ragged edges of her nail polish,

the skin around her cuticles. "Clara has cleft hands, Detective Fitzroy. Her fingers are missing on both of her hands."

Ting.

In cases like this, Fitzroy liked to listen for the music in her mind, and when she heard it, she grasped for it. Some called it gut instinct, a cop's nose, but for Fitzroy, it all happened up in her head, the quiet song of cerebral process. Clara's disability explained why she had left the school grounds on her own, how her vulnerability might have made her an easier target than most.

Her brief upsurge of hope crashed.

It wasn't enough.

"So she hasn't had surgery on them?"

Mrs. Foyle dropped her head. "Clara is quite unusual, Detective. Most children have surgery to correct it when they're eighteen months old or so, and sometimes much younger, but I didn't want her to. I hated the idea of her going through any kind of pain. I thought she'd learn to live with it. My husband didn't agree, especially when the doctors advised us that surgery would become more difficult as she got older. We argued about it horribly. They were reluctant to operate without my consent, but I just couldn't bear the thought of them cutting into her hands." She gave a heavy sigh. "Her case is fairly extreme. The three middle fingers of both hands are missing."

Mrs. Foyle leaned her head back against the sofa and shut her eyes. For a long while they sat like that, the room silent apart from the occasional crack of a shifting log. At first, it seemed as though she had fallen asleep, but then Mrs. Foyle began to cry again, quietly, brokenly. Struggling to shape the words through her distress, she groped for Fitzroy's arm. The need in her face was terrible.

"Is my baby still alive?"

Several hours had passed since Clara had disappeared, and Fitzroy had already lied to Amy Foyle once, when she had arrived at the house and been asked if there was news.

There *was* news, but not of the kind she was prepared to share. The investigating team had been swamped with supposed sightings of the little girl. Always a risk with a Child Rescue Alert, they were buckling under the weight of information, struggling to sift the critical from the crap.

Fitzroy was not prepared to lie again.

"I hope so," she said, refusing to make a promise as empty as the small red Wellingtons she had noticed by the front door. "But I can tell you that many children who go missing *are* reunited with their families."

"What about the ones stolen by strangers?" Amy began to sob again, an edge of hysteria crawling in.

"I know it's hard, Mrs. Foyle, but I can promise you we're doing everything we can."

"You must find her. You must!" Her voice was panicky.

Fitzroy tried to ignore the snapshot of Grace Rodríguez, which floated, uninvited, to the surface.

She chose her next words with care. "Do you have any idea who this man might be?"

But Mrs. Foyle didn't. With no living male relatives except Miles, the police had already moved on to the fathers and husbands of Clara's friends and her own, the male teachers at the school, even the workman who had mended the gutters last month.

Every registered sex offender in the area was being traced, too, although Fitzroy didn't tell Amy Foyle that.

"So it was just a normal school day for your daughter?"

"Apart from being collected by Mrs. Smith, yes."

Fitzroy knuckled her eyes. Although she was tired, there was no point in going home. David, who'd shrugged, unsurprised, when the call came through, had chosen to stay on at the hotel, to celebrate his birthday alone, and she wouldn't sleep now.

A silence opened between them. Etta wondered if David was in bed, or still at the bar, chatting with the night staff. The first time he'd taken her there, she'd been touched by the flowers he'd arranged for the room, his lack of expectation of anything in return. She'd liked that about him. Things were different now that she had expectations of her own.

Much later, when the shifting shadows had taken on their morning shape and there was nothing left to say, Amy called out for her mother-in-law, and Elisabeth materialized with Fitzroy's coat. As she shut the door behind them, Amy took another large swallow of her drink.

"I'm sorry about that, Mrs., er, Detective . . ." whispered Elisabeth. "She's rather overwrought at the moment."

"Understandable."

"She's got MS, you know. Doesn't mix well with pills and alcohol."

Fitzroy pressed her lips together and forced them into a tight smile. "Thank you for the tea."

She picked up her suitcase, and opened the door on a new day.

Outside, the air was golden, that rare quality of light that heralds an early winter dawn. Its luminosity reminded her of a child's skin, the curve of a cheekbone in the muted haze of a bedside lamp, the dragging in-and-out breath of untroubled sleep.

But Fitzroy could not think of light without dark. Seared into her consciousness was the ambush of that youthful bloom by the pallor of death, and she wondered if its creeping fingers were already stroking Clara's face.

NINE

7.38 a.m.

He unlocks the front door, listens for the familiar creak of her voice.

"Is that you, love?"

She is awake, then, and his heart soars.

"Yes, it's me," he calls.

The room is stale with sleep and the yeasty smell of her body. He breathes in her scent, leans over to brush damp hair from her face. Pain twists her features. After all these years, he does not need to ask. Already he recognizes that she will not move from her bed today, and he rummages in the drawer for her painkillers, presses a glass of water to her lips.

"You must be tired," she says.

He smiles at her, shakes his head. What she means is that *she's* tired, even though she has not moved from this bed for years. He lifts the bedpan. There is a faint smattering of talc on the rim. It eases the dragging of metal across delicate skin.

"Tea," he says. "And toast."

When he comes back with the tray, she has managed

to prop herself up against the pillows. They obscure the S-shaped curve of her spine, but the weakness in her back thrusts her face forward, forces her shoulders to hunch.

He has cut the toast into four squares, and he hands her one. The curtains are shut, the room gloomy, but she does not like the world looking in until she is washed and changed.

When she has finished eating, he takes the tray into the kitchen, runs warm water into a basin. Sleep is pushing against him and his eyes feel heavy, but still he does not rest. Instead he turns on the radio, drinks down the morning's news like a man who has been in the desert.

He carries the basin back along the hall, careful not to spill its contents on the dark brown swirls of the carpet. Her eyes are closed again, but she opens them at the sound of the enamel knocking against the seat of the wooden chair. Outside, the first tendrils of a purpling dawn are streaking the sky.

He smiles at her again, a tender smile, and brings the sponge to her face, wiping the rheum from her eyes, the dried saliva on her chin that has spilled from her mouth during sleep. Her skin is lined now, but he does not see it. Even though her body is bowed, her eyes have not changed at all.

Her nightdress is too big, but still it snags as he eases it over the misshapen mound of her back. He washes beneath her arms, between her legs, checks her skin for pressure sores. When he is satisfied, he places a clean nightgown over her head and opens the curtains. The bus stop is right in front of the bedroom window, and he watches the seats fill up with passengers.

"Television, radio, or book?" he says.

She does not ask about his plans for the day. He does not mind. He understands the radius of her world has shrunk to this house, this room.

Only when her eyes are fixed on the television does he speak again.

"I've just got to—"

She waves a thin arm, doesn't move her eyes from the screen. "I know, I know. They need to be fed and watered, too."

Outside, the grass is damp, and the air scorched with fumes. The shed smells of hay. He inhales its sweetness.

When he has finished in the garden, he sleeps for an hour or two. He showers. She is still watching television and she talks to the screen instead of him.

They are interviewing the mother of Grace Rodríguez, she says. The Girl in the Woods. The teenager who disappeared on her way to a ballet exam.

Mrs. Rodríguez has been invited on to share her experience, she tells him, because a five-year-old girl has gone missing.

He listens to the faux sympathy of the breakfast presenters, their Technicolor commiserations at odds with the bruised shadows beneath Mrs. Rodríguez's eyes. They remind their viewers of the salacious details: that when the police stumbled across Grace's remains in Oxleas Wood, most of her body was missing. All except the tips of her fingers and toes, which had been sealed in small plastic bags and neatly lined up.

He closes the door behind him, makes a sandwich, and wraps it in greaseproof paper.

When he carries it through to her, he is wearing his suit. She does not ask where he is going.

TEN

3.46 p.m.

"Is this a joke?" asked The Boss.

Fitzroy studied the picture of Clara that was pinned on the wall of the Major Incident Room in the southern district of the Metropolitan Police's Homicide and Serious Crime Command.

We'll find you, sweetheart. I promise.

Across the room, a dozen or so officers were at work, manning the phones, scribbling notes, their faces ghosted by the glare of their computer screens. The rest were out conducting house-to-house checks, or joining the search.

"Fuck," said The Boss, and slammed down the phone. He popped a tablet from the blister pack in his pocket and dry-swallowed it. Outside, the pinprick lights of the city lit up the gathering darkness.

Fitzroy cleared her throat. "Everything all right, sir?"

"No, it fucking isn't," he said, and rubbed his eyes with the heel of one hand. "Fucking newspapers are planning a story on Miles Foyle."

Fitzroy didn't need to ask what kind of story. A few hours ago, as part of a routine check, she had run his name through CRIS and CRIMINT, the Metropolitan Police's intelligence databases.

Her eyes had widened at what she had read. Two cautions for trawling the streets for sex, less than six months old. One of the girls had been underage. Or, at least, under eighteen, which as far as the law concerning prostitution stood, was the same thing. There had also been an allegation of sexual assault and kidnapping against a student intern, which had later been withdrawn.

"Didn't take them long."

"No, it fucking didn't, and the timing couldn't be worse, what with the press conference on Monday. We want the public to sympathize, not point the bloody finger."

"So, what now?"

"No choice but to ride it out, but I suppose we'd better warn him." He sighed, flicked through a couple of sheets of paper on the desk. She knew what was coming next.

"Get down there, will you? Paying for sex with an underage prostitute does not make him guilty of abducting his daughter, but I want you all over Miles Foyle like a bloody rash."

When Fitzroy walked up the path to Pagoda Drive this time, the front door was wide open, a chandelier lighting up the chessboard floor. A young woman was coming out, her eyes red-rimmed, streaks of blond in her cropped hair. Her hands were resting on the shoulders of a girl around seven or eight.

"I don't want to go," said the girl.

The woman nodded at Fitzroy, then lowered her gaze back to the child.

"It might make you feel a bit better, lovely. You can't stay indoors all day. Perhaps we can get a hot chocolate at that café you like on the way home."

"Is Dr. Foyle in?"

The woman's fingertips whitened as she gripped the child's shoulders. "He's somewhere around. Upstairs, I think."

Fitzroy pressed the bell, then stepped into the hall. Waited. Leaned back out and pressed it again. For a second time, she marveled at the grandeur of this house, so different from the home of her childhood, the austere atmosphere of the two-up, two-down in Kent broken only by her mother's obsession with jazz 45s.

"Gina," shouted a man's voice. "Can you get that?"

Fitzroy wondered what had happened to the Foyles's family liaison officer. When no one appeared, she tried calling out instead.

"Hello? Hello?"

Miles Foyle stuck his head over the bannister. When he saw Fitzroy, he ran his fingers through his hair and started down the stairs. It had now been almost twenty-six hours since Clara had vanished, and every moment of that loss was painted in his bloodshot eyes, the stubble on his chin.

"Amy's gone for a walk. She was going mad, cooped up in here all day."

So that's where the FLO had gone. "It's not Mrs. Foyle I've come to see."

"Gina was here." He looked vaguely around him. "She said something about taking Eleanor to see a friend."

"Dr. Foyle, we're still waiting for that list of patients you saw on Friday afternoon. Can I ask you to give it to me now?"

He glanced up, startled. "Um, I'm not sure I can do that."

"Is there a staff member in your practice who can photocopy it for me? I can send someone to collect it. Or perhaps they can e-mail it."

Miles rummaged in his pocket for his hankie and blew his nose. "I'm afraid that's not going to be possible."

Fitzroy's eyes flicked to the left. Hanging from the key hook in the hall was a laminated identity badge attached to a lanyard, the initials *RSH* emblazoned across the plastic.

"Were you working elsewhere that day? I gather you sometimes see non-private patients."

He followed her gaze. "Yes, at the Royal Southern, but that's usually on Tuesdays."

Fitzroy's impatience ignited.

"Dr. Foyle, do I really need to remind you that your daughter is missing, most likely the victim of an abduction? I have no desire to arrest you for obstruction, so I suggest you try to be a little more helpful—"

"I can't give you a list, because I don't have one."

"You *were* at your office, though? We picked you up from there."

He let out a long sigh. "Yes, I was there."

"So, why don't you have a list?"

"Because I wasn't seeing patients on Friday afternoon."

"Well, I shouldn't think that's too much of a problem. If you were catching up with paperwork, I'm sure your receptionist can vouch for you."

"I sent her home."

Ting.

"Well, there must be someone who saw you in your office, or perhaps you spoke to them on the phone. All we need to do is verify where you were when—"

"—Clara went missing? That's what you're *suggesting,* isn't it? That I had something to do with my own daughter's disappearance."

She could read his outrage in the line of his lips, the fleck of spittle on his chin. She understood it, and would have been surprised by its absence. But Fitzroy had also seen that expression before on other faces, on the faces of fathers who had raped and strangled their little girls.

"No one is saying that, sir. But we do need to know what you were doing. It's a standard line of inquiry."

"Look, I was with someone, okay? Happy now?"

Fitzroy gave herself a moment to allow his words to settle on her.

"Who? We'll need to speak to her. Or him."

"It's a her." His face was a smooth mask. "And you can't speak to her."

"Why not, Dr. Foyle?" Fitzroy waited a beat. "Is she a prostitute?"

He looked away. Fitzroy watched his left cheek moving, his teeth biting into its fleshy interior. She tried a different tack.

"Are you aware that tomorrow's newspapers will be running stories about your predilection for picking up prostitutes?"

His face caved in. "Fuck."

"Does your wife know?"

He looked at her.

"I suggest you tell her."

"I can't." His voice was a whisper.

"Believe me, it'll be worse if she finds out from the papers. In the meantime, I want you to think very carefully about what I'm asking. As I told you before, failure to provide relevant information to an ongoing inquiry could be regarded as obstruction. When you're ready to talk, you know where to find me."

The temperature had dropped by the time Fitzroy found herself outside again. The bite of frost in the air was as raw as her memories of the search for Grace Rodríguez.

The woods had been covered in white needles, the unmistakable hallmark of a hoarfrost. Their feet crunched against the iron earth.

They had moved through the trees, beyond Severndroog Castle, the ancient folly built by a grieving widow in memory of her husband. She had wondered then what horrors this Gothic tower had witnessed.

Deeper into the woods. Into the frozen darkness of a winter morning.

"I don't usually walk this way," the man had said, his dog nosing the backs of his legs. He pointed to the ballet case, its pale pink outline visible against the ground like a moon against the sky.

Fitzroy had stared at the name sticker, peeling now

after days in the damp and cold, but still clinging defiantly to the leather.

"Get forensics here now," she had shouted, and the woods had echoed with her fear.

Even a year after Grace's disappearance, Fitzroy's frustration had not diminished. Her thoughts jumped back to Miles Foyle. He was a conundrum. She did not know yet if she believed him, although his distress had seemed genuine enough.

And yet . . .

Most abductors of young girls were known to their victims. Most were white, unemployed. Most had a record. Three out of four. The odds were not in his favor.

And he had no alibi. At least, none she had managed to confirm. But she was reluctant to bring him in. The tar of an arrest—especially a father's arrest on suspicion of child abduction—took years to scrape clean. But she would be back. She would give him a couple of days, and in the meantime, the family liaison team could keep a close eye on him. If he began to unravel, she would know about it.

From a downstairs window in Pagoda Drive, Miles watched the detective walk down the path to her car, footsteps echoing against stone. As the red taillights turned the corner, he picked up his jacket and left the empty house that no longer felt like a home.

ELEVEN

4.36 p.m.

Mostly, he prefers to wait until they're dead before setting to work with his knife. He enjoys the art of dissection, the careful removal of organs, the peeling back of the skin; the rest he leaves to his colony.

When he has cleaned and oiled his tools and set loose the dermestids, he mops the floor of the cutting room, climbs the basement stairs of his father's house, and locks the door behind him. He will return in a few hours, when the beetles have finished their ghoulish striptease, coaxing the flesh from the fragile bones. He sniffs his pin-striped jacket. The scent of dead matter clings to it.

Up here, the silence enfolds him. He closes his eyes and inhales deeply. Here is where he belongs. Amongst the bones of his family's collection. The Ossuary.

A treasure trove of oddities passed down through countless generations. Seeded in a grave robber's alliance with a king's surgeon, harvested by the male bloodline, *his* bloodline, and displayed here, in this house.

He wanders the rooms. There is no furniture, no family photographs. In what was once the kitchen, a small glass box displays a staved-in human skull. Next to it, the pockmarked ossified remains of a syphilitic. In the wood-paneled hallway, the bones gleam in their glass cases. He knows their secrets, and it excites him. But it isn't enough. Not now.

He checks his watch. He has lingered too long, and will have to drive fast through the rain-slicked streets.

He wonders what Mr. B, the funeral director, will have for him this time, and feels for the brown envelope in his breast pocket. He accepts most of Mr. B's offerings. No car crashes, though. Or jumpers. Too messy. Too much damage. Occasionally, he finds something from their corpses to salvage and sell. Skin perhaps, an organ or two. There is always someone who is willing to pay. But invariably, it is not worth his time. Too much effort and too little return, as his father would say.

Like the living, the dead can be bought.

The house and its shadows subsume him. He lingers in the hallway, drinks in the shape of the boy's skeleton trapped in its twin prisons of glass and bone.

He thinks, then, of the other boy, and the thrill of possibility unfurls inside him.

Frith. Meaning "freedom." He smiles at the irony. The name rolls off his tongue. It cannot be coincidence.

In the stillness of the house, the air vibrates with sobbing so faint he wonders if he imagines it. Obsessively, he fingers the thin silver chain he wears around his neck. Its pendant, a curio inherited from his father, feels warm to the touch, heavy with the weight of its bloody history.

He closes his eyes, grasps the pendant between thumb and forefinger. Shadows enfold him like a lover. All this darkness reminds him of his father, the lessons of his youth.

Memory pokes at him. Takes him back to his eight-year-old self. The look of scorn on his father's face; the burden of his father's hand on his shoulder; the taste of failure on his lips when he cannot do as his father bids.

"It's easy," Marshall had told him. "Imagine you're drawing a curtain, pulling down a blind. Become part of the scenery, like you've always been there. Simple as that."

He had squeezed shut his eyes, tried to do as his father had asked. But he could not make himself disappear.

"Watch me."

Marshall had stood in the busy high street, a blank look shuttering his face. Women were carrying boxes of overripe fruit, the market vendors shouting to one another. Weaving between the stalls, he had melted into the Saturday crowds. Now and then, the boy had caught a glimpse of his father's jacket. And as the traders had gone about their business, Marshall had stolen their money belts stuffed full of bills.

Later that day, they had gone down the road to the tobacconist, and Marshall had turned to him and grinned. Above the cashier's desk, the fluorescent lamp flickered. His father had prowled the shop, helped himself to a packet of Wills Embassy, a bottle of Scotch. He had blown out smoke rings as they had walked home.

"It's easy," his father had said again.

Years it has taken him, to perfect the skills prized by his father and forebears, but now he has learned how to turn down the dial and fade into the background, to move undetected through the shadowy edges of life. Not in an otherworldly way. Not like a ghost. It was just something he could do. Like some people could cross their eyes or were ambidextrous. It just was.

He is late for Mr. B, but no matter. Mr. B can be relied upon to keep his eyes open and his mouth shut. Mr. B understands his needs. He calls him "A Collector of Curious Bones." The Bone Collector. He likes that.

Mr. B's philosophy is uncomplicated. If a family expects their loved one's body to be inside a coffin, why disabuse them of that notion? It's a simple case of mathematics. The weight of an average human body is roughly equal to two large paving slabs.

Yes, mostly he prefers to wait until they're dead before setting to work with his knife. But sometimes it cannot be helped. Sometimes he cannot make himself wait.

Take the girl, for instance. She promises so much. And there is much to admire in a specimen such as her, much to discover. He yearns to experiment, to peel back the layers of her skin and look upon the bone. To display an exhibit that still moves and breathes.

And yet.

He finds himself listening at the door to her childish mutterings. Once or twice, he has let himself in to straighten the sheet covering her sleeping form.

She reminds him of who he could have been in a different sort of life.

But there's risk, of course. Always risk.

The question is: to keep or to kill?

Flesh or bone?

SUNDAY

TWELVE

4 a.m.

The baby's face was red and screwed up, and its cry, an insistent *wah-wah-wah* that carried across the sticky floor of the maternity ward, lodged itself slap-bang in his mother's middle temporal gyrus and orbitofrontal cortex.

Oblivious to the burst of activity in her brain precisely one hundred milliseconds after his first mewl reached her ears, she stretched out a hand to rock the hospital-issue crib. Her eyes were still shut as she tried to cling to the last vestiges of sleep, but it was no use; she was biologically programmed to attend to the cries of her seventeen-hour-old son.

"It's okay," she murmured. "S'okay."

Her stomach was soft from the birth and raw from the C-section, and there was a smear of blood on the sheets. Her breasts flopped out of the front of her unbuttoned nightie, and a bead of colostrum gathered on the tip of her nipple. Her face was blank with tiredness. But she didn't care. She was swollen with love, with wonder.

Two beds down, from behind drawn curtains, a second wail went up, building in volume and intensity. Another baby joined in, then another, until the cacophony of crying babies forced the duty night sister from her flirting with the on-call doctor to soothe her ward back to sleep.

The mother—Nina Harper—reread the message scribbled on the small rectangle of card that had been hand-delivered that afternoon with the shiny *It's a Boy!* balloon.

Congrats! He's gorgeous. Love, Etta x

She hadn't mentioned it to Patrick, but she was worried about her older sister. She was busy, career-driven, Nina understood that, but sometimes she worried that the job would swallow her. Just like it had swallowed their father. As for David, she could see what Etta did not. But how to tell her that the man she'd chosen to remake her life was seduced by promotion, not procreation? That as much as Nina loved her sister, Etta's tunnel vision often blinded her to the needs of others.

Take this afternoon. Etta had staggered into the maternity unit, carrying a ridiculous gigantic stuffed elephant.

"Erm, thanks, sis. That'll fit nicely into our closet-cum-nursery." She had smiled to soften the sting of her sarcasm.

Etta had waved an airy hand. "It's a collector's item."

Nina had thought she was joking, but when she had checked the Internet on her phone after Etta had left, she'd been shocked by the price. She tried not to mind that such a large sum of money would have paid for a shiny new travel system instead of the secondhand stroller they'd borrowed from a friend.

She had tied the balloon to Max's cot before lifting him out.

"Do you want to hold him?"

A look had passed across Etta's face, and she had waved her mobile at Nina.

"Better not. I'm waiting for a call and I might need to rush off in a sec." She bent her head, refreshing the screen. "I shouldn't even be here. The Boss thinks I'm at a suspect's house."

It was a thinly disguised excuse, but Nina didn't challenge her. Her sister had her reasons, even though the dismissal of her son pierced in ways she hadn't expected.

Instead she had guided his mouth to her nipple, ignoring the pull of her scar. *Don't lift anything heavier than your baby*. She felt her sister's gaze and dragged herself from his perfect features to smile at her with the sheer joy of it all, but Etta's eyes had slid away.

"He's such a hungry little one," she said. And then: "If he carries on like this, he's going to drink me dry."

Etta had pushed her chair back. The scrape of its legs made a passing nurse stare.

"I've got to go," she said.

"But you've only just got here." Nina shifted against the pillows. "I didn't hear your phone ring."

"Text."

Etta had brushed her lips against her nephew's downy head, and squeezed her sister's hand.

"You'll make a brilliant mum," she said, then she was gone.

Nina rubbed her eyes and yawned. The air was sticky with the smell of milk and meconium.

A cleaner working the night shift walked past her bed, pushing his ancient mop over the vinyl floor, sticking it beneath the iron bedsteads, and bedside drawers and chairs for visitors. Nina held her breath, praying he wouldn't knock the plastic crib and jolt her son awake. In that way unique to babies, Max was fast asleep again, his tiny hands curled into fists that rested on each side of his head.

The ward settled back into a kind of dazed quiet. Nina dozed off, occasionally opening an eye to marvel at the newness of her son.

Minutes passed. A faint *clink* of china suggested that breakfast was on its way. Soon, the first of these young mothers would shuffle from their dirty sheets in search of sustenance.

Across the city, dawn rinsed the darkness from another night, and its inhabitants went about their business.

The cleaner washed out his bucket and mop, and stowed them in a cupboard. Then he changed out of his uniform and found his outdoor clothes.

Dr. Hassan dried his hands, zipped up his jacket, and thought about the way that new agency nurse had smiled at him, and how his wife rarely smiled at all.

Fitzroy, who had spent a second night in the Major Incident Room, watched a fiery orange sun paint the sky. She thought about her nephew's smell and wondered who was hiding Clara Foyle.

Lilith and Erdman Frith made breakfast without speaking to one another.

Miles Foyle woke at dawn, listening for the treacherous *thump* of the Sunday supplements on his doormat.

And all day, Amy Foyle waited for news. And waited. And waited. And waited.

MONDAY

THIRTEEN

9.54 a.m.

The office of the 387th biggest-selling magazine in the country was fittingly housed in a grimy warehouse conversion off Borough High Street.

Visitors to this unremarkable building could turn right at the reception desk to The Domination Station, an online company selling sex toys with such enticing names as Fuck-a-Duck, or journey upstairs and Sprinkle a Little Magic into Your Life with *Psychic Weekly*.

That glittery, over-the-top pink-and-purple sign hanging above the door yielded a snort from Erdman every time he arrived at work. *Psychic Weekly*'s few but loyal readers might subscribe to that kind of bullshit, but he couldn't take it seriously, not when he was the one making most of it up.

He was now officially Very Late. Usually it wouldn't matter, but Daniel Jarvis, *Psychic Weekly*'s thrusting new editor, was watching the clock in the same way a compulsive eater eyes a hamburger.

"S'all right, he's in a meeting with the publisher," called Amber the Goth.

Thank fuck for that.

Amber swept some papers aside and plonked her generous backside on the edge of Erdman's desk. Her dye job looked like the synthetic hair on a Barbie doll and, despite the early hour, her thick black eye makeup was already smudged. She wore a skull stud in her slightly wonky nose.

"Can't be mithered today. Wanna brew?" Her nasal Mancunian was always more pronounced when she had a hangover. She pointed to the fat white slug on his finger.

"What did you do to your hand?"

"Had a run-in with a carving knife."

"Self-harming, were you . . . ?"

"Nah, sex game gone wrong."

A low laugh rumbled up from Amber's belly. " 'Course. Should have guessed."

Erdman switched on his computer and leaned back in his swivel chair, gazing around the office. The wallpaper seemed shabbier than usual. He had to find his way out of this dead end.

He had long fantasized about writing a book. He just hadn't got 'round to it yet. He'd always assumed it would feature his experiences as a journalist for *National Geographic* or *Paris Match,* but he hadn't got 'round to that yet, either.

When he'd finally gotten back from the hospital on Friday night, soaked through, his finger throbbing and desperate for a beer, he found Lilith in the spare room, brandishing a recycling bag.

"Do we really need these?" she had asked, gesturing at the piles of mint-condition back copies he'd painstakingly tracked down online or bought from his favorite store, the Vintage Magazine Shop on Brewer Street.

He snatched one up and waved it at her. It had a black background and a black-and-white image in the center of the cover, *Mort de Kennedy.* A collector's item.

"This is a collector's item."

"No, it's an old copy of *Paris Match* taking up valuable space in the study."

"Tell you what," he said. "I'll stick 'em in the loft."

An hour later, the magazines were neatly packed into boxes, waiting to be photographed and sold on eBay. There was no room in the loft, apparently.

Not that there hadn't been the odd chance to boost his career. The news editor at his first newspaper, Russell Shoesmith, had landed a job at the *Daily Mirror*, and had invited him to come in for shifts, but Erdman didn't want to spend his weekends being some full-of-himself journo's gofer when he'd been working all week. Besides, the pay was crap. So, he slept the hours away, or played computer games, and then he met Lilith. Now Russell was the head of content at the *Sunday Times*, and Erdman was a feature writer at *Psychotic Weekly.*

Amber looked up from her computer. Her face was scrunched up, her head cocked to one side.

"Erd," she called across the office. "Do all angels have wings?"

He almost spat out his tea. Amber appeared to be suggesting that angels existed. That was like believing in the tooth fairy. Or ghosts.

Before he had a chance to answer, a familiar voice

echoed up the stairwell. Erdman quickly began a one-fingered tap: *A unicorn is the physical representation of Divinity; its arrival is often heralded by the sound of tinkling bells. It is an incarnation of purity, and it has the power to bestow wisdom upon those who are lucky enough to see one.*

"Gooooooooooood mooooooooooooorning, *Psychic Weekly*," boomed Jarvis, all slicked-back hair and designer glasses. Erdman doubted he'd ever given a moment's thought to the nuanced commentary of the Oscar-nominated Vietnam War comedy.

Daniel Jarvis was everything Erdman was not. At only twenty-six, he'd been promoted from a features editor role at a men's magazine to his first editorship. His boss was going places, thought Erdman gloomily, while he was still at the bus stop.

"Right," shouted Daniel, rubbing his hands together. "I'm assuming that everyone's copy is ready to go, as per my request last week. Deadline day tomorrow, folks."

Fuckety fuck.

"Which means"—he grimaced at his team—"we'd better get on with the Christmas issue. Pronto. We're running seriously behind. Editorial meeting in five."

Double fuckety fuck.

Erdman clicked on the FESTIVE COPY folder on his desktop. It was empty. He racked his brain. It was empty. He prepared himself for another bollocking.

Daniel Jarvis sat at the head of the table, sipping coffee and shuffling papers. Erdman watched him watching his newly inherited team. Jarvis stared at Amber's dyed-black hair and sacklike dress, his lip curled back in a sneer. His disdain was palpable. Then his eyes flicked to Elodie, *Psychic Weekly*'s young trainee, before dropping to her cleavage.

On Jarvis's first morning, while Erdman was waiting outside his office for what his new boss termed his "Getting to Know You" sessions—the staff had renamed them "Getting to Blow You"—he had overheard him on the phone.

"Yeah, right bunch of losers," said Jarvis. There was a pause while the other person spoke, and then Jarvis had guffawed loudly.

"They'll close it down if it doesn't start making money. Bet none of their psychics have told 'em that."

Jarvis hadn't mentioned layoffs again. But it was a worrying development.

"Right, my earnest team of Hemingways," he said, chortling at his own brilliance. "I'm in charge now, so no slacking. I've never seen such a bloody shambles. We're almost three weeks behind schedule, so it's noses to the grindstone from now on. Okay, any great ideas for our festive edition?"

There was an uncomfortable silence as three sets of eyes looked at their notepads.

"Um, could we introduce a section called 'Ho Ho Holistic'?" suggested Amber eventually. "Lots of info on how holistic therapies can help you cope with the trauma of Christmas."

Daniel nodded. "Like it. Next."

Elodie's timid suggestion followed. "How about something like 'Dreams Can Come True'? We can ask our readers to send us their best examples of dreams that have actually happened in real life."

"Not bad. Get 'em to send in their photos, too."

Elodie gave a tight smile and scribbled a note on her pad. The silence in the room seemed to grow and blossom. Daniel fixed Erdman with a pointed stare. "What about you, Nerdman?"

"I was, er, thinking we could do something about the symbols of Christmas and what they mean, er, like a holly leaf or a candle."

"Crap. We did that last year. Did you seriously think I wouldn't bother to check?" He shook his head. "What else?"

"Um, what about—"

Jarvis didn't wait for Erdman to finish. "I want a piece on the mystical qualities of the pomegranate. And make it good. Remind our readers that there's more to Christmas fruit than a bloody satsuma."

In the Bank, Erdman ordered a reviving lunchtime pint and a Laphroaig, just to take the edge off.

The Orange Tree Pub—the Bank's official name—smelled of toilet cleaner and stale beer. Long ago, Erdman had devised a clever scheme for when he fancied a quick one. "Just popping to the Bank," he'd tell his boss. Strictly speaking, it wasn't a lie, just a . . . nickname.

Huddled over a menu with Amber and Elodie was Erdman's friend and colleague Axel.

"All right, mate?" said Erdman, raising both glasses at him. He looked around the pub. "Where's Jarvis?"

"Coffee, Borough Market." Axel licked the foam from his lips. "Is it true that prick called you Nerdman?"

Erdman slid his eyes away and changed the subject. "Where were you this morning?"

Axel looked shifty. "Doing a bit of this and that."

When it was Axel's round, Erdman offered to help him carry the drinks. As they walked to the bar, Axel bumped shoulders with a skinny dude in a pin-striped suit, who, in turn, bumped up against Erdman. "Sorry," muttered Axel. The man held up a placatory hand, his fingers splayed like sticks, and disappeared into the men's room.

"Actually, mate, I've got a bit of news," said Axel, his attention back on his friend.

Erdman set his empty pint glass down carefully on the bar. When people said things like that, it meant one of two things: Either they were having a baby or they had gotten a new job. As Axel was single, he could guess which it was.

"Where you going then?"

His friend beamed. "To LA. To a lifestyle magazine. Can you believe it? Cool or what?"

"Yeah, way cool."

Listening to Axel jabber on about where he was going to live, and all the hot women he was going to meet, was almost as uncomfortable as that morning's editorial conference.

Fifteen minutes later, Erdman told his colleagues he was feeling unwell and took himself home to bed.

FOURTEEN

2.17 p.m.

Jakey screwed up his eyes so he didn't have to look at the walls of his classroom and the drawings that never changed. The classroom where he practiced his phonemes, where he ate his lunch, where he'd spent every playtime since starting Year One at South Side Primary School.

Outside, he could hear his classmates shouting to one another, the high-pitched shrieks of children playing football or tag or hopscotch.

He was allowed to pick one person every day to stay inside with him and play cars or Legos. Today, he had chosen Joshua Carruthers. On hearing this news, Joshua had wrinkled his nose and said, "Oh, but Miss Haines, I promised I'd play football with Samuel," but their teacher had shaken her head, and said, no, no, he had to stay in with Jakey.

It wasn't that Jakey didn't have friends. He was a personable child, well-liked by his classmates, but the lure of fresh air and freedom to run was difficult for small boys to ignore.

When they had eaten their afternoon snack, and Mrs. Husselbee, his aide, had told them she was popping to the restroom, Joshua had gazed longingly out the window.

"I'm going to the toilet, too," he said. He still hadn't come back.

Jakey placed his car on the table, drew it back, and let it go. It flew off the edge and bounced onto the carpet. He picked at a spot of dried cereal on his trouser leg. He tried to ignore the pain in his arm, the growing ache in his chest. Then he limped over to the window and looked out at the playground, and the playing field beyond.

Without thinking about what he was doing, Jakey opened the door and went outside.

Children whirled past him, shouting to each other, running, running, running everywhere. One child, a much bigger boy, almost crashed into him, but he swerved around him at the last minute, the fronds of his scarf brushing against Jakey's face. A gaggle of girls, Year Two, screeched at him to move out of the way, to stop blocking their running game.

Jakey wasn't allowed on the playground. There were dangers everywhere, his mother said. He could get knocked over and break an arm. Or he could trip over his feet and bash up his knee.

Or—and this was not a reason his mother ever voiced—no one would want to play with the poor little boy who couldn't run or catch. And so he had to stay inside. With Mrs. Husselbee. Even though school, with its central heating and overattentive staff, was so suffocating that at times he couldn't breathe.

The November air slapped his cheeks, and he shivered, suddenly aware that he had forgotten to put on his coat.

He should go back inside. In a few moments, Mrs. Husselbee would return, see his empty chair, and come looking for him. But he didn't want to be in that stuffy classroom. He wanted to be like everyone else.

Jakey inched his way around the edge of the concrete rectangle that was South Side Primary's playground, towards the field that bordered it.

A few boys were playing football, matchstick figures against the grey winter sky. He watched them for a bit, marveling at the ease with that they ran, ducked, controlled the ball with a fluidity of movement that was alien to him.

He lurched a couple of steps closer.

Outside the school, a man watched his faltering progress across the damp earth towards the perimeter fence at the far end of the school grounds that kept children in and strangers out.

The man buttoned up his pin-striped jacket.

Jakey hadn't noticed the way his shoes sank into the mud as he made his way across the field, or heard the distant whistle that signaled the end of South Side Primary School's afternoon break. He hadn't realized how much his arm was hurting, or how his breath came in wheezy gasps. He rested his face against the cool mesh of galvanized wire, and counted the cars driving by.

A movement on the other side of the pavement caught his eye. A man was crossing the road. He was wearing a dark suit and hat. He saw Jakey peering through the diamond-shaped gaps in the fence.

"Hello," he said.

"'lo," mumbled Jakey.

"Not playing football?"

Jakey gave a sort of half shrug.

"Never mind. You can talk to me instead."

Jakey looked at the man's black eyes. He should go back. He shivered again.

"Rabbits grow a special winter coat at this time of year." He pointed to Jakey's sweater. "Looks like you could do with one of those."

Jakey thought for a moment. "That would be cool."

"Do you like rabbits?" said the man.

Jakey did not have much movement in his neck, but he tried to nod anyway. "Ye-es," he said, "but I like dogs best."

"I've got a dog. She's at home. Do you want to come and see her?"

"I'm not allowed out of school."

"I thought you liked dogs."

"I do."

The man shrugged. "Doesn't sound like it."

"But I can't. I'll get into trouble."

"I'm sure you could if you really tried."

Jakey had wanted a dog for his birthday. Dogs didn't care if your arms wouldn't work, or if your head was all wonky. When he had opened his presents to find a mechanical puppy, he had cried for two hours. Then his mother had cried, too.

He should go back to his classroom, but the man was smiling at him, and his eyes had crinkly lines around them, a bit like his father's.

If his father was here, right at this very moment, he'd make Jakey stop talking to this man and go back to class.

Jakey decided to do the opposite.

"I suppose I could see if the playground gate is open," he said. "I sometimes see the Year Threes go through it for PE when my teacher, Miss Haines, is reading us a story."

"Attaboy!"

Jakey didn't know what that word meant, but he thought it must be good, as the man was still smiling.

"If it's not open, same time tomorrow?"

He smiled shyly in reply, and had just turned to walk back up the field when he saw Mrs. Husselbee running towards him, the belt of her coat flapping behind her.

"Jakey! Where have you been? I've been looking for you everywhere. You must never leave your classroom without telling me."

"I was only . . ." He turned back towards the fence, to show Mrs. Husselbee the person he'd been talking to, but the man in the suit had gone.

FIFTEEN

5.11 p.m.

When Erdman told his colleagues he was going home to bed, it wasn't a lie, exactly. He *was* going home, but only after a teensy diversion.

Six pints and one game of pool later, he lurched past the site of the old Cross Bones graveyard and staggered towards London Bridge Station. He wasn't sure if it was the beer or the rush-hour traffic making his head whirl.

What was it Samuel Johnson had said? *When a man is tired of London, he is tired of life.* What a load of bollocks. Samuel Johnson had never caught the sodding 5.16 p.m. to Lewisham.

Fighting to keep his balance, Erdman stumbled the length of the platform, scouring the crowded cars for just enough space to fold himself in. Commuters thumped on the windows and shouted at passengers to move down, to make room. Erdman favored the stealth approach, and elbowed his way in a moment or two before the doors slammed shut, forcing the mass of bodies to absorb him.

He pressed his face against the cool glass doors and shut his eyes. When he opened them, a blank-faced man in a pin-striped suit and a bulky holdall at his feet was staring at him from across the compartment. *What you looking at, weirdo?* But he daren't voice it. Alcohol made him bolder, but he didn't have that instinct for trouble, however aggrieved he felt. A frisson of recognition tingled his synapses, but was washed away on a wave of giddiness as the train juddered home. He closed his eyes again. That lucky bastard, Axel. This was all his fault.

By the time he forced his eyes open again, the man had been replaced by a black woman reading a newspaper. Her multicolored dreads partially obscured the headline, but he could see enough to recognize the mother of that missing girl, Clara whassername again, splashed over the front page, on a pilgrimage to the sweetshop where her child was last seen. Her face was mangled by anguish.

When the train pulled in, Erdman weaved the short distance up the hill from Lewisham Station, but didn't make it home in time and pissed against the low wall outside their flat. He wiped his hand on his trousers, then patted his pocket. Better switch his mobile back on. It beeped loudly at him, and he grimaced at the sound. Three messages. Probably Axel or Amber. He'd check when he got in.

In the dusk, the converted Victorian apartments on his street were stacked upwards like packing crates. Retching and wretched, he fumbled in his pocket for his key. It took him three tries to slide it into the lock.

Lilith was watching the press conference on the early evening news. Mrs. Foyle was barely coherent, distress plastered onto her features like makeup. Mr. Foyle was shrunken and grey, desiccated by grief.

"Please, if you have any information, get in touch with the police," stuttered Mrs. Foyle, the contours of her face ragged with suffering.

Her husband was more composed, but his eyes gave him away, those hollowed-out pools of desperation.

"Clara, if you're watching, Mummy and Daddy love you very much." Mr. Foyle looked directly into the camera. "Please, just bring our baby home."

Erdman wasn't so drunk that he couldn't sense the atmosphere as soon as he put down his keys. Lilith kept her back to him, eyes glued to the screen, hands in the sink. Jakey was at the breakfast bar, pushing chicken casserole around his plate, his attention snared by a woman police officer describing the suspect who had been seen leading Clara away.

"What's up, champ? Does your arm hurt?" Erdman sat on the stool next to him and gently touched his son's stiffened limb, but Jakey wrenched it away.

"You didn't come, Daddy." His big brown eyes were accusing.

"I'm here now, aren't I?"

Lilith whirled around, sending suds flying. "You forgot, didn't you?"

What was he supposed to have forgotten? His booze-befuddled brain searched for the answer, but it eluded him. He grinned stupidly at Lilith, whose arms were folded across her chest.

"You look beautiful."

She refused to take the bait. "You were supposed to be at Take Your Dad to School Day. Remember?"

Erdman groaned, a vague memory pressing at the

edges of his brain. "I thought that was tomorrow afternoon."

"We tried to call, but your mobile was off—"

"The battery was—"

"DON'T INTERRUPT ME. Jakey was gutted." Lilith's eyes spoke the words that she couldn't say aloud. That they didn't know how much longer their son would be physically able to go to school. That it was bad enough he wasn't allowed on the playground at break time, or to take part in PE, or that he had to sit at a specially adapted desk, or that the other mothers were all too terrified to invite him over. That Jakey's needs should come first. Always. Always. Always.

He opened his mouth to say something, and shut it again. He slid onto the stool next to Jakey.

"I'm sorry, sweetheart. I'll buy you a toy tomorrow. Will that cheer you up?"

"You can't *buy* forgiveness, Erdman. You have to earn it. Didn't anyone ever teach you that?"

"You're not helping, Lilith." He held his arms open for a hug. Then dropped them to his sides when Jakey didn't budge. "Daddy's really sorry."

"Joe's daddy was cool." Jakey's voice was sulky. "He came in a police car. And Harry's dad earns loads of money and buyed us all sweets."

Cops and robbers. The officer and the lawyer. Erdman had met them both at a family social at the start of the term. Groping for conversation, they had settled on football, that great equalizer. Except Erdman had never quite perfected the art of small talk. He had plenty to say about Messi's sliding tackle or Fergie's replacement. But somehow he could never get the words out. Three minutes of awkward silence followed, and then they'd made their excuses.

"You smell funny, Daddy."

"Oh God. You're drunk."

Lilith didn't speak to him for the rest of the evening.

Her spikiness was one of the reasons he'd fallen in love with her. He had always admired the way she could skewer an adversary with words alone, but these days Lilith's barbs were aimed at him. He'd read in some weekend supplement or the other that marriages rarely survived once contempt had crept in. Well, contempt hadn't just crept into theirs; it was stomping about with bloody great boots on.

When once they'd sung along to the radio and discussed the day's news, now they'd fallen into the habit of snarling at each other like wounded animals. Erdman couldn't remember the last time Lilith had slung her arms around his neck and smiled *that* smile.

When Erdman first met Lilith, she fizzed and sparked with an invisible energy, always laughing, always moving. Now she barely spoke to him at all. He knew why, but he didn't know how to make it better, so he did what he usually did. Nothing.

Naturally, his darling wife had stalked off to bed without saying good night. When he'd gone up a couple of hours later to try and smooth things over, she was asleep, slack-mouthed, a slug trail of dribble on the pillow.

In the early days, he'd have slid in beside her and gathered her naked body to his, murmuring an apology. They might have made love or spooned, like two pieces of a well-worn puzzle.

Now she slept in faded pajamas and didn't like being disturbed, so he inched his way under the cold sheets, careful not to touch her.

On nights like these he missed her the most.

SIXTEEN

11.59 p.m.

Miles Foyle counted to ten and knocked on his bedroom door.

"Who is it?"

"Me."

"Go away."

He tried the handle, but it was locked. "Please, Amy."

"I said, go away."

"I want to talk to you."

"Try talking to one of your whores instead."

He rapped on the wood until his knuckles turned pink. After a couple of minutes, he heard the sound of the privacy bolt being drawn back.

"You'll wake Eleanor, you selfish twat."

He tried to grab her hand, but she pulled it away.

"Please. Give me a chance to explain."

"What's to explain, Miles? There's a prostitute in today's *Sun* telling the world that my husband fucked her for money."

"It was only once."

"So?"

"I was lonely."

"So?"

Amy sat on the edge of their bed, poured herself a glass of wine from the bottle on her nightstand. She swallowed a large mouthful.

"She's old and raddled and disgusting, and you *paid* to fuck her." Her words were laced with disbelief, her lips stained with tannin.

He knelt on the floor next to the bed, his knees sinking into the thick carpet. He could see the skin under her nose had been rubbed raw from endless crying, and that vulnerability made him weak with regret.

"I was lonely, Amy. I'm sorry." His voice wavered. "I'll make damn sure it doesn't happen again."

"You lied to me," she said, refusing to look at him. "You promised you'd never had sex." Amy swiped at her eyes. "That you liked to *talk*."

"Look, we're going to get through this." He was crying now. "The police will find Clara, and I'll prove to you how much I love you, and we'll be a family again."

"But it's the not the first time, is it? That you've been accused of something"—her voice was barely audible—"unsavory."

He flinched, as if she had fired a slingshot at him instead of words.

"She withdrew the allegation," he said. "It was a horrible misunderstanding."

"She was fourteen."

"She was a hormonally charged teenager who completely misread the signals." His sigh was impatient. "We've been through this before, Amy."

"And we'll go through it again, *Miles*."

"Look, she was an intern who tried to seduce me and when I didn't respond, she set me up."

Amy stared fixedly at the carpet.

"It's the truth," he said. "I certainly never held her against her will."

"No, the truth is, you're a cheating bastard who pays for sluts and can't keep his thing in his pants."

"It was *once*."

But Amy would not answer.

A quiet knock on the door.

"What is it, Gina?"

"It's Eleanor, Mrs. Foyle. She's crying again. She's asking for you."

Amy walked across the bedroom floor. The light from the lamp reflected the sheen of tears on her face. Gina was waiting for her on the landing, the belt of her robe tied tightly around her waist, slim legs visible beneath its hem.

"I think she's had another of those nightmares. She was shouting for her sister."

Amy stood very still. She leaned towards the nanny, whose shattered face already wore the answer to the question that Amy now hissed into her ear.

"Have you stopped to consider that all of this might be your fault, Gina? None of this would have happened if you'd just been there to pick up my daughter."

TUESDAY

SEVENTEEN

3.04 a.m.

Before Erdman even opened his eyes, he could hear the low gulps of Jakey's distress. He dragged himself to the surface of sleep.

"All right, champ?" he mumbled.

His son didn't answer.

Erdman rolled out of bed, reached for his robe, and padded down the half-lit hallway to his son's bedroom.

Jakey was sitting up, holding his bruised arm against his chest. His breath came in short, sharp gasps. The night-light cast shadows across the walls.

"Everything hurts," he said, misery rolling across his features.

Erdman fought to keep his face very still. "Does Mummy know about this?"

"No," said the little boy. "I tried calling, but she didn't wake up."

Erdman sat on the bed, the weight of his body on the mattress causing Jakey's body to briefly rise, and uncurled his son's fingers.

His "good" arm was now hot and swollen, a lump

already forming on the flat of his forearm. His son's breathing sounded labored, his face much warmer than usual.

Jesus.

He calculated how many doses of medication his son had taken in the last twenty-four hours. They would have to wait until morning before they could give him anything else, even a painkiller.

His son leaned into him, his body burning through the thin fabric of his pajamas, despite the chill of the room.

"Stay, with me, Daddy," he said. "Just 'til I fall asleep."

"All right, champ."

Erdman swung his legs into his son's bed and pulled the covers over them both. A pale moon threw down its light through a crack in the curtains. He stroked the hair from his son's face. The sounds of Jakey's ragged breath filled his ears and his heart.

Although neither of them knew it then, father and son had only a few hours left together, before their lives were as ruined as Jakey's bones.

EIGHTEEN

8.12 a.m.

Clara scraped at the patch of mold on the wall with her fingernail. Her nose was blocked, and it was getting harder to breathe. Her mother would blame it on her allergies. She hated it here.

Her eyelids were heavy, as if someone had sewn miniature weights inside them. She was tired all the time, but she could see grey light through the window, so she knew it must be morning. She crawled under the sheet, which hadn't been changed since she'd wet herself two nights ago. It was smelly and cold against her skin, and she wanted to go home.

There was ice on the inside of the window. The freezing air made her shiver.

It had been several hours since Clara had eaten a proper meal. For two nights now, he had brought up a glass of milk, a slice or two of bread and butter, and once, a bruised banana, which he had peeled for her. There had been no need. Despite the awkwardness of her hands, Clara could manage simple tasks, had been doing so since she was tiny. She wolfed down the food first, because when she drank the milk, the darkness came. The funny thing was that even when she wasn't hungry, her stomach hurt. Nothing seemed to fill up the emptiness inside.

At night she slept, but daylight was no protection. Sometimes she hid under the bed just so she didn't have to see the cold, damp walls pressing down on her.

This room frightened her. Like everything about this place. Especially the Night Man.

She had begun to call him that after a horrible, vivid dream a few hours after she had been taken. She had woken, with a *thud* of dread, into the sort of dense blueness that signals the hour before dawn. There was a chalky taste in her mouth. The room was empty, the house silent, but all Clara could see were his black eyes and carved-out face.

On his last visit, he had brought a cardigan with him. It was yellow and knitted and he had buttoned it up for her, right to her chin. She didn't like the way he looked at her hands as he did it.

If anyone had asked Clara how his gaze upon her made her feel, she might have said like she was shrinking. And one day soon she would disappear altogether. He made her want to hide.

Clara sat up, and stilled herself as tiny stars danced about inside her head, like the fireworks she had watched through the slats last night. The fireworks had baffled her. She knew it couldn't be Bonfire Night, because she had spent it on the Heath with her parents and Eleanor. She remembered it quite clearly, because her mother had complained about the mud, the cold, the crowds. She had rummaged in her handbag for her little silver flask, and shouted at her father when she couldn't find it, and everyone had stared at them. Clara had said to Eleanor that her mother was always cross about *something*, and Eleanor had shaken her head and put her finger to her lips.

"Don't forget me," Clara whispered.

On the street below, she could hear the muffled hum of rush-hour traffic. On the first day, she had tried to look out of the window, but she was so small she couldn't reach the sill. On the second day, she had pressed her back against the door and pushed, but it was locked.

She had no idea how long she'd been in this room that smelled of cabbage and a sweet, sickly scent she hadn't come across before.

Sometimes she cried, but mostly she talked to herself, muttered imaginings with her "pillow" doll.

They went on long journeys. To the beach near her old home. To the swimming pool with Gina on a Saturday morning.

A footfall outside caught her ear, and her stomach fell through her bottom. He did not touch her in places he shouldn't or look at her in the way she sometimes saw men glance at Gina. He had not hurt her. But she knew what was coming, and that made it worse.

Clara drew the urine-stained sheet up to her chin, and listened as the lock clicked and the door swung in.

The Night Man was pushing a grey machine on wheels with a box attached to it and a long metal arm that stuck out. She watched as he plugged it into the wall and it made a whirring sound. His mouth twisted.

"Time for your X-ray, my dear," he said.

NINETEEN

10.57 a.m.

On Tuesday morning, when Erdman blew in late on a gust of rain and a hangover, Daniel Jarvis was waiting for him. It was four days since he had cut his hand.

He should have been at the office an hour ago. But Jakey was acting up, clinging to Erdman's legs as he laced up his shoes, begging him not to go in today, not to go *anywhere*.

"Can't you work from home, Daddy? Please. Pleeeease."

When Erdman had explained that no, unfortunately he could not, the little boy had become hysterical. Coughed and coughed until he was sick. Erdman had spent ages trying to calm him down, promising to get home as early as he could, but Jakey had refused to listen. Eventually, Lilith had forcibly peeled him off. He'd tried to ignore the sound of his son's screams as he jogged down the garden path, grateful for his wife's no-nonsense attitude. Both of them knew how Jakey could get after taking his medication.

And then his train had been delayed.

"Erdman?"

His boss was perched on the edge of Erdman's desk, staring pointedly at his watch. A freelancer Erdman didn't recognize was working quietly in the corner.

"Daniel."

He didn't mean to sound quite so brusque, but he'd hardly slept. He'd been up until late, trying to finish off last week's features, and he still had to write that crap on the healing properties of the amethyst, as well as squeezing in a break to buy Jakey's guilt gift.

"A word," he said, unsmiling. As Erdman followed Jarvis into the editor's office, he caught a glimpse of Amber's agonized face. He rolled his eyes at her, but for once, she didn't grin back.

"Sit down, Erdman."

It was bad, then. No stupid nickname, no pretense that everything was all jolly-jolly. But the question was, how bad?

Jarvis began a well-rehearsed spiel about magazines facing tough times, what with tightened budgets and dipping circulation. "You get the picture, mate."

Erdman stared hard at a patch of grease on Jarvis's jacket and wondered where this was going. It didn't take long to find out.

"So the point is, I'm afraid we're going to have to let you go," said Jarvis. "You're just too expensive for us these days."

A bubble of nausea worked its way up Erdman's throat and he swallowed it back down. Jarvis was talking shit. They both knew it. It was a clash of personalities, as simple as that. To his shame, he found himself struggling to speak.

"We'll sort you out some redundancy. And you'll

obviously get your notice period. A month, I believe. Thanks very much for your loyal service. Ten years, isn't it?"

"Twelve."

Erdman stood up. Jarvis clapped him on the back. "Chin up, Erdman. You'll easily walk into another job with all your experience. Oh, I almost forgot . . ."

To his credit, Jarvis flushed as he handed over the plastic bag filled with old notebooks, chewed pens, and paper clips. Erdman spied an empty Crunchie wrapper in there, too.

"Sorry," he said awkwardly. "It's company policy. We prefer employees to leave ASAP now, you know how it is."

Erdman wasn't a violent man, but as Jarvis dialed down to Pete, the aging security guard, he experienced a profound longing to smack his smarmy bastard boss—ex-boss—one right in the mouth.

TWENTY

11.07 a.m.

DS Fitzroy returned home to shower and change as soon as she was sure David had left for his job as a commodity broker in the City. Sleep was an extravagance she could ill afford. Every hour that passed pulled Clara Foyle further into darkness. But even she needed to wash now and then.

A plate of congealed fish pie sat on the kitchen counter. Her husband loved to cook, often making her elaborate meals. Fitzroy acknowledged the rebuke and served her penance by microwaving it and eating it for breakfast.

Hair damp, she sat on the edge of the perfectly smooth bed and tapped out a text to remind David of their appointment at the clinic on Thursday. Halfway through, she stopped and deleted it, suddenly worried he might phone in response. She pulled a pad from her bedside drawer and scribbled a note instead. She did not have the energy for that particular conversation.

When she had finished, she placed it on David's pillow. Her message was brisk, businesslike. Once upon a time, she had drawn doodles and kisses while he had slipped his own scraps of paper, full of love, into books for her to find. On their first date, he had surprised her by taking her to a basement salsa club in the east of the city, moving with a rhythm that had excited and exhilarated her, which made it all the more painful they were so out of step.

At first, his age—he was twelve years older than she—hadn't seemed to matter. His stability, his financial acumen, his focus on career over family, had steadied—and aroused—her.

But now her desire for a child was stretching the distance between them, dragging them both into uncharted territory. If she—or he—moved a single step backwards, something would surely snap.

Detective Constable Alun Chambers was picking her up in five minutes, in time for a briefing with The Boss. She already knew what he was going to say. That they were frighteningly, dangerously short on viable leads. That they needed to eliminate Miles Foyle without arresting him, if possible. That he needed lateral thinkers on his team. That finding Clara was the priority.

But there was nothing.

So far, Mrs. Foyle was coming up clean, and Mr. Atwal, the shopkeeper, was about as useful as a chocolate teapot, changing his statement every five minutes about who had been in the shop on the afternoon that Clara had vanished. There had been one confirmed sighting of the little girl—dozens of others from Land's End to Mallorca—and a vague description of her abductor. Someone had reported a silver or grey van speeding away a few minutes after she was last seen, but they didn't get its registration plate, not a single letter or number. And the CCTV cameras close to the school *had* been filming—but in the opposite direction.

Fitzroy knew exactly the type of individual who stole girls like Clara, and prayed she wasn't suffering.

She wondered what her father would do if he was running this investigation, and called up his face, unsmiling, hard. Even in repose, the lines around his mouth fanned downwards.

Years later she could still hear him, strident and unwilling, the first—and last—time she had approached him for help with a case, a stabbing in a neighborhood that protected its own.

"Don't think about what I would be doing, silly girl. Find the patterns yourself."

She should have known better. No special favors. A patronizing dismissal. Even though she had scored the highest exam marks of her class at Hendon, and at twenty-one, was no longer a girl.

It was nothing new.

If only she had been more like Nina, who had laughed off a childhood lashed by his critical words and charmed him into paying for drama school.

When Nina had played Rosalind in *As You Like It,* he'd led the standing ovation and clapped until his palms were sore. But not once had he told Etta he was proud that she'd followed him into the force.

Too late now. Her father had moved to Greece with his new wife two years ago, and she hadn't seen him since.

Fitzroy wandered into the living room. The sofa was the same grey as the sky outside. Every magazine, every book, every *thing* was in its place. She tried to imagine a heap of toys in the corner, spilling across the expensive rug that David had brought back from his last business trip to Italy. She tried to imagine the cry of a baby with David's muddy eyes, his dark curls, pulling at her from its crib. She tried to imagine a future for her and David without a child, but the pages were blank, unwritten.

Outside, Chambers sounded his horn and she slipped from the flat like a ghost.

TWENTY-ONE

11.15 a.m.

Shit, bollocks, fuck. Shit, bollocks, fuck. Erdman's feet pounded out the rhythm of his misery.

He was officially Unemployed. Out of Work. Up Shit Creek Without a Paddle. Any of the above would do.

Humiliated Erdman Frith was sacked yesterday. The loser, 39, couldn't even hold down a job at a magazine for nut jobs.

Behind him, a young boy laughed. He sounded so much like Jakey that Erdman spun around, but the pavement was empty, apart from a couple of people with their heads down, immersed in their mobile phones. *Should be called antisocial media*, he thought.

He pounded the heels of both hands against the heavy wooden door, but even though the glass shook, it wouldn't budge. The Bank didn't open until 11.30 a.m., and it was fifteen minutes shy of that.

There was always the liquor store. Nah, maybe not. He wasn't desperate enough to risk being seen with a six-pack in the park. That was the province of tramps and winos. And he wasn't there. Yet.

Not that he could go home, either. It was Tea Bread Tuesday, and Lilith was hosting some hospital fund-raiser at the house. She'd been up since the crack of, making cakes that cost more than she'd raise. Should have just donated a few quid and saved herself the trouble.

What the hell were they going to do for cash when the money ran out?

And what the hell was he going to do for the rest of the day?

He couldn't face a museum, full of camera-happy tourists and noisy schoolkids. Wait for the pub to open? Possibly. But he couldn't afford to drink all day in more ways than one.

The splats of rain that had drenched him on his way to work had stopped, and although the skies were grey, he hoped it might stay dry for a couple of hours at least. Of course. He knew what he'd do. He'd go and see Ma.

One of Erdman's earliest memories was of seeing his mother cry. Shirley Frith didn't cry much, which was why he remembered it.

He'd been three the first time he'd asked where his brother had gone, and pretty soon he learned not to. Not long after that, all the photographs had disappeared. As the years faded, so had his memories of Carlton.

And so Erdman grew up in a house where two should have been four, where grief wore the soft edges of his mother into sharpened points, where he was smothered and shunned in equal measure.

Back then, whenever Erdman caught a glimpse of his reflection, he always saw an echo of himself, a skewed mirror of his own face. These days he tried not to think about his childhood at all.

As he got off the bus and walked up the street, his legs felt heavy. He was getting older, there was no denying it. At least his eyesight wasn't going. Every morning, before he got up, he checked he could still read the Phases of the Moon poster Lilith had stuck on their bedroom wall. *A waxing gibbous moon is one that is illuminated by more than half but less than full.* It was as much a part of his routine as brushing his teeth.

God, he hated visiting his mother. Why had he decided to come, today of all days? Must be his masochistic streak. It didn't make him feel any better and it certainly didn't help her. Christ, it was all of six months since he would have last visited her.

He trudged up the path, nodding at the gardener, who was clipping the edges. He imagined what Ma might say, that slow stretching out of her vowels, her eyebrows knitted into an unrelenting expression of discontent.

"It's been far too long, darling. I'm still your mother, after all."

Erdman stepped off the gravel and onto the spongy grass. A bouquet of lilies dangled from one hand. He knelt before his mother's grave.

SHIRLEY FRITH

B. 13 MAY 1947 ~ D. 25 MAY 2012

LOVING MOTHER AND WIFE

Taken Too Soon

The weeds had beanstalked since her funeral, and they twisted around the headstone, almost obscuring her name. He tugged hard at them, careful to avoid his bandaged finger, and allowed his past to engulf him.

He'd been a lonely child, always in his mother's way, always dressing the wounds inflicted by her knife-sharp tongue.

Always playing with his dead brother.

He'd hated taking friends home. She'd bombard them with questions, never noticing that as she became more personal they would shrink into themselves, faces as pink as the canned salmon sandwiches she served up for tea. Invariably, the conversation would turn to him.

"Do you spend all day in your bedroom too, pretending to play with imaginary friends?" she'd asked one young visitor. For the next three years, Erdman's schoolmates had teased him mercilessly.

As a teenager, it had got so bad that the few friends he did have would wait in the car, unwilling to face her intrusive probing. The sly digs dressed up in fancy clothes.

Mostly, though, Erdman had stayed in his room by himself, and the conversations with his brother had eventually petered out. He'd learned how to distract himself with books and computer games.

Not once had he spoken of it, not to his mother, or to Lilith, but buried it deep in the murk of his memory.

Now it was Jakey who had imaginary friends. A few nights ago, he'd come across Lilith on the landing, an ear pressed to the door, an indulgent smile on her lips.

She'd beckoned to him, inviting him closer.

"Listen to this," she'd whispered.

Erdman had stood next to her. He'd inhaled the warm, sweet scent of her skin and briefly forgot himself. But at the sound of Jakey's high, clear voice, his stomach had turned over.

"Don't know."

Silence for a few beats.

"I can't."

Another silence.

" 'kay. How 'bout ten?"

His son's tone had been sulky and reluctant. A *thump*, and a muffled yelp. Erdman had started towards the handle, but Lilith had laid her hand on his arm to stop him.

"Twenty?"

A sigh.

"Tell me, then."

A pause of a few seconds, and then Jakey had spoken again, a note of incredulity creeping in.

"Two hundred and six?" Another pause. "I do believe you. I do."

Erdman heard Jakey moving around, and the sound of his toy cupboard door opening. Lilith had given him another conspiratorial smile, but Erdman couldn't bring himself to smile back.

"Did you know that having an imaginary friend is a mark of superior intellect?" she'd whispered. "Cute, isn't it?"

"Don't. I don't want you to."

Jakey's voice was sharper. Erdman thought he heard an undercurrent of fear and, ignoring Lilith, he'd opened the door.

"Everything all right, champ?"

Jakey jumped, a guilty look on his face. "Fine," he'd mumbled, Mr. Bunnikins under his arm.

Erdman shoved a handful of Legos into their box. "Bedtime in a bit, okay?"

" 'kay."

As he'd turned to go, Jakey called softly after him. "Daddy, do you know how many bones there are in a skeleton?"

Erdman looked around in surprise. "A human one?"

"Yes," he'd said, his thumb finding its way into his mouth.

"Um, no idea. Do you?"

"Two hundred and six."

"Wow," said Erdman. "That's a lot."

"You're strong, Daddy, aren't you? Really strong."

Erdman had laughed and flexed a skinny arm. "As an ox."

"So you could fight anyone?"

Erdman's grin faded. "Well, I wouldn't go that far. But no one's going to be doing any fighting around here, champ, so you don't need to worry about it."

And Jakey had given him a sad little smile.

Later that night, in between checking his online bank account and an hour or so fighting the Horde in Pandaria, Erdman had called up an article about the human body, just out of curiosity. Jakey was right. Must have been something he'd learned at school.

The ground was damp, the moisture seeping into his jeans, but he ignored it. He unwrapped the cheese roll that Lilith had made for him and took a bite.

Eeugh. Pickle. Thanks, Lilith.

His wife was obviously still pissed off with him, but

the gesture was so Lilith it sort of made him smile. She was a woman who could hold her own. The only woman he'd dared introduce to his mother.

"Hello, darling, a joy to meet you at last. Erdman tells me you're a foster child. You poor girl. How could anyone do such a thing? Such a terrible shame."

Twelve years later, Erdman still cringed when he recalled it, but Lilith had handled the comment with customary aplomb.

"Hello, Mrs. Frith. It's a pleasure to meet you, too. That happened a long time ago, and I'd prefer to leave the past where it is. My foster parents were wonderful, by the way. But I like your dress. Marks and Spencer, is it?"

Shirley had frowned then. "And we haven't met before?"

"I don't think so," said Lilith, smiling. "I'm sure I'd have remembered you."

The women circled each other warily, but, over the years, their defenses were weakened by his mother's vocal bombardment, and gradually, their visits had stopped.

His mother had too much pride to patch things up. Before long, they were down to birthday and Christmas cards. And then, six months ago, he'd received a call from a nurse at a hospice in Brighton.

"Your mother's asking for you. She's being most insistent."

He'd gone alone, not sure what to expect and ashamed he didn't know. The nurse told him his mother's chemotherapy had triggered a stroke, which had affected her speech and ability to swallow.

He hadn't recognized the emaciated creature on the bed with bird's-nest hair and the kind of flowery nightie she'd always despised. Her head was skewed at an awkward angle, her chin resting on the jetty of her collarbone.

"It's me, Ma."

One drooping corner of her mouth twitched, but she didn't open her eyes. Erdman felt for her fingers. They were warm, the skin papery. His eyes stung.

"I won't leave you again, I promise."

"She died once, you know." The nurse's tone was conversational, but Erdman had recognized a dig when he heard one. "She suffered an allergic reaction to one of the chemo drugs, and went into anaphylaxis. She was clinically dead for about two minutes or so." She dabbed at Shirley's forehead with a sponge. "But she's a stubborn old thing. She obviously wasn't ready to go without seeing you first."

Erdman had covered his face with his hands.

"Better late than never," the nurse relented, patting him on the back.

For hours, he'd waited by her bed, never letting go of her hand, even when the nurse checked her blood pressure and the dark night floated in. He'd been dozing when he heard her voice, so low, so *un-Ma*, that, at first, he thought he'd imagined it.

"Sree."

Erdman opened his eyes, but his mother hadn't moved.

"Ahm sree."

Her fingers were plucking at the covers, and she was moving her head against the pillow.

"It's okay, Ma. I'm here."

His voice seemed to soothe her, and she had stilled. A few moments later it began again.

"Ahm sree. Ahm sree."

A silence.

"Ah-m sorr-ee. Jay-key."

"Oh, Ma, don't worry about all that. We're sorry, too. But we try not to think about the future. We prefer to concentrate on the here and now."

Her head had jerked from side to side and her voice became louder, more insistent. Unsure how to calm her agitation, he chose the coward's route.

"I'll just go and ring Lilith, shall I? Let her know how well you're doing. Perhaps she'll put Jakey on the phone."

He'd gone downstairs to call his wife, knowing full well that he would not expose his son to Shirley's ramblings, but desperate to get away from the grunts coming from the place where her mouth used to be. By the time he came back, his mother was dead.

The nurse had explained that sometimes stroke patients could sound lucid but talk gibberish, that sometimes they held on until a loved one arrived before they allowed themselves to leave, that after the cancer but before the stroke, Mrs. Frith had talked about her family with warmth and love. It was a picture of his mother he couldn't reconcile with her vagaries of mood, her selfishness, her martyrdom.

After her death, he didn't cry once, not even when her body arrived in London and he buried her in a cemetery close to his home.

A fine drizzle had begun again, but there was intent behind it, so Erdman balled up his foil and scrambled to his feet, brushing the crumbs from his trousers. He placed his lips on the marble headstone. "'Bye, Ma. See you soon."

The cemetery was empty as he wended his way back to the exit, apart from the gardener and a lone figure in a black suit, sitting on a bench, with a bag at his feet.

The man's face was familiar. Erdman stared at the razor-sharp cheekbones, convinced he'd seen them before. Who *was* he?

"Are you following—"

But he was talking to empty air. The figure was already sliding into the backdrop of the day. Erdman caught a glimpse of him moving between the headstones, his suit a blot of ink against the paper-white sky. An unpleasant smell lingered, like decaying animals.

"Are you okay, sir?" called the gardener.

"Did you see that man? In a black suit—"

"Can't say I did, sir." The gardener stuck out his lower lip, his weather-beaten face confused.

Erdman started to run, scanning the graves for the stranger, but apart from an elderly lady in the distance, the cemetery was deserted. Who was that man? Where had he seen him? The Tube, was it? Or the train? He was sure he recognized him from somewhere else, too, but where? The wind was picking up now, and he shivered in his damp jacket. Perhaps his memory was playing tricks on him. Frankly, he had bigger problems than a half-imagined freakazoid stalker to worry about.

As Erdman walked home, a sudden thought seized him. Jakey. He'd said he'd buy him a present. He shouldn't spend much, not now. But he couldn't break another promise.

He was tossing up the merits of a toy car and a Spider-Man figure, when something in a shop window caught his eye.

Something shiny and wonderful and completely inappropriate.

He imagined Jakey's face when he gave it to him, the way his eyes lit up from the inside. He imagined that joy spreading across his face, his whole body, sparking a smile, a glorious jig of limbs.

He couldn't afford it. He wasn't even sure if Jakey would be able to ride it.

He bought it anyway.

TWENTY-TWO

2.19 p.m.

The man in the suit was waiting in exactly the same place.

"Hello," said Jakey, stumbling across the mud, two pink patches high on his cheeks.

"Hello," said the man.

"I'm not supposed to be here. Mrs. Husselbee will be mad. She told me I have to stay in the classroom, or she'll take me to Mrs. Gaynor's office. She's the head of South Side Primary School. I only came to tell you that my mummy's coming early, to take me to the doctor's, so I can't come and see your dog."

Jakey felt an unexpected surge of relief when he'd finished.

"That's a shame." The man's stitched-on smile unravelled, and he stuck his fingernail between his teeth. "I was going to ask if you wanted one of her puppies."

Jakey's eyes widened. "A puppy?"

"If you don't want one . . ."

"I do. I do." His face fell. "But I can't come today. It's my arm, see. It's going all wrong."

The man's eyes gleamed. "Can I see?"

Jakey looked back towards the school building. Mrs. Husselbee had appeared in the door of the classroom. Her hand shielded her eyes as she scanned the field.

"I've got to go," he said.

"Why don't you come and choose your puppy tomorrow? I'll meet you, if you like." The man fished inside his jacket for an envelope. Two words—*Miss Haines*—were scrawled across the back. "Give this to your teacher. It's from your mum. Says she's giving me permission to pick you up early." He smiled at the boy as he pushed it through the gap in the fence. "Not until tomorrow morning, mind."

Jakey's fingers closed around the paper, his eyes snagging on the inky loops of the man's handwriting, already smudging in the light drizzle that had just begun to fall. He shoved the letter into the pocket of his school trousers.

"Yes," said Jakey. "Tomorrow."

TWENTY-THREE

3.12 p.m.

"Has Miles Foyle been in touch?" asked The Boss.

"Not yet, sir, no."

"We need that name."

"I know."

"Tell him if he doesn't givc it to us, we'll have no choice but to bring him in."

TWENTY-FOUR

3.23 p.m.

The house was empty, which was a relief. Erdman weighed the merits of oblivion, but put the Laphroaig bottle back on the shelf and drank a glass of water instead. Then he sat on the sofa, and waited for his family to come home.

"Good God, you scared me."

Erdman squinted into artificial brightness as Lilith switched on the light, and Jakey flung himself into his father's lap as if it had been years since they had seen each other rather than a matter of hours.

"Steady, champ. Careful you don't fall."

He didn't voice the unspoken thought. *Could be catastrophic, champ.* He ran his fingers through Jakey's bangs—they needed cutting again already—to the back of his head, and gently dragged them back again. Was that a new swelling on his son's skull? He swallowed down the lump in his throat.

Lilith was tugging at her top, but it kept rising up and he could see a strip of her pale belly above the band of her skirt. Unusually, she was smiling at him. He wanted to kiss her, not make her cry.

"How come you're home so early?" There was a teasing warmth in her voice that had been absent for too long. He felt himself unfurling in her presence, like a leaf in the spring sun.

"Jarvis gave us the afternoon off." He paused. "What did the doctor say?"

She pulled a face. "The usual. Hospital if his arm gets worse. Watch out for a chest infection. Keep a close eye on him. Blah bloody blah."

"I'll take that," he said.

"Me too," she said, smiling. "Jakey's insisting on school tomorrow, so he can't be that ill."

In his head, he'd practiced telling her about his job, breaking the news with a suitably somber expression, but now she was here, right in front of him, and since she was grinning fully for the first time in weeks, he couldn't bear to.

Instead he stood up and wheeled out the bike he had hidden behind the sofa.

Jakey and Lilith gasped in precisely the same way. Erdman had always loved that about his family: the discovery that his son was a miniature version of his wife, from the way his eyebrows knitted together when he was angry to the identical mole on his neck.

"Thank you, Daddy, I love it."

"What do you think you're up to?"

"Can I go out on it now?"

"You should have discussed this with me."

"Please, Daddy. Pleeease."

Erdman looked from Jakey to his wife. It was a lesson in contrasts.

"Five minutes," he said to his son. "Go and get your shoes on."

Jakey shrieked with glee and disappeared to find his sneakers. Lilith's face was a collage of emotion.

"What if he falls off? What if he doesn't have the strength to push the pedals or hold the handlebars?" She was shouting now. "What the bloody hell were you thinking?"

"We have to let him live a little, Lilith. We can't protect him all the time."

"Yes," she said, "we can. It's our job to protect him, not put him in unnecessary danger. He's not well, remember? And where's his helmet? Shin pads? Wrist guards? Honestly, Erdman, you're useless."

There it was, that word again.

He wheeled the bike from the room without looking back.

The street was almost empty, still too early for rush-hour commuters. Darkness was settling on the city, but Jakey didn't seem to care.

"Better not go too far, champ. Mummy's not very happy with me. We'll just try you out on this stretch of pavement here."

Erdman helped his son onto the seat and guided his hands onto the handlebars. The skew of his head, his locked-in elbow tipped his weight to the left, and the stabilizer on the right of the back wheel lifted two inches off the ground.

"Whoa," said Erdman as the bike wobbled, but his son just giggled.

Carefully, Erdman closed his hand over Jakey's,

used his own weight to balance it out. His son's feet flailed, searching out stability. As he connected, he pushed backwards and the pedals windmilled crazily.

The bike lurched forward less than half an inch.

"You need to push down with your legs, champ," said Erdman, trying not to listen to the wheeze of his son's breath. "Do you think you can manage that?"

Jakey gave a brief nod of his head and tried to do as his father suggested.

Still, the bike barely moved.

Perhaps Lilith was right and his legs weren't strong enough. Perhaps this was a stupid idea. Perhaps he *was* a useless father.

"C'mon, Daddy," said Jakey. "Let's try again."

Erdman blinked into the darkness, unexpectedly moved by his son's determination.

"Hold on," he said, and grasping both handles, gently pushed Jakey and his bike forward.

Jakey's feet moved in motion with the pedals.

"I'm doing it," shouted his son. "I'm riding a bike."

"Yes, sweetheart, you are."

Jakey spent the next ten minutes practicing his newfound skill, his lower lip protruding as his thin legs pumped the pedals uphill, a grin splitting his face as he freewheeled it down, Erdman slowing his progress with a cautious hand.

And then the bike's front wheel caught the edge of an uneven paving slab.

As if time were treacle, thick and sticky and slow, Erdman witnessed his son's journey headfirst over the handlebars, heard the elongated cry that spilled from his lips. A car drove past, its headlamps splashing over Jakey's face. A light drizzle began to fall again. Erdman was able to register all of this before grabbing a fistful of Jakey's coat and jerking him back to safety.

The fear in his chest receded to a tight, dark spot.

Roughly, he pulled his son towards him. "You're all right, champ," he said, as much for himself as for Jakey. "You're fine."

Lilith opened the front door. "Tea's nearly ready," she said.

Erdman and Jakey locked eyes, waiting for her anger to detonate the calm of the street, waiting for the accusations, the threats to lock the bike in the garden shed, or worse, sell it on eBay.

"Did you hear me, boys?" she said. "Tea in five minutes."

Father and son released a breath and laughed together, a joyous, free sound.

"Can we do this every day, Daddy?"

"Try and stop me."

Neither Erdman nor Jakey noticed the man in the pin-striped jacket watching them from his grey van parked on the opposite side of the road, his nails gouging crescents in the palms of his hands.

"Let's hope nothing gets broken," the Bone Collector said.

Later, while Lilith did the dishes, Erdman gave Jakey his bath. It had been a while since he'd done that, and it shocked him.

Jakey's spine was a xylophone of bony bumps, and there was a misshapen protuberance beneath his left shoulder blade that he hadn't noticed before. He rubbed at it with Jakey's Moshi Monsters flannel and felt his son felt wince at the pressure, despite his tender touch.

On the pretext of working up a lather, he counted three soft-tissue swellings on Jakey's head. A bridge of extra bone was visible above his collarbone. The lump on his good arm was bigger. His bones looked like they had been fused together in all the wrong places, an uninvited alien presence lurking just beneath the skin.

A squirt of water hit him square in the face, and Jakey giggled and waved his Super Soaker with his good arm. He wondered how long it would take for it, too, to fuse to his body. For once, Erdman was glad; nothing like a drenching to disguise the tears.

He lifted Jakey from the bath and dried between his toes. The two big ones were malformed and turned inward, and they always reminded him of the day his son was born. The concerned cluster of doctors in the corner. The catastrophic sense of shock. The beginning of the fault line running right through his marriage.

"Daddy . . . am I going to die?"

The question stunned Erdman. Quickly, he regained his composure and buttoned up Jakey's pajama top.

"Not for a very long time, champ. Why d'you ask?"

"Josh's mum told him I was."

Erdman cursed Alyson Carruthers and her big mouth.

"You know you've got a little problem with your bones, right?"

It was the understatement of the decade, but Jakey didn't know that. "I've got extra ones, haven't I, Daddy?"

"That's right. And you're going to keep on growing extra bones, so there'll just be more of you to love."

Erdman didn't think it was necessary to explain that by the time he was a teenager, those extra bones would have bridged his muscles, tendons, and joints, restricting his movement and forming a second skeleton. A prison of bone.

Jakey seemed satisfied with his answer. "Cuddle."

His neck was twisted towards his shoulder, and he couldn't lift his left arm, but Erdman could see sleepy love shining from his son's eyes. Gently, he circled Jakey's rigid body and squeezed him as tightly as he dared. Somewhere in the house a telephone was ringing.

"Whatever happens, Daddy will always look after you, I promise," he murmured, breathing in the sweet apple scent of his son's hair.

When Erdman came downstairs, Lilith was knitting, and the vicious *clack-clack* of her needles should have warned him, but he was still lost in his moment with Jakey.

"That was Amber Collins on the phone." Her voice was dangerously calm. "She wanted to know if you're all right. Because, *apparently,* you've lost your BLOODY JOB."

Erdman stopped pouring his glass of red wine. "Ah."

"Is that the best you can do? Bloody 'ah'?" She slammed her fist on the table. "We've got a mortgage to pay, in case you've forgotten. Why didn't you tell me?"

She was shouting again, pacing up and down the sitting room and rubbing her belly, as she often did when she was agitated. Erdman hoped, like Buddha, it would bring good luck.

"I didn't want to worry you."

"Bullshit. You were too scared. So, you let your colleague tell me instead. Good call, Erdman. Really great job."

"It'll be fine."

She spoke slowly, as if Erdman was incapable of understanding words of more than one syllable.

"We haven't got any savings. You spent them on that heap-of-shite car. A *steal,* remember? Which it was. That charlatan"—she spat out the word—"*stole* good money from *us*."

It was an old resentment, one of many, and Erdman wasn't surprised to hear it come up. Lilith wheeled them out during every fight. He liked to visualize it as a hostess trolley filled with a selection of tempting desserts. This was tonight's after-dinner offering. *The Suzuki special, a real humdinger. Served with a generous side order of whipped backside.*

"You'll have to get a job. Any job. The Sun in the Sands is hiring."

"I'm not working in a pub. I'll e-mail Russell, see if he's got any shifts." He didn't tell her he'd done that already, and Russell couldn't help. *Sorry, mate. We're on a budget freeze, like the rest of the planet.*

"You can't be picky. You'll have to take whatever comes up."

"Lili, I've been a journalist for nineteen years. I'm not about to switch careers now."

She laughed bitterly. "Exactly what 'career' are you talking about? You've never been promoted, and you haven't had a decent pay increase in God knows how long. You've been at the same crappy magazine for a decade. You're unreliable, you never have anything interesting to say, and, frankly, I don't think I can take another forty years of this." She grabbed a breath. "We were happy once, Erdman. Do you remember how that feels? Before you decided to give up on us. Before"—she closed her eyes—"Jakey."

"Now, hang on a minute . . ." He raised his hands, as if that would somehow dam the verbal torrent, but Lilith wouldn't meet his gaze, and her mouth was fixed, unyielding.

"It's true."

She might as well have kicked him in the stomach. He looked at his wife. She seemed all hard, disappointed edges. Had she always been so out of focus? Was it only now, after years of blurred vision, that he was seeing her clearly?

He remembered a time when it seemed like they'd never stop talking, when they'd sneak out of the cinema early because staring in silence at a screen had seemed such a waste of time, when they'd spent hours in the kitchen, cooking together. Christ, he even used to sit on the edge of the bath with a beer while she lay amongst the bubbles, chatting nonstop about her day.

In the weeks before Jakey was born, he had rubbed oil into her growing belly and gone on late-night dashes for Marmite and cheese-and-onion crisps. They had pored over books about pregnancy, never suspecting the bomb inside her that would blow open their lives.

He remembered when they were *interested* in each other.

"Is that really what you think of me?"

The expression on her face spoke more eloquently than any words. For the fourth time in less than twelve hours, tears threatened to overwhelm him, and this time it wasn't the trickle and sniff, just-chopped-an-onion variety, but the kind of sobs that turned a man inside out.

"Fuck you," he said.

Then Erdman Frith slammed the door on his wife and stepped into darkness.

TWENTY-FIVE

7.56 p.m.

Upstairs, Jakcy stirred as the front door shut on his father's anger. He was neither asleep or awake, but somewhere in between. The halfway world of awareness and dreams.

A shadow man with sharp teeth and long, skinny arms who looked just like the bogeyman on the cover of Daddy's book was leaning over him, but Jakey gave a muffled scream, kicking out with his legs, and he disappeared in the dusty black hole beneath the bed, or inside the toy cupboard, Jakey wasn't sure.

All Jakey knew for certain was the man meant to hurt him. Just like that little girl he'd heard them talking about on the television. And that dark things liked dark places.

He pulled his Spider-Man duvet up to his nose, and tried to reach out with his sore arm. His fingertips brushed the hard plastic of his flashlight and knocked it on the floor. The door had been open when his daddy had said good night, but now it was shut. Jakey didn't like it when the door was shut.

Ol' Tommy Rawhead's here, Ol' Bloody Bones.

As soon as the name came into his mind, Jakey fought against the rise of panicked tears.

He's in my bedroom. He's come to take me away. And there's no Daddy to scare him off.

He tried to shout for his mother, but something was stopping him, something was crammed in his mouth. He clawed at it with his right hand, but it was only his old stuffed rabbit, Mr. Bunnikins.

Jakey squeezed his eyes tight, and counted to three, the way his father had taught him to when the pain was too much.

Underneath the silence of the room, he could hear the quiet rattle of Ol' Tommy's breath. Could he make it to the door? *No, nooo.* Those bony fingers would wrap around his ankles as soon as he got out of bed. What about the window? *Too high in the sky*. If only he could turn on the light. That would scare the bogeyman away.

His eyelids fluttered, heavier now, the twin ropes of imagination and sleepiness binding Jakey to his bed. *Ol' Bloody Bones has stolen that little girl, and next he's coming for me.*

The boy lay unmoving, trapped by fear and the limitations of his body, but by the time his mother came to check on him, Ol' Tommy was gone and he was asleep.

TWENTY-SIX

7.58 p.m.

Miles Foyle was slumped in a chair. Since Fitzroy had last seen him on Saturday, he hadn't shaved. A scratch scored his cheek; his eyes were swollen and baggy from lack of sleep.

He wore the look of a man sentenced to death by public condemnation.

She might have felt sorry for him if he wasn't being so bloody stubborn. Even when she had read him his rights, he'd refused a lawyer, insisting it wasn't necessary, that he had nothing to hide.

"For the benefit of the recording, it is Tuesday, November twentieth, 2012. I'm Detective Sergeant Etta Fitzroy, and I'm here with'—she paused to allow Miles Foyle to mumble his name—"the father of missing child Clara Foyle. Interview is resuming at 7.58 p.m."

Miles did not look up.

"Dr. Foyle, are you prepared to tell us the name of the woman you were with on the afternoon that Clara disappeared?"

He didn't answer.

"Dr. Foyle, you are obstructing an inquiry into the disappearance of your daughter. If you cannot tell us the name of the woman to verify your alibi, it suggests that you are lying. Do you understand that?"

He lifted his head. A spiderweb of tiny red veins was visible in the whites of his eyes.

"What happens if I don't tell you?"

"We can keep you here for another twenty-two hours or so. After that, we can apply for an extension."

He slammed his fist onto the table, making Fitzroy jump. "Why can't you just take my word for it?"

"What if the police had taken the word of Roy Whiting? Or Ian Huntley?"

Miles's chin dropped onto his chest, but she could see his weak mouth trembling. She pushed a box of tissues across the table.

"Look, we *will* find out. Why don't you make it easy on yourself?"

She waited for him to compose himself, then changed tacks.

"Dr. Foyle, is it correct that a teenage girl undertaking work experience at your private practice made an allegation of sexual assault against you last year?" Fitzroy consulted her paperwork. "I believe that she claimed you held her at your workplace for three hours against her will?"

A flush spread across his face.

"It's crap," he said. "She made it up. The allegation was withdrawn."

"Did you force her to drop the allegation, Dr. Foyle?"

Miles stared at the detective, wet lashes fringing his eyes like iron spikes.

"You've already made up your mind about me, haven't you?"

"So, change it."

Rain drummed its remorseless beat on the roof of the building. Fitzroy obsessively plucked at the fabric of her skirt over and over, as if that might restore order to the chaos confusing her thoughts. She waited an hour for him to challenge her, to fight back, to do *something* to defend himself.

But Miles Foyle refused to say another word.

While she had been in the interview suite, the stain of night had deepened around her. Fitzroy, on a brief break, ducked across the road, caught the DLR to ride the escalators at Cutty Sark.

She stepped onto the steel staircase and allowed herself to climb, to let the smooth motion carry her thoughts to a place where connections could be made.

What was stopping Miles Foyle from telling the truth? What was so bad that he'd rather be accused of his daughter's abduction than come clean?

Fitzroy stepped off the top of the escalator, turned left, walked a couple of yards, and placed her feet on the parallel moving staircase, heading downwards now. The young couple behind her nudged each other and grinned, but Fitzroy ignored them. Riding the escalators helped her to organize her thoughts, to listen to the music in her mind.

Miles Foyle was niggling at her, discordant and jarring, a clanging of cymbals in the strings section. In her experience, most child killers did not place themselves so squarely in the frame, preferring to loiter at its edges.

But that did not excuse one unassailable fact.

Miles Foyle's whereabouts were still unaccounted for at the time when Clara disappeared.

TWENTY-SEVEN

7.59 p.m.

It was drizzling and the moon was smudged, its curves rubbed soft by scudding clouds. The houses, as tightly packed as a line of dominoes, were silent. One by one, the street lamps turned talisman against darkening skies. Erdman stomped towards Tranquil Vale, and the lure of a drink.

His cheeks were wet. His fingertips swabbed the moisture, but his skin was damp again in seconds.

Lilith doesn't love me.

And then . . .

How did it come to this?

A longing to see Jakey filled him. He half-started back towards the house, towards the muted square of his son's bedroom window, but a shadow moved against the curtain, and he turned away. He couldn't face Lilith again.

Up Granville Park he strode. Right into Pagoda Gardens. Left towards Mounts Pond Road, following the bend where it joined Hare and Billet Roads, the thoroughfare into the village.

Lilith had persuaded him to buy in Blackheath eleven years ago, back when they were still high on life and each other. They had scraped together every penny they had and some they didn't, and sweet-talked the bank manager into lending them too much.

On the day they moved in, it had rained and rained until the storm drains overflowed, splashing rivers of water down Lewisham Hill. Their cardboard boxes were sodden, the polished wood of their furniture slick with moisture. At dinnertime, they had raced across the waterlogged heath in search of a meal, but Lilith's boot had got stuck in the mud, and she had tipped over, face-first.

Erdman had slid his hands beneath her armpits and hauled her to her feet, but Lilith was laughing so hard that her body went limp. She had mud on her chin, and in her hair. As her knees buckled and she slid back down into the dirt, she dragged him with her. They had lain together in the grass, rain drenching their faces, laughing until their stomachs ached.

Too filthy to venture into any of the village's restaurants, they had bought fish and chips, and eaten it with their fingers on the doorstep of the Conservatoire.

Lilith had turned to him, breath steaming, hair hanging in strings around her face.

"I hope we stay like this forever."

He had slung an arm around her shoulder and pulled her damp body to his. She was shivering beneath her jacket, but she hadn't complained of being cold, not once.

"We're a team, aren't we? We'll still be doing this when we're eighty."

"And we'll have dozens of grandchildren and a house by the sea—"

"—and a couple of dogs and some chickens," he finished for her.

She had swatted his chest lightly, but her eyes were smiling at him. They both loved building castles in the air.

Later that night, they had lain down together again, but this time on clean sheets instead of grass. It was late, but the lack of curtains and the trains rattling along the track at the bottom of their garden kept them from sleeping.

"Our own home at last," said Lilith, for the tenth time that day.

Erdman laughed, and she had rolled towards him. His fingers traced the dip and curve of her bare skin.

"I still can't believe you chose me," he murmured into her hair.

Lilith had propped herself up on her elbow, and touched the stubble of his chin with the back of her finger.

"I was waiting for you," she said.

Lilith made Erdman happier than he could remember. It didn't matter they had only been together for a year when they bought their house. It didn't matter that he'd flunked university or had a string of disastrous relationships behind him. It didn't even matter that he hated his job at a magazine that peddled claptrap. He would find a new job, propose to Lilith, and life would be perfect.

And it was for a while. Weekends on the Essex coast in their tent; long, laughter-filled nights at the Railway;

painting the walls of their first home. They had sex. They got married. They still had sex. Lilith got pregnant. Jakey was born. And their perfect life unraveled, stitch by stitch.

A sharp wind was driving the drizzle into his face, so Erdman dug his hands into his pockets and bowed his head. The streets were empty. He would have a pint, cool off, and head home.

A gang of teenagers was messing about by the bus stop, their catcalls fracturing the evening still. One of the boy-men, hooded, low-slung jeans, was dancing to a beat in his head, each elaborate step for the benefit of the girl sitting alone beneath the graffitied shelter.

"Dat is fit. Wassup, mama? Bin workin' out?"

She pretended to ignore him, fiddling with her mobile phone.

"Party wit us, mama? Hither Green, innit."

She flashed a smile, but didn't meet his eyes. Mumbled a reply. "Can't tonight. Sorry."

The teenager stood, wide-legged, in front of the girl, and grabbed his crotch. He thrust himself at her. "Wan' sum?"

His crew laughed, backslapped him, but it wasn't enough. Infuriated, the ringleader lunged for her handset. The girl shrieked, and Erdman ran towards them from across the street.

"*Hey!* What the hell are you doing? Leave her alone."

Five heads swiveled in his direction, five faces wearing the same mask of hostility.

"Wha' da fuck da matter wi'cha? Tryin' to get yoself some pussy, old man?"

The gang circled him, and he rifled through his

mental filing cabinet. When surrounded by a pack of dangerous-looking youths do you (a) act confidently and come out fighting, (b) beg for mercy, (c) play dead until it's all over? Erdman favored (b), but when he held up his hands in a *Look, lads, let's forget about it* kind of gesture, someone shoved him in the chest and he stumbled backwards. The girl, it turned out, was nowhere to be seen. His insides liquified.

Another of the gang, a rat-faced boy with a studded belt and a rope of gold around his neck, flicked a fist at Erdman and the blood sprayed from his nose and collected at the back of his throat. He spat it out, then ran his tongue around his mouth, feeling for loosened teeth. A second punch to the stomach from Rat Boy and he was on his knees. A heavy sneaker booted his kidneys, and he grunted in shock.

As his body was buffeted by kicks and punches, his mind muffled the pain, slowing time to a second-by-second stopwatch. Someone eased his wallet from his pocket, his mobile. He saw a red shoelace trailing in a puddle, the glint of a gold sovereign ring before it cut him on the chin, tasted earth and copper.

At first, he was sure it was a knife. The cool metal of a blade across his cheek. Less than a couple of seconds, and he realized it was heavier than it should be, and the wrong shape. Rat Boy waved it in front of his eyes. An unpleasant warmth filled his trousers.

"Bitchin' out, Big Daddy?" he whispered. A final kick. "Yo pissed on my shoes, fucker."

The gang whooped and high-fived, pumped up by the violence. Someone stamped on Erdman's arm, and they laughed and swaggered off.

Perhaps it was *Daddy,* whispered an hour earlier by

his sleepy son. Perhaps it was his sheer contrariness, which Lilith was always complaining about. Perhaps he was humiliated and angry. But the words were out of Erdman's mouth before he could stop them.

"Good. *Fucker*."

Rat Boy, who had lingered to tuck in his lace, uncoiled himself. In one fluid motion, he pulled a Webley 8mm from the band of his boxer shorts.

"Booya," he mouthed and fired.

Erdman barely took in the gun before the bullet punched a hole in his outer thigh. He registered warmth, then a pain that blazed brightly. Fire with white flame at its center. People talked about the smell of cordite, but he caught only the faintest whiff of rotting vegetation.

Underneath the ringing in his ears, he heard shouts, laughter, and running footsteps. Erdman closed his eyes and rested his cheek against the pavement.

A father was gunned down in southeast London last night. Erdman Frith, 39, should have minded his own bloody business.

His fingers found his leg. His jeans were sticky but the flow of blood was more of a trickle than a spurt. Erdman wasn't a doctor but he guessed the bullet had grazed his skin. Hurt like hell but he wasn't about to bleed to death. He didn't believe in God but thanked Him anyway. He'd been shot and survived. How many people could say that? He could write about it for the magazine. No, no, he didn't work there anymore.

A swell of jubilation, and then his eyes were heavy as he fought against the urge to close them again. Wasn't he supposed to stay awake? Or was that hypothermia?

As he lay still, his body roared back to life. His lower back burned with every intake of breath—kidneys?

spleen?—and his face was puffy and raw. His eyes were swelling rapidly. He imagined his flesh as a map of bruises and cuts.

Slowly, he rolled onto his side. He tried to speak, to call out for help, but his mouth didn't seem to be working.

Erdman hefted himself across the grass verge. He waited for a comforting voice, strobing blue lights, strained to hear a siren above his still-ringing ears, but the Heath stayed empty.

He shut his eyes, one foot on the ledge of unconsciousness, and prayed that someone had witnessed the attack.

As it happened, someonc *had* witnessed the attack, but if Erdman had realized who that someone was, he would have recanted his prayer.

TWENTY-EIGHT

8.07 p.m.

The father's bloodied body is lying in the grass, a couple of hundred feet away. He steps down from the van, his polished shoes sinking into boggy ground. As he gets closer, he sees that his eyes are closed, swollen. He does not move.

The Bone Collector skirts around him. He could help him. He could call an ambulance. But he does not. For once, the road is deserted. No cars drive by, no dog walkers or runners across the Heath. He smiles, teeth flashing in the sodium gleam of the streetlight. With the father *incapacitated,* it will be easier to get to the boy.

He has been watching this family for a few days now. At work. At school.

It is almost time.

He shifts the bag on his shoulder. The contents are not heavy, but he feels the weight of its significance. He carries it everywhere. He dare not let it out of sight. His fingers slide into the bag's opening, grazing cardboard, lingering on the smoothness of bone. A present for the boy, an exchange, of sorts. It is only fair.

It amuses him that the father did not notice the grey van crawling after him, prying, uninvited. His fury was a gift; it blinded him.

The Bone Collector is building a picture of this family. He wants to expose its weaknesses, its vulnerabilities. To find the chink that he can slip through to claim his prize.

He is sure now it is this man. He has seen the truth, written down in black and white.

He gazes down at the father, the drizzle coming harder now. His face is wet with bloody tears. The man's eyelids flicker, close, flicker, close. Flicker. Close.

The wind lifts, chilling his dampening skin. He will be late for work tonight. In the distance, he hears the wail of a siren. He pauses, cocks his head. Its voice is rising, climbing the hill. Closer now, almost to the Crown.

He turns and runs.

At first, he makes progress, but his shoes slip beneath him on the grass, and he loses his footing, sprawls into soft earth. The bag flies off his shoulder, lands upside down a short distance away.

Now the sirens are almost upon him, screaming their way past the church. He scrambles to his feet, snatches up the strap. Takes up his stumbling run.

He does not notice his bag is empty.

TWENTY-NINE

11.56 p.m.

"Are you sure?" said The Boss.

Fitzroy lifted her eyes from the profiles of local child sex offenders that were sullying her screen, glad for a moment's respite. It was making her feel grubby and depressed.

Miles Foyle was still in custody. Last time she had checked, he was sleeping. In a few hours she would try again, tell him they were planning to apply for an extension. Perhaps desperation would loosen his tongue.

"Fuck it," said The Boss, and chucked his mobile on the desk. A couple of officers looked up in interest. He rubbed his chest in a circular motion, and tipped an antacid from the tube in his pocket.

"Do you want some water with that?"

He nodded towards the computer screen. "You've seen a man's been shot on the Heath?"

"Yeah, but the night shift is handling it. It's not our problem, right?"

"It is now. The super wants us to have a have a look."

"What for?" Fitzroy was surprised.

The Boss was writing something down. Fitzroy could read his irritation at the prospect of losing a couple of officers in the way his pen serrated the paper.

"Some teenage girl saw a grey van." He looked weary. "Look, I know it's a long shot, but when a little girl vanishes and a man is shot less than half a mile apart, we need to be sure these incidents aren't connected." He sighed. "It's probably nothing. Check it out, will you? DC Chambers can go with you."

"What about Miles Foyle?"

"I'll get someone else to interview him."

"Yes, sir."

As Fitzroy shut down her screen, her phone rang. Nina. She ignored it and tried not to think about why she hadn't been back to see her new nephew. Although she had braced herself, the baby's downy hair, his milky, sweet smell, had been more difficult to endure than the most brutal of crime scenes.

She had never had a chance to lock eyes with her son, to feed his searching mouth. Her own baby, unblemished and beautiful and born a week before his due date, had not moved at all.

"And, Fitzroy—"

"Sir?"

"Be as quick as you can. I need you back on this."

Fitzroy folded her sadness into a small, neat square and stuffed it down. Someone, at least, needed her.

WEDNESDAY

THIRTY

12.00 a.m.

Midnight: **Come home, Erdman. It's pouring outside.**

12.15 a.m.: **I'm sorry, OK? I don't think you're crap at your job. Or unreliable.**

12.30 a.m.: **That's right, run away, like you always do.**

1 a.m.: **I'm going to bed. If you stay out all night, don't bother coming home. Ever.**

The trouble with Erdman was that he just didn't think about other people. He stormed off when it suited him, and now he was making a ridiculous point. If he'd applied this much effort to his job, he'd be the bloody managing director by now.

Lilith shifted in bed, trying to sleep and pretending to herself that she wasn't listening for the beep of her mobile, and yes, she was sorry for what she had said, but, actually, it *was* true, Erdman had let his family down.

She had kept it a secret, never even told Erdman, but she used to pity her foster parents. Although she loved them, the flicker of their ancient television seemed to her the only color in their grey, suburban lives. Now she was just like them, spending night after night in front of the TV, or in Erdman's case, on the laptop, playing endless games or posting messages to a bunch of strangers.

She listened to the rain hammering on the roof. Sometimes her own life felt like a weather forecast: dreary and overcast with no prospect of sunshine. Beneath the covers, she worried her slim silver wedding band, the only jewelry she wore. Erdman couldn't afford an engagement ring when he proposed, and had never got 'round to buying one. She was sick of pretending it didn't matter. Recently, she'd developed a habit of fiddling with it whenever she was anxious, and it slid around with ease. She couldn't figure out why her fingers were thinner now while everything else just got bigger.

Where the bloody hell was he? Jakey would be up in four hours, and she had no idea how to explain his father's absence.

Finally, the anger that had spun her insides finished its cycle and, wrung out, she lapsed into a fitful doze, jerking awake every now and again to check her phone on the bedside table.

She didn't want to admit it, not yet, but she was starting to feel the first stirrings of worry. This wasn't like him, not at all. But she had been so angry about his losing his job, pushed all his buttons, and now he was somewhere in the city, probably drunk. Most certainly vulnerable.

For the first time in months, she found herself wishing for the reassuring mound of her husband in bed next to her. Tomorrow—technically, tonight—she would cook his favorite meal for tea, perhaps splurge on a bottle of wine. She would apologize. He would find another job, even if it took a few months. And she would try harder. If only he would call and let her know he was okay.

A whimper caught her ear, so faint she might have dreamed it. She sat up, listened to hear if it would come again. Before she could get out of bed to investigate, Jakey appeared in the doorway of her room. His eyes were open and watching her, and there was a scratch on his cheek that hadn't been there when he went to bed.

"Jakey? Are you okay, sweetie? Did you have a bad dream?"

She threw back the covers and held open her arms, inviting him in as she'd done countless times before, ever since he was old enough to run to her bed when nocturnal shadows chased him from his. But Jakey didn't move. He continued to stare at her, a sheen of sweat coating his skin like oil.

His lips began to move, muttering words she couldn't hear, just a jumble of meaningless sounds.

She swung her legs over the side of the bed, placed a hand on his shoulder, and gently shook it. She could feel the dampness of his pajama top beneath her fingers. The heat from his swollen arm. His eyes flicked over her, unseeing, his breathing fast and shallow.

"It's a dream, Jakey. Just a dream."

The dark puddles of his eyes swept over her. She opened her mouth to soothe him again, but the bleakness of his expression silenced her.

Jakey took a step towards her, then made an abrupt half turn to the left. Eyes unblinking, he jerked himself forward and cracked his forehead into the sharp angle of the door frame. A sickening sound reached her ears. The sound of skin and bone being violated.

Before his mother had time to react, he did it again. A trickle of blood slid down the bridge of his nose, but Jakey didn't flinch.

"Stop it," she half-shouted, horrified, and grabbed him by his shoulders as he threw his head back, ready to pitch himself into the door for a third time. He didn't struggle, but stood passively, as if he was waiting for her to let him go so he could begin to hurt himself again.

Light spilled from the landing onto Jakey's face. A bloody welt dissected his forehead, and a bruise was already forming. A streak of blood decorated the white paintwork. Lilith could hardly bear to think of the damage he might have caused himself, already picturing the swellings, the misshapen nub of bone disfiguring his face.

She shook him again, more roughly this time. "Wake up, Jakey. You're having a nightmare, that's all."

His eyes regained some of their focus, and a look of confusion crossed his face, as if he was surprised to find himself standing in his parents' bedroom in the early hours of morning.

"It's all right, darling. It's over now, all gone," said Lilith. She lifted him up and carried him over to her bed, brushing his bangs to one side.

His forehead was a mess, but already his eyes were glazing over, dragged under by the pull of sleep, and she was reluctant to disturb him with antiseptic cream, a cold compress, and the harsh glare of the bathroom light.

He was almost gone now, the rise and fall of his

chest slowing as he tumbled further towards oblivion, but as she leaned over to tuck in the duvet, his hand grabbed hers and pulled her to him. His breath on her face smelled sour.

"He's coming," he whispered. "Ol' Bloody Bones is coming."

Lilith's skin prickled. That damn book of Erdman's. She had no idea why Jakey was still obsessing about it. When she had found it discarded near the laundry bin on the night he had hurt his arm, she had hidden it away. Perhaps this whole episode was a side effect of the medication he was on, overloading his still-forming brain. And he was at that age when his imagination was beginning to take flight, when there was darkness around every corner. She would talk to him in the morning and try to get to the bottom of it.

Lilith slumped back on the bed, her gaze resting on a chair shrouded with clothes. The shadows in the bedroom seemed to thicken and pulse with life, and for the briefest of moments, it seemed like the clothes were an amorphous, shifting mass. Lilith's heart ricocheted in her chest before she gave herself a mental shake. She was jittery waiting for Erdman to come home, that was all.

Jakey opened his eyes for a moment, then shut them again. It was only as she watched him drift deeper into sleep that she realized he hadn't once asked where his father was.

When the knock came, as soft as the grey dawn breaking, Lilith was still awake and staring, grainy-eyed, at the ceiling.

Pulling on her robe with a growing sense of inevitability, she looked down onto the quiet street below.

The car gave it away. Those fluorescent Battenberg markings, the long nose that poked its way into everybody's business. An unmarked vehicle was parked behind it. She hurled herself down the stairs before they knocked again and woke Jakey.

A woman in a belted green coat and black trousers was holding up an ID card. Her face, which, under different circumstances, looked like it would be friendly and open, was somber, her mouth a pencil line. The damp air frizzed her mop of brown curls. A tall man with fleshy cheeks and a paunch stood next to her.

"Mrs. Frith? I'm Detective Sergeant Etta Fitzroy. This is Detective Constable Alun Chambers. May we come in?"

Lilith clutched her robe around her. "What is it?" *Tell me, just tell me.*

"Is there somewhere we can sit down?" said Chambers.

Later, whenever Lilith replayed the events of that morning, *that* was the sentence she remembered. It was what officials always said when they were handing out terrible news.

DS Fitzroy perched awkwardly on their leather sofa. With her smart jacket, she looked out of place amongst the shabby furnishings. Her eyes, full of pity, locked on Lilith's.

"Is your husband at home?"

"We, um, had an argument." She searched their faces for reassurance. "Is Erdman all right? Please, can you tell me what's going on?"

"There was a shooting at the junction of Mounts

Pond and Hare and Billet Roads at about eight fifteen p.m. last night." A pause. "We think your husband was involved."

The mirror on the wall above the fireplace seemed to lurch to one side. Lilith's vision blurred, and she dug her nails into the brown leather. "Erdman's been *shot*?"

Chambers gave a brief nod. "A witness, a young girl, saw a man fitting your husband's description being attacked by a gang of youths. We understand a gun was fired, but we're trying to establish the sequence of events."

The detective lowered his voice, as if the drop in volume would somehow soften the blow. "We found your husband's wallet at the scene."

Lilith processed his comment, and smiled in sudden, unexpected relief.

"How do you know it's Erdman? I mean, he probably just dropped his wallet on the way to the pub. He drinks at the Crown, in the Village. He's so careless like that, he's always losing things. Last week he mislaid his keys, and once he lost his passport for a whole year, and the other day he dropped his checkbook down the back of the fridge."

Fitzroy gave her another pitying look. "The witness. She was sitting at the bus stop when the fight kicked off. She ran away and called the police, but came back when she heard all the sirens. Your husband's press card was in his wallet. She's had a look at the photo ID, and thinks it was him."

"Oh my God." Questions whirled in her head. "Is he all right? Is he in the hospital? He's not—" She couldn't say the word.

Fitzroy and Chambers shared an uncomfortable look.

"That's the problem. We don't know. We understand he was taken to the hospital, but by the time we got there, he'd been treated and left. We're investigating a separate missing persons case and we need to talk to him about a van seen at the time of his attack. It's extremely urgent. Do you have any idea where he might be?"

This couldn't be happening. She was going to wake up any minute, and find Erdman asleep in bed next to her, and she would make Jakey's packed lunch and walk him to school, and, later, she and Erdman would share a Wednesday-night curry, and probably have another argument.

"He doesn't have many friends."

"What about work colleagues, that sort of thing?"

"I don't think that's very likely. He's just lost his job."

The detectives exchanged another meaningful look.

"Mrs. Frith," began Chambers, "has your husband ever been involved with drugs?"

The mirror tipped a second time and then righted itself. "Of course not." It wasn't necessary to mention the odd joint, surely. "Why are you asking that?"

"We think the teenager who shot him belonged to one of southeast London's most notorious drug gangs. There's a possibility your husband was attacked because he owed them money."

"You're saying he's been shot by a drug gang?"

"That's one theory."

Lilith's laugh was a harsh bark. "You're not serious." The officers didn't answer. "Oh my God. You are." She could tell what they were thinking. *He's lost his job, he's got money problems, why else was he with them?*

The room swam again, and she forced herself to focus. She thought about that time they'd been clubbing, when Amber had offered round lines of coke and produced a see-through sandwich bag containing pastel-colored pills. "Nah," he'd said, shaking his head. "Not my scene." But how much about her husband did she *really* know?

Upstairs, a toilet flushed. Jakey. What the hell was she going to tell him? She had never lied to him, not even about his illness, and had promised herself she never would. But this could destroy the fragile confidence they had fought so hard to build. Did withholding the truth make it a lie?

A thought slammed into her, snatched her breath. *Oh God, what if he's dead?* What if they were sitting here, discussing theories about where he might be, and ways to find him, and he was already several hours' cold, the life stripped from him. But no, he'd walked out of the hospital himself, the officer said. He *was* alive. She just didn't know where.

From somewhere, Chambers appeared with a pot of tea. He'd poured sugar in a bowl and found an ancient milk jug they never used. He put three spoonfuls in Lilith's cup, even though she'd stopped taking it when she was twenty.

She took a sip, noting that, in spite of everything, she still had the capacity to feel embarrassed about her chipped crockery.

No, no, no. This had to be a mistake. Her husband was boring. Things like this didn't happen to people like them. Erdman would walk through the door any moment, and everything would go back to how it should be. Dull and predictable.

"What happens now?" she asked.

Chambers was grim. "We wait for your husband to come home, Mrs. Frith."

The house filled up with people. When Jakey came downstairs, hair sticking out at all angles, his arm red and swollen, Mrs. Cooper from next door was in the kitchen buttering toast while Mr. Cooper made another pot of tea.

Lilith found him hiding in the study, spinning 'round and 'round in Erdman's chair. He had a large bruise on his forehead, and dried blood in the jagged edge of his cut. His chin was skewed towards his collarbone, but his eyes lifted to meet hers. The sight of his face, so like his father's, made her eyes fill. He removed the thumb corking his mouth. Watched in silence as Fitzroy and Chambers put down their mugs and left.

"Where's Daddy?" he said, as soon as they had gone.

She picked him up then, and the sharp edges of his bones dug into her flesh, but she didn't care. Like a baby monkey, he wrapped his legs tightly around her waist. She registered the movement and let out the breath that she hadn't realized she was holding. There was still mobility in his legs. No extra lumps on his back. It was a game she played every morning, uncertain what changes the night might bring. Unconsciously echoing Erdman's gesture from a few hours earlier, she squeezed his body to hers, and her fingers played the bones of his ribs beneath his pajama top. She felt the heat from his arm. His back.

She tried to frame the words so a six-year-old would understand them.

"We're not sure, sweetie. We're looking for him."

"But what if you don't find him?"

Lilith set him on the floor and half-crouched in front of him, gripping his twisted shoulders. She could read the doubt in his face.

"Of course we'll find him," she said. "Daddy will be home soon."

Jakey tried and failed to shake his head, and he made an exasperated sound. Frustration was a common side effect, the support group had warned Lilith, especially if he remembered what it felt like to move freely.

"Are you okay, sweetie? Shall we go and get dressed?"

But Jakey couldn't speak, his young mind full of dark imaginings, magpied from his father's tattered storybook and the television coverage about Clara Foyle.

Instead, he reached for Erdman's notepad, and flicked gently through the pages. They were covered in his father's mostly indecipherable scrawl.

The boy followed the loops and whorls with his finger, but his eyes were dead.

THIRTY-ONE

10.06 a.m.

A few miles away, in Lincoln's Inn Fields, a figure slips into a museum.

Anyone who happens to glimpse him would assume that sickness has sucked the meat from his bones. His cheeks are sunken, the skin so stretched it looks ready to split. Clothes hang off his spare frame, a set of aging bones held together by the flimsiest threads of sinew and flesh. When he smiles, it seems like a warning.

Anyone who stands too close might catch, beneath the musky, deodorized notes, the faintest whiff of something. They won't be able to place it, will discreetly move away, too polite to comment, noses wrinkled in distaste. For those few who work in mortuaries or abattoirs, recognition will cleave through them as cleanly as a blade.

The Bone Collector treads softly across the marble floor with its dark twists that mirror the diseased bones upstairs.

It has been three days since his last visit, and the

dead welcome him. He breathes in the odorless air, closes his eyes, and steadies his heart.

John Hunter is everywhere. In the shrunken quintuplets from Blackburn, the teeth of soldiers lost on the battlefields of Waterloo, and the thousands of other tempting curiosities that are his legacy.

And walking in his shadow is Hunter's faithful sidekick, Mr. Howison. The body snatcher. The Bone Collector's own flesh and blood. The one who began the family collection with grim treasures plundered from the graves of others, and passed down through the gen erations, each son carefully selecting the rarest, most perfect, of specimens. A collection his own father curated, and handed down to him.

The ties that bind cut deep and bloody.

As he enters the Crystal Gallery, the Bone Collector allows himself to be pulled, briefly, in the direction of a three-month-old fetus, filleted down to its fragile bones. A dolly in a cigar-box bed.

From habit, he peers through the glass, but although its skeleton is no thicker than a splintered match, it no longer holds the same appeal for him.

Not now that he has one of his own.

He hurries across the gallery floor, ignoring the cylinders of animal tongues and amputated limbs, until he reaches a glass case displaying the remains of the skeleton that once was Charles Byrne. This is what he has come for. He sinks to one knee and bows his head, a worshiper at the altar, reverent and humble.

It began here. And it is his pleasure and his privilege to continue Howison's work.

Eventually, the Bone Collector lifts his face, flicks

out a tongue to wet his lips. The Irish Giant. Seven feet, seven inches of mystery and bone.

Decades later, professors discovered what Hunter had never managed to. The mutated gene, the cause of his unnatural height. But the Bone Collector is grateful to Byrne, and the way his skeleton beguiled and bewitched the surgeon. Because authorizing the theft of Byrne's body gifted the Bone Collector's ancestors with a legacy more wonderful than Hunter could possibly have imagined.

His eyes linger on Byrne's femur and travel the length of his body, drinking in the ischium, ilium, and scapula. He puts a finger against the glass and traces his vertebrae and rib cage bound together by brown string. Some bones are missing from his feet. He wonders what secrets those missing bones will yield.

Marshall first brought him here as a young boy, despite his mother's disapproval. But Sylvie need not have worried. The displays did not frighten him, even then. They intrigued him.

His father had been gratified by his interest. He encouraged questions. Told stories of grave robbers and spirits. How Howison had switched the giant's body with paving stones and stolen it for Hunter. Of their family's connection to this place, to the men behind the exhibits.

It was here that Marshall introduced his son to the concept of familial duty. Began the education that would culminate in killing sprees born of a desire to preserve and protect medical rarities.

And he was eager to learn, to carry on the traditions of his bloodline.

An hour passes, then another. But the Bone Collector doesn't notice the stiffness in his legs, or the tourists nudging into him for a closer look. He stares at the display case that houses Mr. Jeffs, his twisted back a trophy on display. He thinks of his own trophies, and the promise of the one he has yet to acquire.

After a while, he glances at his watch. He hopes she will be eating the lunch he has left on the chair by her bed. She has hardly been touching it lately, a bite here and there. He will buy her a treat to tempt her appetite, which dwindles with each passing day.

He thinks about going back, feels the pull of her. But he has a meeting in Woolwich in an hour or so. If he doesn't move quickly, the dealer will sell the new colony to a rival collector, and that will not do at all. The beetles belong to him.

And then there's the boy. He must get to the school for the close of the day. He has much work to do.

Twelve miles away, in a faceless room at the top of a house, Clara Edith Foyle was practicing spelling her name. She said the letters over and over. She knew that each part of her name contained five letters, and that her whole name had fifteen. She repeated her name to remind herself that she still existed.

When she had first arrived, Clara had called out for her mother and father. For Gina and Eleanor. After a while, she had come to understand that they were not coming. That the only one who ever came was the Night Man.

A few hours earlier, Clara had watched a spider scuttle across the floor to the corner nearest the door. It was spinning a web, following its natural instinct to hunt prey, even though the freezing temperatures meant that Clara had seen no other insects during her captivity.

A bit later, she had found herself drawn back to the web. To her surprise, a small creature was snared in its sticky strings, moving with a frantic, wasted energy. It was flat, and shiny black. A beetle, she thought, rolling the vowels on her tongue.

Lying on her tummy, studying the spider, she had nodded off, and in her dreams, she had been back at home, tucked safely in her own bed with her night-light on, and Christmas just around the corner. She dreamed of a door opening and closing, of her mother coming in, kissing her on the forehead and smoothing down her covers.

When she opened her eyes to the pockmarked walls of her cell, Clara gave a little sob, the memory of her mother's touch already fading. The girl wiped away her tears with the back of her hand and began to repeat the letters in her name again. The school playground had taught her that crying wouldn't change things, and the pointing and stares of others had helped Clara to solder each painful experience into a steel core.

This inner strength—the Don't Cares, Clara called it—was keeping her alive.

Stiff and uncomfortable from falling asleep on the hard floor, Clara tried to pull herself upwards, but her arms wouldn't move properly. At first, she was certain the Night Man had tied her wrists together again and, panicked, she tried to free them. They came loose easily, and her heartbeat slowed. It was just her bedsheet, tangled around her limbs.

She didn't remember wrapping herself in a sheet. Especially not a sheet like this. It didn't have *that* smell, like the one on her bed where she'd had an accident. This sheet was soft, with faded printed roses on it, and it smelled clean, and she had never seen it before.

It was getting colder, so Clara wrapped the sheet around her shoulders and bent to take a closer look at the beetle in the web.

While she had been sleeping, the spider had wrapped its prey in silken threads.

THIRTY-TWO

1.46 p.m.

Fitzroy was cursing the rain. Not only was the downpour fucking up her crime scene, it was ruining her shoes.

As she stared down at the watery traces of blood on the grass, she wondered if The Boss was still punishing her.

Although Fitzroy had a keen sense of justice for everyone, it was the children who clamored for her attention, who drove her to spend long nights sifting the evidence for patterns. Which was why she was so angry that he'd sent her on this wild-goose chase when she should be directing all her energies towards finding the little girl.

So Erdman (what the hell kind of name was that?) Frith had been beaten up and shot. Clara Foyle was missing, believed abducted. Both incidents had happened less than a half a mile apart. As far as she could see, that singular fact of location linked the cases. As for the "grey" van, the witness didn't have the faintest idea if it was silver, dark grey, or even light blue. But

The Boss was under pressure from on high, and this was a lead, no matter how tenuous.

Served her right for staying at work all night instead of grabbing a few hours' sleep at the flat. For the first time in their four-year marriage, David hadn't bothered to text to see if she was coming home. He'd left a terse message just after dawn, presumably while he was getting ready for work, telling her that Nina had rung twice. Fitzroy hadn't called either of them back yet. She would see David at the fertility clinic tomorrow, try to smooth things over. As for Nina, she still couldn't face the smug triumph of a new mother.

Etta would never say that to her sister, of course. But although she loved her, she could not bear that Nina had trumped her again. Except this time, it wasn't about exam results or who could persuade their father to smile, but something that Etta had no control over, which made it all the more cruel.

It was this rend in her own life that drove her to fill the space by searching for Grace and Clara, to push David in a direction he was reluctant to travel. She was dreading tomorrow, and the prospect of David's detachment, the way he sighed out his displeasure. But that was then, and this was now.

So here she was. On Blackheath Common, deserted apart from a few officers scouring the ground, soaked to the skin in freezing rain and up her to ankles in mud.

The weak afternoon light would be fading soon. A few weeks ago, The Boss had made a big song and dance about how he was ready to give her more responsibility again, and she felt its weight like a monkey on her back.

She watched the forensics team combing the grass,

framed against the pretty church with its spire clock, every passing minute a rebuke that Clara was still out there, still lost. They'd be lucky if they found a cigarette butt in this weather, but The Boss had ordered teams to scour the vicinity until they found a clue, any clue, to her whereabouts. Five days on and they were still looking. Chambers thrust an expensive coffee from the village in her face and bent down to wipe his mud-spattered trousers with a napkin.

"Clean today, these were."

"Makes a change."

Fitzroy blew on her drink. It was hot and bitter, and just what she needed.

"Thoughts?"

"Well, I'm cold, my trousers are filthy, and I quite fancy a pint."

Fitzroy rolled her eyes at Chambers, and he shrugged, took a slug of his own coffee.

"Mr. Frith doesn't seem like your average drug dealer."

"That's my instinct." She looked at the photograph in her hand. He was an unusual-looking man, so rangy, and with his pale, freckled skin and reddish hair, he looked like a Renaissance painting, and had one of the saddest faces she had ever seen. "But we all know that appearances can be deceptive.

"Look, he's not known to us. He lives in neither a slum nor a penthouse. His wife seems genuinely distraught. Even if he's a small-time user, why would he be messing with these boys? They're hard-core. Until yesterday he worked at a little-known psychic magazine. Something doesn't add up."

"You're right." Chambers moved the cup to his other hand. He breathed out a curl of white smoke as he spoke. "Wrong place, wrong time?"

"Could be. But why shoot him? Sounds like they'd already kicked the shit out of him."

"Because he saw something he shouldn't have?"

"Possibly."

"So, where is he now?"

"Had a fight with his wife, lying low with a mate?"

"But what about the van?"

"Coincidence? Human error? It's difficult to be precise about color when it's dark."

"So, what's the connection to Clara Foyle?"

Fitzroy bit her thumbnail. She was groping for a link between the cases, but couldn't see one, couldn't feel its hard mass in the shape of evidence. She was used to relying on her instincts, to listening for the *ting* in her brain that drove her on, exploiting every lead, no matter how flimsy, until the clanging stopped and the answers were found. But not today. Today all she could hear was Clara's voice, urging her to hurry, and the fainter echo of Grace Rodríguez. She tapped a reminder into her phone to ask Mrs. Foyle if she knew the Frith family, but already she could guess the answer.

"Come on." She jerked her head at Chambers. "This is a waste of time. Let's go."

The officers were walking back to their car when one of the white suits suddenly crouched down and let out an excited yell. The rest of his colleagues clustered around him, peering at the same spot on the ground. Someone held an umbrella over his head. Fitzroy exchanged a look with Chambers, then ran back across the heath, ignoring the squelching beneath her feet.

"What is it? What have you found?"

From his hunkered-down position, he pointed to the grass. Lying half-submerged in a puddle of muddy water was an old shoe box. Inside it was the carcass of an animal. Stripped down to its skeleton, which was a sort of dullish, pale color, it had a small, slightly elongated skull and a curved vertebrae. Its feet were spindles of bone.

"What the fuck is *that*?" said Fitzroy, her mind already tearing ahead, rifling through the evidence, sifting the pieces of the puzzle, slotting them into what she already knew.

Building a new and wholly unexpected picture.

"What the fuck, indeed," said the officer who had found it, signaling for a crime scene photographer. "Take a look at this."

Gingerly, he lifted the fragile skeleton from the puddle. The bones were bare, but just enough of the animal's connective tissues remained to hold them together. With gloved hands, he removed a small plastic tube attached to its hind leg.

"Interesting," he murmured. He delved into his pocket for a pair of tweezers, used them to extract a thin cigarette paper from inside the tube. With a deftness that belied the size of his hands, he carefully unrolled it and scanned its contents.

"I think you'd better read this."

Fitzroy leaned over his shoulder, the printed ink jumping before her eyes.

". . . the bones came together, bone to bone."

Adrenaline sluiced through her. "Bag it. Now."

Her hands wouldn't stop trembling, and she buried them in the pockets of her jacket. She turned to Chambers. "Get onto the Identification and Advisory Service at the Natural History Museum. Tell them it's urgent, tell them not to go until we get there. I'm going to make a call. I need to speak to The Boss."

THIRTY-THREE

2.11 p.m.

Erdman swallowed down a painkiller and switched on the TV. Then switched it off again.

Even that simple movement set off several flashes of pain. Every part of him hurt, and not just his body.

He shifted against the cushion, trying to get comfortable. Amber had left a plate of biscuits on the coffee table, but he wasn't hungry. He wasn't exactly sure what he felt.

Lilith would be worried, he knew that. But he couldn't bring himself to call her. Last night, when he'd been taken to the ER and realized that his phone and his wallet were missing, he'd had every intention of asking one of the nurses to call her.

But by the time they had finished patching him up, the embers of his anger had reignited, hot and immediate.

A tiny piece of him wanted her to suffer for all the terrible things she had said. He felt bad about Jakey, but Lilith would have to deal with that. This was her fault, after all.

It didn't occur to him that the police might wish to speak to him. Nor did he properly consider the repercussions of his unexplained absence on his family. *He* knew he was okay, and that was all that mattered.

And Amber had been fantastic, not blinking an eye when he rocked up on her doorstep at 1 a.m. She had taken in his pulped face, the gaping slit in his jeans where the doctors had sliced through denim to treat the gunshot wound.

"I didn't realize you were *that* into S&M," she said drily, tightening the belt on her skull-and-crossbones robe, and he had let out a snort of laughter, even though it was the last thing he had felt like doing.

He could have gone to Axel's, but his friend lived in a grubby flat-share, and he couldn't face the curiosity of strangers. Amber had a spare room, and she didn't ask questions.

Before she had left for work that morning, she had opened the thick velvet curtains and touched him lightly on the shoulder.

"Make sure you call Lilith," she'd said, but he'd pretended to be asleep.

He knew he ought to go home, or at the very least, pick up the phone as Amber had suggested. That would be the *right* thing to do. But the part of him that was selfish and irresponsible, and all the other things that Lilith had accused him of being, stayed his hand. He wanted her to understand that her words were not bits of confetti, to be tossed around and lost on the wind, but blocks of concrete that could fell a man.

There was another, deeper truth that Erdman acknowledged quietly to himself. That he wasn't ready to return home yet. That he welcomed this unexpected reprieve from a wife who had allowed fear to shrink her, and from the unrelenting effort of worrying about his son.

For a few hours, he could breathe.

Amber's landline rang, its shrillness making him jump. He ignored it and let voice mail kick in.

"Pick up, mate. I know you're there." Axel. Erdman made no move to answer it, unwilling to face his friend's pity.

"Okay, I get it. You're in the bathroom. Or something." There was a pause. "So, the thing is, I've got this mate who's the news editor at a local newspaper and he's looking for staff. No guarantees or anything, but I can put in a word, if you like. It's not far, Essex, I think. Near the coast. It's a bit of a trek, but easily doable. To be honest, you'd be doing him a favor . . ."

A lump lodged in Erdman's throat at the generosity of his friend.

"Anyway, let me know. Er, hope you're feeling okay. Right. Um. See you later."

Erdman eased himself off the sofa, limped to the window of the purpose-built flat in Camberwell. It looked out on a residents' garden, where an old man was pulling crusts from a plastic Hovis bag, tearing them into strips for the birds.

He hoped the police would catch the fuckers who had done this to him.

The old man was tipping the bag onto the grass now, pigeons and starlings at his feet like disciples. He was just a pensioner, whiling away the loneliness of his days. But something about the wisps of his silver-grey hair triggered a memory in Erdman.

Last night, while he was lying, bleeding and broken, in the grass, he had seen a face. He didn't know who this man was or why he was following him or why he had seemed so familiar, but some instinct warned him that he needed to find out.

THIRTY-FOUR

2.54 p.m.

Jakey Frith was in the toilet cubicles at the back of his classroom, and he was crying. The itch in his arm was a burn that would not stop. And his chest really, really hurt.

It had been a while since he'd felt like this, but he could tell that this flare-up was not good news. He was used to the frustrations and restrictions and irony of a disease that, even while creating extra bone, diminished him. But this pain and heat was a bad sign. He just didn't know *how* bad.

He thought about telling Mrs. Husselbee, but she was still cross with him for wandering off.

"You'll get me into trouble," she'd said yesterday, frowning, when he'd limped back up the field. "I'm supposed to be looking after you."

But he didn't want anyone looking after him. He only wanted his father.

His mother had been reluctant to let him come to school today, but Jakey had remembered the man's promise of a puppy, and had insisted he was feeling better.

He clawed at his arm, his nails raking the tender mound of his flesh. The swelling on his arm was getting larger. He knew it was. And that meant his mother would do as the doctor had told her, and take him to the hospital.

But he didn't want to go, in case Daddy came back for their bike ride.

What if Daddy doesn't come back?

Two tears leaked out of his eyes.

He sat on the toilet lid and listened to the rise and fall of Miss Haines's voice, and knew that Mrs. Husselbee would knock on the door in a moment and ask if he was okay.

The urge to scratch overtook him again. His nails dug into the site of the inflammation, lacerating his arm in his frenzy to turn the skin inside out. He scratched until his flesh was bleeding, but it only fanned the fire in his arm, so he scratched it again and again.

Jakey forgot all about the letter and the man in the suit who had promised to give him the puppy that day. He forgot about the worry etched into the lines of his mother's face. He even forgot, for a moment or two, about his missing father.

The itch in his arm and the burn in his chest pushed every thought from his brain.

THIRTY-FIVE

4.01 p.m.

Some days, taking the Tube, with its delays and never-ending tourist rush hour, was even slower than going by car. Even so, Fitzroy did not hurry as the escalator carried her out of South Kensington Station.

Around her, the voices of the city merged until she could hardly hear them, lost as she was in the rhythm of constant motion.

She shut her eyes, allowed her mind to wander as the steel staircase climbed upwards. Was it possible? Could this be the breakthrough that she'd been waiting for? It was the last thing she'd expected when The Boss had sent her out to check on the van.

Fitzroy stepped off the escalator, walked briskly through the tunnel, left and up the stairs.

It was darker now, and she could see the cold white lights of the ice rink on the corner of Cromwell Road, where she and David had toasted their second anniversary, drinking mulled wine and wobbling on too-tightly tied skates. The skeleton trees outside the Natural History Museum, bare save for hundreds of fairy lights, reminded her that Christmas was little more than a month away. She prayed that Clara's family would have something to celebrate.

She ran up the steps, past security, into the cavernous hall with its black-and-white mosaic floor, past the replica of *diplodocus*, turned left, past the gift shop, past the Mammals, Blue Zone, and there it was: the Darwin Center.

Down the steps, turn left again, and she was standing in front of a set of glass doors, decorated with bluebells and butterflies. The Identification and Advisory Service. She pressed the buzzer, and a serious-faced young man with dark hair appeared in the glass. He spoke through the intercom.

"Detective Sergeant Fitzroy?"

"Thank you for seeing me at such short notice."

He shrugged, and she stepped through the door. The walls were unnaturally white, illuminated by strips of fluorescent light. A row of green chairs, all empty, lined the corner.

"I'm Dr. Dashiell Hall. We spoke on the phone." He put out his hand, held her eyes. "You have heterochromia iridum." His voice lifted in surprised pleasure.

"Yes."

"It's beautiful, so distinctive." He took a step closer, peered at her face. "Brown and blue is my favorite combination."

Fitzroy was aware of her cheeks coloring, but Dr. Hall didn't seem to notice.

"You have something to show me?"

Carefully, she removed the plastic evidence box from the carrier bag and lifted the lid.

He raised his eyebrows above his glasses. "This

would have been much better left in situ, you know. One of our forensics team could have been with you by tomorrow."

Silly girl, she could hear her father saying.

"We don't have the luxury of time, Dr. Hall."

"Your call," he said, already turning away. "Follow me."

He led Fitzroy past a series of cubicles, each with a computer and microscope, to a row of metal filing cabinets. A stuffed hedgehog in a display case was sitting on top of them, next to a fox. He indicated for Fitzroy to set her box on the table.

"Haven't had the police here in a while," he said, pulling on a pair of plastic gloves.

"That's a good thing, surely," she said.

His laughter was rich and warm, and reminded Fitzroy that it had been a long time since she had heard David make a similar sound. He used to laugh all the time, mostly at her cooking. "I suppose it is. I don't look at the specimens as part of the crime scene, more from a scientific perspective."

"Do you know what it is?"

"Depends on your definition of 'know.' I can tell just by looking that your skeleton is a member of the lagomorph family."

"And that means what?

"Well, it's a hare or a rabbit, not a rodent."

Her face remained neutral, but her heart was galloping in her chest. "I see. Can you tell how old it is?"

"The skeleton, or the specimen itself?"

"Both."

"From its size, I'd say it's an adult. Look, the bones of the skull and the epiphysis are fused. As for the specimen, it can't have been in situ for more than a day or so. See, the connective tissues that would have been eaten by carrion insects are still intact. Which is odd." He frowned. "Was it found in a sealed box or bag?"

"A shoe box, but it wasn't sealed. It was falling apart in the rain."

He moved away from Fitzroy, towards the filing cabinets, pulled out one of the metal drawers.

"Take a look at this."

Fitzroy came and stood next to him. He smelled faintly of sweat and the musky scent of andostrenol. In a plastic tray was the skull of a small mammal, its jaw open to reveal teeth as curved as claws. Written on the bone specimen, in black pen, was *Oryctolagus cuniculus*.

"Now," said Dr. Hall, "let's compare these beauties."

He removed the skull from the tray and placed it next to Fitzroy's skeleton, pointed to its jawbone.

"See, the shape of its head and the line of its jaw are pretty much identical."

"You can narrow it down?"

"I don't know if it's wild or domestic, and I can't tell you the species, but I'd say it's *oryctolagus cuniculus*."

"Say what?"

"I assume you know that *Homo sapiens* is the collective word for 'humans.'" Fitzroy gave him a look. "Well, *Oryctolagus cuniculus* is the one for 'rabbits.'"

"So, it's a rabbit skeleton," she said.

"Correct."

He placed the specimen tray back in the drawer, pulled off his gloves, and turned to Fitzroy with a triumphant grin. She was sagging against the table, her face the same off-white color as the rabbit skull. His smile faded.

"Oh hell, are you feeling all right? Shall I get you a drink of water?"

Fitzroy didn't know what she was feeling. Grace Rodríguez's case file was flicking through her mind, like the pages of a book. She placed a finger between two of the pages. Brought up the image of a photograph taken in the woods a few hours after her remains had been discovered. *Deeper into the woods, they had gone. The dogs had snuffled the ground in search of reward, twigs cracking beneath their claws. Fitzroy's flashlight had bounced against the trees, no longer a beacon of hope in the darkness, but of sorrow.*

The wind sliced through her jacket, but she was determined to search these woods until she had found what she had come for. The ballet case had belonged to Grace. There was no doubt. But she needed to find the girl.

The dogs were a short distance ahead when they began to bark, rupturing the still of the twilit woods.

A thin moon slid between the clouds. A shouted warning from one of the handlers. Fitzroy had run then, felt the branches beneath her dig into the soles of her shoes.

And then.

The horror of discovery, sealed tidily in little sandwich bags.

Fitzroy and the team had spent hours at the site, collecting evidence and searching for the rest of Grace's body.

Then one of the dogs had found the perfectly preserved bones of a small mammal's skeleton nearby.

The crime photographer had taken a couple of pictures, but no one had paid it much attention, blaming it on the brutality of the natural world. Everyone knew these woods were teeming with life. With death.

"Here, drink this."

She swallowed a mouthful of warm water, and wiped her lips with the back of her hand, aware of Dr. Hall's eyes upon her.

"I need to know more. As soon as you can."

"I can do that," said Dr. Hall. "If you give me a couple of days, I'll tell you its bloody life history."

"Thank you," she said, holding out her hand, not quite able to look at him.

His fingers closed around hers. His skin was warm, smooth. "My pleasure."

She stumbled back across the museum's pale wooden floorboards, dropped to tie her laces. The grain was riven with the same crooked sewing-machine sutures as the fused bones of the rabbit specimen she'd just seen. Hintze Hall rumbled with voices, with footsteps, even this late in the day.

The Christmas tree outside the gift shop blurred, its silver baubles spinning and drifting in front of her tear-filled eyes. The Boss had warned her last year about getting too emotionally involved in her cases, but she couldn't help herself.

In her bleaker moments, when she was suffocating in the memory of her son, the perfectly formed dip between his nose and mouth, the pain of giving birth to a baby who would never draw breath or cry, she blamed herself for his loss.

For all their losses.

A child ran, tripped, and his cry pierced her heart.

THIRTY-SIX

4.09 p.m.

By late afternoon, the Frith house was ablaze, its windows a fierce orange. It was the only brightness in the day for Lilith, whose optimism was sinking as rapidly as the afternoon sun.

There had been no word from Erdman. His phone was dead. He wasn't replying to e-mails or Facebook messages. Where *was* he? This was so unlike him. He wasn't the sort of man who just disappeared. Occasionally he'd forget to call during a bender with Axel, but he always came home to his own bed. To her. Always.

A couple of weeks before their wedding, he'd gone drinking with a few old friends from university. She hadn't been too bothered when he wasn't back the next morning. It was a Saturday, but she was working, snared in the vise of a deadline. By the time she had come up for air it was late afternoon. She had showered and dressed, and stood by the window, watching for him. When the late summer shadows had begun to creep across their garden, a coldness had claimed her and she had gone looking for him.

The city was stifling, dust and fumes clogging her senses. She had scoured the pubs of their courtship, eyes scanning the crowds for a flash of rust, a pint glass held in a certain way.

After an hour or so, she found him. He was sitting in a beer garden, a bottle in hand, condensation peeling the label from the glass. The last rays of the evening sun had turned his hair into a burnished crown. Across the chattering drinkers, he had looked up, waved, and beckoned her over.

"Lilith," he had called. "Come and have a drink."

She had turned on her heels and left.

He had caught up with her on the way home, panting slightly in the heat. The dampish smell of his sweat, his two-day-old T-shirt, was in her nostrils. She wrenched her hand away.

"What's the matter?" he said.

"I was worried." Her voice had wavered on the last syllable, loosened by unexpected tears.

His face had collapsed, stricken.

"We got a bit carried away. I should have called or something." He brushed her tears with his thumb. "I'm sorry."

She wouldn't look at him, but instead made a performance of rummaging through her handbag, pretending to search for her keys. To show she didn't care *that* much.

He had taken her hand again and this time she let him.

"It won't happen again, Lilith. I promise. No matter

how drunk I get, or how late it is, I'll always come home." He had cupped her chin, looked into her eyes. "Deal?"

She had made him wait a moment or two, but relief had weakened the masonry of her anger.

"Deal."

And he had kept his word. Until now.

She telephoned family and friends to ask if they had seen him. Amber Collins didn't pick up but Lilith left a message, asking her to check with the rest of her colleagues. She made lists of the places he might be. Even though his phone was off, she sent him a text. **I love you. Come home.**

On her way to collect Jakey from school, she had walked across the Heath, right past *that* bus stop, and seen the fading imprint of blood on the pavement. Erdman's blood. A wave of dizziness caught her unawares, and she clung to a lamppost, as if holding on to a lump of iron would help rid her of this strange, untethered feeling. It reminded her of the day Jakey was born. *Don't*, she told herself. *Just don't.* Tears overwhelmed her. *I'm so sorry I didn't appreciate you. I'll make it up to you when you get home, I promise. Just come home, please.*

Jakey looked exhausted, purpling semicircles beneath his eyes. Heat radiated from him. The school welfare officer had rung her at the afternoon break, suggesting she pick him up early.

"Is Daddy back yet?" he said dully, as if his question was a formality and he already knew the answer. He dropped his Spider-Man backpack and duffel coat on the floor, and winced.

"Not yet, darling. I'm working on it." She bit her lip. "How's your arm? Can I see?"

But he wouldn't let her. Instead he trudged up to his room, and no amount of coaxing would make him come out. So she left him alone to read his books and play with his toys, to process what was happening.

He'll come and find me when he's ready. He always does.

But he didn't.

At teatime, Lilith carried up a sandwich and a glass of milk, but Jakey wasn't in the mood for talking. Not to her, at least. As she pulled the door shut behind her, she heard his voice. It had an oddly pleading quality to it.

"Go away. Leave me alone."

A pause.

"Daddy, where are you? I need you to come home."

She almost went back in to comfort him, but told herself it was his way of dealing with things, that she should leave him to it.

When she went up to check on him later, he was asleep on top of his duvet, so she carefully undressed him.

Her hand flew to her mouth.

A flare-up, that's what they called it. No one knew why or how it happened. Sometimes it happened after a fall. Or sometimes for no reason at all. The soft tissue swellings could be large or small, lasting a few days or a year, traveling around the body at will.

Jakey's "good" arm was disfigured by four new lumps.

She pressed her lips against his burning forehead, and cried until her tears dampened his hair.

Her heart constricted with love as she looked at his face, the last vestiges of babyishness still evident in his plump cheeks. She knew it wouldn't be long before that disappeared, too, along with the diapers, pacifiers, and Wooby, which was now stuffed in a drawer in her bedroom. She wanted to keep this soft lump of rag that smelled of milk and baby powder and hope, even if Jakey didn't.

At some point Lilith must have dozed off, because when she jerked awake the darkness had deepened and there was a dragging, gone-to-sleep feeling in her leg.

She wandered downstairs, through dark, empty rooms. In the hall, she reached for the handset and pecked in Erdman's number. The flat, female tone of voice mail greeted her. She hung up, suddenly furious with her husband for putting Jakey through all of this. As she stared, vacant-eyed, at the television, she wondered if she would ever forgive him such selfishness.

THIRTY-SEVEN

9.14 p.m.

Erdman had a pounding headache. Trying to sleep in an unfamiliar bed always did that to him. And that was when he hadn't been beaten to a pulp by a gang of feral youths, and shot in the thigh at point-blank range. *Permit me a little slack.* He snorted to himself.

He turned over, wincing at the pain in his body, and at the feel of Amber's black polyester sheets. Perhaps he should have stayed in the hospital, after all.

Ordinarily, he wouldn't have taken himself off to bed so early, but Amber had been on his case since coming in from work, Chinese takeaway in hand.

"Ring your wife," she'd said, dumping a mountain of chow mein on his plate.

"Gee, honey, I'm fine, how was *your* day?"

She'd sighed then, ignored his sarcasm. "She's left two messages on my phone, Erd. I haven't called her back because I don't want to lie for you, but I can't ignore her for much longer." She loosened another cardboard lid. "She sounds desperate."

Guilt had coated each mouthful of his meal, and

he'd pushed it away, half-eaten. If he was being honest with himself, he was starting to feel a bit of a heel, especially about Jakey.

In fact, he hadn't done much else except think about his family, and the stranger who'd been watching him.

Cautiously, he eased himself onto his back. It required more effort than he had expected.

He'd spent most of the day trying to recall his encounters with the man. He'd been on the train. At the cemetery. And he'd seen him somewhere else, he was sure of it. But where? The pub, was it? Yes. That's right. The Bank. Monday lunchtime.

If he counted the night of the attack, that made it four times he'd seen him. Four times in two days. *But why?*

Perhaps he should confront him? But what good would that do? Because he was in a fit state to physically take on this weirdo. Yeah, 'course he was.

Raindrops hammered the roof. He pulled up a mental image of this stranger: the narrow line of his shoulders, the gun-metal strands of his hair. It set off a quickstep of recognition, which whirled and danced, confusing his thoughts. His face was familiar, like a long-forgotten song that comes back slowly in snatches of melody. He *knew* him. He did.

But who the hell was he?

Erdman heard a quiet, rhythmic tapping. It took him a second to realize his teeth were chattering, and he pulled the duvet up to his chin. He could hear the low sounds of the television in Amber's sitting room, the murmur of traffic in the distance.

Sleep drifted towards him, luring him with its siren song.

Lilith, I love you. I'm sorry.

He dredged his memory for their wedding day. Long ago he had buried it in the very depths of his mind, and here he was, dragging it through silt to the surface. Not his finest hour. He'd been late, hungover, but, worst of all, had forgotten to confirm their booking at a castle near Bristol, and that oily bastard of a manager had given their suite to someone else. There had been a music festival on and every hotel for miles was booked up. So they spent their wedding night at a Premier Inn on the M5.

No, he preferred to remember that golden day when he'd proposed. Lili, sun-kissed and relaxed at Lulworth Cove, the wind lifting tendrils of hair from her freckled face, her throat exposed to the sun every time she gave a languid stretch. And him, laughing and still full of hope, in a pair of faded denim shorts, snapping the ring pull from a can of Coke, and sliding it onto her finger.

"Will you marry me, Miss Lilith?

She had laughed at first, not taking him seriously. But as he bent in the sand on one knee, her face had grown serious, and she cupped his chin in her hands.

"Do you mean this, Erdman Frith? Or is this another of your silly games?"

"I want you to be my wife, Lili. I want you at my side for the rest of my life."

She had cried then, and that's what he remembered most. The sun's benevolent warmth, and the sheen of tears on her perfect skin. He still hadn't gotten 'round to buying her a proper engagement ring, even though he knew she kept that bent old ring pull in a velvet case at the back of her jewelry box.

Tomorrow he would go home. He would speak to the police, apologize to his family, and try to become a man worthy of their respect.

His eyes were growing heavier now. He called up pictures of Jakey, to comfort him on his walk towards oblivion: his laugh; the way he slept; his tongue poking from his lips as he practiced his reading.

Jakey-boy. My champ. I'll see you tomorrow.

He clung to those pictures of his son, his precious boy. The flaxen highlights in his hair. The dancing spirit in his eyes. His tender body, perfect to him in spite of its lumps and contortions.

But they drifted away as gently as gossamer until, finally, he was asleep.

THURSDAY

THIRTY-EIGHT

7.49 a.m.

The rabbit blinks, unsuspecting. With one swift *crack* of its neck, it is dead. The Bone Collector cradles its still-warm body in his hand, then picks up his knife and skins it, dropping its sodden coat into a bucket beneath his workbench. A careful incision, and the blood spools out, staining the galvanized metal. Another flick of his wrist, and the heart and kidneys thud against the rim, followed by its tongue, eyes, and brain.

For his sixth birthday, his mother had bought him a rabbit. It was white and black, and its whiskers twitched as it sniffed his hand. He could feel its heart beating beneath its fur, a vibrant reminder of life.

He loved that rabbit. Played with it, fed it, brushed its coat for hours at a time. When it bit him, he hit it on the head with a cinder block, and fractured its skull.

He turns his attention back to his task.

Using his scalpel, he saws at the excess flesh that clings defiantly to bone. A spindly finger dips into the spatter and he smears it on his lips like salve. Globules snag on the chapped skin. He wipes his latex gloves on his white coat and offers a bloody smile. He has searched everywhere for the lost rabbit bones. No matter. A few more hours and this new skeleton will be ready.

It is only right that he leave it behind as a gift. A thank-you. A badge of his devotion to duty, and a sign for the detective. One likes to be recognized for one's work.

And the beetles must feed to stay alive, killing two birds with one stone.

He reaches for his magnifying glass and plucks a dermestid from the creeping mass in one of seven Perspex tanks he stores in the cutting room. He peers closely at its legs, and between its head and thorax. One stray mite and he will have to destroy the whole colony.

The Woolwich dealer didn't ask awkward questions when he said he worked for a museum, and the Bone Collector didn't quibble over price. At £700 for three thousand adults, larvae, and pupae, it was more than the going rate, but he could ill afford to draw attention to himself. He paid in cash without a murmur.

"So, right, yer know not to let 'em get too wet and make sure the body's been left a few hours. They don't like 'em fresh. Dunno what size animal yer wanning to use 'em on, but if yer wanna mount the skeleton, yer gotta check 'em every few hours, make sure they ain't eaten through the joints and connective tissues."

The fat man, who had a shaven head and a tattoo of a ladybird on his forearm, lit a cigarette and took a deep drag, then blew out the smoke through his nose. It made his nostrils flare.

"If yer wanna grow more, yer gotta keep 'em warm

and dark. But make sure it don't go moldy, or too dry. Then they won't lay no eggs."

The Bone Collector nodded, and thanked the man for his help. He did not tell him about the ten-thousand-strong colony he already owns, stored in the unplugged chest freezer at his father's house. Or the girl imprisoned upstairs. Together, they decanted the beetles into a plastic tank with some wood shavings and a foam block, and packed it into a cardboard box.

Early Thursday morning, he comes back. The butchered remains of the rabbit have already begun to give off a unique perfume, and the Bone Collector knows it will ripen. He revels in its cloying scent, will later lick his own skin to see if he can taste it in the dead cells and follicles.

The beetle man has warned him to air-dry his specimen for a few hours before setting his army to work; now it is time. He places the rabbit carcass into the tank and watches his newest battalion advance, thousands of dung-colored soldiers ready to unmask the enemy. Like a sentinel, he keeps watch as his colony strips down its quarry, until nothing remains but an almost-perfect set of bones: tarsus, atlas, ulna, metacarpus. The top of the cervical vertebrae is broken, but it doesn't matter.

The boy won't care what the Bone Collector leaves as his calling card.

He is pleased, surprised even, with the speed and efficiency of his newest colony; soon, he will be ready to set it to work on something larger.

He croons to his beetles, calls them home. In one undulating mass, they swarm up his arms, 'round his neck, down the back of his jacket. He enjoys the sensation of thousands of insects crawling over his skin, prefers it to the touch of human hands. After a few moments, he coaxes them back into the tank, and they follow as one.

The Bone Collector leaves the cutting room and bolts the door, climbing the concrete stairs up to his father's house. He sniffs the air, picks out a faint scent beneath the unemptied garbage cans. He has been so intent on the rabbit that he's forgotten to check on the girl, but it will wait. Now he needs sleep, just an hour or so, to prepare himself for the next phase.

The liquid sunrise drips beneath the blinds of his house, a nondescript building on an anonymous road. He is weary but excited. As always, the siren song of his collection lures him. He shouldn't linger, but he does.

He is drawn first to the glass cabinet labeled *S*. The bones are discolored and crumbling. He learned long ago from his father that boiling in ammonia is quick, but the damage it wreaks endures.

He patrols the room; there is *G* and her missing distal phalanges; the beautiful, misshapen skull of *Q*, a sufferer of Paget's disease, with its cruel weakenings and distortions; and the complete articulated skeleton of a horse. *F*, the perfect form of a stillborn fetus, is on show by the window, protected from the light by blackout blinds used in nurseries the breadth of the country. The irony does not escape him.

Today, he makes himself wait. And the thrill, when it comes, explodes inside him. The sight of *C*'s lumpen bones renews him. Reminds him of his father. He wonders what secrets the skin of *J* will unveil, already dreams of displaying his skeleton in a familial embrace.

Shutting the door on his personal museum, he permits himself a smile. His collection is a pleasure to behold, but by no means complete. There is still much work to be done: new specimens to prepare, exhibits to display, a colony to care for.

Fresh targets to track.

His wife is sleeping when he lets himself in. She is breathing through her mouth, and he listens to every breath as it flutters and flies. He takes off his jacket, hangs it on the back of her chair.

The bedpan is full, but the smell does not bother him. He is used to it. He checks to see if she has taken any medication, if the pain from her joints has wrenched her from sleep in the depths of the night. The foil is intact, and relief washes through him like warm water.

While she sleeps, he sees the sadness in her aging face. A crisscross pattern of blade-thin threads, some woven into the fabric of her skin, some fresher, newly minted. She wears the lines of her motherlessness like scars.

He sits on the edge of the bed, removes his shoes, his trousers, and folds them neatly. Daylight is pressing through the gaps in the curtains, and still she sleeps on. He rests his body on the cold strip of sheet next to her, feels her warmth pulling him in. Her hand finds his. He shuts his eyes.

THIRTY-NINE

7.56 a.m.

Fitzroy was not supposed to be drinking coffee, but she downed the triple espresso and prayed it would be enough to get her through the morning.

Her eyes felt full of grit. She tried to rub away her exhaustion, but the only salve was sleep, and there was no chance of that. Not until the *ting* in her brain had quieted, and with every passing hour, the volume was rising.

She had almost canceled, *should* have canceled, but it had taken her months to persuade David to come. A light drizzle was varnishing the pavement. Fitzroy threw her paper cup into the bin and pressed the buzzer.

The seats were pale pink and comfortable. Four of them were occupied by couples holding hands and looking anxious.

"Can you fill this in, please?" said the receptionist, and handed her a printed form attached to a clipboard.

She sat alone, head down, and tapped out a couple of e-mails. The clock on the wall said 7.58 a.m. She checked her phone. At 7.59, she sent him a text.

Where are you?

Nothing.

At 8.01 a.m., her phone pinged.

I'm sorry, Etta, I'm not coming today. I can't.

She stared at the words on the screen, hardly able to process what he was saying. What he was *not* saying.

"Mr. and Mrs. Fitzroy?" called the receptionist.

Fitzroy rose to her feet. "I'm sorry," she whispered. "My husband has been held up."

"That's fine, you can wait, if you like."

"Um—"

She couldn't think clearly, couldn't accept that David had allowed her to come here, hopes raised, only to let her down. He was many things, her husband, but the casualness of his cruelty was unexpected. She wondered if it was because he didn't care anymore.

She had been a fool.

Her mind drifted back to Nina and Patrick's engagement drinks three years ago, the flushed glow of her younger sister's cheeks, despite the bottle of fizzy water in her hand.

"Fun, wasn't it?" she'd said when they got home, flopping onto the sofa and kicking off her shoes.

"She's pregnant." David's tone was dismissive, even then.

Oh, right. Of course.

Several glasses of wine had fueled Fitzroy's courage. She'd stood up, wobbled slightly, and taken his dry hand in hers. This was the solution to their marital teething problems—she just knew it.

"Why don't we try for a baby, too?" She'd started to unbutton his shirt. "Right here and now."

"No."

"When, then?"

He had sighed, batted her hand away, and sat down, resting an ankle on his knee as he unlaced his shoes.

"I don't want to have children."

She had laughed, a shocked, surprised sound.

"You never said."

"I think I did, Etta."

And he was right. He *had* said. Not when she had met him during the police investigation into the suicide of one of his overstretched colleagues. Then he had been respectful and polite, although he'd held her gaze for a fraction too long. Nor when he had pressed his business card into her hand and invited her out to dinner. No, that came later. Mostly during drunken conversations at the wine bar down the road during those early heady days when they had found each other as intoxicating as the contents of their glasses, when his experience and stability had been exactly what she had been craving, the antidote to the toxicity of her loss. He was a broker, for heaven's sake. He was used to negotiation. She had just assumed he would change his mind. That *she* would change his mind.

A week after those engagement drinks, Nina had miscarried her baby. Her indifference had been startling.

"I'll have another in a couple of years," she said. "Anyway, I don't want to be a fat bride."

Fitzroy had thought then that she wouldn't care about being fat for the rest of her life if it meant she had a child.

She worked hard to change David's mind, and for a while, she thought she had. She shared with him her dreams of becoming a mother. When that didn't work, she had shown him those heartbreaking photographs in a box in her wardrobe. Then she'd begged. Reluctantly, he'd gone along with it; the unprotected sex, the midcycle couplings, but still it hadn't happened. "Unexplained infertility," the doctor said.

Slowly, the intimacy between them dried up like a stain on a sheet.

Soon, she was spending every spare moment at work. So was he. And Fitzroy and David slipped between the cracks of each other's lives.

But this. This was what had sustained her, this had allowed her to hope, and even as she had stepped through the doors of the clinic that morning, she had still believed they would make it.

But he hadn't come. Which was as good as saying their marriage was over.

"Shall I make you another appointment?"

"No. Thank you."

Outside, the November morning was raw. And she had work to do.

The escalator carried her deep into the underground, and as the motor turned on its endless cycle, so did Fitzroy's brain.

Most of the night had been spent rereading statements and scanning the contents of Grace Rodríguez's case file.

But she didn't need to search amongst those pages to know that the rabbit skeleton found on the Heath was identical to the skeleton they had discovered—and dismissed—at the site of Grace's remains.

There had been no tube attached to its leg, though. Not like the one they'd just found on the Heath.

So what? If we weren't looking for it, it could easily have been lost.

Perhaps that was why he had sent the note. This time, there was no room for confusion. But she was still baffled. Was that skeleton intended as a calling card for Clara? If so, why had it been found on the opposite side of the Heath when she was last seen at a sweetshop in the Village? There was no trace of a body at the site of the shooting, no trace of anything at all, except Erdman Frith's blood. And what about the grey van at the scene? Was *that* the connection? She had to talk to Mr. Frith, to see what he remembered.

When she boarded the train at London Bridge ten minutes later, her phone was ringing. Her stomach jolted, but it wasn't David.

"Where the fuck are you?" said The Boss. "I thought you were only going for coffee."

"Sorry, I got tied up."

"Well, untie yourself and get back here. I want to talk about the rabbits."

Back in the office, there was the buzz of a major investigation. The Boss beckoned her over.

"Tell me everything," he said.

Even though she had already written a memo several hours ago, she repeated what Dr. Hall had told her.

"Forensics are all over it," said The Boss. "But we're not going to get much. The rain's washed away our chances." He stifled a yawn. "Although it wasn't the rain that washed away the evidence left by Grace's attacker. We managed that all by our bloody selves." He shut his eyes, rubbed at the center left of his chest with the heel of his hand. "Oh, and the note got wet. What a fuckup."

"Sir—"

"And Clara Foyle's disappearance is giving me a major fucking headache. We've traced every known sexual offender in the area, bar one or two. The team's still checking out their alibis. We need more warm bodies, fucking pronto, but we're not going to get them."

"Sir—"

"So now we've got two major bloody investigations and not enough specialist officers to work them. How do I decide which is more important? The search for a teenager who's been missing for a year and is almost certainly dead, but whose family is in pieces, or the abduction of a five-year-old girl? I can't decide, that's the bloody nub of it. I shouldn't have to." He took a breath. "Are you okay to have another crack at Miles Foyle later? He's still saying nothing."

"Yes, but sir—"

"What is it, Fitzroy?"

Now The Boss had finally stopped talking, Fitzroy wasn't sure if she was brave enough to say it out loud. She felt foolish, but the *ting* was telling her that she ought to speak up, that she'd regret it if she didn't. She jumped in.

"Has anyone checked the sweetshop for a rabbit skeleton?"

He took off his glasses. His face was naked without them, the lines around his eyes more prominent, an indent on either side of the bridge of his nose. He took a cloth from his pocket and polished them.

Fitzroy blundered on. "I mean, the skeleton in the woods was just a few yards from Grace's fingertips, right? It was meant to be found. But there's no sign of Clara on the Heath, where the other skeleton was left.

Shouldn't we be looking for a more"—she paused, groping for the right word—"*concrete* connection between the cases?"

He put his glasses back on, rolled his tongue around his cheek. His tone was patient, but she still felt like an overeager trainee on her first day at Hendon.

"The forensics team has already checked the route Clara walked when she left the school playground, Fitzroy. They've checked the Heath twice. They've checked the sweetshop, her house, even her parents' car. They've checked everything they can bloody well think of."

The shame of that morning's events at the clinic began to crowd out her confidence, and she dropped her head, suddenly weary of fighting everyone, at home and at work. Of David and his lack of empathy, his inability to see beyond his own restricted horizon. On their wedding day, an elegant but low-key registry office affair in central London, she had believed he was her future, but now even that seemed uncertain.

Her lack of progression in her job. She'd been so sure that The Boss had been hinting at promotion before that incident last year. Now she was lucky to be here at all.

She thought of the *New Grandson* card she had seen by Nina's hospital bed. Her father had never acknowledged what had happened to her, and couldn't understand the point of coming to the funeral of a baby who had died before he'd lived, that he had never known and would never know. She had barely noticed at the time, her own grief deadening the pain of his lack of interest. But now it consumed her, and was one of the reasons they barely spoke anymore.

And she was beginning to realize that unless she moved on from David she might never have a child of her own.

She was messing things up in every part of her life.

Sometimes she felt more like a seven-year-old than a thirty-seven-year-old.

Silly girl.

"It was just a hunch," she said. "A stupid hunch."

"Fitzroy—" said The Boss, and something about the way he said her name made her square her shoulders and lift her head. Made him more of a father than her own ever was.

Her eyes met his.

"Check again."

FORTY

8.31 a.m.

On Thursday, 22 November, two days after his father disappeared, and less than an hour after Fitzroy had concluded her marriage was over, the unwelcome light of dawn climbed over Jakey's windowsill and declared it morning. He squeezed his eyelids shut, and a tear trickled down his cheek, causing a stain to bloom on his Spider-Man pillowcase.

His heart hurt. Not like his body did when the bones had begun a fresh incursion, and his mother gave him medicine, and it stopped for a bit. Or that teeth-grinding pain that kept him awake at night, and made his mother cry when she thought he was asleep. This went deeper, like he was carrying something heavy inside and it was dragging him down.

Go away, Ol' Bloody Bones, Ol' Tommy Rawhead. Leave me alone.

Jakey hadn't slept much. And when he did, his dreams were filled with pictures of a shadowy man with sharp teeth, and skinny arms, and his father.

Oh, Daddy.

Jakey made a noise somewhere between a gasp and a sob. His father had promised to protect him, but he'd left him behind.

Daddy, please come home.

In the playground of his imagination, Jakey saw the figure from his father's childhood stories reaching for him, his fingers outstretched, black eyes watching.

Jakey was only six, and in the way that children have, the man in the book and the man everyone was talking about on the television had become muddied, and then distilled into the same creeping threat.

Ol' Bloody Bones had taken the little girl. He had seen it on his television.

Now his daddy was gone.

If Ol' Bloody Bones was real, as the boy believed he was, it would mean that all his fears and anxieties had been made flesh.

And he, Jakey, would be next.

As for Clara Foyle's mother, her own imagination was dragging her down a dark path that she did not wish to travel. Her days and nights were simply defined by the ebb and flow of light and shade, and she often found herself dozing off at odd moments and then jerking to, discovering afresh on each awakening the distress and horror of her daughter's disappearance.

The black box of her curtainless window signaled it was night again. *Clara, Mummy misses you. My precious girl. I hope you're sleeping.*

She reached for the glass of clear liquid by the side of her bed. She swallowed, took another burning sip.

She wasn't sure if it was the vodka or the MS blurring her vision.

The bedroom was quieter than usual without the animal grunts of Miles's snoring, but his side of the bed was cool and empty. He was still with the police. Her hand was shaking as she laid their silver-framed wedding photo facedown.

She had always insisted on the best of everything. Designer clothes, expensive linen, luxury holidays, but as she lay in the yawning darkness of her home, she had much to regret.

At barely thirty, Amy was a mother without one of her daughters and the wife of a cheat. A woman who had taken for granted a life of privilege, greased by money and prestige.

But she would give it up, every last penny, if she could just see Clara again.

FORTY-ONE

9.04 a.m.

Dharamdeep Atwal was tipping bags of coins into the cash register when Fitzroy walked in. He shook his head slightly.

"What you want now? This not good for business."

"A little girl is missing, Mr. Atwal. Surely you don't begrudge me half an hour of your time?"

He slammed shut the drawer. The coins jangled. "Of course not. But the police, they already turn it upside down."

"I just want to have another look around. It won't take long."

Fitzroy didn't wait for an answer. In situations like these, she felt a bit like soiled goods. The police had swarmed Mr. Atwal's shop on Friday, as soon as it became clear that Clara was missing. Her colleagues had spoken to him several times since. By the time it was her turn, he'd had more than enough of Her Majesty's finest.

But she needed to be here. It was the last place Clara had been seen alive.

Mr. Atwal's was a proper sweetshop. It didn't sell tins of beans or frozen pizzas or shiny rolls of biscuits, just dozens of jars of brightly colored confectionery, slabs of chocolate wrapped in foil and paper, lavishly beribboned gift bags of retro sweets. The smell of sugar stuck in her throat. She saw Clara, beguiled by choice, walking up to the counter, a coin clutched in her hand.

Mr. Atwal kept his shop tidy. Nothing out of place. The shelves filled with stock. She stood between the lollipops and the prepackaged cones of fizzy cola bottles, and tried to imagine where he might have hidden it. If he had hidden it.

She walked forward, back through the front door, heard the *ting* of its bell, and the answering *ting* in her mind. She corrected herself. He wouldn't have hidden it at all. He'd have wanted it to be found.

Fitzroy looked in the garbage can outside, down the alleyway at the side of the shop. She went back in, scanned the shelves, behind the counter, the tiny room at the back, which held Mr. Atwal's coat and packed lunch, a chair and kettle, and not much else.

I'm wrong, she thought. But she didn't feel wrong.

A delivery truck pulled up outside the shop, its engines running. Fitzroy watched its driver carry in a stack of cardboard boxes, watched Mr. Atwal exchange a joke with the man, and sign for them.

He lifted one on the counter and slit open the tape with a Stanley knife.

Packets of sherbet lemons spilled out.

Mr. Atwal began to put away the sweets straight onto the shelves. He hummed while he worked, a tuneless sound that grated on Fitzroy's already shredded nerves. When he finished, he placed the box on the floor, and started on the next one.

In her mind's eye, Fitzroy glimpsed the collapsed shoe box on Blackheath Common.

Ting.

"Mr. Atwal," said Fitzroy, "where do you store your empty cardboard boxes?"

He kept his back to her. "At the back of the shop, mostly. We leave them out there for the recycling guys."

Fitzroy could hear, inside her head, the *whoosh* of blood in her veins.

"When do they come?"

"Thursday mornings."

She ran.

The boxes were stacked against an overflowing garbage bag in a small alcove that smelled of urine behind the shop. Some had been flattened to make space, but the smaller ones had not. They were damp and soft with rain. Something unpleasant was leaking from the bag, but Fitzroy ignored it.

She pulled a plastic glove from her pocket, and reached for the pile of boxes, felt the texture of disintegrating cardboard between her fingers. She flipped open the first set of flaps. Nothing. Reached for the next one. Nothing. The third box fell apart in her hands, sending dirty rainwater or worse onto her shoes. She forced herself to slow down, to stop fumbling. If Clara had been snatched by the man who had taken Grace Rodríguez, hope was almost certainly lost.

Only a couple of boxes remained, and Fitzroy felt the sick twist of failure in her gut. The traffic crawled by. Commuters pounded the pavement just a few feet away.

She reached for a small box with black lettering on the side, its ink beginning to run, and opened its flaps.

Fitzroy's heart was a trapped bird in her chest.

In the corner of the box, its bones stripped and fragile, was the huddled carcass of another rabbit skeleton. A note rolled in a tube, just like before. *"Behold, I will cause breath to enter you."*

Lying next to those bones was a torn paper bag of strawberry bonbons, pink icing sugar spilling across the cardboard like coffin silk.

FORTY-TWO

11.31 a.m.

Like Fitzroy, Lilith had now been awake for hours and hours. Doubt had been her bedfellow, and in those lonely predawn hours, when the rest of the world was slumbering, she'd convinced herself that Erdman was in trouble.

Darkness had a way of amplifying one's fears. He was lying in an alleyway, leaking blood onto the pavement, overcome by his injuries, unable to cry out for help.

The cold wash of daylight brought her back to her senses. Not Erdman. He would never have left the hospital if he still needed treatment. He was sulking, that was all.

She tried to ignore the niggling doubts that wouldn't go away. At one time, she'd have sworn he would never give up on their marriage, but she'd been wrong about that, hadn't she? What else was she wrong about?

That detective had phoned earlier and asked to speak to Erdman. She had wanted to lie, to pretend he was out, but her conscience wouldn't let her. She had told DS Fitzroy that he still hadn't come home, that she had heard nothing from him. The silence at the other end of the phone had felt like a judgment on her wifely virtues.

"I need to talk to him," the detective had said.

You and me both, thought Lilith.

After the call, she had climbed the stairs to check on Jakey. He was asleep again, his breath rattling in and out of his lungs. School was not an option today. She would take him back to the doctor later this afternoon. Ask for another prescription of steroids, perhaps some antibiotics. She hoped it was no more serious than that. The thought of those long hospital corridors closed up her throat.

While Jakey slept, she prepared a simple lunch. A chunk of cheese, a green apple cut into slices, a buttered roll. She ate alone, listening to the radio, covered Jakey's share with plastic wrap in case he woke up hungry.

The soft chime of the doorbell cut through the presenter's phone-in on the new director general of the BBC.

Erdman? Is that you?

"Hello, lovey," said Mrs. Cooper from next door. "I just wondered if your husband was back yet."

Lilith drew in a breath to steady herself, her eyes filling. Mrs. Cooper's wrinkled face softened in sympathy, and she patted the younger woman's hand.

"I'm sorry to hear that. Is there anything I can do? Anything you need?" Her motherly concern was comforting.

Lilith pictured Erdman, lost and hurting somewhere in the city.

"Actually, there is something," she said. "Would you mind sitting with Jakey for a couple of hours? I'm going to look for my husband."

When Lilith stepped outside, it was clear that winter had arrived. Sleet was stinging her face as she hurried down the road, uncertain where to start.

The pubs wouldn't be open yet. She tried to think where he might go, whom he might be staying with. Most people had replied to her increasingly frantic messages, but Amber Collins hadn't called her back. Erdman had told her once that his colleague lived near the Blue Elephant Theater. Perhaps she should start there.

She dithered briefly by the car. There was no guarantee she would cover a greater distance in it, not with London's traffic. In the end, she walked down to the bank of bus stops by the Lewisham police station. The 436 would take her straight to Camberwell.

As the sleet turned into rain, Lilith could make out the top deck of her bus, rumbling along the road. As she reached into her bag for her Oyster card, her phone began to ring. She fished around amongst the tissues and tampons until she found it. The name on the screen made her mouth go dry.

Home.

"Lilith?" The panic in Mrs. Cooper's voice caused the pulse in her throat to *flick-flack*. "You need to come back, lovey," she said.

"What's happened? Is it Erdman?"

Mrs. Cooper's voice sounded far away, as if she was speaking to Lilith from the other end of a long tunnel.

"No, dear, it's Jakey," she said. "I'm afraid he's collapsed."

FORTY-THREE

2.17 p.m.

He waits by the fence and watches the children play, but the boy does not come. He was not here yesterday, either. He had walked through the school gates, hidden amongst the harassed mothers with toddlers, the nannies pushing their wide buggies, the awkward grandparents, but the boy with the burnished hair, the eager freckles, was nowhere to be seen.

The Bone Collector wonders if he is ill.

If the missing father will make the mother more careful, or less.

He burns to know.

He returns to his grey van, and drives hard through rain-slicked streets. Not far, just a couple more roads. He wonders if the boy will come willingly, or if he will have to be coerced. The prospect excites him.

Already he knows the boy will not disappoint; he has watched him, followed him. Witnessed for himself the twists and distortions beneath his skin. But the father, he is perplexing, and not at all as he expected.

He pats his jacket pocket, makes sure his tools are in place. The colony will not consume living matter, so a blade will have to do its job.

And then the glass case, empty for so many years, will be filled.

The lights are on, and he spies movement through the windows.

Droplets batter the windscreen, capturing pinpricks of reflected headlights. "It's raining stair rods," Marshall used to say. He wonders what Marshall would say now, if only he could see him.

He crawls along the street, looks for a place to park. The van bounces as it mounts the curb, the angle just right.

He will kill the mother if he has to.

And then he hears it, and his heart freezes.

The rise and fall of a siren.

He forgets to breathe.

They have found him.

The strobing lights cast an eerie blue flicker over the watching houses and flats, and slowly, slowly, he lets his breath go.

But it is not the police.

It is an ambulance.

FORTY-FOUR

2.51 p.m.

It was an unhappy coincidence that the opposing forces converging on the Frith family home like points on a compass would not cross paths.

Erdman had woken late, still bruised and sore. He had helped himself to Amber's cornflakes, showered (a painful experience), and dressed in the baggy black clothes she had borrowed from her boyfriend (even more painful). He had switched on the television. Flicked through one of her books. He was planning to go home, but he'd wait until Jakey was back from school. By staying away, he'd conceded the moral high ground. But his son's presence would dilute his wife's anger. Which was why he was only just walking across Camberwell Green when the ambulance arrived at his house.

The Bone Collector, who had intended to abduct Jakey Frith that afternoon, did not like dealing with the unexpected. As the ambulance pulled in, he pulled away, circling the nearby streets like a bird of prey.

DS Fitzroy had wondered if she was being fobbed

off. Mr. Frith's wife had sounded distracted. She would pop by, she decided. The house was not far. Which was how she came to be there less than a minute after the paramedics had parked and the Bone Collector had left.

As for Lilith, she had run all the way up the hill from the bus stop, the blood in her veins pumping faster and faster until she thought her heart might burst from her chest.

She arrived exactly sixty seconds before the ambulance, and did not register a grey van on the opposite side of the street.

The front door was open, Jakey just visible in the hallway. Mrs. Cooper's arm was around his shoulders. He had fallen forward onto his knees. Eyes screwed up, he tugged on his sleeve.

"It hurts," he moaned.

His breath came in short, labored gasps.

Lilith half-stumbled, half-ran towards him, her own arms outstretched, like a sleepwalker, or a drowning sailor.

Jakey tried to stand, to reach for her in return, but as soon as he was on his feet, he wobbled, and moaned again. A moment or two later, he crumpled as if his legs had turned to butter.

Fitzroy, who had sprinted up the path, was just in time to catch him as he fell. She set him gently on the grass. His eyes were closed, and his dark lashes curled against his cheeks.

The paramedics ran towards him.

"It's okay, sweetheart," said Lilith, cradling her son. "It's okay." Tears streaked a fresh path down her face.

Fitzroy felt something shift inside her, and she looked

away. She remembered another lifetime, before she'd met David, before things had become complicated and confused and broken. She remembered another little boy, his tiny fingernails touching hers, the bluish tinge to his lips. Eyes that never opened.

The paramedics were bent over Jakey, who was pale and still.

"He's got a bone disorder," said Lilith. She was talking very quickly. To Fitzroy, it sounded like she was spewing up glass with every word. "He's having a flare-up. A really, really bad one. Try to avoid intramuscular injections, they accelerate the condition. And don't be too rough with him. We don't want any unexpected breaks or traumas.

"There's a general rule of thumb. Unless you need to save his life, don't touch him."

"He's USC," Fitzroy heard one of the paramedics say. "Let's get him to the hospital now."

Lilith climbed awkwardly into the ambulance, and Fitzroy watched as the doors slammed shut, and it pulled away. She'd been in the game long enough to know what "USC" meant. *Up Shit Creek.*

At the hospital for the second time in less than a week, Lilith sat by Jakey's bed and waited. They had given him a heavy dose of anti-inflammatories to ease the swelling, the pain. His eyes were closed and he coughed, then moved uncomfortably against the sheets.

The doctor spoke to her in a low voice. He was concerned about Jakey's breathing, his temperature. He wanted to do a chest X-ray. To rule out a chest infection. Or pneumonia.

"We'll monitor him overnight," said Dr. Garvey. "Let's just see what happens. Everyone is different, but when new bone is forming, the pain can be excruciating. Let's hope it's just that."

As soon as the doctor was gone, Jakey rolled onto his side, his back to her. His shoulders began to shudder. In alarm, Lilith reached out to touch him, and realized he was crying. She gathered him into her arms. Several moments later, she deciphered what he was trying to tell her.

"I-I-I'm frightened, Mummy." Jakey's face was blotchy, and a thick stream of snot trailed from his nose and over his top lip. He began to cough again.

Lilith held him until the spasms racking his body subsided. Then she took his hot hand in hers and brought it to her lips.

"You're in the best place, sweetheart. The doctors are going to treat you, and you're going to be fine. Do you understand me? You're going to be fine." Her voice was fierce, and she was aware that she was trying to convince herself as much as her son.

"I don't want to die, Mummy."

"Oh, Jakey. You're not going to die. What on earth makes you say that?"

But Jakey wouldn't answer.

Her own eyes filled with tears, but she blinked them away and pasted on a smile. She would not allow him to see her unravel.

The little boy turned back towards the wall. His pajama top gaped at the collar, revealing the bony lump on his shoulder, an unwelcome intruder lurking beneath his skin, stretching it into an unnatural shape, just like their lives.

A woman visiting a patient walked by, carrying her young daughter. The toddler twisted around her mother's shoulder, eyes drawn to Jakey's distorted body.

Lilith turned her head away. She didn't blame the child, but it was a painful reminder of all the stares they'd endured over the years, even though she should be used to them by now.

On his first day at school, a small girl had run up to Jakey, her smile as bright as her curls.

"Can't catch me," she teased, already sprinting away from him in anticipation.

Jakey had returned her grin and started after her, his limp becoming more prominent as he ran.

Aware of the pitying glances, Lilith had resisted the urge to chase after him, urging him to be careful, not to exert himself. She'd always promised herself she wouldn't wrap him in cotton wool, but that had proved more difficult than she'd ever imagined. Although school had given Jakey a newfound freedom, it had bound Lilith in chains of fear and worry. When he was a toddler, it was easier to track his movements, to watch over him. Now, every day, she prepared herself for a call from the school to say Jakey had been taken ill, or knocked over. It wasn't that Jakey didn't have friends. But those friendships would never be the rough-and-tumble kind, the let's-go-out-on-our-bikes-after-school kind.

And now he was in the hospital again.

She was filled with a fierce urge to protect her boy, who had come into the world fighting and who continued to fight every day. *It isn't fair*, she thought savagely. *First his illness, and now all this shit with Erdman. It isn't fair.*

Where *was* he? Over the last twenty-four hours the guilt that was taunting her had solidified into self-righteousness. She was right. He was never there when she needed him. But it wasn't about her this time. It was their son who was suffering now.

She stayed with Jakey, holding his hand and singing to him, until his breathing deepened and the burden of fear and worry slid from his face to hers. It took him almost an hour to fall asleep.

FORTY-FIVE

3.43 p.m.

Erdman limped up the hill as quickly as his injuries would allow. Which was not very. That suited him just fine. The closer he got to home, the more he found his feet dragging, reluctant to face the music that two nights' unexplained absence was about to unleash.

A woman was sitting outside his house in her car, staring up at the windows. As he stepped into view, she opened the door. Given the events of the last few days—especially the stranger at the edges of his life—Erdman approached with determined caution.

"Can I help you?"

She absorbed his bruised face, his ill-fitting clothes, hair slowly turning the color of burned gingerbread in the rain.

"I think it's a case of me helping you, Mr. Frith."

Erdman narrowed his eyes. "Is that so?"

The woman stuck out her hand. "DS Etta Fitzroy." Her grip was firm, no-nonsense.

"Is this about the other night?"

"Yes and no. I do need to talk to you about that,

about a grey van that a witness saw, but . . ." She paused, the words catching in her throat. Even experienced officers struggled with unhappy news.

"Do you want to come in?" he said. "I, um, haven't been home for a while. I should probably go and see my family." He had already started towards the door when he felt the pressure of her hand on his shoulder.

"They're not there."

"Oh." He swung around to face her, his face screwing up at the jolt of pain in his back. "I don't suppose you know where they are?"

The detective caught his eye, held him there. "Your son's not well, Mr. Frith. An ambulance came. He's at the hospital."

Erdman blinked twice, the bricks of the houses blurring into monotone sky. Dusk had begun to swallow up the daylight. Something tight and heavy lodged itself in his chest.

Fitzroy saw guilt streak across his face, felt a sudden rush of sympathy.

"Come on," she said. "I'll give you a lift. We can talk on the way."

As it turned out, there wasn't much to talk about. Erdman stared out of the car window, barely speaking at all.

No, he hadn't seen a grey van.

No, he had no idea of the identity of his attackers.

No, he had never taken drugs.

Headlamps from passing cars lit his eyes, twin beacons of fear and self-reproach. It astounded her, the excuses these men came up with. Miles Foyle, all buttoned-up denial, protecting himself before his daughter. Erdman Frith, a man suffering because of his *self-imposed* absence, and her own father.

Chief Inspector Boyd Fitzroy.

Living in Greece. She wasn't exactly sure where. Somewhere on the coast, near Athens. A man whose anger had grown as his own career faltered. Who had glossed over his own failings by abandoning his family.

The television had been on, one of those fresh, bright evenings that hinted at spring. The teatime news. She remembered it because he was never at home at teatime.

Riots in a northern city, police with shields, with batons.

"Hit the bastards," he had shouted at the TV. "Smack 'em."

Etta's mother had looked up from her sewing. "Surely that's police brutality."

"Those louts deserve it. The police force is the foremost authority in this country. It holds us all together, stops us from descending into anarchy. That must always be respected. We are the Law."

He'd said it like he truly believed it.

"But, like Mum says, the police shouldn't go around hurting people," said fifteen-year-old Etta. "That's the very opposite of what they're supposed to do."

"Don't listen to your mother, Etta," he'd said. "She doesn't understand much apart from cooking and cleaning. Make sure you do something decent with your life."

Her mother had quietly set down the skirt she was making and left the room.

The unmarked car pulled into the hospital car park. Fitzroy crawled around for a space. Erdman's face darkened in the shadow of this building. Again, she felt that twist of sympathy. He must have spent many months here with Jakey.

"I'll come with you," she said. "I'd like to check on your son."

He acknowledged this small act of decency with a nod of his head.

The receptionist said words like "pediatric" and "intensive care." Fitzroy watched him absorb this news, watched him swallow several times as if it wasn't just nerves controlling his actions but the taste of an unpalatable truth.

The moment, when it came, was not one of high drama or hysteria, but of an ordinary family reconnecting. Through the small window in the unit's door, Lilith Frith was talking to a nurse. Her eyes passed over the glass, then back again. She stood completely still for a moment. Then she was running through the doors, slamming into her husband, and he was putting his arms around her, stroking her hair, her face, touching any part of her body that he could.

Fitzroy tried not to stare, tried not to think how she would react if David had disappeared for two days without telling her where he was. She waited for the recriminations to spill from Mrs. Frith's mouth, the accusations, the sense of betrayal and outrage.

But she only repeated two words. Over and over and over.

"Thank God," she said. "Thank God."

FORTY-SIX

5.10 p.m.

The first time he smelled the damp, raw-meat odor of the inside of a dead body, he'd bit down until his eyetooth cut through his lip. The pain distracted him from the urge to faint.

His father thought it would be instructional for him to watch the preparation of an exhibit. To watch the slitting open of the corpse, the Y-shaped incision, the removal of the organ groups: cardiothoracic, gastrointestinal, and urogenital. He was ten.

"With a little skill, you can remove them all in one go, but I prefer to do it like this." Marshall grinned, holding the lungs aloft in one hand, the heart in his other, forearms slick with blood and matter.

The boy had watched the parenchymal fluid leak from the two sacs that had once inflated and deflated with air, with life. Watched Marshall pack them into containers surrounded by slushy ice, ready to take to their contact at the research laboratory in Hertfordshire.

"Don't just stand there, son. Gotta get the innards

out next." Marshall picked up the scalpel. "Innard out, innard out, shake it all about." He had laughed, a harsh sound that jarred the quiet of their cellar.

Gingerly, the boy moved towards the eviscerated corpse, drew in a shallow breath so he didn't have to inhale the stink of the woman. His eyes met hers, only for a moment, but there was no rebuke, no recognition, just a flat, empty stare. His stomach clenched, but he would not let his father see. Marshall had a way of knowing things. Secret things.

"Get on with it."

Retching, shoulders heaving, he had reached down into the pulpy mess of her abdominal cavity.

"*Hands,*" roared Marshall. "Wash your hands first, idiot boy."

He'd smacked the boy across the face, and the force of his blow sent him flying against the hard surface of the sink. He staggered to his feet, back towards the body on the table, and caught, beneath the blood and organs, the coconut scent of her hair.

"Get the colony instead," his father said. "Time to strip the lying bitch."

In the stillness of the cutting room, the Bone Collector hears his father's voice, traveling towards him down the years.

Once, during dinner, when his father was in an expansive mood and he was feeling daring, he'd asked him if he'd ever had any doubts, if he'd ever worried that what they were doing was wrong. Marshall had levered a sinew of meat from his tooth with a cocktail stick.

"It doesn't matter how we feel, son. We have a duty."

"But—"

"But nothing. Family loyalty comes first. Always. It was the same for my father."

Marshall rarely spoke about his family, so he held his breath, waiting for his father to expand.

"It's like this. I never think about the rights or wrongs. Your grandfather was the same. He was proud to be entrusted with the collection and believed that to truly accept responsibility, he had to prove his commitment and worth by continuing our family's"—he casually put down his toothpick—"work."

Marshall had taken one look at his son's face.

"Are you loyal, son?"

"Yes, Dad."

"So, you'll always do as I ask?"

"Yes, Dad."

The Bone Collector locks the door on that memory and begins the slow tread up two flights of stairs.

A lamp is lit, its arc of muted light pooling on the floor, the corners of the room resolute pockets of black. He stands, all shadow and bone, framed in the doorway, listens as the clock ticks the silence away.

As his eyes grow accustomed to the half darkness, he picks out some old tools on the floor, an ancient drill, a discarded chisel. A decaying wooden and glass cabinet.

The heels of his black shiny shoes do not make a sound as he crosses the room to a long table bearing a small casket with wooden sides and pries open the lid.

He is preparing himself for the arrival of the boy.

Inside, he pictures a collection of human bones, as pale and clean as moonlight.

He talks himself through the process.

First, he will begin in the cutting room. He will peel back the boy's skin, remove the organs, amongst them the brain and the tongue, and leave the remains to dry in the flat, still air of his father's house. Then the beetles will finish the job, consuming the already-decomposing flesh. They do not enjoy fresh meat.

Every few hours, he will check the body, making sure his colony does not eat through the connective tissues, that the skeleton still hangs together.

Then he will carry him up here, to this casket. Ready for the First Hanging, the first time he will bear witness to the glories of his labor.

He closes his eyes, imagines touching the bones he is yet to possess. The most malformed skeleton he is ever likely to see. To secure this for the collection will immortalize him in their family history. He thinks of the glass case downstairs. Of his father's whispers in that cool room with its altar and crosses all those Christmases ago. "Hurry," Marshall had said, as they swaddled the small boy's body in a sheet and carried him away through the quiet, empty corridors. "Before somebody sees us."

But this will eclipse even that early prize.

"The femur," he will murmur, thin fingers trembling across the length of the thighbone, and downwards. "The tibia, an elegant example."

His hands will move upwards, past the torso and neck, until his fingers find the dip of the cheek, exploring the hollow, following the curve of the bone. "An interesting rendition of the zygomatic arch."

He wonders what it will feel like to trail his hand across the slats of his rib cage, to stroke the kinks and perversions in osseous matter.

Unsheathed, the skeleton will be the most perfect specimen he has ever seen.

A stray beetle scuttles across the empty casket, and he pulls a matchbox from his pocket, flicks it inside before sliding it shut.

A cool rush of air brushes his face, and he turns sharply, eyes probing the far reaches of his museum, but it is nothing, just the draft of a winter dusk.

He sniffs the air, licks his chapped lips. A distant cry splits the silence, and the Bone Collector curses under his breath. For now, the girl will have to wait. He is busy here.

He thinks again of the boy, lying in his hospital bed.

It is a sign. A gift.

But he will not rush.

When he has claimed him, he will gather this jumble of bones and drag himself up the stepladder. He will fix the skull to a hook embedded in the ceiling, and carefully let go. The skeleton will sway and still, and the specimen labeled *.I* will be complete.

Then he will press his face up against it, and inhale its bone scent.

When he steps back to admire his handiwork, he will know that this specimen will not be abandoned to ruin and decay in the attic of this house, like others before him. Others with their smooth, unending, *ordinary* bones.

This rarity he will bring downstairs, to his special gallery.

These bones will be worthy of his care.

His protection.

FRIDAY

FORTY-SEVEN

9 a.m.

"And for those of you just tuning in, good morning and welcome. It's nine a.m. on Friday, November twenty-third, and time for the news.

"There have been dramatic developments in the disappearances of missing schoolgirls Clara Foyle and Grace Rodríguez. Exactly a week after Clara vanished, police have confirmed they are looking for the same suspect after identical rabbit skeletons were discovered at the scene of both abductions. Catherine Murray has more . . ."

He lifts a spoonful of porridge to her mouth, and she swallows.

"Did you hear that?" She shudders, even though the heating is cranked up.

The detective is talking now, Detective Sergeant Etta Fitzroy. He slides another spoonful between her lips.

"Yes, we are looking for the same suspect in connection with these abductions, but I'm not prepared to comment on anything else at this time. This is an extremely difficult time for their families. Please bear in mind that any kind of speculation is unhelpful."

He detects a frisson of panic below the surface, and he smiles. It whets his appetite. He almost feels sorry for her. By the end of tonight, when he has taken the boy, her panic will be full-blown.

Perhaps he will send her a little something. Something personal. A gift to fan the flames. To up the ante. To taunt her for her failure to "detect."

He nods to himself. Yes, he will enjoy the sport of it, to watch her scurrying around like one of his beetles.

He puts the bowl on the chair and switches on the twenty-four-hour news channel. The same story is running, the same detective, but now he can see the strain, visible in her taut jawline, the bags beneath her eyes.

"Did you hear that?" his wife says again. "Who in their right mind would do that to a rabbit?"

"There are some terrible people in the world, my love," he says, and pats her papery hand.

While the Bone Collector was attending to his wife, Clara Foyle was drawing stick pictures of her mother on the floor with a crumbling lump of concrete she had worried from the wall.

Her cleft hands made it tricky but not impossible, and she was satisfied with her clumsy efforts.

She couldn't be sure that her mother was missing her. She *wanted* to be sure, but her mother was always so busy that Clara wondered if she might be pleased to have a bit of peace and quiet for a change.

What if they had decided that a family of three worked better than a family of four? But then she remembered what Gina always whispered to her when she was dismissed by her mother or ignored by her father. *No matter how busy your parents are, they do love you.* Clara clung to those words, and they kept her afloat.

Clara pulled out a stale biscuit she had stowed in her pocket. He had brought biscuits with her milk last time. Real biscuits. She savored the shortbread's buttery sweetness.

A couple of crumbs fell onto the floor, and she dabbed at one with the tip of her finger. The spiderweb was still there, and she placed the crumb on its sticky strands.

In the cartoons she sometimes watched with Eleanor, the good guys always beat the bad guys.

Clara sat back and waited for someone to rescue her.

Amy Foyle was also waiting. It was all she ever did now. Waiting for the police, and when they arrived, waiting for news. Waiting for sleep. Waiting for Miles to come home.

She was in a state of suspended animation, unable to resume her life until Clara was found.

She hadn't dared to tell a soul, was horrified at herself for feeling like this, but lately she had found herself furious with Clara. What on earth had possessed her to leave the playground? She wanted to shake her daughter, to scream at her for dragging them into this unfamiliar landscape of fear and anguish.

It wasn't just Clara she was angry with. At school, she had seen Miranda Smith—Poppy's mother—laughing with another parent, and she had marched over to her, dragging a reluctant Eleanor behind her. She had wanted to scratch the woman's eyes out.

But when Poppy's mother had seen her coming, her face had frozen, her eyes flicking desperately from side to side, searching for an escape. As she drew closer, Amy noticed her jeans were hanging loosely, and a patch of foundation on her neck hadn't been rubbed in. A set of keys was looped around her trembling fingers, the metallic *clink*s like a distress signal.

Amy had walked straight past her.

And she had realized then that Clara's disappearance had damaged other families beyond their own, that the thief who had stolen her daughter had left a mark on this community as creeping and corrosive as acid.

FORTY-EIGHT

12.30 p.m.

Fitzroy pulled up outside her flat and rested her head on the steering wheel. She had no desire to go in, but David had called her early that morning, pleaded with her to come home for lunch.

"You have to eat," he said.

"I have to find Clara Foyle," she said.

"Just a quick sandwich, Etta, and then you can go. I haven't seen you for days. Please." David didn't say "please" very often.

"Okay," she said, and hung up.

When Fitzroy slid her key into the door, she was hit by the overpowering aroma of chili and garlic. In the kitchen, the table was set with flowers, and a basket of sliced baguette rolls. A pan of pasta bubbled on the stove, steaming up the windows.

"Bloody hell, what *is* this? A pop-up Italian restaurant?"

David whirled around. "You made me jump." He half-moved towards her, arms outstretched. When she didn't respond, he satisfied himself with an awkward pat on her shoulder.

"How *are* you?"

"David, I can't stay long. I need to be at work."

"Lunch will be two minutes. Sit down."

She watched him work, draining the spaghetti, dishing up the sauce. "Parmesan?" He held up the block of cheese with a smile. She didn't smile back.

He sat down at the table, poured her a glass of water.

"So, what's new? Have you met your nephew yet?"

She frowned at him. Small talk wasn't his usual inclination.

"Our nephew," she countered.

"You should call Nina, you know. She's desperate to see you." His voice softened. "She's worried about you."

"I'm in the middle of a major investigation, David. I don't have time for fussing over new babies." *Or for pandering to the whims of my younger sister.*

He shoveled in a mouthful of spaghetti. For a moment or two, they ate in silence.

"Etta, I'm truly sorry about yesterday. Leaving you there on your own was a shitty thing to do."

She sipped her drink. "To be perfectly honest, it told me everything I needed to know."

"Don't be like that," he said, putting down his fork. "I just got overwhelmed by it all." That was putting it politely. For all his concern, she knew David was the sort of man who believed that once his wife had gotten this baby business out of her system, they could get on with enjoying their lives again.

He did not know that Etta had refused to give up her

stillborn son, that a funeral director with more compassion than most had encouraged her to take him home for a day or two, that she had, weeping, shown him the garden and his crib, and had slept in a cool room with him next to her bed. That her family had found it disturbing. That another man, living another life, had no idea he'd become a father at the same moment as losing his son.

"Shame you didn't think to tell me that before I got to the clinic." She bit into the bread. Its hard crust cut into her lip, and she put it back on her plate.

"You do know that wasn't the only reason?" His tone was gentle.

Her eyes flashed at him. "Don't start that again."

"We have to talk about it," he said.

"I don't want to talk about it."

"Etta, if you can't talk to me, perhaps your work can put you in touch with someone who's trained to deal with this sort of thing. A grief counselor, perhaps." He reached under the table and pulled out the box of memories she kept in the wardrobe. Her private things. *His* private things.

Fitzroy dropped her spoon, and it clattered against the plate. "I have to go now."

She pushed back her chair, bumping the table in her haste to escape, and then he was beside her, pulling her into his arms.

"Let go," she shouted, pushing at him. "Let me go."

But David was stronger than she was, and his hand circled her wrist, pinching the delicate skin. She raised her other hand, struck him hard across his cheek.

His face was a portrait of shock.

"Satisfied?" A drop of her spittle landed on the lens of his glasses. She yanked up her sleeve to examine her reddening skin, shoved it under his nose. "You couldn't leave it, could you?"

"Etta, I—"

"Don't," she said.

His hands hung by his sides, his body lumpen with the sorrow of seeing his marriage unspool.

She shut the door carefully on her way out.

She made herself walk down the stairs, keeping her mouth open, taking small, even breaths. During a trip to Pakistan, in the days when she'd spent her annual leave working for a children's charity, she'd come across a newspaper article that reported most victims in a bombing die from bleeding in the lungs. In an emergency, victims naturally hold their breath, but the lungs become like a pressurized balloon and rupture. That fact had stayed with her, the way random snippets sometimes do, and so she inhaled and exhaled shallowly. It didn't matter that she wasn't waiting for a real blast wave to pass, that this was just an emotional explosion. The breathing helped to focus her mind.

In her distress, Fitzroy did not notice the broken window until she was inside her car, until she smelled the raw earth and iron of her grandfather's butcher's shop.

She turned her head slowly, her eyes already on the box on the passenger seat. One side of the cardboard was sodden with blood. Using the tip of her fingernail, she flicked off the lid.

Blood had pooled in the corner, thick and dark. Lying in the middle was something small, the shape of a bean.

Oh, fuck.

That looks like a kidney.

A child's kidney?

No.

Too small.

Then, what?

Oh no.

No.

NO.

Ting.

It's from him.

I know it.

It's a kidney.

From a rabbit.

A rabbit.

She touched it with the tip of her finger. It was still warm.

Fitzroy fumbled with the door, jumped out, spun around in a circle. The street outside her home was empty, save for a dust cart rumbling away.

She reached for her phone. Tapped out a text to Chambers.

Is Miles Foyle still in custody?

His reply came within seconds.

Yes.

Shit.

Their best lead was telling the truth.

Nothing else was inside the box. Carefully, she lifted it up. Blood smudged her coat, a droplet landed on her cheek. Taped to the underside was a plastic wallet, a piece of paper. Written in a hand she recognized. The same hand as the notes she had found with the rabbit skeletons.

Are the kidneys demolished? I will leave it to you as to what is to be done with his bones.

FORTY-NINE

4.44 p.m.

My husband abducted my daughter.

Amy Foyle tried the sentence out in her head. It felt clunky, awkward on her tongue. She said it again. This time it sounded a little smoother, a little more *plausible.*

Shock was a bit like that, she'd discovered. It jolted you out of reality and into the unknown. But as the hours and days pass, the unknown becomes reality, and reality, the everyday.

Miles had now been in police custody for almost seventy-two hours. When that woman detective, Etta Fitzroy, had come to arrest him, he had turned to his wife, his face perfectly calm.

"I didn't do it," he said. "I didn't take Clara."

She had flown at him then, clawed at his face.

She didn't believe him.

I am married to a child killer.

Amy had always believed in the sanctity of her marriage vows. *Through thick and through thin.* But when the moment came, when those vows had been tested, the doubts, it turned out, had come sprinting in.

At the kitchen table, Gina shook the dice and threw it.

"Six," laughed Eleanor. "Not again."

Amy ignored them both as she poured herself a little pick-me-up. A moment later, she felt Gina's hand on her arm.

"Do you really need that?"

"Yes," she said, adding ice. "I do."

The tears were rising again, but she pressed down on them. She had cried so much they had become meaningless. Inside, she was as dry as a nub of bone.

She called up Clara's face, her shiny smile, the babyish curve of her tummy.

Mummy, Mummy, will you play with me?

All those times when she'd shooed her younger daughter away, telling her that she was too busy. All those times when she'd been reading a magazine, or buying clothes on her laptop, or just plain couldn't be bothered.

Her daughter's voice was already fading. She groped for it. Nothing. The weight of panic began to crush her.

"Mummy," said Eleanor. "Will you play with me?"

She heard her own voice from a distant place.

"Not now, darling. Play with Gina instead."

And then, he was there, standing in the kitchen, eyes weary, shoulders hunched. He placed his keys on the worktop with deliberate care.

His eyes found Amy.

"They've let me go."

"So I see."

"They've realized it couldn't be me. The detective, Fitzroy, she received some sort of package relating to the case while I was in custody."

"So they haven't charged you?"

How do they know that he's not in this with someone else? That it wasn't a deliberate ploy to divert attention? Her brain paused a moment, then whirred crazily back into action. *Perhaps they've done it on purpose, to follow him.*

"No."

Amy stood by the counter, Miles by the table.

"Come on, let's give Mum and Dad some space," murmured Gina, ushering Eleanor away. The room was quiet, but the silence rang loudly.

"Can I have a hug?" said Miles.

Amy put her arms around her husband but their bodies barely touched. He buried his face in the silk of her hair.

"You do believe me, don't you? I would never, *ever* hurt our daughter."

Amy could not bring herself to tell him that her trust was a gift, hard won and easily lost. That the look of him, the smell of him, even the sound of him now filled her with a curious sort of disgust. That she would, in all probability, never trust him again.

FIFTY

6.05 p.m.

The streets are wet and just dark enough. He wears the weather like a disguise, drifting through the drizzle that obscures London. It is past six.

He smiles as he recalls the look on the detective's face, the disgust, the fear. He likes it. He dreams of seeing it again. He longs to witness her expression when she finds out the boy is gone.

The Bone Collector drives on through the darkness, the taillights of cars snaking their way back to their owners' little lives, their homes. The boy will never go home.

As for the girl, he has not yet decided.

Marshall encouraged him to push boundaries, to see what he was capable of. To experiment. He considers it.

When she is lost in her drugged sleep, he could flay the skin from her hands. He yearns to see those prehensile digits without their covering of tissue, the technicality of their grasp and pinch. He wants to study them at work, bone claws attached to living matter. He wants another first for his collection.

But there is a chance she may die, of course. From shock and blood loss. From infection and pain. There is a chance she will escape. Attract unwanted attention.

And he is growing used to having her around.

But his decision can wait. Tonight, he has other important business to attend to.

The boy. The backbone of his collection, the cervical vertebrae, the spinae.

Fate has handed him another chance. There is another prize awaiting collection. Another Frith.

The Bone Collector wants this one very, very badly. And he always gets what he wants.

FIFTY-ONE

10.31 p.m.

The pediatric intensive care unit was on the seventh floor of the Royal Southern Hospital, just above the maternity ward.

Although its medical equipment could be noisy, and the children seriously ill, it seemed to Lilith to give off an aura of calm, an antidote to the emotional mayhem of her life.

Lilith's eyelids drifted downwards, but the sound of snoring from the woman opposite startled her back to awareness, and she sighed and sat up. The springs of her chair squeaked, and she heard the mother across the ward move on her own makeshift bed before her snores resumed, louder than before. She rolled her neck. Foldaway beds were not allowed in the PICU, and the relatives' accommodations were too far away. A chair would have to do, but it didn't make for a comfortable night's sleep.

Who was she kidding? Even with a king-size bed and total silence, Lilith would not have been able to sleep. How could she contemplate something so mundane when Jakey was so ill? What if he died while her treacherous self was dozing? No, her body would not betray her.

The machines in PICU beeped and hummed as the nurses' footsteps echoed on the floor, even at this late hour. There were always checks to be done, children to be brought back from the precipice. The rhythmic squeak of the cleaner wiping the floor was oddly comforting.

Jakey was on a ventilator. A machine was breathing for him, inflating and deflating his little lungs. A machine, for fuck's sake. Lilith had always taken the simple act of breathing for granted. But the events of the last few hours had taught her that it wasn't simple at all. It was the product of half a dozen or more of the body's complex processes.

His body was as stiff as an exclamation mark, his lips slightly parted. The shadows thrown by the nighttime lighting made his face look grey. A tube trailed from his nose. He was in a bad way.

An X-ray had revealed the depressing truth.

The growth of bone in his chest was restricting his lung function, and he had developed pneumonia.

The consultant had warned her to prepare herself for a rocky ride, but she was barely listening when he explained, in that brusque tone of his, that even if Jakey survived the pneumonia, the new bone could prove catastrophic. In the pauses between his words, she had nodded her head, but she refused to believe him. Her son would not die. The force of her love would keep him alive.

Her kidneys ached. She didn't know if it was because of the awkward, half-twisted way she was sitting, or because she needed to use the toilet. She weighed up the chances of Jakey needing her in the next five minutes. Of leaving him alone. She wished Erdman was up here with her. But he was in the canteen, refueling with yet more coffee.

Ever since he had turned up so unexpectedly yesterday, he had struggled to cope with spending more than a few minutes at Jakey's bedside. He had wept when he had seen his son, Jakey's eyes shuttered against the world. Against him.

As Lilith had witnessed his distress, her anger had melted to nothing. She understood. He couldn't bear to see his son this way. Neither could she.

Jakey had not moved, not so much as an eye twitch or a muscle spasm.

Why did it have to be her family?

Always her family.

She hated this hospital. The memories that stalked the corridors. The reminder of that terrible day when Jakey was born, a life not yet two hours old, but already with a sentence of death.

"I'm so sorry," the doctor had said, his face grave, leaden.

"Sorry about what?" Erdman had put his arm around her, a tired, baffled smile on his face, while Lilith had taken a taut breath, pulling her baby in closer.

"Your son has fibrodysplasia ossificans progressiva."

She could still remember the sight of Erdman's mother, Shirley, raking her fingernails through her permed pouf of hair.

"My son?" Lilith laughed. "No, he hasn't." Then, "What's fibrodis . . . ?"

And so he had told them. Shirley had shut her eyes, but Lilith hadn't noticed. She was too busy watching her future fall apart.

Later that night, Erdman had brandished a sheaf of papers at her, printouts from the Internet. The doctors had counseled them to wait, to process Jakey's diagnosis before seeking out information, but he had ignored their advice. When Lilith had sent him home for forgotten maternity pads, he'd gone straight to the computer and searched online for hope amidst the despair.

"Perhaps he'll have a mild form," he said. "It says here that a handful of sufferers live into their sixties."

"What kind of a life is that?"

Tears filled her eyes at the memory, and she rested her head on the bed next to her son's sleeping form. She longed for the uncomplicated days when she'd spent her time looking after Jakey and resenting Erdman. She wanted her old life back, with all its imperfections and frustrations. She wanted to be a mother and a wife. Now she might no longer have the chance. The foundations of her marriage were weak, unstable. Her son was dying.

And then his mouth began to move.

"Daddy," he murmured. "Daddy."

Her heart swelled with an unexpected sort of hope. Jakey had a breathing tube going through his nose into his windpipe. Physically, he shouldn't be able to speak.

"Nurse," she shouted. "Nurse."

Footsteps slapped across the floor of PICU. "What's happened?" said the nurse, panting slightly. "The alarm didn't go off."

"He was talking," said Lilith.

The nurse, a ward manager called Anna Murphy,

looked at Jakey. His eyes were shut, his breathing wheezy but even.

"Do you think that perhaps he may have been grunting in his sleep?"

Lilith was suddenly unable to speak.

"It can happen occasionally," said the nurse. She checked the monitors measuring his pulse, the levels of oxygen in his blood, and squeezed Lilith's shoulder.

The nurse arranged the sheet over Jakey.

"I've got a bit of good news, actually. The doc says I can tell you." Her face broke into a smile. "The results of the second X-ray have come back, and it seems as if the bone growth in his chest isn't as invasive as we feared. If it stops growing, stops pushing into his lungs, and if we kick this blasted pneumonia . . ." She left the possibility of his recovery unspoken, but Lilith heard it. "There are no promises, mind. There's still a long road to travel."

Lilith grinned faintly. Was it in relief or disbelief? She wasn't quite sure. The nurse squeezed her shoulder a second time, and was gone.

Her back throbbed again, and she stood, slipping on the flip-flops she had tucked beneath the chair.

She hadn't imagined it. Jakey had been calling for his father.

He must have been dreaming.

Now Jakey's nurse had left, the room was empty, apart from the sleeping patients, and one or two parents, also asleep, and she blinked as she stepped into the corridor, disoriented by the sudden brightness. There was a whiteboard on the wall with Jakey's name written in green marker pen, the times of his obs, his next medication.

The cool air of the parents' bathroom was a relief from the stultifying heat of the unit. The cleaner nodded at her as he left, pushing his mop in front of him. She splashed her face with water to wake herself up, and looked at her reflection. A ghost stared back. Her eyes were red-rimmed from crying and lack of sleep, and their fan of fine lines had deepened into grooves. She couldn't remember the last time she had eaten properly, and her clavicles were prominent above the scooped neckline of her cotton top.

She braced her hands on the sides of the sink, and closed her eyes, letting the tears fall against the porcelain. They trickled into her mouth and she tasted anchovy saltiness.

She looked at her pale fingers gripping the white porcelain, and took a deep breath. Jakey was going to die before her. On some instinctive level, she knew that. But he was still alive, and she had no choice but to build a citadel around her emotions to protect him from the force of her grief.

She washed her hands. Toilet paper was sticking to the floor, and she could smell urine beneath the disinfectant. Lilith sat on the toilet seat, and stared at the blank, hard tiles on the wall. Minutes ticked by.

A sudden waft of cold air filled the cubicle, and she turned, half-thinking a window had broken free from its catch, that it had swung open to let in the frozen night, but there was no window, just a wheezing vent. An overwhelming urgency to get back to her son gripped her, and before she registered what she was doing, she was out of the stalls, running towards the ward, stumbling over her flip-flops in her haste to get to him.

Please, no. No, no, no.

A team of medical staff (was that a senior house officer? She didn't want a fucking SHO, only a pediatric respiratory specialist) was clustered around his bed. To Lilith, it seemed as if their arms were flailing all over the place, without direction or success. Jakey's pillow was on the floor.

Please, God. Let him live.

She knew she shouldn't go to his bed, that it would only distract the medics who were focused on bringing him back, but she could not help herself.

As she ran towards them, their movements seemed to slow down and there were so many bodies around his tiny one that she could not see him.

She could not see him.

A nurse grabbed her by the arm—*ease up on the pressure, bitch*—and then she was being propelled along a corridor, into a room, and told to wait.

But she knew. She knew even before she had gone to the bathroom. She had seen it written in the architecture of his body, in the limpness of his arms, the pallor of his cheeks.

Only half an hour, but in that time, Lilith aged a decade. Fear tightened the muscles around her mouth, hunched her shoulders. She thought how fear had reduced Clara Foyle's father to a husk of a man, how the disappearance of his daughter—how *suspicion*—had rinsed him of all color, and she understood how that could be.

Erdman was ushered in, jaw taut, nerves stretched wire-thin. "What's going on?" he whispered. And she had looked at him, and his body had deflated, as if air were slowly seeping from a pinhole.

A junior doctor came to tell them, not even the specialist, but a *junior* doctor. It said so on his badge. The tremor in his hands triggered a flash of insight. This was his first time breaking bad news to parents.

She watched his mouth as he spoke. There was a smattering of stubble on a jaw soft with youth. It hadn't hardened into experience yet. Today was one of the steps in that particular journey.

"Mr. and Mrs. Frith—" His voice was scorched with tiredness and emotion, and there was a hesitancy to it. She almost felt sorry for him.

She dipped her head in acknowledgment but didn't trust herself to speak. He couldn't meet her eye, and the words, when they came, were a mumble.

"I don't know how to tell you this, but I'm afraid we've lost your son."

A ball of anger seemed to catch in the pit of her stomach, and her hands tightened into fists. If the doctor hadn't been so young, she might have thrown her bottle at him, but instead she let it drop to the floor. She hadn't put the lid on properly, and water gushed in rivulets across the relatives' room, like the day when Jakey was born, almost two weeks late, and the doctor broke her amniotic sac with a hook. She remembered the matter-of-fact way he had put on a glove and torn a hole in the very thing protecting her baby. Now here was another doctor, tearing a hole in her heart.

"Wha—" She made a sound as convention dictates when one is in the middle of a conversation. She didn't know what she was trying to say, it was just a collection of vowels and consonants that came out of her mouth.

The doctor misunderstood her.

"The police are on their way."

He shifted awkwardly and fiddled with a button on his white coat. She wondered whether his mother or girlfriend washed it for him, or if he did it himself.

I'll never get to wash Jakey's clothes again.

A tunnel of emptiness yawned before her.

Oh my God, there'll be a postmortem.

She'd seen a TV program on postmortems. They sawed through the rib cage and cut open the skull. They couldn't desecrate her little boy like that. She wouldn't let those bloody butchers anywhere near him.

Erdman said nothing, just stared blankly at the doctor. She would have gone to him, if she could. But her legs didn't appear to be working.

A nurse came in, wringing her hands, and she saw it was Anna Murphy, the PICU manager who had checked on Jakey earlier.

"Mrs. Frith, Mr. Frith, I'm so sorry about this . . ."

"I . . ." Lilith hesitated, suddenly unsure of what to say. A rolling wave of grief hit again, and she swallowed down a mouthful of snot and tears, not caring if anyone saw her wipe her nose on the cuff of her cardigan.

Tears trickled from beneath her lids. Once she had said a last good-bye to Jakey, once she had held his hand and kissed the soft petals of his eyes, once she had fulfilled her necessary duties, she would find a bottle of pills and she would go to sleep for a long time.

Erdman continued to stare at the young doctor, who fiddled with his pen and could not meet his gaze.

The nurse was now chewing her lip and shooting worried glances at them. Lilith took a shuddering breath. She had just begun to accept that Jakey would die before she did, but she had never expected it to be so soon, and in such heartbreaking circumstances.

How to tell people? His school? His friends? Those terrible phone calls would make his death a reality in this horrific new dreamscape of her life.

The nurse touched her arm, and Lilith rose.

"I want to see him," she whispered. "He's frightened of the dark. He won't even go to the toilet on his own." She turned towards the nurse, trying to muster a watery grin, but the expression on the nurse's face stopped her. "What is it?"

Nurse Murphy opened her mouth, then shut it again. She looked at the junior doctor, and he lowered his eyes. When the nurse spoke, it seemed to be an enormous physical effort.

"I'm not sure you've quite understood."

Erdman spoke for the first time. "Understood what?"

"I'm so sorry to be the one to break it to you, but I don't believe in beating about the bush." She drew in a deep breath. "Jakey is missing. As far as I can gather, he disappeared from PICU between forty and fifty minutes ago. We're in the process of checking everywhere in the hospital, but, as it stands, we cannot locate him. We *will* find him, Mr. and Mrs. Frith. Seriously ill children don't just vanish. But this is mortifying and embarrassing for the hospital, and in all my years of nursing—" She stopped suddenly, a mottled blush climbing her throat.

"He's not dead?" Lilith sucked at the air and let it fill her lungs. Held it there. The nurse gave a brisk nod. Lilith let her breath go.

"I don't understand," she said. "Jakey was just here.

Someone must have taken him for another scan while I was in the bathroom."

"That's not possible." Nurse Murphy softened her voice. "We've already checked."

"Let me get this absolutely clear," Erdman said slowly. "You're telling me that our son has vanished?"

The nurse looked him straight in the eye. "Yes, Mr. Frith. I'm afraid that does appear to be the case."

Lilith took a step forward, but her knees buckled and then she was pitching straight towards the floor. The young doctor, who had been sidling closer to the door, to his escape route, made a halfhearted lunge and just caught her, his fingers digging into the hollows of her armpits.

She hadn't fainted. There was no loss of consciousness, no letup in the feedback screeching in her temples. More a weakening of her limbs, the taken-for-granted gravity that held her upright simply dribbling away. She leaned against him. He smelt of deodorant and peppermints, and an underwash of sweat, and the lapel of his coat was rough against her cheek. The reality of what he represented slammed into her, and then she was snatching at the air for breath, gasping and crying.

A look of panic passed over his features and he guided her into a chair, prying loose her fingers as one might remove a child who didn't want to be left. Someone in another time, another moment of unknown tragedy, had picked lumps of foam from the chair, like a giant scab. It was uncomfortable against the back of her legs, but it didn't matter. Nothing mattered.

Erdman's arms hung limply by his sides. He gazed at Lilith as if he had never seen her before, shock erasing all expression. All feeling.

Nurse Murphy helped her to stand. Her hands were gentle as she tucked Lilith's arm in hers, and Lilith sagged against the motherly bulk of her body, as if the taut strings holding her up had been cut.

Her limbs felt heavy with the weight of the nurse's revelation.

"The chief executive of the trust has been contacted at home. He's on his way to see you. So are the police. In the meantime, let's get you both a cup of tea."

Lilith allowed herself to be guided to a lift, but she had no idea which floor she was being taken to, or where. All she remembered was somebody pressing a scalding cup of tea into her hands—proper china, not the plastic kind that always seemed on the brink of collapse—and the nurse who had brought her here making a series of telephone calls.

Erdman didn't speak at all. Not a word. After a few minutes, his hand reached for hers. Its warmth offended her. Inside she was frozen. Numb.

She wasn't really aware of the passing of time, only in the very loosest sense, and no one was paying her much attention. Occasionally, she was aware of the nurse glancing in her direction, a worried expression on her face. At one stage, she was vaguely aware of a message over the loudspeaker.

"Attention, all hospital staff. This is a Code Amber Warning. Repeat, this is a Code Amber Warning."

But for the most part, she sat there quietly, literally staring at the wall.

My little boy is missing.

Missing.

Someone has abducted my son.

No, it's just a silly misunderstanding.

He'll be back any minute.

Someone has taken him for a walk.

Someone has taken him.

Jakey.

Come back to Mummy.

Jakey.

My Jakey.

She longed to stroke the rusty curl of his hair, trace her finger down his cheek. She wanted to inhale him, to preserve every detail of his beautiful self in her memory.

In three terrible days, she had lost her husband and now her son. Her husband had come back to her, but in some deep part of herself she knew that Jakey might never return. A whisper—disloyal, enticing—curlicued its way into her mind. *If only it could be the other way around.* She pushed it away, flicked a guilty look at Erdman.

He was staring at the floor, his tea untouched.

Some faceless individual had taken a sledgehammer to their lives. How would they ever begin to piece themselves together again?

No, they will find him.

The police will find him.

That's what they do, they find missing children.

But they haven't found Clara Foyle yet.

Why should Jakey be any different?

She must have dozed off. The nurses had obviously decided to leave them alone for a bit, and now they looked busy, caught up in someone else's drama. It didn't matter. It was easy to sit here, and she was just so tired.

As far as she could tell, Erdman had not moved. He had barely spoken. Instead he sat, statue-still, but she sensed a slipstream of anger and distress beneath his veneer of control.

A few seconds later, she heard a familiar voice and footsteps running down the corridor. Detective Sergeant Etta Fitzroy's coat was streaked with blood, her brown curls greasy and unkempt. Behind her, Lilith saw a handful of officers in uniforms, already flooding the hospital, locking it down, searching for Jakey. For the person who had taken him.

"Mrs. Frith—is it true?" She grabbed her shoulders. "Is. It. True?"

Lilith lowered her eyes.

Fitzroy let out a low moan of disbelief, and slammed her hand into the wall. She sank into a chair and bowed her head. It gave her a crumpled, shrunken look, as if all hope had been sucked from her.

"It was a warning," she said, under her breath. "It was a fucking warning."

Erdman, who had begun to pace the corridor, caught her muttered words. He stood before her, outrage corrugating his forehead. "You knew this was going to happen?"

"No, no, of course not. But he left"—she hesitated, unsure how much to reveal—"a message in my car."

"A rabbit skeleton?" Erdman was brusque.

"Um . . ." Fitzroy could not bring herself to tell him about the bloodied lump of flesh.

Lilith covered her mouth with her hand.

A couple minutes later, she forced her lips to form the sounds. "You think—same man—Clara Foyle?"

Fitzroy swallowed audibly.

"So, these rabbits, the ones on the news, they are"—Erdman fumbled around for the word—"significant?"

"It would seem that way."

"But what do they mean?"

"I wish I knew. The newspapers are having a field day with this one, but don't believe everything you read."

"Who can we believe, then?" Erdman's voice was dull.

"Me. I will always tell you the truth, Mr. Frith."

"Then tell it to us now."

Fitzroy looked uncomfortable. "We're doing everything we can to find this man."

Lilith believed her. But she also recognized that the detective was trotting out a line, that she was holding something back from them.

Her instinct was right. As Lilith watched Erdman mark out his fear in footsteps back and forth across the shining tiles, Fitzroy was recalling her earlier phone conversation with The Boss.

"Talk me through everything," he'd said, as she'd hurried to the hospital, scarcely able to believe that another child was gone. "I want to hear it out loud." He had fired the words at her, urgency clipping his vowels.

She had taken a deep breath and begun to speak.

"When Grace Rodríguez's remains were discovered in the woods, over a year ago now, a skeleton of a small mammal was found a couple of feet away. But we dismissed it, didn't realize its significance.

"A couple of days ago, we found a shoe box containing an identical rabbit skeleton on the Heath, close to where Erdman Frith was attacked and not far from where Clara Foyle—a little girl with cleft hands—was taken. Attached to its leg was a small plastic tube, the type used by carrier pigeons, and inside was a rolled cigarette paper with a quotation written on it."

"Remind me what it said."

She hadn't needed to consult her notebook, had memorized it. "It said, '. . . the bones came together, bone to bone'."

"Taken from?"

"The Old Testament, the book of Ezekiel." She had waited for him to speak, but The Boss was silent. "Ordinarily, we might not have given it too much weight. Could have been the work of a religious nutter, or a crank, or a random coincidence, but because of the Grace Rodríguez connection, we couldn't just ignore it. Then we found another skeleton, at the sweetshop, where Clara was last seen alive."

"With a quotation, too."

"Yes. Same modus operandi. This one said, 'Behold, I will cause breath to enter you'. Verse thirty-seven, chapter five. But we still haven't got a clue what he's trying to tell us, or why he left a skeleton on the Heath without a body. By God, we've looked. But there's no signs of disturbance, nothing at all. We've been running a DNA trace, but we've got nothing so far."

"What about the quotation he left for you?" said The Boss.

"From the Bible, too, I'm guessing."

Neither of them had needed to articulate what they both already knew: that extensive research into the background of serial killers had shown that many had endured a strict religious upbringing, that many, when captured, quoted Bible phrases to justify their crimes.

"And now Jakey Frith—another child with a bone deformity—is missing from the hospital?"

"Yes, sir."

"Fuck." One word, but it had been laced with exhaustion and fear.

Fitzroy was running through the hospital's double doors when The Boss spoke again. This time, he was brisk, adrenaline and authority saturating his orders.

"Go and speak to the Frith family. The medical team. Find out what happened. Make sure you turn the place upside down. I want to see if he's left us his little calling card."

With two children missing now, both with some kind of bone malformation, Fitzroy made a mental note to check which hospitals Clara had been treated in, and to call Mrs. Rodríguez first thing. Grace had no bone deformities—she knew that already from the previous inquiry—but perhaps there was another connection.

"Yes, sir."

"And, Fitzroy?"

"Sir?"

"If you do find something, keep it to yourself, won't you? Just for a while. This investigation is becoming leakier than a bloody sieve, and the papers haven't got hold of this yet."

He had hung up then, and she had gone looking for the Friths.

Fitzroy glanced warily at them both, and repeated her mantra. The one she used when children were abducted and when children were found dead. "We're doing everything we can to find this man."

Lilith closed her eyes, as if that simple act would shut out the detective's voice as effectively as the despair embossed on her face.

Erdman kicked the legs of his chair, stalked off down the corridor, colliding with a doctor who opened his mouth to chastise him, but upon seeing his face, thought better of it. Lilith let him go.

The two women sat side by side on the hard-backed chairs while all about them lives were won and lost. Silence hung between them, contracting and dilating, muffling the sounds of the hospital. Both mothers, each one's arms as empty as the other's.

Lilith stared at the wall, grief dislocating her features, taking her apart, turning her into someone else.

A sudden, horrific thought occurred to her.

"Did you find a ske"—she stumbled over the word, could not bring herself to say it—"anything near Jakey's bed?"

"My officers are searching that area now."

"But it's him, isn't it? You think it's him."

Fitzroy looked down at the floor.

"Find him for us. Please."

The spotlights at the rear of the hospital flooded its sprawling, well-tended grounds, making it seem more luxury hotel than a place for treating the sick. Only the green-gowned patients, loitering by the double doors and sucking on their death sticks, hinted at the happenings inside, the ebb and flow of lives lost and found.

No one paid much attention to the man pushing a wheelchair towards a grey van or, beneath the pile of blankets, the slumped form of a child.

FIFTY-TWO

11.13 p.m.

"Etta, it's me. Please, just answer your phone. Or give me a call back." A pause. "Max wants a cuddle with his auntie. And I'd really like to see you, too. Can you believe he's got the same color eyes as you? And my nose, apparently." A laugh. "Poor child."

Another silence.

"Etta, I spoke to David. Please pick up. I miss you."

SATURDAY

FIFTY-THREE

3.14 a.m.

"Where shall I drop you?"

Lilith Frith was either asleep in the backseat, or she hadn't heard. Fitzroy winced at the grinding sound as she struggled with the unfamiliar gear stick. Her own car was still with forensics.

"Mr. Frith?"

"Call me Erdman." His voice was a cracked whisper.

Fitzroy swore under her breath as a speeding car cut her off, a beer can bouncing off of their windscreen. Weekend nights in the city were as busy as rush hour.

"Is there someone I can call for you? Or perhaps I can drive you to a friend's?"

"No."

"I'll take you home, then, shall I?"

"*No.*" Erdman's voice was sharp and unnaturally loud in the quiet of the car. "Sorry," he said. "It's just that I don't want to go home."

Fitzroy understood. She felt the same way. "Well, I can't let you wander the streets."

"I know where I'd like to go," he said, and reeled off an address in Hither Green.

As soon as they drove past the gaudy lights of Lee High Road and into Northside Road, Erdman was ambushed by memories of his mother.

Sandwiches made from the leftover meat of the Sunday roast joint, buttered right up to the crusts. Biscuits gone soft in the tin. A painted wooden cuckoo clock on the wall.

A face like his own.

A house of secrets, of unanswered questions.

The spare key was still under the boot scraper.

Inside, the house had that neglected feel that empty houses do. Dust had settled over the furniture and the air smelled stale, with a hint of mice droppings. Erdman had refused to sell it, to even rent it out. Lilith had been furious about that. Now that he was thankful he had stuck to his guns. Even in six months, property prices had risen. Now he no longer had a job, perhaps he could fix it up and sell it. Use the cash to buy some time with Jakey in that house he dreamed of by the sea. And then he remembered that Jakey was missing.

Fitzroy stood awkwardly in the door.

There were a few cards on the mat, from old acquaintances who had no idea where else to send them. He could see the sloping letters through the flimsy envelopes. *With Sympathy.*

Cards like that will be arriving on my doormat soon.

Tears were laminating his eyes, a sick disbelief skewering his insides.

"Are you sure you want to be here?" said Fitzroy.

Strands of grey that hadn't been there a few weeks ago streaked Erdman's temples. He dragged the sleeve of his jacket across his eyes. "Yeah," he said. "I'm sure."

He stumbled upstairs and into his old bedroom, still preserved by his mother. In hope? Or for posterity? He wasn't sure. His *Star Wars* duvet cover was crooked and, tenderly, he straightened it. He stared up at the ceiling, painted with the planets of the solar system.

Where are you, Jakey-boy, my champ? Who has stolen you from me?

But he was just as unlikely to find the answers in the shaky lines of those faded orbs as in the spangled sky outside, which was cold and clear and crisping the leaves.

Erdman could pick out the figures of Han Solo and Luke Skywalker in the wallpaper, the thick cords of dust hanging from the lampshade. A boy's faint laughter filled his ears, identical to his own. In the room of his childhood, he could hear the echoes of the past.

He lay down on the bed and offered up his life for his son's.

Downstairs, Fitzroy was in a kaleidoscope of confusion. She should get back to the office. The Boss had already rung twice. But she didn't want to wake Lilith, who was, blessedly, still asleep in the back of the car.

The house was freezing, the dark night closing in. She was cold, and she pulled her coat tightly around her.

Despite the absence of a skeleton, the *ting* in Fitzroy's brain was telling her it was the same man.

She wondered what depravity he would be visiting upon those two children, lost somewhere in the night, and she used the burn of that anger to cauterize the fear that was threatening to cloud her thinking, to strip her of all clarity and detachment.

She scrolled through the evidence. Three missing children: Grace Rodríguez, Clara Foyle, and now Jakey Frith, two with skeletal deformities. Three rabbit skeletons: one she had failed to recognize the significance of; one found on the Heath, seemingly unconnected; and a third, left at the scene of Clara's abduction. Nothing—so far—at Jakey Frith's bedside.

Two messages concealed in the tubes, one warning left in her car.

It didn't make sense.

She knew there must be a link, a connection, somewhere, but she was groping around for it and it wouldn't come.

Find a motive, find a killer. But there was no motive, none that she could see.

Apart from the geographical connection.

His victims were not from the same ethnic group.

His victims were not the same gender.

His victims were not all the same age.

She fumbled in the darkness, trying to piece it together, trying to listen for the symphony in her brain, but it would not play. In another minute or two, she would tell Erdman that she had to leave.

She wandered around Shirley Frith's living room, sensed the traces of a life unhappily lived. No family photographs on the walls, no smiling grandchildren in school uniform, no memories at all.

Fitzroy slumped back in an armchair and felt something hard dig into her back. She pushed the cushion aside, and drew out a silver-framed picture.

It had that washed-out, warmed-up look of photographs taken in the 1970s.

Her heart stuttered out a beat.

Two boys: the same rust-colored hair, the same infectious grin, and one of them with the same face as Erdman and the same skewed bones as Jakey.

"Have you found anything else up there? Any other"—she hesitated—"photographs?"

Fitzroy's voice drifted up the ladder and into the loft where Erdman was plucking twenty years' worth of cobwebs from his hair. Although it had been six months since his mother's death, he hadn't got 'round to clearing it out, yet another task on his *can't-be-bothered* list. Perhaps he would find the answers he was seeking in here.

"Not yet. But there's boxes and boxes up here. It's going to take ages to get through them all."

He stuck his head through the hatch. Tendrils of grey dust floated down. "Come up."

Shirley's loft was crammed full of cardboard boxes, ancient pieces of furniture—including a baby's white wooden crib and a matching rocking chair—a collection of battered suitcases, and a leather chest with a padlock across the front. Erdman and Fitzroy stood side by side, surveying the chaos.

"Look at this," said Fitzroy, holding up what looked like a flattened piece of khaki cloth.

"That's Grandpa Frith's field service cap." Erdman fingered the thick fabric. "Missing in action at El Alamein." His throat tightened at the mention of his grandfather, the unspoken specter of the other missing loved ones.

"So you had a brother . . ." she said softly.

"I did," he said, his gaze drifting to the photograph that Fitzroy had handed him.

"What happened to him?"

Erdman frowned, struggling to dredge his memories. "I don't know. Ma didn't like talking about him." He faltered, looked again at the picture in his hand. "I was so young, I can barely remember. He was unwell, I think. One day, he was at home, playing with me, and the next, he was gone. My mother was never the same after that."

In the shadows of the loft, Erdman looked so bereft that Fitzroy's heart constricted with the memory of her own loss.

"What's in that chest, I wonder?" she said.

Erdman bent down and yanked on the padlock, but it wouldn't give. "I'll look for a little key," he said, and scrabbled around on the dusty floor.

Fitzroy looked around. Balanced on a bureau pushed against the sloping roof was a shoe box of letters, but the ink was so faded in places that it was impossible to read who had sent them, or what they contained

Fitzroy pulled one from the batch. A spidery scrawl covered the page. She could just about make out the name "Erdman." The ink had run, the handwriting almost indecipherable. It might have been signed *Love*

Derek, but she wasn't sure, and she guessed it must have been sent to his mother when Erdman was little. It was dated March 1976. That date was written in pencil and a different hand.

But what about this other little boy, the one who looked so like Erdman and Jakey?

"Found it." Erdman was brandishing a key, a weak smile on his face. "It was inside those weird shoes."

Fitzroy followed his finger, which was pointing to a cardboard box with collapsing sides, just hidden behind the padlocked chest. Contained within it was an old pair of children's shoes. Plain with no adornments, no buckles or laces, they were made from a dark brown leather, which had cracked and split over the years. The contours of the owners' feet were still visible in the shape of the shoe. There was a sheet of yellowing paper on top, and Fitzroy bent over to retrieve it.

> *These shoes were placed here as part of a topping out ceremony when this house was reroofed in April 1976. Do not remove them under any circumstances.*

Fitzroy frowned. What on earth was a topping out ceremony? She would Google it later. She folded the letter and slid it into her pocket.

Erdman's key fitted the rusting lock, but years of neglect had made it stiff. After several minutes of wiggling it around, it turned and the padlock clicked open.

In the corner, nestled amongst the silken folds of a christening gown, were a tiny pair of shoes and a see-through box with a pale red curl in it. A tatty bear lay next to them. Next to the teddy was a collection of newspaper articles, bound together with a faded ribbon.

"What is it?"

"Not sure yet," murmured the detective, untying the ribbon and pulling free a newspaper. It was the *Daily Mirror*, dated 25 October 1976.

She began to read it aloud.

> The heartbroken family of Carlton Frith yesterday held a private memorial service for the missing three-year-old.
>
> His mother, Shirley, 29, carried a bouquet of forget-me-nots in memory of the little boy, whose body mysteriously vanished from the Chapel of Rest at the Royal Southern Hospital ten months ago.
>
> His twin brother, Erdman, was understood to have remained at the family home in Hither Green, southeast London, during the moving 90-minute ceremony. Guests were asked to wear white.
>
> Detective Inspector Felix Tapp, who is leading the investigation, said: "We will not stop until we find Carlton's body."
>
> Carlton's father, Derek, was not at the service. In a tragic twist, he died from a heart attack in April.

The detective passed the cutting to Erdman. Reflexively, he took it, but his eyes were unseeing, his face set in hard lines of shock.

"Do you remember anything of this?" Erdman shook his head, a violent, angry gesture. While he scanned the smudged newsprint, Fitzroy's brain whirled and ticked.

So, Erdman had been a twin, and his brother had

suffered from the same bone disorder as Jakey. His body had disappeared, too.

It was too much of a coincidence to ignore.

"Look, is that another box up there? I think I see something." She pointed to the gap between the eaves of the roof.

Fitzroy wandered over to the dark opening and felt around inside. Her fingers brushed against something rough, and she snatched them free.

"Ugh!" She wiped her hand on her black trousers and fished in her pocket for her flashlight, which she shone into the gap.

Its beam picked out thick, cobwebby dust and what looked like dozens of caraway seeds, the unmistakable hallmark of mice. Lying amongst them was something grey and shrunken. The bones of its back legs were exposed, while patches of leathered skin still covered its breast. Fitzroy saw a thin wisp of a tail. Extended claws. Half its face was gone, but a row of pointed white teeth were drawn back in a snarl. A dead cat.

Revolted, she dropped the flashlight, and it clattered on the floorboards and rolled away, plunging the loft into semidarkness again.

"What was it? What did you see?"

Fitzroy picked up the flashlight and pointed it into the gap.

"Fuck," said Erdman. "What *is* that?"

A desperate need to get away consumed her. To swap the cloying atmosphere of Shirley Frith's attic for some fresh air. To check on Mrs. Frith, still sleeping in the car.

The breakfast china was still on the draining board, waiting to be put away. The sight of the Royal Worcester plate with its dusty garland of pink roses made Fitzroy want to weep. Something unspeakable had happened to this family, but how did that fit together with Carlton's disappearance, with Jakey's? With Grace and Clara?

It was time to find some answers.

The practice of topping out is a centuries-old custom, often used by the construction industry. Traditionally, trees were put on top of new roofs when they were laid. There are also instances of people leaving children's shoes in concealed places to ward off evil spirits. The innocence of the young, and the fact that shoes are the only piece of human clothing to hold its shape, was said to be powerful enough to repel malignant forces.

It was not unusual for superstitious families also to hide dead cats behind chimney stacks, over door lintels, or under roof rafters to act as protection.

Erdman stared at the image of a mummified cat on his iPad, a half-eaten slice of toast abandoned on a plate next to him. He wasn't hungry anymore. Not that he had much of an appetite these days.

He called up Google and, using one finger, tapped out two words: *Carlton Frith. 8,900,000 results (0.22 seconds).*

He clicked on the first story. It was dated 11 April 1999. A headline in blue writing. Local newspaper, front page: After Twenty-Four Years, I Still Hope My Boy Will Be Found.

This story had been published a few months before he met Lilith. When he had spent a miserable three months in India, trying to decide what the hell to do with his life. His mother must have waited for him to leave the country. Anger burned the back of his throat, and he swallowed it down. His family, built on secrets. He read on.

> It was a balmy June afternoon when Carlton Frith was playing on the beach at Southend-on-Sea with his twin brother, Erdman.
>
> As his mother, Shirley, watched her son, then two, potter about on the sand, she noticed a lump on his chest.
>
> That was the beginning of a nightmare for this ordinary family from south-east London.
>
> Medics were convinced that Carlton had developed an aggressive form of cancer and biopsied the growth.
>
> But this proved to be a disastrous course of action. Carlton was suffering from the rare condition Stone Man Syndrome, which causes extra bone to grow in the body's connective tissues, either at sites of trauma or due to spontaneous flare-ups.
>
> Victims of this debilitating disease often grow a second skeleton, which effectively traps them in a prison of bone.
>
> In Carlton's case, this invasive procedure triggered an unusually rapid progression of the disease. The growth of extra bone in his chest cavity restricted his lung function.
>
> Six months after his visit to the beach, Carlton Frith was dead.

This tragedy would have been enough to last this family a lifetime. But the Friths' story of heartbreak does not end here.

On Christmas Day 1975, while most people were eating turkey and listening to the Queen reflect on a year of record inflation, Carlton's young body was stolen from the hospital's Chapel of Rest.

It was the holidays. The hospital was short-staffed, and in the days before CCTV, nobody saw a thing.

More than two decades on, the fate of her son still haunts his mother.

"I often wonder where Carlton's body is, and, even after all this time, I would love to be able to give him the burial he deserves," said Shirley, now 51.

"Even though he was dead when he was taken, I feel cheated of the chance to say good-bye to him. I would like to see the sick person who stole our son's body—and with it, our chance to grieve—brought to justice."

Carlton's twin, Erdman, has never spoken publicly about his brother's disappearance, but Shirley, an insurance broker, revealed he has never gotten over it.

"Erdman was only a baby, really. The twins had just turned three when Carlton died. He couldn't understand where his brother had gone for a long time, and it was difficult for all of us."

There are around 35 recorded cases of Stone Man Syndrome—also known as fibrodysplasia ossificans progressiva—in the UK. It can be an inherited condition, but it seems the family escaped a double tragedy.

> While Shirley would not discuss her surviving son, she did confirm that he is free from the disease.

Carlton had *Stone Man Syndrome*? In all those lonely years of his childhood, of his teenage angst, of his adulthood, Ma had never so much as hinted at the possibility. Not in those early, euphoric years of his marriage, when he had announced that Lilith was pregnant, and Ma had just tightened her lips. Nor on that awful night, six years ago, when the doctors had told them the truth about Jakey's illness, and he had watched Lilith cradle their new baby and thought he might die himself.

True, he had never talked about his twin, not as he had grown older while his brother never aged. But that was only because she refused to discuss it. Maybe she *couldn't* talk about it. And then, he found, neither could he. His memories of Carlton had been replaced by a sort of blank numbness. *But why?* a voice whispered. Why the hell hadn't she warned him about the genetic time bomb of Carlton's illness? Especially after all that Jakey had endured.

He couldn't shake the sense of betrayal.

With both of his parents dead, there was no one left to ask.

Together with Fitzroy, he had riffled through the rest of the newspapers in the attic, most of them dated the same month. One article contained a photograph he had never seen before: Erdman and Carlton as babies, chubby arms and matching sun hats, squinting into the camera, full of toothless smiles. Another black-and-white image showed a much-younger-looking Shirley dressed in a suit, entering the Royal Southern, surrounded by journalists and photographers.

His mother had kept secrets from him.

The knowledge stung.

Erdman's vision was now so blurred he was forced to stop reading. How could he have forgotten all this? Had he blocked it from his memory? Perhaps he had never known. He was only three, after all, and there had been no photographs of Carlton at Shirley's house, no mementos of his short life at all.

And what about his mother? Had her actions been designed to hurt him? Or protect him?

Oh, Ma. Had he ever bothered to consider why his mother had built, brick by unyielding brick, a wall around herself? When he thought of their easy disdain, their determined withdrawal from her life, Erdman's cheeks flamed with guilt and shame.

Shadows edged the study, sullen and silent. Rain smacked against the window, like handfuls of loose gravel. Erdman stared at the screen until the letters jumped in front of his eyes.

Was Jakey's abduction somehow connected with the stranger who had been following him? No, he was being ridiculous, paranoid. All the same, perhaps he would mention it to Fitzroy.

Lilith was upstairs, sedated into somnolence. She had woken, groggy and disoriented, in Fitzroy's car as the detective was driving them back from his mother's home, back from the discovery of his brother's illness. His wife had cried out for Jakey and wouldn't stop crying until the emergency doctor had arrived.

He thought how easy it would be never to wake up.

But while there was the tiniest spark of hope that Jakey might still be alive, he would do his damnedest to find him.

The phone began its strident call to action, and he rose to answer it.

FIFTY-FOUR

10.16 a.m.

When Jakey Frith opened his eyes, he was in a room he didn't recognize.

He drew in a breath, and felt a tightening belt across his chest. Cold air wrapped itself around him. He snatched another breath, felt pain and panic rattle in his rib cage.

"Mummy?"

His throat was raw and swollen, like something too big for it had been shoved in or pulled out, or both. There was a chair in the corner, a bucket. A metal vent screwed into the wall. It was dark, apart from blade-thin strips of daylight bleeding through slats across the windows.

Ol' Bloody Bones is here.

Jakey felt a wet trickle between his legs.

The boy sat up. It hurt his chest. Every breath he took hurt his chest. He was feverish. Hot and cold. He wondered, for a second, if he might be dreaming.

His body began to tremble, and although his sheet

was soaked, he pulled it over him anyway, tried to ignore its clamminess against his skin.

He shut his eyes.

He listened.

The house was quiet, the darkness whispering at him from the shadows. Although he was only six, Jakey knew that death lived here. That death would be coming for him.

And then, from the vent in the corner, he heard a little girl singing.

FIFTY-FIVE

10.45 a.m.

Fitzroy was on the phone.

"Mr. Frith—"

"Is there—news?"

The detective's voice was hesitant.

"A grey van was seen driving away from the hospital last night, the same type of van spotted on the afternoon of Clara's abduction."

Erdman gripped the receiver. He and Lilith had been counting on the absence of a rabbit skeleton, on Fitzroy having misinterpreted the warning left in her car. "Are you sure?"

"We don't know if it's the same guy, but it's a strong possibility. We're pulling footage from nearby CCTV cameras, but it's going to take a while. I'll let you know if anything changes." She paused, asked the same questions that she had of Amy Foyle.

"Has there been anything troubling Jakey? Anything odd or unusual that he may have mentioned?"

A guilty silence. "That's probably a question for

Lilith, but, no, nothing I can think of. He was worried about dying, someone had said something to him at school, but that was all."

"And you're sure you don't remember seeing a grey van on the night you were attacked?"

Erdman cast his mind back to that night, which now seemed a lifetime ago.

"No, I—"

The stranger's face loomed in his memory.

"What is it, Mr. Frith?"

"It's just that I think someone might be following me."

A pause.

"Tell me more."

He explained about the man he had seen in the days leading up to his attack, Jakey's abduction.

"Do you think perhaps you should have mentioned this sooner?" Her voice was ice.

"I didn't think it was important."

"Can you describe him?"

"Tall, grey hair."

Fitzroy's brain flicked to Miles Foyle. He was tall, grey.

"Have you see Clara Foyle's father in the paper, on the news?"

"Yeah."

She was blunt. "Is it him?"

"No." He sounded shocked. "No, definitely not."

"We'll need an electronic image. Do you think you can remember him clearly enough for us to create his likeness on the computer?"

"I think so."

"And we'd like to hold that press conference we talked about last night. Most likely this afternoon, with you and Mrs. Frith."

The rise and fall of a siren, broadcasting another tragedy somewhere in the city, cut through the buzz in Erdman's head.

Jakey's been abducted by someone who cuts the fingertips off young girls.

When Fitzroy spoke again, there was a faint edge to her tone. "Mr. Frith? Are you happy to do that?"

If he hurts my little boy, I'll kill him.

"Mr. Frith? Did you hear me? As well as helping Jakey, it could lead us to Clara, to Grace."

He needs his medication, proper hospital care.

"Mr. Frith?"

"Yes?"

"The press conference?"

"Yes, of course. We'll do whatever you need."

"Good." Her tone was clipped. "I'll pick you both up after lunch."

Upstairs, Lilith was emerging from a drug-induced sleep. She stared at the ceiling, at a tiny white light that danced in the corner of the room.

Jakey?

She was struggling to sit up, reaching out a hand, when she realized it was just the reflection of her watch as she moved her wrist.

What has he done to my baby? She stuffed her knuckles in her mouth, bit down so hard she broke the skin. *Stop it. Stop.*

A shaft of pain in her chest threatened to fell her,

and she forced herself to take in a breath. And another. Jakey's absence became an acid burn in her throat. Her joints ached, her fingers, her knees.

Belinda Chong, the family liaison officer assigned to them last night, had warned her about this. How emotional pain could translate into physical pain.

She ignored the hurt, used it to push herself upright.

Surely he would have left behind a rabbit skeleton. Some kind of sign. If it was him.

Hope flared inside her, bright and hungry, but she snuffed it out. Hope made a person vulnerable.

Not for the first time, she wished her foster mother was around, that she had parents of her own to lean on. But Valerie Thrupp's hands were full with three young sisters whose mother had abandoned them for a two-week holiday to Tenerife. She closed her eyes. Her real mother was dead, that much she knew. And she didn't even know her name.

Downstairs, she could hear the slow, uncertain tread of her husband pacing the hallway.

Erdman had always let her lean on him. But now he barely had the strength to hold himself up.

Many times over the last year she had contemplated a life without him, had imagined packing a suitcase for her and Jakey. She had even contacted a solicitor, just to find out the process.

But now she realized that Jakey's birth had left her winded by shock, by grief. Six years later, she was still struggling to catch her breath. And that wasn't Erdman's fault. It had never been Erdman's fault.

And now that Jakey was gone, there was a wound inside her that would never close.

In those horrific days after he was born, when she

had functioned in a weird daze, lost halfway between loving her baby and grieving the loss of the life she had planned for him, her Caesarean scar had become infected. It had taken weeks and weeks to heal. But the disappearance of her son would take years—a whole lifetime, even.

Jakey, darling Jakey.

She shivered when she remembered their last night at home together, before he'd become so sick and a new kind of hell had begun.

She'd found him kneeling at the window seat, looking out into the blue-black expanse of the front garden, watching the thin, miserable rain drift down.

Beneath the security lights, the grass shone glossily, each blade a freshly painted work of art. The crazy paving gleamed.

His face was pushed up against the glass, and every now and then he would lean back slightly and doodle steamy stickmen. His breathing was rapid and uncomfortable.

A couple of teenagers ran by, their footsteps slapping the pavement, shrieking with laughter as the rain soaked their skin. She'd watched them until they were gone.

"Time for night-nights, sweetheart," she'd said, and she'd carried him, unprotesting, up the stairs.

Then she'd bathed him, helped him with his teeth, and tucked the sheets around him, ready for a story.

"Mummy?" he'd asked, yawning. "What about the little girl? She needs help. Will *you* help her?"

"What little girl, darling?"

"She's frightened, she . . ." Tiredness was thickening his voice, and she'd rubbed the pad of her thumb along the line of his eyebrow as her heart quickened. "Jakey," she said, "what little girl?"

"The one on my TV. That one."

"Do you mean *Clara Foyle*?"

"Yes." The little boy had given a surprised laugh. "That's her name, Mummy. How did you know?"

FIFTY-SIX

10.54 a.m.

Fitzroy stared at the receiver. She'd handled it badly, let her impatience show.

Behind her, The Boss was pacing back and forth. His eyes were sunken holes, but there was fire in his voice. "Come on, people," he shouted. "We need to catch this fucker. I want an arrest by tomorrow."

Don't we all, Boss? But you can't arrest thin air.

The Friths were understandably distraught. She couldn't blame them. Fitzroy pulled out a printed copy of the same article that Erdman had found on his computer, reread it. She wondered whether Detective Inspector Felix Tapp, the police officer mentioned in the story, was still alive. She began a search for his address.

There was still no word from Conchita Rodríguez. Fitzroy had tried her twice already that morning but her landline had gone unanswered, and she knew that Grace's mother refused to use a mobile after a series of prank calls following her daughter's death.

On her desk, the phone rang.

She snatched it up. "Mrs. Rodríguez?"

"Fitzroy?"

It was the desk sergeant from downstairs, PC Jared Fox.

"Foxy, it's you. Everything all right?"

"There's a guy asking for you in reception. But don't get too excited. Says you know him. Dashiell Hall, from the Natural History Museum."

Dr. Hall was lounging against an advertisement for Crimestoppers. His dark hair had been slicked back with styling spray. He was wearing contact lenses instead of glasses. He smiled with half of his mouth.

"Thought I'd drop by and see you in person, rather than send an e-mail. So impersonal, don't you think?"

Fitzroy touched a hand briefly to her hair, mirrored his smile. "There's a coffee shop across the road."

Bakes & Beans was one of those small independents that sold wedges of home-cooked cakes and neat bags of Colombian coffee. The smell made Fitzroy happy.

A waitress brought Dr. Hall's black coffee and her own flat white. Fitzroy waited for her to put the drinks on the table and leave before she spoke.

"So, what can you tell me?"

Dr. Hall pulled a folder from his briefcase. "Quite a lot, actually. This specimen is fascinating. It's an adult male rabbit, almost certainly domestic."

"How can you be sure?"

He pointed to the photographs of Fitzroy's skeleton, and another he had brought with him for comparison. His eyes glittered. "Take a look at this. Your rabbit has a more rounded head, a shorter skull. That's the way artificial selection works. It's like comparing a wolf and a bulldog. Domestically bred rabbits are selected to produce much more meat, so naturally, they'll have different proportions. We weighed it, just to confirm, and your domestic rabbit's bones were much bigger and heavier than this wild rabbit."

He wrapped his hands around his drink. He had very long fingers.

"So, can you narrow it down to breed?"

"It's difficult. It's not foolproof. But because of its wide chest, its short neck, I'd guess at Blanc de Hotot."

He flicked through the photographs in his folder, and pulled out another. It showed a white rabbit with black rings around its eyes. "Bred for its beautiful white fur and meat. Originated in Normandy, France."

Fitzroy leaned back against her chair, let the noise of the coffee shop wash over her. Did this mean he was a rabbit breeder? How many of those lived in the southeast? They'd have their work cut out, trying to track them all down.

"But that's not all." Dr. Hall's face was ablaze with the joy of discovery. "Any forensic expert will tell you that everything leaves a trace. And that's certainly the case with your skeleton."

Fitzroy's skin began to prickle.

"I was surprised by the state of your specimen, I must admit. Its skeleton was intact, the connective tissues still in place, but the bones were stripped of all flesh." Fitzroy was listening intently, and he met her eyes. "That's unusual, to say the least." He swallowed a mouthful of coffee. "So, I dug a little deeper."

"Go on."

"When I looked at it under the microscope, I discovered that several of the bones had tiny nicks, which suggests that the fur, the organs, and some of the meat was removed with a knife."

Fitzroy was sitting up straight now, oblivious to the curious glances of the couple at the next table.

"But what happened to the rest of the meat?" Dr. Hall went on. "No one, however skilled with a knife, could remove every last trace of it. Unless . . ." He gave Fitzroy a shy smile.

"Unless what?"

"Unless he had a little help from *Dermestes maculatus*."

Dr. Hall produced another set of photographs. An animal skull swarming with thousands of tiny black insects.

"He's been using carrion beetles. They clean the flesh from dead animals. I found traces of their DNA in saliva on the bones."

Fitzroy's mind was racing. Where did these beetles come from? How easy would it be for him to obtain them? Dr. Hall was ahead of her, already explaining.

"Some scientists use chemicals to strip the flesh off of skeletons, but that can eat into the bones and change their structure. At the Natural History Museum, we use something very similar to clean our specimens. *Dermestes haemorrhoidalis.* But in the past, we've used *maculatus.* Many people still use that species now.

"We maintain our own colony, but some breeders will sell you batches of hundreds or thousands of adult beetles to start your own." He set down his empty cup, and tore a lump from his chocolate muffin.

"Find the breeder, Etta, and you've found this sick-minded bastard."

FIFTY-SEVEN

1.03 p.m.

Why had no one warned her how difficult it was to sum up, in one photograph, the son she loved? Should she portray him as a laughing, carefree boy on his daddy's shoulder, or sick and fragile, in a hospital bed? The public would search harder for a poorly child, Lilith decided.

Erdman placed a sandwich on the table, and plucked a picture from the pile, running a finger across his son's glossy, frozen smile. Lilith reached for his hand, not hungry, but appreciating the intent behind his gesture.

"How you doing?" he said.

She shrugged. There was nothing to say.

"They'll find him," he said. "We have to believe that." But he wouldn't meet her eyes.

PC Jemma Maslan, a specialist in electronic facial identification technology, had just spent the last two hours with Erdman, constructing an image of a potential suspect. She had shown him hundreds of noses and chins and eyes and hairstyles. Erdman had cursed the holes in his memory; the man's features were as elusive as smoke.

"I'm afraid that can happen," she said. "You think you can remember a face, but when it comes to pinning it down, it's always much more difficult. It's confusing, you start to doubt yourself."

While they had worked, a couple of police officers had searched Jakey's bedroom. Lilith had resisted the temptation to ask them to leave.

But now the house was empty, apart from Belinda, their newly assigned family liaison officer, who was washing up mugs and teaspoons.

"They'll be back," she said to Lilith. "Just as soon as they've got something to tell us." Lilith resented the way she said "*us,*" as if Belinda knew and cared about the fate of Jakey, and wasn't being paid to stand in their house up to her elbows in the kitchen sink.

She'd been dreading this moment. The Press Conference. The words loomed large in her mind. The morning had whirled by. She'd made endless cups of coffee and escaped on the pretext of buying milk when the atmosphere of the house became too suffocating. One of the mothers—Alyson Carruthers—from Jakey's school had driven past, and offered her a lift home. She'd helped Lilith up the path, holding her by the crook of her elbow as if she were an old lady. Lilith had wanted to scream at her to go away, but even in the face of tragedy, self-preservation restrained her.

Then she'd cried at photographs of Jakey, stared at the walls, and now—she checked her watch—DS Fitzroy would be here to collect them in a few moments.

Lilith hated being the center of attention, especially

when she was at her most vulnerable, but Fitzroy had persuaded Erdman it was essential, that they needed to do it to raise public awareness, that it might help them find Clara Foyle—Grace Rodríguez, too.

Please let Jakey be alive.

She wasn't naïve. She was fully aware that the police used press conferences to put suspects under pressure, to see if they tripped up or cried crocodile tears. Fitzroy had assured them that wasn't the case and, numbly, she'd agreed.

The doorbell rang. Fitzroy stood on the step, bruised smudges beneath her eyes. "Sorry I'm late, Mrs. Frith. This morning has been rather, um, busy."

And that was how Lilith and Erdman found themselves, that Saturday lunchtime, at the Novotel Hotel, a glass-and-brick edifice that squatted on Greenwich High Road. It had been more than fifteen hours since Jakey had vanished, eight days since the disappearance of Clara, and a year and four days since Grace had left for ballet and never come home.

A small table had been set up at the back of the large conference room with three chairs, a jug of water, and a microphone. The photograph that Lilith had chosen was projected onto a screen behind them.

The steady hum of conversation lapsed into respectful silence as Lilith and Erdman took their seats. Lilith's stomach churned queasily at the sight of all those expectant faces. She saw a round-faced woman with dark hair and black-rimmed glasses, her chewed pen poised over her pad. A young man with a microphone and sound recorder was crouched by the table, there were cameras trained on her from the back, and a selection of Dictaphones had been laid out in front of her. Erdman was chewing his lip, darting anxious glances around the room, filled with so many journalists that they'd had to move the press conference from the police station to here.

I can't do this, she thought, and her legs turned to rubber. She wanted to cry. She didn't want to be in this characterless hotel, putting herself out there for the public to gawp at. But Fitzroy was grasping her elbow and guiding her to her chair. The detective gave her an encouraging nod, and before she knew it, Fitzroy was introducing them and Lilith began to read, haltingly, from a prepared statement. About halfway through, she looked up and saw two journalists whispering, and she lost her focus and stumbled over Jakey's name, so she crumpled the sheet of paper in her hand, and let it fall, like her tears. Erdman's fingers laced hers, squeezing gently. He swallowed once. A moment's pause, broken by the strobing of camera flashes. And then he spoke, in unconscious imitation of Miles Foyle, straight into the camera lens.

"Please, please help us find Jakey, and bring our son home."

Fitzroy stood up and addressed the assembled media. "That's it, folks. We're not taking questions today, but thank you all for coming."

As the journalists and news crews packed up equipment, tapped out e-mails, or called their news desks, Fitzroy murmured to them both, "Well done. You did a good job. It should make the teatime bulletin, and we'll see what that brings."

Our son. I hope it brings our son.

Fitzroy was walking Erdman and Lilith back to the car when they heard footsteps on the pavement behind them. It was the dark-haired woman from the press conference, the *Daily Mirror*'s crime reporter, and she was calling Fitzroy's name.

"Have you got time for a quick word?"

"No," said Fitzroy shortly, not turning around.

The reporter raised one eyebrow and waved her Dictaphone at Fitzroy's back. Even with a blustery wind, Lilith couldn't help noticing that the young woman smelled of stale cigarettes.

"That's a shame. I wanted to give you a heads-up."

Fitzroy took a deep breath. "Excuse me for a moment, Mr. and Mrs. Frith . . ." She stepped away from the couple, and drew the journalist to one side. Even though their backs were angled towards her and their voices lowered, they could still hear most of the conversation.

"We know about the rabbit kidney," the journalist was saying. "We're going to lead with it tomorrow."

Fitzroy's hands curled into fists, which slowly unfurled as she turned a half circle to face the woman. Lilith was worried that the detective might punch her, but Fitzroy's voice was calm. Too calm.

"Please don't. We're not ready to make that public yet. For operational reasons."

"C'mon, Fitzroy, it's a great story. A potential serial killer leaving rabbit skeletons in place of his victims. A kidney left in your car as a warning. The desk already knows about it. They love it, so does the editor. They're putting it all over the front page, so if you want me to pull it, you're going to have to give me something bloody brilliant to replace it."

"Don't be crass, Sarah. These are someone's loved

ones, not a way to boost the circulation of your newspaper. And don't blackmail me. You know as well as I do that all it takes is one call to your boss."

"I wouldn't bet on it. He's still pissed off that you tipped off the *Sun* about the Girl in the Woods fingertips story last year."

A muscle jumped in Fitzroy's cheek. She slid her hands into her pockets. "We didn't tip anyone off. I believe it was Mrs. Rodríguez's sister-in-law who shared that particular nugget with the press."

Sarah laughed without humor. "Same difference. They got a massive story that we didn't get. We need one that they haven't got. I know what you're thinking. You want to be able to separate genuine callers from the cranks, but you'll never be able to sit on this. It's going to leak, you know it is."

Lilith felt oddly detached from the exchange, as if she was listening to a play on the radio and couldn't see the faces of the actors. Erdman was staring at the journalist, disgust staining his features. Fitzroy's curls bobbed slowly from side to side in disbelief.

"I really don't think it's appropriate to be having this conversation with Mr. and Mrs. Frith standing so close, do you? But I will say this. If you're hell-bent on running this story, we'll have to manage it, I'm afraid. That means releasing this information to the rest of the media . . ."

"You wouldn't dare. It's *our* exclusive." Sarah was outraged, her face flushing down to her roots.

"Just wait a couple of days until we're ready to release it, and then it's all yours."

"What if someone else gets it first?"

"They won't. Give me a call in a couple of days."

The journalist stalked off, and Fitzroy gave the Friths a wry smile. "She won't use it," she said.

"How do you know?" said Erdman.

"Trust me," said Fitzroy. "She'll hold out for the bigger story, I know she will. Journalists always do."

FIFTY-EIGHT

4.14 p.m.

The bucket was full, and it was starting to smell. Clara wrinkled her nose. The Night Man hadn't come for a long time. She was hungry and, although he frightened her, he always brought something to eat.

She slumped back on the tangled sheets. An unpleasant odor rose from them. Her tongue felt thick and dry in her mouth, and her back ached. She reached for her lumpy pillow.

"It's okay, Rosie," she crooned. "Mummy's here."

She sang softly to herself, made-up words and fragments of tunes that she remembered from home and school, although those memories, now a week old, seemed fuzzy and distant.

Usually, he came when the morning light spilled through the bars onto the floor, the bare walls, but it was darker now, the room veiled in shadow.

She was dozing, drifting in and out. She had been doing the same that afternoon when a muffled *thud* had jerked her from the peripheries of sleep. She had sat up, clutching Rosie-Pillow to her chest, and listened.

Should she shout out or stay quiet? Perhaps it was her mother, or the police, come to rescue her.

She fixed her eyes on the door and willed it to open.

Another *thud*. And with it a low cough, and the light tread of footsteps, not like the Night Man at all. She wanted to call out, to urge whoever it was back. She waited. A door shut somewhere.

Other people are here.

That delicious thought curled its way into her brain. Never before had she heard anyone apart from *him* within this strange place.

She pressed her ear against the door until it turned pink, straining to pick up something, anything.

But she could hear only silence.

"What do you think, Rosie-Pillow?"

"I don't know, Clara. It doesn't sound like the Night Man." Clara's voice was high-pitched as she waggled Rosie-Pillow in the air.

"Hmmm . . . maybe it's someone who can help us. Maybe it's Mummy."

That possibility prompted such a moment of unexpected giddiness in Clara that she hopped on the spot and twisted her ankle. She ignored it. She could handle any amount of pain if there was a chance she'd be sleeping in her own bed tonight with Mr. Snuggles, and Raggedy the Cat.

"I don't think it's Mummy," said Rosie-Pillow.

"Shut up," said Clara, disappointment souring her childish lilt, and threw the pillow on the floor.

The lightbulb in the lamp in the corner kept flickering, casting half shadows across the walls. It wasn't dark enough for bed, but it was too dark to be daytime.

With all her limited strength, Clara heaved a chair, the only piece of furniture in the room, apart from the bed, over to the door. As she tried to scale the precarious mountain, to look through the keyhole, it wobbled and she lost her balance, falling hard to the floor.

Winded, she lay motionless. When the black dots stopped flashing, she felt a sudden urge to make herself as small and as hidden as possible, and squeezed into the narrow gap beneath the bed. Perhaps he wouldn't see her there.

Twenty minutes later, she dragged herself the short distance to retrieve Rosie-Pillow before crawling back to her hiding place.

By the time the Night Man came to empty her bucket, she was asleep, and he was in too much of a hurry to move her. He righted the chair and left a glass of milk containing the sleeping tablets on top of it. From his pocket he pulled a soft knitted dog—made by his wife decades ago, but never played with—and laid it on the floor next to Clara.

FIFTY-NINE

6.12 p.m.

The streets are surprisingly empty for Saturday evening. The rain is keeping people away. Lady Luck is on his side. He hopes she will stay true.

The detective's car is long gone, a wide and empty space left in its wake. He watched the men load it onto a truck, a bag of shopping in hand, a song in his heart.

They will find nothing. He was careful. He is always careful.

There is a light at her window, but the Bone Collector knows she is not home. She will be looking for him. But she will not find him.

The detective intrigues him, crowds his mind. He swims in the warm waters of her despair. It adds a new dimension to his work, and he finds he yearns for her to know that the boy's time is short, that within hours he will begin to prepare him for his final honor.

Tick-tock, Detective. *Tick-tock*.

He thinks of the girl, hidden in the shadows in the corner of the room, and tries to imagine what a child of his own might have looked like, but its face is featureless and empty.

He thinks of the boy, lying on the mattress. He is sick, but it does not matter if he dies. It will save him the task.

He wonders how long he can keep them hidden in this city of eight million souls, and whether he should move them to a place of silence and safety.

Death is not the end. His collection allows them to live forever. But he will not be rushed: He wants time—hour after languid hour—to savor the unsheathing of these rarest of bones.

The windscreen wipers are too slow to clear the endless weeping rain. Almost there.

He will heat some soup for his wife's supper, perhaps swirl in some cream. Her arms are so wasted now. If she doesn't eat soon, she, too, will become a skeleton, encased in the thinnest covering of skin.

He hurries up the street. She was not well when he left her. Not at all. He is worried. He hopes she has managed to drink. He wants to get home, to see her. Her sheets need changing, she needs a wash, a new nightie.

When he turns the corner, his stomach folds in on itself.

Every window is ablaze with electric light.

SIXTY

7.01 p.m.

Jakey eased himself off the mattress. His pajama bottoms were damp and cold, and every breath, a scissors blade to his side.

Shadows probed the corners of the room. Almost twenty-four hours since he had been taken. He dragged himself across the floor, to the wall with its shiny metal vent. He pressed his mouth to the gash between the slats.

"Hello," he croaked. "Hello."

Nothing.

Exhaustion was pushing down on him with heavy hands, painting a sheen of sweat on his brow. He shuffled backwards on his bottom, until his back was resting against the wall.

He must have dreamed it.

He shut his eyes. Two warm tears trickled into his mouth, and he swallowed them, wincing at the violation of his swollen throat.

Mummy, I want you.

Come rescue me, Daddy.

But there was no hope of escape. Ol' Bloody Bones would see to that. Jakey dozed for a couple of minutes. His breathing was labored and fast. At the hospital, the intravenous antibiotics had only just begun the work they would not now be permitted to finish. If Ol' Bloody Bones didn't kill him, the pneumonia would.

He was going to die here.

His young mind wandered. He thought he could hear his father singing to him, thought he was falling down a rabbit hole.

"Hello," said the wall. "What's your name?"

SIXTY-ONE

7.03 p.m.

If an owner takes on the characteristics of his dog, it stands to reason that the same might be said of his house.

Number 46 sort of bulged in the middle, more flatulence than subsidence, and the bamboo grass in the front garden was not unlike the wisps of his nicotine-stained hair.

Retired or not, if Detective Inspector Felix Tapp had heard a whippersnapper like Fitzroy describe him like that, he'd have given her a clip 'round the ear.

She rang the bell. A blurred outline appeared in the glass of the door.

It had been a while since Felix Tapp had received an evening visit from someone who wasn't one of his caregivers, and when he shuffled into the hallway, his swollen feet jammed into a tatty pair of slippers, the house had that moldering smell of unwashed clothes and sweaty bodies.

Felix was wearing a checked shirt with a stain down the front, and he led Fitzroy into a cramped sitting room and over to a sofa with cushions that didn't match. Crammed on every available surface were photographs of family and friends. An old *Australia* tea towel was draped over a stool that held a basket of flowers in lurid purples and pinks that didn't fade like the furnishings.

His body was squashy with age, his skin as lined as a piece of aluminium foil that had been scrunched into a ball and then smoothed out. His eyes were vague, but his mind was as sharp as his tongue.

He made tea, which they drank with milk that floated in spots to the surface.

"Sir, do you remember I mentioned on the phone that I needed your help with a case?"

"I'm going blind, not deaf."

"Of course. Sorry, sir."

He peered at her.

"You Boyd Fitzroy's daughter?"

"That's right."

"Bastard to work for. Good officer, though. Now, young Carlton Frith, wasn't it? Christmas 1975?"

"Yes, the young boy whose body was stolen from the hospital's Chapel of Rest."

He was nodding now, a thoughtful look spreading across his features. "Damn well nearly killed me, that case, trying to find that young lad. Killed my marriage, too."

"Sorry to hear that, sir. Curse of the job."

"Gah. Modern-day policing. Not the same, is it? Not with the Internet, the massive leaps in forensic techniques. My generation had to pound the bloody pavement until our feet bled."

Fitzroy gave a respectful dip of her head. Felix

shifted his body until he was comfortable. When he moved, Fitzroy detected the faint whiff of potatoes.

"No bloody CCTV, nothing like that. We interviewed hundreds of people, but no one saw a bloody thing. Christmas, wasn't it? Skeleton staff, people turned in on their own lives."

He slurped his tea, and the brown liquid collected at the corners of his mouth.

"His family, in bits, they were. His poor mother. She just wanted to bury her little lad, have a place she could go, to sit and talk to him. To lay flowers. It was a bloody tragedy. Their whole family was a bloody tragedy."

Fitzroy looked up sharply. "Why was that, sir?"

"Well, she'd already lost one son, hadn't she?"

"What, you mean she'd lost another child, before Carlton?"

"Didn't say that, did I? Call yourself a bloody detective. No, what I mean is, she'd already lost one child and now she was going to lose another." Felix's face clouded over and he stared at the unlit gas fire, a removed look in his eyes. "I often wonder what happened to him. I tried to keep in touch with the family, but she didn't want to, you know, not after her husband died, and it became clear we were never going to find the little lad."

He was silent while Fitzroy tried to organize the ringing in her brain.

"Sorry, sir, you've lost me. Why was she going to lose another child?"

"Carlton, he had that bone disease." His parchment hands fluttered in his lap. "Damn, what was it called?"

Fitzroy spoke slowly. "Fibrodysplasia ossificans progressiva."

He looked at her, surprised. "Yes, that's right. Bloody terrible burden. Well, his twin, Erdman, he had the same thing."

Fitzroy thinned her lips, shook her head. "No, no, I don't think that's possible. Erdman Frith, he's never shown any signs of disease."

"Well, I'm blowed. I was sure he'd be dead by now." The retired detective inspector frowned. "But I know I'm right. I remember it distinctly, because I was interviewing his mother at the time." He paused for a shaky sip of tea. "That poor woman. Not only was she dealing with the death of her three-year-old son, but she'd just been told his body had been stolen. She was in a terrible state. And then Erdman was sick all over the head honcho's office, and they had to call someone to clean it, and amidst all the chaos, Carlton's bloody doctor arrived and chose that moment to tell her that he suspected Erdman—as Carlton's identical twin—would develop it. And perhaps future generations, too." He scratched his head. "But he didn't, you say?"

The clock ticked rudely in the silence. Erdman did not have Stone Man Syndrome. She knew that as surely as night follows day. But his son, Jakey, did, and then there was Clara, with her poor ruined hands.

Through the banging and the whirring and the clanking, Fitzroy heard the familiar *ting* of her synapses.

Was it really possible that the man who had abducted Jakey and Clara was the same man who had stolen Carlton's body almost four decades earlier? Had he been keeping tabs on the Friths all that time, all the while expecting Erdman to develop the disease and moving on to his son when he hadn't? Or had he come across him more recently?

But if the connection between Carlton and Jakey and Clara *was* the bone deformities, how did the Girl in the Woods case fit in?

She hurried outside to try Mrs. Rodríguez again.

SIXTY-TWO

8.14 p.m.

"I'm Jakey."

The boy did not have the energy to move very far, so he rolled himself onto his tummy, and pressed his mouth against the vent for the second time that day.

"How old are you?" said the wall.

"Six." He screwed up his face. "Who are you?"

"My name's Clara. I'm five-and-a-quarter." A pause. "Are you a goodie or a baddie?"

"A goodie." His voice was a scrape of wood against brick. "Like Spider-Man."

"I like Spider-Man," she said, her own voice high and clear. "I wish you could spin a web. Then we could escape." A wobble. "I don't like it here."

"Me, either," he said, as if talking through the wall to a little girl was the most natural thing in the world.

The children sat in silence for a moment, their mouths just a few inches apart, their bodies separated by a brick wall. Jakey closed his eyes, fighting the burn in his chest. Clara, so starved for company, couldn't stop the words from tumbling out of her mouth.

"Did the Night Man bring you? He brought me. In a van. I didn't like it. He hurt me. Did he hurt you? He's got a machine. Have you seen his machine? You have to stay still. It doesn't hurt, but you have to stay still. He gets cross if I move. I'm hungry. Have you got anything for me to eat?"

"No," he whispered. "I don't feel well."

"Have you got a poorly tummy? My tummy hurts. It really, really, really hurts, but I can't do a poo. My mum says doing a poo can help if you've got a tummy ache, but I can't do one, so I don't know. Have you seen my mummy?"

"Yes," he murmured. "On my television."

"Oh," said Clara. "When is she coming to get me?"

Jakey tried to sort it out in his head. He wasn't really sure why Clara Foyle's mother was on the television, but he kind of had an idea. He tried to form the words through the pain, which was spreading to his back, his bones. "She doesn't know where you are."

Through the vent, he heard an intake of breath and the girl began to cry.

"S'okay." His eyes would barely open, his tongue thick and loose in his mouth. "S'okay."

Gradually, Clara's sobs became sniffs. A stream of snot was running from her nose, and she wiped at it with the back of her hand, smearing a stringy residue across her cheek.

"Is your mummy coming to get you?" she said.

"No. I don't know." Speaking was becoming an enormous effort, his words beginning to slur. "I don't think she knows I'm here, either."

Both children absorbed the painful significance of this.

"When I get home, I'm going to have chocolate for breakfast. And jelly," said Clara.

"I like jelly."

"And I'm going to let Eleanor borrow my heart necklace. And my Sleeping Beauty dress." She paused. "Are you hungry?"

Jakey's head was full of black bees buzzing.

Puzzled by his silence, Clara pulled the last half slice of bread from her pocket. Her secret stash. "You can share, if you like." She pushed a piece of the stale crust into the vent. Two or three crumbs waterfalled onto Jakey's side, but he did not notice. His eyes were closed.

Clara nibbled at the rest of the bread.

"When bad things happen, the police come," she whispered.

"Police . . . looking . . ." he managed to say, eyes still shut.

"This is a scary place." She started to cry again, quietly now. Jakey rested his fingertips against the vent. Clara caught the shadow of the movement through the narrow slats, pressed her own fingers to his.

They sat like that for ten minutes, or more. Neither spoke, but each child was comforted by the presence of the other. Eventually, Jakey's fingers slipped from the metal, but Clara didn't notice. If she tried hard enough, she could pretend this was just a game of hide-and-seek.

And then Clara's head jerked upwards.

In the distance, she heard the faint squeak of wheels. Panicked, she scooted beneath her bed. A second later, she crawled back across the floor on her hands and knees, put her mouth to the grille.

"He's coming," she said, her voice an urgent whisper. "The Night Man is coming."

But Jakey didn't hear her warning, lost, as he was, in a sleep that walked the fine tightrope between death and life.

SUNDAY

SIXTY-THREE

11 a.m.

Lilith forced herself to get up about eleven, didn't bother eating breakfast, and spent half an hour staring into the garden at nothing much at all.

This unbearable state of not knowing was killing her.

After a while, she shuffled into the kitchen and retrieved the plastic bottle of sleeping pills the doctor had prescribed and placed it on the table.

If Grace Rodríguez's fingertips were hacked off and left in a wood, what will he do to my son?

Lilith pushed her chair backwards, ran to the downstairs toilet, bringing up the contents of her stomach. It was empty, apart from the water she had just drunk. The retching pulled at the muscles of her hollowed-out abdomen. She was a mother without a child.

A hand rubbed slow circles across her back, held her hair away from her face.

"That's all right, sweetheart. You let it out."

Erdman helped her to the table, went to fetch another glass of water.

Outside, bloated grey clouds rolled across the sky. She longed to drift away with them, far from this unyielding, unending bleakness.

She tipped the tablets onto the table, felt their smooth promise of oblivion, then counted them back into the bottle.

A noise behind her. Erdman again.

"What are you doing?" he said, setting the glass down on the table. She let him wipe the vomit from her chin, heard the fear in his voice.

"Just counting them," she said. "To see how many I've got left."

She could tell from his expression that he didn't believe her.

"Don't give up, Lilith," he said brokenly. "Please."

She tried to answer him, but the words wouldn't come. He looked so much like their son. She closed her eyes, felt the tears leak from beneath her lashes. The truths that had anchored her life had been reduced to flotsam. Now she was part of that wreckage, adrift on storm-tossed seas, and like wreckage, she would simply float away.

Jakey is dead.

In the garden of the house opposite, colored fairy lights blinked on and off. Signs of festive cheer were all around. Carols on the radio, cheap tinsel in the shops. In a rare flurry of organization, she had bought some presents for Jakey's stocking a few weeks ago. Smug, that was how she'd felt. Now that red sock would remain unfilled, limp and empty, just like her life.

A blank darkness filled every sinew and cell.

Erdman pulled her unresisting body into his arms, rocked his wife back and forth. After a minute, he buried his own face into her shoulder.

He's dead.

My son is dead.

And Erdman thinks so, too.

They sat there for an hour.

And another.

They sat there until Lilith's left foot, tucked beneath her bottom, filled up with loose sand and she had to stretch to shake it out.

Eventually, stiff and cold, they let each other go. Erdman took off his sweater, eased it over his wife's head. Slipped the bottle of pills into his pocket.

She let him.

There was tomorrow.

Always tomorrow.

SIXTY-FOUR

1.30 p.m.

Less than half a mile away, Eleanor Foyle was trying to talk to her mother.

"Fleur's going to have a party where you make your own CD," she said. "You can choose the song you want to sing, and they record it."

Amy's eyes did not open, nor did she move, or so much as acknowledge her elder daughter's presence. Eleanor thought about stroking the stray strands of hair from her mother's face, but decided against it. Instead she perched carefully on the edge of her parents' bed.

"I might wear my pink dress with the sparkles. And my silver shoes. Or my red ones." Her mother still hadn't opened her eyes. Eleanor leaned over her. She smelled a bit funny. Not of her usual perfume, but of something else. Like she hadn't showered in a while. "What do you think, Mummy?"

When her mother didn't speak, Eleanor gently pushed her shoulder. "Mummy? Red shoes or silver ones?"

A muscle in Amy Foyle's cheek twitched, but she did not answer, not immediately. Instead, she turned, very deliberately, from her daughter.

"Mummy?"

Her back was a wall.

"Mummy?" A pause. "Mum?" Eleanor touched her again on the shoulder.

Slowly, Amy pulled herself into a sitting position. Her voice was controlled, but her body was rigid with a tension that Eleanor was too young to read.

"To be perfectly honest, I don't care which shoes you wear."

Eleanor's head drooped, but not before her mother had glimpsed the naked disbelief flash across her daughter's features. Amy placed her hands over her mouth to dam the dismissal, mumbling through her fingers. "Sorry, sweetheart. Sorry. Mummy didn't mean it."

But Eleanor had already fled.

The girl flew down the stairs. She wanted Gina. Gina, who still noticed her, who dried her tears and told funny stories about Clara, who didn't scold her for laughing, even though nobody in this house laughed anymore. She looked in the kitchen, the sitting room, her mother's library. The cloakroom was empty, too.

Gina, where are you?

From across the hall, Eleanor heard the low murmur of Gina's voice in the study. She spun around, wrenched open the door handle, tears still wet on her cheeks.

Gina.

There you are.

I've been looking for you everywhere.
Oh, Daddy's crying.
Gina's got her arms around Daddy.
Gina and Daddy.

SIXTY-FIVE

8.52 p.m.

The lad behind the counter at the late-night tea hut on Shooters Hill Road was no older than twenty, but he was giving Fitzroy the Look. If she hadn't been so exhausted, she'd be flattered. When she got back into the car, Chambers pointed out the tomato ketchup on her chin, and she blushed at the memory of the lingering stare she'd given him in return. No fool like an old fool. She'd be getting her evening caffeine hit from the convenience store at the gas station in the future.

It was days since she'd been home for anything but a shower and a few hours' sleep. She wondered whether David had noticed. How Nina was coping with the baby.

She didn't call to find out.

What a mess. Clara had been missing for nine days. They were no closer to finding her. And there were still no sightings of Jakey.

Some of the team had begun the time-consuming task of investigating rabbit breeders, while Fitzroy was trying to trace anyone selling beetle colonies, posting messages on Internet forums and contacting pet stores with a particular interest in insects, but it took hours, not minutes, to generate those kind of leads, to track down and talk to people. To rule them out. And Fitzroy knew that time was slipping away from them like so many grains of sand.

What she needed was a fucking break.

Miles Foyle was in the clear. He had phoned her a few hours ago, tearful and apologetic. Eleanor had caught him in a compromising situation with Gina. Fucked up, yes. But she wasn't surprised; his confession only confirmed what she'd already known.

But with Mr. Foyle out of the picture, who *was* in the frame?

To make matters worse, that dirty bastard Chambers kept farting. If he did it again, she might throw up. She took out her a small bottle of perfume and sprayed it in the car.

"That smells like cat piss," he spluttered.

"Better than dog shite. Or the puke that's going to land in your lap if you do that again."

Chambers rolled his eyes, but Fitzroy didn't notice. She was listening to the voices crackling over the radio.

At the sound of her name, her ears pricked up. She shushed Chambers, who was nattering on about the differences between eau de parfum and eau de toilette. She was being recalled to the Major Incident Room. As a matter of urgency.

By the time she found her voice—"Take me back. Now!"—Chambers was already pulling away.

Thc Boss was waiting for her downstairs, explaining as they ran back up the steps together.

"It arrived a couple of hours ago, addressed to you, but we had no idea of its significance. Not until we got a phone call. Bloody unregistered pay-as-you-go. We're trying to triangulate the signal, but he's too damn clever to make a call from anywhere that's going to give away his location. Might help us with CCTV, though. Get us a look at his face."

Fitzroy hurried into the Major Incident Room. Officers were clustered around her desk. They stopped talking when she walked in.

Lying on her desk was an envelope, with her name across the back. His handwriting, its extravagant loops and whorls, was unmistakable.

A heady combination of fear, shock, and excitement began to drum its way through her veins.

The Boss handed her a plastic glove and she slipped it on, used a paper knife to slit the flap. A single unlined piece of paper drifted onto her desk. And a lock of soft red hair.

Jakey's hair.

We cannot divide the bones, like the soft parts, into vital and non-vital.

Fitzroy stared at the letters until they jumped and blurred. *Another warning, another fucking warning.* But this time the threat was implicit, and she knew at once he was referring to Jakey. To what he planned to do with his body. His bones.

Her mouth filled with fear.

"Fuck," she said. "What does it mean? What is he trying to tell us?"

Chambers was writing something in his notebook. "He's trying to play God. Same as the note with the kidney. It's got to be some Bible quote. Ezekiel again?"

Fitzroy frowned. "Doesn't sound like the Bible to me."

Chambers raised his eyebrows. "Since when were you an expert? I bet the only time you've been in a church was when you got married."

"We had a civil ceremony, actually," she said.

"Shut up for a minute, you two," said The Boss, leaning over the computer. He pointed to the letter. "Get that sent down to Forensics, while I check online. I've found a site with a complete list of Bible references." He tapped at the keyboard, frowned. "That quote's not coming up."

"Let me see," said Fitzroy.

She hovered at his shoulder. The Boss was right. Wherever this quotation had been taken from, it wasn't the Bible.

"But the note with his little present in Fitzroy's car—you know, the one about the kidneys—that was from the Bible, you say."

Fitzroy bit her lip. "I assume so."

"What do you mean, you *assume* so? Didn't you bloody check?"

She caught Chambers's eye. He gave a slight shake of his head. A bad mistake. She imagined her father's reaction. *Silly girl.*

"No, sir, we didn't."

"For fuck's sake." He slapped his hand on the desk. "What am I running here? A bloody kindergarten?"

"Sorry, sir."

He raised his eyes heavenwards. "For the love of God, what are you waiting for? Do it now."

"I don't want to sound like a twat here," said Chambers, rubbing his nose. "But why don't we just try Googling it?"

The Boss snorted. "Why the hell didn't I think of that? You're a fucking genius, Chambers. An Einstein. A fully paid-up member of Mensa."

Fitzroy ignored their bickering and bent over the computer. It took less than a couple of seconds.

"The quotes are taken from"—she read from the screen—"*The Works of John Hunter, with Notes*, edited by Sir James Frederick Palmer."

"Who and who?" said Chambers.

"Get me a full biography of both men," said The Boss. "Let's see if it will help us nail this fucker."

•

While Chambers delved into the history books, Fitzroy checked the message boards again. *Bingo*. One reply. She rang the mobile phone number included in the post. A man answered after seven rings.

"Yeah?"

"Is this James Davenport?"

"Who wants ter know?"

"I'm DS Etta Fitzroy, calling from Operation Flute, a major missing persons investigation."

"Right." His tone was wary.

"Can I come and see you?"

"I ain't done nothing wrong."

"I'd like to talk to you about the beetles you breed, that's all." She heard the *click* of his lighter, the blowing out of smoke. "It won't take long, twenty minutes tops."

"S'pose so," he said, and named a pub in Woolwich.

* * *

He was sitting at a table, an empty pint glass in front of him. Fitzroy ignored the heads of the customers that swiveled from the bank of fruit machines against the far wall when she walked in.

"Pig," she heard someone mutter. Even though she wasn't in uniform, she gleamed with the patina of the police: her smart overcoat, her polished heels, the corrugations in her forehead that set her two decades apart from the young lads pissing and gambling away their dole.

"Ignore 'em. Ain't got nothing better to do," he said. Tattoos covered the length of his arms, his hair was grey and greasy, his belly nosing greedily out from under the hem of his T-shirt. "Pint?"

"No thanks," said Fitzroy.

He looked her up and down. "I mean, mine's a pint. Black Sheep, if yer buying. Expenses, ain't it?"

She paid for their drinks and brought them over. His face was slightly pink, and as he leaned back into his chair, she saw that he'd relaxed into the idea of this meeting, enjoying the sense of self-importance, the interested glances from the other pub-goers.

"Who gave yer me number?"

"I posted on a message board. Said I wanted to buy a beetle colony. Someone passed on your mobile."

He gave a self-satisfied smirk. "My customers trust me. They know I ain't gonna rip 'em off."

"So, you have lots of customers?"

"I do, all right. Only geezer in the south of England selling colonies, ain't I?"

"Regulars?"

"Sometimes. But most of 'em know what they're

doing, don't need to buy new beetles once they've got a colony established. Newbies, though. They forget you gotta feed 'em to keep 'em alive." He laughed.

"Sold anything lately?"

His face closed down. "Why'd yer wanna know?"

Fitzroy wondered how much to tell him. She decided the truth would net her more than a vague fob-off.

"Two young children have been abducted. We have reason to believe that our perpetrator is using beetles to clean the rabbit skeletons he leaves behind as his calling card."

He stuck out his lower lip. "Can't stand them nonces that take kids."

"Nor can I," said Fitzroy. "So help me find him."

Davenport ducked his head at his empty glass. "Same again, ta."

Fitzroy forced herself to count to ten. This time, she returned with two pints for him.

"Cheers," he said, holding a dimpled tankard in each hand and clinking them together. He slugged down half a pint, and the fluctuations in the muscles of his throat reminded her of the movements of a snake.

"Come on, then. Let's have it."

He licked the frothy moustache around his top lip. "Truth is, business has been a bit slow, ain't it? Always the way, this time of year." He looked at her slyly from beneath surprisingly long eyelashes. "Bit strapped for cash, ain't I?"

God, he was so bloody predictable, but this was a familiar dance and she knew all the steps.

"I might have a little something to put your way. If

you help me," she said carefully. "And Clara Foyle's father is offering a £100,000 reward."

"One hundred thousand smackers. Fuck me." A smile hijacked his face, and he took a long swallow, finishing his pint.

"Fuck me, indeed," she said.

"Well, if you're asking . . ." He snorted. Fitzroy couldn't be bothered to challenge him. She'd asked for that.

She scraped back her stool. Her stare was granite.

"Look, Mr. Davenport, if you can't help me, I've got better things to be doing. Like trying to save the lives of two children."

He held up his hands. "Calm down. I'm jus' messin' wiv yer. Look, I've only sold one colony in the last coupla weeks. To some guy. Dunno his name."

"What did he look like?"

"Old, ain't he? And tall. Six foot one, maybe. Silver hair, skinny."

"Did he pay by check?"

"Strictly cash, innit?" Davenport looked awkward. "You ain't gonna tell the Revenue?"

"I'm not interested in that," she said, trying and failing to quell the impatient tone that was creeping in. "I want to know more about this guy. Did he say what he wanted the colony for?"

When Davenport rubbed his hand over the stubble of his chin, it made a rasping sound. "I don't ask me customers for their life histories, but he might have mentioned something. Can't remember now."

He downed the dregs of his third pint, then picked up her untouched bottle of Corona, raising his eyebrows. She nodded. "If yer come back to my place, I might have written it down in me book."

Ordinarily, Fitzroy would not have gone alone. But the team was stretched to the breaking point, and she couldn't afford to wait.

Davenport set the empty bottle on the table and belched. "C'mon then."

Eight minutes later, they arrived at his flat. Alone, it would have taken Fitzroy less than four, but Davenport kept stopping to lean on the park railings to catch his breath. Fitzroy wondered how he managed to stay upright against the gravitational pull of his beer belly.

He lived on the ninth floor of a high-rise tower block, not far from the leisure center. For once, Fitzroy prayed the lift was working. Usually, she couldn't abide the stench of piss and disappointment, but even that was better than walking up nine flights of stairs with Davenport. She couldn't be sure he'd make it to the top without having a cardiac arrest.

"Here we are," he said, his key in the lock. "After you."

Fitzroy stepped in, and her heart stopped.

A bird, with a bridal train of white feathers, was sweeping towards her, its claws outstretched. She gasped, instinctively ducked her head and covered her face so it couldn't scratch at her eyes, but even half-crouched, she felt the touch of tail feathers in her hair, and the sensation made her skin crawl.

She wasn't ornithophobic, but there was something about birds that spooked her. Their glassy eyes. The cruel shape of a beak. She thought she heard its wings flap somewhere behind her, and pressed herself against the wall, braced for the moment it would fly back, its claws catching in the mess of her curls.

When that didn't happen, she dropped her hands from her face. A fox was in the hallway, its teeth bared in a snarl. Its black eyes watched her as she stumbled backwards, trying to find the door.

Behind her, Davenport was laughing.

"Gets 'em every time," he said. He grabbed the bird by its tail, and drew its body back along the wire-and-pulley system Fitzroy could now see above her. "It's triggered when the door opens."

The fox was still snarling, still watching. It hadn't moved.

"They're stuffed," said Fitzroy, heat staining her cheeks.

"That's right. This beauty here is a bird of paradise, and old Foxy is the first one I stuffed. He's looking a bit threadbare these days, but I still love 'im. I like to think of it as me own little collection."

Fitzroy considered Davenport's beer belly and tattoos. *Sometimes,* she thought, *you just can't tell.* Slightly calmer now, she noticed dozens of eyes following her. A mouse climbing the telephone cable. The outspread wings of the magpie balanced on the back of a chair.

The proud ears of a rabbit.

"Right, let's have a look in me book," he said, rummaging in a drawer.

"Where do you keep your beetles?" Fitzroy kept her voice light, her eyes fixed on the soft fur of the fox.

"Over there." He waved an arm in the vague direction of a doorway. "Don't take thc lids off."

The room was quiet and dark, warm, but not hot. The curtains were drawn. Seven or eight large fish tanks rested on a couple of tables, the only furniture in the room. Inside the aquariums were thousands and thousands of tiny black beetles, feeding on the remains of mice and rabbits.

She risked a quick glance behind her. Davenport was still rooting around. She heard the hollow echo of pencils rolling around the wooden drawer, the *clink* of spare coins knocking together.

The beetles. The rabbit. Can it possibly be Davenport? Is he somehow involved?

She was suddenly aware of her own vulnerability, her foolishness in coming here alone.

A sickening, meaty smell filled her nostrils, one she recognized from the most horrific of crime scenes. From the mortuary slab.

Decomposing flesh.

A movement behind her. Above the scent of death, Fitzroy could smell beery air. Davenport placed his hand in the dip of her spine, and dangled the mangled remains of *something* in front of her, pale pink and slippery.

Fitzroy recoiled from it, and Davenport laughed again. It was a cruel sound.

He lifted the lid off the nearest aquarium and dropped it in.

"Takeaway's here, lads," he said, wiping his hand on his T-shirt.

His other hand found its way to Fitzroy's back again, pressing lightly against the fabric of her coat. She resisted the impulse to shake him off. Not before she'd gotten what she'd come for.

"Right," he said. "Where were we?"

"You were looking for your book."

"Ah, that was it."

Davenport drew the tattered notebook from the waistband of his jogging bottoms, where he'd stuck it when he'd found it in the drawer, and flicked through dozens of pages filled with scribbled pencil notes.

"I know it's in here somewhere."

He stopped flicking at a page near the back.

"So, yeah, I found the ol' geezer I was telling yer about. I ain't got his number no more, 'cos me ex-wife borrowed me phone and dropped it in a glass of wine, silly cow, and those spotty-faced bozos at the phone shop couldn't get me contacts back, but I did write something down."

He grinned hopefully at her.

Fitzroy took in his absurd stomach, his balding head, the ladybird tattoo on his arm, and suddenly Davenport seemed less of a sinister presence, and more one of ridicule. She could quite understand how his wife was now his ex-wife, but at his next words, even *she* was tempted to kiss him.

He waved his notebook at her. "It ain't much, but it's always helpful to know who's buying what, in case yer can tempt 'em with another order. I was right. I dunno his name, but he did tell me he works for a museum."

SIXTY-SIX

9.18 p.m.

His hands tremble as he warms the milk in the pan, pours it into her favorite mug. She is still jittery. He does not blame her. So is he.

She calls his name again, insistent, querulous, and he is back in the now of that moment. It's yesterday teatime, and he is arriving home to shining windows in every room, fear biting into him.

In less than a minute, he weighs the risk.

The windows are lit, which means someone is there. But who? The police? Has he pushed his luck too far?

Or has something awful happened to her?

His blood pumps through his arteries, his veins. His lips are cracked and dry. He moistens them with his tongue. There are no cars, though. No flashing blue lights. He starts up the path, his mind whirring through possibilities. But he cannot abandon her.

The fear of discovery drags him down, and he fumbles with the lock. In the face of opposition, Hunter and Howison stayed true to their beliefs, their methods. And so will he.

"Is that you?" Her voice is shrill.

His heart swells in his chest. He hangs his jacket on the peg, puts down his bag, and begins to untie his shoes.

"Is that you?" she calls again, and he hears a rising tide of panic in her voice.

"Yes," he says. "It's me."

"Come quickly."

He lines up his shoes, and goes straight to her bedroom, but his eyes are deceiving him, playing cruel tricks. The bed is empty, the covers thrown back. He hears the *whump-whump* echo of blood in his ears.

"Where are you, my love?" He forces his voice to stay calm.

"The kitchen. Come quickly. Please."

She is sitting, hunched, at the table, her face almost touching the sunflower oilcloth, her stick propped against the chair. A thin nightdress covers her body, and she has managed to reach her robe. It has been two years or more since she has ventured from her room, and the curve of her spine snatches his breath.

He remembers the first time he saw her, smiling up at him from her hospital bed. Before her deformity claimed her completely.

There is something on the table in front of her. He closes his eyes, steadies his heart.

Her face is wet with tears, and her thumb circles the sleeve of her robe, over and over, as if she's trying to rub out the stain of what she has seen.

"I'm next," she whispers. "I'm going to be next."

"No," he soothes. "No, no, my love. No."

"I knocked my drink on the floor. I was so thirsty, and I didn't know when you'd be back." He lets her know he forgives the reproach by stroking her arm. Her fragile body is shaking. "I found it, by the sink. Just now, just lying there, it was." Her voice rises again. "You heard what they said on the radio. It's his calling card. I'm going to be next."

She lifts her glass to her lips. The surface of the water is disturbed by her trembling hands.

"I don't know how he got in. I turned on all the lights down here, but—" She looks up, falls into his eyes. "We should call the police," she mutters.

Pale meat still clings to the rabbit's skeleton, ragged lumps of its skin. He wonders whether the blowflies have laid their eggs yet. If there's death, they'll find it. He should never have brought it here. But he hadn't wanted to leave her alone for any longer, had planned to finish skinning it while she slept, before taking it back to his father's house for his colony to feed on.

But now this. He knows she is like a dog with a bone. She will not let it rest.

"Probably just local kids," he says, "having a laugh. They know you're here on your own. See, it's not even a skeleton. The meat's still on the bone. Someone's having a joke at your expense. A not very funny one."

The milk has cooled now, and he tips in the crushed remains of the pills. If he does not hurry, he will be late for his shift tonight. He carries the mug through to his wife, places it by her bed.

He takes her shaking hands in his own, strokes the yellowing skin, the gnarled nails. He begins to talk to her, calms her until her breath is even and the color is back in her cheeks.

He stirs the drink, lifts it to her lips.

"Leave it to me," he murmurs. "Leave everything to me."

SIXTY-SEVEN

10 p.m.

"Please, Etta. You can't ignore us forever." The thin wail of a baby in the background. "Oh God, he's crying again. Look, I have to go. Call me, please."

SIXTY-EIGHT

10.30 p.m.

"John Hunter was a surgeon, lived in the seventeen hundreds," said DC Chambers, leaning back in his chair and stretching both arms above his head. "Says here, he was born in Scotland but lived in London. Served as the royal surgeon to King George." He peered closely at the screen. "A distinguished anatomist, he carried out dissections on bodies stolen from graves by his assistant, Howison, and collected loads of weird shit."

Fitzroy tore off a nail with her teeth. "What, it actually says 'weird shit'?"

"Hunter was married and kept a collection of living animals so he could study their anatomy. Some people even donated their bodies to him, postmortem, in the interests of medical science. He was profoundly influential in his day."

"I don't think we need to look very far to see that he's still having an influence."

Fitzroy closed her eyes, imagined keeping them closed. Sleep lured her. But Clara and Jakey were out there. Were they still alive? Truth be told, she didn't think so. But she badly wanted answers for their families. For Conchita Rodríguez. Wouldn't sleep until she got them. But those answers eluded her, darting along her neural pathways in a dozen different directions instead of contributing to the more intimate communications between her little grey cells.

The hours, the days, were passing by with terrifying speed. All of them knew that the chance of a happy outcome was trickling through their fingers like water.

Their faces haunted her.

"I need some air," she said.

London Bridge Tube was Sunday-night quiet. Fitzroy placed her feet on the escalator and allowed herself to climb, to become subsumed by the low thrum of moving metal. Her thoughts settled like dirt in the grooves beneath her feet.

Three victims. Two of them with bone deformities. But, if that theory was correct, how did Grace fit in? She had no bone disease, no medical issues at all. But the answers remained out of reach, and Mrs. Rodríguez was still not at home to ask.

Fitzroy stepped off the escalator, turned left, and rode to the summit again. The station was almost empty now, and she was grateful for it. The handrail moved stickily beneath her hand.

Three rabbit skeletons. Found at the woods, the Common, the sweetshop. But none yet for Jakey Frith. What did that mean?

She was certain the cases were connected, but she couldn't make all the pieces fit.

Two messages quoting Ezekiel. A rabbit kidney, and

two personal letters addressed to her quoting the scientific notes of anatomist John Hunter. But was Davenport right? Did his client—a tall, thin man with greying hair who carried the smell of death—really work for a museum? And if so, how many of those could there be?

And then she remembered what Dashiell Hall had told her when she'd e-mailed him earlier. Fourteen hundred staff worked at the Natural History Museum. It would take months of police work to talk to them all. Months and months. And that was just one museum. What about the British Museum? The Horniman? Then there was the Science Museum. The V&A.

Off she stepped, back down the escalator again. Fitzroy drew in a troubled breath and blew it out over the heads of a couple of late-night drinkers who scurried across the concourse below.

Her eyes rested vaguely on the posters that lined the walls of the station, designed to snag the interest of a captive audience.

Posters advertising West End shows, and art exhibitions, and Christmas concerts, the fodder of the metropolis. A dancing girl, the smiling face of a singer, a poster of a skull.

A skull.

Visit London's Best Kept Secret.
THE HUNTERIAN MUSEUM
In the ROYAL COLLEGE OF SURGEONS,
Lincoln's Inn Fields.

In her mind's eye, Fitzroy saw the words he had scratched into paper and offered up with the rabbit bones, heard the rise and fall of Chambers's voice, reading aloud from the book documenting Hunter's medical notes.

The words on the poster swam in front of Fitzroy's eyes, the tinging in her brain as loud and as sweet as a bell.

MONDAY

SIXTY-NINE

7.31 a.m.

He has always enjoyed the way that night segues seamlessly into the glory of morning. He visualizes a giant vacuum cleaner sucking up darkness to reveal the winter white of dawn. There is a bite in the air as he makes his way home from work, the streets unfurling into life: dust carts and milk floats, and a fox slinking slyly behind the garbage cans.

He is dog tired. He will fry himself a bacon sandwich when he gets in. Pour a glass of cold milk. If Vishnu has managed to get himself a new paperboy, there might even be a newspaper waiting. Apparently, they're a bitch to hire these days, banging on about minimum wage and employee rights. When he was a kid, you got what you were given, and you were bloody grateful at that.

There is something special about an unread newspaper. These days everyone is stuck to their iPads, or their mobile phone apps, or whatever the hell they are called, barely looking up to make eye contact with the person sitting opposite them. Nothing beats turning those virginal pages. Once his wife has been attended to, he likes to read his paper, the radio on in the background, sipping at the dregs of his drink, perhaps with a digestive biscuit or two.

Same as his father. Always the same as his father.

Fatigue dogs his footsteps, but he pushes on. Only a handful of streets to go and he'll be there. Food, an hour or so's sleep, and then he'll head out again.

This place has changed in the years he has been here, but he has stayed still. He isn't one of those desperadoes, always wanting to move on to something better. This is something better, as far as he is concerned. He loves his job, the daily human contact, the opportunity. There is a drama to it, more compelling than any of those murder mysteries on TV, and it encapsulates the ebb and flow of life, as constant as the tide, washing up the detritus and the pearls.

But perhaps the time has come for him to move on.

At last he is home. The house is silent. It smells of stale food. He trudges up the stairs, and washes his hands, a routine almost as old as he is.

He flexes his fingers, crooked and misshapen. The cold air is making them ache again, but he is used to it. Another of his father's legacies.

Absently, he rubs at them, and memories submerge him.

He had been down in their basement, and he was eleven, and he had forgotten to wash his hands again. His father had called him up to the kitchen, and he'd found him standing by the table, a smile on his lips, an arm behind his back.

"Sit down."

He had sat, an expectant look on his face. Perhaps

his father was going to give him some pocket money at last.

"Lay your hand out flat."

"What for, Dad?"

"Just do it."

He had done as his father had ordered, the palm of his hand sticking to the vinyl tablecloth. He was used to his father's strange behavior, and his instinct for self-preservation warned him it was safer to oblige. His stomach rumbled. He was hungry.

He was looking at the kitchen clock, wondering if his father would buy chips or make fish-paste sandwiches for tea, when his fingers detonated in a blaze of pain. He screamed, fire shooting up his wrist until the sensation blurred into one pulsating flare of agony.

A claw hammer dangled from his father's hand.

"Next time, make sure you wash them. One finger for every time you forget."

His father had an obsession with cleanliness.

He pads through the hallway, into the kitchen, and lets himself out the back door. The shed is unlocked, and he scoops up a large handful of pellets, which he carries over to the hutch. A warm feeling that he identifies as pleasure engulfs him.

Once the rabbits have eaten, it is his turn.

Still she has not opened her eyes, so he makes one sandwich and one cup of tea. He enjoys the simple act of preparing his breakfast. He picks up the newspaper. More stories about the missing children. Endless speculation about where they have gone and who might have taken them. When he has finished, he carefully washes his plate and cup, and shuts the kitchen door behind him. He dislikes the smell of grease and the way it clings to his hair and clothes. He changes into an old T-shirt and some baggy sweatpants that also smell, not of bacon fat, but of bedtime funkiness.

He sets his alarm. There are things that need sorting out. Like the girl. Today, he thinks. Today. But sleep is whispering its seductive song, and before he knows it, he has crawled into bed and his eyelids are drooping shut.

He wakes an hour later, refreshed but still tired. No more time to sleep, though. No time at all. After a shower, he rifles through his wardrobe and selects his clothes with care. He shuts the front door behind him, and heads out into the cool morning.

SEVENTY

9.54 a.m.

Fitzroy heard him before she saw him, footsteps slapping across the pavement.

"Got here as fast as I could." Chambers panted. "All the pool cars were taken, so I had to catch the Tube."

"Sounds to me like you could do with getting reacquainted with the gym," said Fitzroy, pushing open the door. "Let's get a move on. They're expecting us."

At the sound of voices in the lobby below, the Hunterian's deputy director appeared at the top of the staircase and hurried down. She was small, dark, with a patterned scarf wound elegantly around her head.

"Professor Hayley Abrahamson," she said. "Let's go to my office. We can talk in there."

They followed her back up the staircase and through a small door in the side of a wall. As she entered, Fitzroy glanced behind her, and glimpsed rows and rows of glass jars with specimens floating inside. She was used to seeing dead body parts, but this gave her an odd feeling, as if they were in a state of suspended animation and might spring to life at any moment.

Professor Abrahamson's office was homely, with framed family photos and hundreds of books, haphazardly piled. Her face was expectant.

"As I said on the phone, we're in the middle of a major missing persons investigation," said Fitzroy, "and we're hoping to speak to someone who may be connected to this museum."

"Name?" she said, tapping on her keyboard.

"That's the problem. We don't have one."

Professor Abrahamson's fingers stopped moving. "Yes," she said. "That is a problem. Do you know anything about this person at all?"

"He's older—"

"Well, lots of retired surgeons work here. You should see the looks on people's faces when they realize they're buying a postcard from the world's foremost authority on conjoined twins."

"—and very thin and tall. Silver hair. About six-foot-one. Smells a little odd . . ."

Professor Abrahamson wrinkled her nose. "Doesn't sound familiar to me, but he might be one of our volunteers. I've been off for a while"—she touched her scarf self-consciously—"and only came back to work last week, so I might not have come across him yet. Clive, one of our longest-serving guides, might know. Let's go find him."

Clive was with a knot of tourists, explaining how John Hunter once cured a coach driver of a popliteal aneurysm by tying the artery in his thigh.

"When the driver died just over a year later, from unrelated causes, Mr. Hunter naturally acquired the leg to examine the results of his handiwork." The group tittered in appreciation.

Professor Abrahamson caught his eye. "A word?"

"Why don't you take a look at that fake nose and spectacles, custom-made for a syphilitic woman?" he said, pointing to a cabinet across the way. "She sent them back to him after she remarried. Apparently, her new husband preferred her without them." The crowd aahed obediently, and did as he asked.

Clive moved towards them. "Everything all right, Hayley?" He had toilet-brush hair and a Welsh lilt.

"These are police officers," she said. "We're trying to locate a member of the staff, but he doesn't ring any bells with me." She repeated Fitzroy's description.

Clive furrowed his brow, lending him the appearance of an agonized politician. "Are you sure he works here? He doesn't sound like any of our staff members."

Fitzroy swore under her breath.

"But, to be honest," said Clive, "he sounds like the spitting image of one of our regulars."

"Go on," she said.

"I don't know his name, but he's in here, what, three or four times a week? Keeps himself to himself, you know. Doesn't much like talking to me, anyway." Fitzroy detected in Clive a faint sense of disappointment at a lost opportunity to show off his knowledge.

Frustration kicked its heels against her. Davenport had said his customer *worked* in a museum.

And yet.

There was something about this place that pulled at her, that sat up and demanded attention.

Clive was scratching his head. "I don't like to judge, you know. Lots of our visitors have a reason to study our specimens up close. Trainee surgeons writing a thesis. Schoolkids drawing a picture. But it *is* a little strange. He only ever looks at two exhibits, stares at them for hours on end, he does."

A look passed between Chambers and Fitzroy.

"And which exhibits would those be?" said Chambers.

"It's always Charles Byrne, the Irish Giant. He's seven-foot-seven, you know. One of our most famous displays. Yep, old Charlie Byrne—and Mr. Jeffs."

"Mr. Jeffs?" said Fitzroy.

Clive's face came alive. "That's right. Lived in England, died in the eighteenth century. His skeleton is fascinating. His vertebrae are fused in a curve, leaving him permanently hunched, and he has knots and plates of bone where there shouldn't be any."

Ting.

"Poor fellow. There's still no cure for it today, although advancements are being made, I understand."

"Cure for what?" said Fitzroy, although she already knew what he was going to say.

"Sorry," said Clive, laughing guiltily. "I assume everyone knows this collection as well as me. Mr. Jeffs had a rare bone disease: fibrodysplasia ossificans progressiva. Otherwise known as Stone Man Syndrome."

SEVENTY-ONE

9.57 a.m.

Erdman's eyes were tiny specks of grit, his mouth as dry as dust. He swung his legs off the sofa. The muscles in his back, his neck, ached like hell. His head was thick and fuzzy.

His toes connected with the empty bottle of Laphroaig.

"Shit," he muttered.

He vaguely remembered pouring himself a glass last night, while Lilith slept on and on, and the walls closed in around him. As the heat in his throat spread to his chest, he drank another, and another, trying to loosen the splinter in his chest. He must have crashed out about 3 a.m.

The door opened and Lilith shuffled in, hair unbrushed, her face grey and old. She bent down, picked up the bottle. "That's not going to help, you know."

Neither are the pills you're popping every five minutes. He wanted to shout at her, to shake some fight into her. But he didn't. Because he understood that those pills were the crutch keeping her upright. Kick that away, and she'd come tumbling down, and he couldn't bear to lose her, too.

He made coffee, black and strong.

"Is Belinda coming today?" He liked the family liaison officer. She didn't care whether Lilith was rude or tearful or whether she wanted to sleep.

"No," said Lilith, filling her glass from the tap. "I'm sick of strangers in my home. I want to be on my own."

"What about me?" he said, half-joking.

"Whatever," she said. "I'm going back to bed."

"Lilith—"

She turned back towards him, sorrow staking its claim in her unwashed body, the grooves around her mouth. Framed in the doorway, she looked like a painting. Or a premonition.

"I will find him."

"So you keep saying . . ." She left the rest unspoken. That his grand plans, his ambitious schemes, always came to nothing.

The trudge of her feet on the stairs matched the unhappy beat of his heart.

He was tired of letting everyone down. For once, just once, he wanted to do something right.

But he didn't know where to begin. Or how to find Jakey.

And then he remembered the man who had been following him.

If he wandered the streets, made himself *available*, perhaps the stranger would find him instead.

SEVENTY-TWO

11.26 a.m.

She was running as fast as a rabbit being chased down by a pack of dogs. Her breath came in short gasps and she clutched at her side, pain tearing her features in two. She threw a glance over her shoulder and darted through the trees, one hand on the damp wood as she bent over, sucking in lungfuls of air.

She needed to find her. She scanned the dark woods, calculating her chances of success.

On the right side of her body, in the concave dip of her rib cage, a burn had taken hold, but she forced herself on, her old shoes slapping the forest floor.

He was here. And so was Grace. She heard a scream, and put on a spurt. Every breath became a struggle, until it seemed as if her heart was beating so quickly that the tiny gaps between each pulsation would run into one continuous sound.

She ran into a clearing.

A glint of a blade in the moonlight, and another, and another, and they bit into Grace's skin like the steel teeth of a trap, and then a scream that perforated the darkness, and a low, rattling laugh, and the sounds of insects clicking and feeding.

Fitzroy jerked awake. Even in sleep, beyond the periphery of consciousness, the dead shook her from her dreams. Around her, the overland train rattled and shook. She lifted her head from Chambers's shoulder, discreetly wiped the drool from her chin.

"You look like you needed that." He nudged her gently. "Ours is the next stop."

An image of Grace, her body brutalized, ruined, floated in front of her.

Even in sleep, the dead spoke to her still.

On the platform, Fitzroy hesitated, then pulled her phone from her pocket, praying she would answer this time.

Conchita Rodríguez had been waiting for news for twelve months.

Most mornings she knelt before a framed photograph of Grace, and her late mother's painting of *Jesucristo*, in the shrine that had once been her living room, and prayed that this would be the day. But this was the first time she'd been in here this week. That other little girl's disappearance had unsettled her, and she had gratefully accepted an invitation from her brother and his wife to stay with them for a few days at their home near Bath. At the sound of the telephone, Conchita Rodríguez rose from the carpet, her knees stiff and painful.

"*Sí?*"

"Mrs. Rodríguez, it's DS Fitzroy. Um, Etta."

The pace of her heart picked up.

"I'm so sorry to phone you out of the blue, but as part of an ongoing investigation, I need to ask you for some more information about Grace. I know this will bring back some terrible memories, but I've been through the case notes a dozen times, and I can't find what I'm looking for."

"The memories are with me every day, Mrs. Detective Etta Fitzroy. Your call will not make that any worse."

"Thank you," said Fitzroy.

Mrs. Rodríguez tucked the receiver in the crook of her neck, and with her other hand, struck a match and placed its blazing tip to the candlewick next to Grace's picture. She placed her lips against her daughter's. The glass was a cold reminder.

"This question may sound a little peculiar, but Grace was a healthy girl, wasn't she? She didn't have any illnesses?"

"No, she was strong girl. She loved swimming, net ball."

"Yes, I remember. She was part of the school team."

"Ah, *sí*." Mrs. Rodríguez's voice was wistful. "She couldn't wait to play in school competition the week she disappeared, but her neck was sore and she didn't go. So disappointed, she was."

On the end of the phone, Fitzroy was silent. In the background, the PA boomed an announcement about a canceled train.

"What was the matter with her neck, Mrs. Rodríguez? Can you remember?"

Of course she could remember. What kind of mother did this Mrs. Detective think she was?

"She had been for an X-ray a few days before she

disappeared. Doctor said she could have them removed if they were giving her too much trouble."

"Have what removed, Mrs. Rodríguez? Please, this is important."

"Grace had bilateral cervical ribs, Mrs. Detective Fitzroy. An extra rib on each side of her chest."

SEVENTY-THREE

12.11 p.m.

Lilith ignored the squawk of the bell. She was counting the sleeping pills back into the bottle again.

The flap of the letter box lifted. "Open up. Mr. Frith, are you there? Mrs. Frith? I need to talk to you."

That bloody detective.

Fitzroy rang the bell again, and rattled the letter box. "Answer the door, please. It's urgent."

Lilith shuffled to the front door. Dark brown strands of hair hung greasily around her face, leaching all trace of color from her skin. If Fitzroy noticed she was squeezed into a Spider-Man T-shirt, ages five-to-six, she didn't mention it.

The police officer stepped into the hall, her partner behind her. "Can we come in?"

A bit bloody late to ask that now, isn't it?

"Have you found Jakey?"

"Not yet."

Lilith felt anger catch inside her like a match.

"Then get out there, do your bloody job, and leave me alone."

"I *am* doing my job, Mrs. Frith," said Fitzroy. "This is part of it."

Lilith hitched up her pajama bottoms and shuffled back into the dining room. She'd been dead inside for days, feeling nothing more than a flat kind of numbness, but when she looked into the detective's face, she was floored by the pity she saw.

She saw Fitzroy take in the tablets on the table, then hold up her palm to Chambers, silently warning him to back off. She didn't care that they had seen them. She didn't care about much at all.

"Is Mr. Frith here?"

"He's out."

Fitzroy was fiddling with the camera on her phone.

"Perhaps I can send this to his mobile instead."

"He hasn't got one anymore," said Lilith. "It was stolen, remember? Funnily enough, he hasn't got 'round to buying a new one yet." Her sarcasm was heavy. "He's had other things on his mind."

Fitzroy ignored her. She held her screen towards Lilith.

"Take a look at this man, and tell me if you recognize him."

Lilith glanced at the grainy snapshot of an old man, shook her head, passed it back. Fitzroy refused to accept it.

"Look again, Mrs. Frith. Closely. We have reason to believe he may have been involved in the abduction of your son." She paused, to allow the power of her statement to sink in. "This might help us to find him."

Lilith sank into a chair. She studied the image, more intently this time. Little creases dented her brow.

"Where was this taken?"

"We obtained it from CCTV footage at the Hunterian Museum." A beat. "Do you know him?"

Lilith didn't answer for a long time. A tear rolled down her cheek, and *plipped* onto the screen of Fitzroy's phone.

"I thought I did, just for a second. But now I'm not sure."

"Who do you *think* he is, Mrs. Frith?" Fitzroy reached for Lilith's hand and squeezed it. Lilith didn't squeeze back, but she didn't pull away, either. The detective leaned into her, trying to shore up the intimacy of the moment. "Who *is* he?"

Lilith did not take her eyes from the photograph. Uncertainty danced delicate steps across her face. He *was* familiar. But where had she seen him? Where? The pressure to identify him was bearing down on her, crushing her with its magnitude.

"I don't need to tell you that we're in the middle of a major missing persons investigation. Potentially a murder investigation. I'm trying to help you and your family, as well as another family in extreme distress." Her voice was insistent. "If we find this man, we may be able to find them all."

Lilith thought she might break under the weight of Fitzroy's expectation.

She groped around in the darkness of her memory. She did recognize him. But where from? Where had she seen that narrow face, that long, thin body?

She was aware of Fitzroy's anxious glance, shining on her like a spotlight. Of Chambers fiddling with his watch strap.

The silence stretched between them. Eventually, Fitzroy stood. She had to get back to the office. To get this image printed and circulated.

And then, in her mind's eye, Lilith saw him.

She went very still.

Then she drew in a shuddering breath and squared her shoulders, as if steeling herself to unburden some great truth.

"I have. I've definitely seen him before."

Fitzroy resisted the impulse to cry out, and forced her voice to stay even.

"Where? Time's against us, Mrs. Frith."

Grief, and guilt, and fear were written in the lines of Lilith's face.

"I'm not certain, you understand, but I think I've worked it out."

"Where, Mrs. Frith?"

Her expression crumpled, like a pile of bricks stacked high and knocked down.

"At the hospital. He works at the Royal Southern."

SEVENTY-FOUR

1.01 p.m.

Even as she watched her trembling fingers punching in The Boss's number, Fitzroy cursed herself for not having seen it before. She tried to collect her thoughts into a tidy pile, but they were muddied and curling up at the edges, and refused to be smoothed down.

It was horribly, blindingly obvious.

He was a collector of bone curiosities.

His "specimens" were all patients of the Royal Southern Hospital.

Bile filled her mouth, bitter and burning. The taste of fear. The taste of failure. It would drown her if she let it, because Fitzroy knew *what* he was, but not who, and sometimes that was worse than knowing nothing at all.

The Boss redirected thirty of his officers to the hospital to interview staff and patients. He arrived with several A4 close-ups of Fitzroy's suspect from the

Hunterian's CCTV. He was brisk and focused and determined.

"Let's nail this fucker," he said. "But I want to be discreet about it. We don't want to scare him off."

Fitzroy was dispatched to a poky office on the first floor with Chambers and the hospital's Human Resources manager.

Department heads came and went. None recognized the man in the photograph. Fitzroy felt the first stirrings of panic. Her fingers drummed the table in front of her.

"Bit awkward for you, all this, isn't it?" said Chambers, leaning back in his chair for a better look at the head of Human Resources. "Didn't a couple of bodies disappear from your hospital last year? In fact, haven't you got a bit of a history of vanishing bodies? And now the police are here again, investigating one of your employees."

The Man with No Name waved an airy hand. "There was a bit of a mix-up, but it's all sorted now. We settled with the families out of court."

"Sign a confidentiality agreement, did they?" said Fitzroy.

He smiled thinly, gave her a look that said *I've come in on my bloody week off, so don't push it.*

"Send the next one in," she said.

Clouds were gathering now, the afternoon preparing to give itself over to night. He stuck his head out the door, beckoned someone in. "This is Karen Matthews. She's our Cleaning Operations manager."

A middle-aged woman with burgundy highlights sat down opposite Fitzroy. She smelled of perfume and disinfectant. Chambers perked up, leaning forward on his elbows. Fitzroy nodded at her and slid the photograph across the table.

"Do you recognize this man?"

A couple of seconds was all it took. "Yeah, I know him. He's one of my team. His name's Brian Howley." She picked up the glossy print. "What's he done, then?"

Fitzroy did not hear her final question. Time was slowing, the room fading to a blur. Inside her body, her blood pressure was rising, the veins constricting and expanding to flood her brain with oxygen.

She shared a brief, triumphant glance with Chambers.

We have a name. Halle-fucking-lujah, we have a name.

"I'd appreciate it if you could keep this conversation to yourself," she said instead. "Just for the moment."

The Human Resources manager—she couldn't for the life of her remember his name—handed her a pale brown folder from the stack on the desk. BRIAN HOWLEY was typed on a white label stuck on the front.

"He's a domestic," said the Man with No Name. "Cleaning floors, that kind of thing. He's here at night, been at the hospital a long time, you know."

Fitzroy didn't know. She rather hoped that this Brian Howley might enlighten her. But she needed to find out whom she was dealing with first. She poured a glass of water and wished it was coffee. Or Red Bull.

"How long?"

"Forty years or so."

She heard again the words of retired Detective Inspector Felix Tapp: "*Then Erdman was sick all over the head honcho's office, and they had to call someone to clean it.*"

She tried not to think of the families, of Lilith and Erdman Frith, of Miles and Amy Foyle, of the brief flare of hope she had heard in Conchita Rodríguez's voice. She could not bear to let them down.

"So, he works nights?"

Karen gave a slow nod. "That's right, and the odd day, here and there."

Fitzroy glanced at the notes in the folder. "On the maternity ward?"

"Usually, yes. But sometimes he gets moved around if we're short-staffed."

"Has Mr. Howley ever behaved in a manner that has caused you or your colleagues concern?"

"To be honest, I hardly notice he's there. He doesn't say much. Just gets on with the job. I do know he lives at home with his wife. She's not well, I believe."

Chambers wrote something in his notebook.

"Is he a good employee?"

Karen laughed. "Who is? He's a bit late, now and then. Could do with a decent wash and a squirt of deodorant."

"Is he at work now?" said Fitzroy.

Karen pulled a crumpled rota from her pocket and unfolded it.

"No, he left at seven a.m."

"Due in tonight?"

"Monday's his night off."

"Do you know where he lives?"

"Should be in his file. Near Catford, I think. Or Bromley. Somewhere like that." Karen gnawed at the skin around her nail. "Is that all? I'm happy to help, but I need to get back to work. I've got to leave by six, to collect my son from nursery."

"Of course," said Fitzroy, standing up. "Let us know if you remember anything else, won't you?"

The Boss moved quickly. An elite team of senior officers was put together to raid Howley's address in a few hours' time.

"I want to be there," said Fitzroy.

He rested his hands lightly on her shoulder, looked into her eyes. "I don't think you're ready for that yet."

"I'm fine."

"Fitzroy—"

"I said I'm fine."

"And I said no. I know what this means to you, and I want you in the interview room when we bring him in. But I can't have you in a high-pressure field situation, you must realize that."

Every syllable resonated with empathy. Fitzroy couldn't bear it.

"Don't tell me it's because of last year. I know what I did was wrong, but I've paid for it a hundred times over. I lost my temper, but it won't happen again, I promise."

"You leapt to conclusions, Fitzroy. It was a mistake, yes, but it diverted our attention from the search for Grace." He gave her a pointed look. "It cost me an experienced detective sergeant."

"But I'm back now, aren't I? So use me. Please."

But The Boss wouldn't budge.

"As soon as he arrives in the interview suite, hit him hard. Don't give him room to fucking breathe. I'll keep you updated, I promise."

She waited for him to leave before punching the wall and proving his point.

Evening fell upon the city. The hospital corridors filled up with visitors, laden with carrier bags of sandwiches and biscuits to supplement the mealtime slop. Fitzroy slipped past them all, like a fish swimming against the surging tide.

The familiar tang of antiseptic reminded her of bleaker times. Of that awful weekend she had spent here, alone and bereft. Before David. Before she had properly understood what it meant to be a mother. It was another time, one she had worked hard to lock away beneath the layers of her life.

Unwelcome tears pricked her eyes, and she blinked them away. Crying on the job wouldn't do.

Outside, the cold air hit her like a slap.

They would be planning it now, meticulous, detailed. Who would lead it? Whether to set up covert surveillance first? How many specialist firearms officers to utilize? How soon could they safely move in? Chambers was on the operation. She was not. Despite everything, The Boss was not ready to trust her again. She had let emotion get the better of her during the Girl in the Woods investigation, and he seemed to think she would do so again. She rubbed her knuckles. Perhaps he was right.

Fitzroy wandered across the hospital car park, towards the alleyway that would take her back to her flat. She had a few hours, at least, before she was needed. David would be at football training. She could grab a snack, a shower.

A frost was already beginning to settle on the cars. A

figure hurried past, hood pulled up. The stars were hard jewels against the sky.

And a set of footsteps, echoing across the concrete path.

Her fingers found the keys in her pocket. She turned around, not sure what to expect, but always prepared.

It was Karen Matthews, the Cleaning Operations manager.

"I've been looking all over for you," she said.

Fitzroy released a breath, and let the keys drop back down into her pocket. Karen was pulling a pair of leather gloves from her bag.

"Got Mum to pick him up in the end. She didn't half-grumble, but she loves to see her grandson and I did say I'd bring in fish and chips."

At the mention of food, Fitzroy's mouth watered. She couldn't remember the last time she'd eaten, let alone a decent meal. Karen was now buttoning up her coat.

"Blimey, it's freezing. I'm sure I heard on the radio that they're forecasting snow. I love it when it snows." She grinned. "Or at least I do until I have to drive in it."

Fitzroy gave a smear of a smile. She was tired and pissed off. She wanted to be on her own. Away from this brick edifice of a hospital with its secrets and its sadness. "You said you were looking for me."

"Yes, that's right," said Karen, pulling down her hat over her ears. "I was just about to go home when I remembered something else about Brian Howley."

SEVENTY-FIVE

9.14 p.m.

Lilith was sleeping again. It worried him, this endless sleeping. Like she was shutting herself off from the world until, one day, she simply wouldn't wake up.

Gently, Erdman pushed on the door, peered into the room. Her bedside lamp was lit, a glass of water and an open bottle of sleeping pills resting on the table. She was pale and still.

Time stopped.

She exhaled.

Time started again.

Her breath was slow and steady, but even in sleep, the lines on her face marked out her grief.

He shouldn't have taken off like that. He should have stayed with her. She was prickly, yes. But she shouldn't be on her own. He loved her. He should be taking care of her. Instead he had spent all day walking the streets of the city, visiting his usual haunts, looking over his shoulder. And for what? "*Come and get me*," he had wanted to yell to the widening grey skies.

But the man was nowhere to be seen.

Erdman arranged a blanket over his wife, and shut the door on his pain.

The landing was cold in the winter gloom, Jakey's bedroom door slightly ajar.

An invitation.

He hadn't been in there since he'd walked out on Tuesday. But now he wanted to punish himself.

Erdman Frith was crowned Loser of the Decade last night for failing to protect his only child. The father of one had only himself to blame.

The police had tried to leave the room tidy, but how were they to know that Jakey preferred his Lego models on the windowsill because he couldn't reach the shelf? That his robe was never hooked on the back of the door, but hid the "eyes" of the wardrobe knobs instead?

A guttural sound—base, anguished—tore from him.

Erdman moved around his son's bedroom. He gathered all of Jakey's soft toys, arranged them on his pillow. He folded his Spider-Man pajamas, slipped them into his cold bed.

Picked up his school sweater, flung carelessly across the top of the wash bin, and inhaled its worn, dirty smell, seeking traces of his boy. Threw it, along with his disappointment, into the jumble of unwashed uniforms.

Silence, endless silence, was everywhere.

He looked back at the row of soft toys watching him, and felt a prickle of panic.

Mr. Bunnikins. Where's Mr. Bunnikins?

A compulsion seized him. He must find Jakey's stuffed rabbit. The one he'd had since he was born.

The one he took everywhere with him. The one he *knew* smelled of his son, because he was always teasing Jakey that it needed a wash.

Erdman's fingers groped the dusty underside of Jakey's bed, the gap between the mattress and the wall, behind the toy boxes, the little nooks and crannies of his bedroom, the hidey-holes. Nothing. Where could it be? *Think, Erdman, think.*

Perhaps Jakey had taken it to school. They were allowed, he knew, to take one pocket-sized toy with them. "Pocket-sized" would be stretching it, but it wasn't the first time Jakey's illness had allowed him some exemption from the rules.

He cast around for Jakey's school bag. No luck. Thudded downstairs, to the hall cupboard filled with old coats and shoes and memories.

And there it was. His son's Spider-Man backpack.

Erdman's hands were shaking as he fumbled with the zipper. His fingers closed around a Lego brick, a pen missing its lid, a couple of football trading cards.

But no Mr. Bunnikins. *Did Jakey take him to the hospital?* He racked his brains, tried to remember the soft rabbit, tucked in his son's limp arms.

He checked again, as if, by some miracle, he had missed it. Jakey's reading book. His water bottle. An unopened envelope.

Erdman slid out the white rectangle and stared at the handwriting. It was addressed to Miss Haines, Jakey's teacher. But neither he nor Lilith had written it.

He tore it open, scanned the lies scratched into paper in a hand he didn't recognize.

Fucker. The fucker had been planning this all along.

He grabbed his jacket, laced up his shoes, tucked

the letter into his pocket to show Fitzroy. He would let Lilith sleep on, but his son was out there, and he was going to find him for her.

And he would start with Mr. Bunnikins and the hospital.

A couple of streets away, a family was sitting around a big kitchen table in a beautiful house. Anyone glancing through the window would have believed that the light of good fortune was shining upon them. A lamp was warming their faces, and the expensive artworks on the walls. A young girl was talking animatedly to her parents, hands flying about. The mother was sipping from her wineglass; the father, his head slightly bent, enjoying his girls.

Inside, though, the Foyle family was breaking apart.

Eleanor *was* waving her arms around, but in distress, not joy.

"Where's Gina?"

"Her mother's ill. She's had to go home." Amy almost believed it herself.

"Daddy?"

"That's right, sweetie." He didn't meet her eyes.

"So, when's she coming back?"

Silence filled the kitchen.

"Mummy?"

Amy rose from her seat and put an arm around her daughter, smoothing back her hair. "I'm not sure she is, El. Her mum's pretty poorly."

"She was the only person left in this house who cared about me, and now she's gone, too."

Eleanor had run, crying, from the room. Amy let her

go. She wasn't quite sure what had happened, only that her eldest daughter had been very upset after their argument, and wouldn't talk to either her or Miles. She had her suspicions, of course. Gina could barely look at her when she'd mumbled she needed to return home to Lincolnshire in a hurry, and when Miles had got back from running her to the station, he was wearing that hangdog expression she had come to recognize. She wasn't even sure she cared. She was beginning to realize how disengaged from her family she had become, how she had gradually withdrawn into her own brittle world of manicures and lunches and shopping, and what an empty and insubstantial place it was.

Miles was still sitting at the table, sipping a glass of red and fiddling with his iPad. She watched him for a while, and feeling her gaze on him, he looked up. His eyes were clouded with—what? Guilt, she decided, the color of lust not red, after all, but a pale, watery blue.

She turned her back on him without a word and climbed the stairs to begin the job of becoming a mother to her remaining child.

SEVENTY-SIX

9.37 p.m.

A surly darkness had staked its claim on the room, the threads of twilight spooling through the window long vanquished.

The lamp glow slipped between the gaps of the vertebrae of the skeletons suspended in a crescent shape from the ceiling, illuminating the curve and length of their bones. The echoes of their former lives drifted through his museum like music.

The glass cases in the strange ossuary downstairs were filled with bone deformities, cortical and cancellous oddities, each a tribute to misfortune and pain.

But the bones of these skeletons—hidden upstairs in the attic of this brick box of a house on an anonymous street—were ordinary, unremarkable.

Abandoned.

Night was falling; the darkness seemed thicker, more dense. The faint sounds of traffic seeped in through cracks in the walls.

Footsteps skittered across the floor. Mice, probably.

Shadows moved and danced as moonlight caressed the horizon.

In the room next door, a young boy opened his eyes and coughed twice. He screwed up his forehead in pain. The burn in his lungs was extreme, but his fever had broken, his skin now cool and dry. The ferocious ache in his forearm had also eased. A new lump of bone had frozen his "good" arm against his abdomen, but he had escaped this flare-up with movement in his hand.

Although he didn't know it or feel it, Jakey had been lucky.

He was no longer on the cold, hard floor, but lying on a lumpy mattress with no recollection of how he had gotten there apart from the memory of a young girl's singing.

Jakey's head swam as he sat up, the light from the lamp making him squint. His pajamas smelled stale and unpleasant. A piece of bread with tiny blue spores of mold was on the floor and he tore at it, crumbs spilling from his mouth. The glass of milk tasted chalky, but he gulped it down, and wiped his mouth with the back of his hand, There was still movement in his wrist, enough to feed himself. But only just.

His bladder pulled at him painfully, and he shuffled to the bucket in the corner. Back to the mattress.

He tried very hard not to think about what had happened that morning.

How he had been awakened by the sound of a door opening, and a child's voice rising, asking questions. A low voice, two sets of footsteps, one lighter than the other. No sounds of a struggle, no tears, and then they were gone, leaving behind them the silence of an empty room.

How, in a state of half delirium, he had crawled across the concrete floor, pressed his mouth to the vent.

"Clara?" he had whispered. "Are you there?"

But she did not answer.

She did not answer when he tried a couple of hours later, or when a weak afternoon sun warmed the cold sky outside, or when night spread its stain across the city and the stars hid their light.

SEVENTY-SEVEN

10 p.m.

Clara was not in his cutting room, nor was she in his museum. She was not in the house at all. The girl the whole country was looking for was asleep in ice-tainted darkness in a place she'd never been before.

Mercifully, she would stay that way until the first rays of dawn touched her skin, and so she would not hear the rats who made their home beneath, or the cries of the barn owls at hunt.

When the Night Man had come to collect her that morning, he had promised to take her home to her mother, if only she would drink her milk, then walk nicely down the stairs and into the van.

That was the conversation, the footsteps that Jakey Frith had heard.

Clara had done as he'd asked, even though its warm sourness had made her gag. Despite the fear stippling her insides, she had climbed into that hated grey box, and she had tried hard not to cry.

On the floor of the van, she had found a stuffed toy rabbit, so loved that its fur was rubbed bare in places.

She had pressed its floppy ears against her cheek and wondered if it belonged to the boy in the room next door.

Jay-key.

She hoped he would be okay now that she was going home.

The motion of the van and the effects of the drugged milk lulled Clara to sleep. She did not know that the city's narrow streets had widened into a highway, or that, in turn, the high-rises and advertising billboards forming an urban guard of honor had become trees and lonely, flat fields, bracketed by the sea.

Eventually, the man named Brian Howley had turned left down a lane, the van bumping over uneven ground until it reached a field with a padlocked gate. The rain-dirty sky was vast above Clara's head as he carried her through a gap in the fencing and across the sandy grass to the new hiding place he had chosen for her.

It still looked the same, even after all these years. He fished in his pocket for a small silver key.

The milk she had drunk would keep her asleep for several more hours, but he tied her hands and feet together anyway. He had decided against a gag. Experience had shown him that this field would stay deserted now, until spring, at least. And she had to eat, to drink, until he decided what needed to be done.

He had piled blankets over the sleeping child, and rested his palm against the damp sofa, the scent of Calor gas and mildew in his nostrils. He knew how cold it could get here, but he'd be back just as soon as he had collected the boy and been to the hospital. It was only an hour's drive or so.

He had trudged back to the van then, returning with

a suitcase filled with money he had squirreled away over the years and a plastic carrier bag, stopping briefly to inhale the salted air. He slid the case under the sofa, took a large bottle of water from the bag and unscrewed its lid, slipped a straw into its open neck. Next, he tore open a packet of biscuits. Crumbs confettied the table. He carefully laid out some grapes. She would be able to reach them with her mouth, he was sure.

Instinct was warning him that the police were pressing in, that he was right to have taken the precaution of moving her.

Part of him was sorry now that he hadn't moved them together. But the risk of transporting both children at once would have been too great. The boy could come later, dead or alive.

He watched a flock of redwings strip berries from a hedgerow before scattering into empty skies, caught a glimpse, in the distance, of the sea. She would be safe here. No one would find her.

The daylight was waning as Brian Howley drew the curtains, locked the door behind him, and began his journey back to the city.

And so, as dusk deepened into night and the darkness filled with a different kind of life, Clara slept on, not yet aware that her mother and father were farther away from her now than ever before.

SEVENTY-EIGHT

11.51 p.m.

Erdman sat in the empty cafeteria, watching the hospital staff come and go, helping themselves to a bar of chocolate from the vending machine or a cup of lukewarm coffee. The lights were dimmed, the brushed-steel counters wiped clean in readiness for the breakfast rush. He soaked up the stillness. Ten minutes passed. Twenty. No one noticed a broken father, his head in his hands. At the Royal Southern, it was not an unusual sight.

It was a stupid idea, coming here. He'd nursed this vague notion that he could talk to the nurses, question them about what had happened the night when Jakey had disappeared. But, of course, half the staff would be on different shift patterns now, and he felt awkward interrupting them, knowing that they were busy, that the children in intensive care needed their attention more than he did.

But he couldn't just sit there. The least he could do was look for Jakey's stuffed toy. It had become a sort of talisman for him. As if by finding Mr. Bunnikins, he would somehow find his son.

He would go up to the PICU, ask the nurses if they had found it, check Jakey's bedside locker, just to be sure.

He had no idea that Fitzroy had been searching for him, driven by that *ting,* that urge to confirm that Brian Howley was the man who'd been following him, to rope the loose threads of her investigation into a net of evidence strong enough to hold a killer.

Erdman found the stairs and began the lonely climb to the seventh floor.

TUESDAY

SEVENTY-NINE

12.21 a.m.

No one pays Brian Howley much heed as he walks softly past the beds, pushing his mop over the mottled blue flooring, an unhurried slosh and sweep.

If they do notice him, they see a thin man with badly cut hair and two deep trenches running from his nose to his mouth. A man who looks like he has the weight of the world on his shoulders; a man who needs a decent meal along with a wash.

A man who has slipped quietly into work without telling his manager, even though it is his night off.

Brian has worked the night shift at this hospital for almost forty winters; 1973 seems like a long time ago, and sometimes it seems like no time at all.

His father had wanted him to take the job. Brandished the newspaper in his face. He had been reluctant at first, but his father was most insistent. *Useful*, that was the word he had used. And it was. Especially when it came to selecting their specimens. But Brian has grown to love it, too.

Forty years has taught him a lot. That the roar of the

working day obscures many things, but there is a clarity to the night that suits him. He can listen, and watch.

And, of course, there is Marilyn. Miss Marilyn Grayson. Brian met her in the winter of 1974, and they'd wed six months later. If some days he finds it difficult to reconcile his bed-bound wife with that pretty-eyed girl full of hope, so be it. He is no looker himself, but the thatch of hair and clear skin of his youth had disguised that. Not now, though. Now he is an old man.

Brian has an important message to convey to Namita Choudray, the senior house officer on the overnight shift in the PICU. She must come quickly. Her specialist knowledge in the field of neonatal head trauma is required on Ariadne Ward.

At least, that is his cover story. He doesn't have a message for Namita Choudray. He just wants to visit the intensive care unit again.

Brian can't work out who in their right mind would name a children's ward after the woman in Greek mythology who had led Theseus to freedom after he killed the minotaur, only to be betrayed by the cowardly prince. Surely it would have made more sense to call a children's ward something innocuous—after some type of tree, perhaps, or after a fish. Although there is nothing innocuous about a stonefish or the Japanese fugu.

There is no one at the reception desk when he rings the intercom and waits to be buzzed through. When they aren't busy saving lives, the nurses tend to cluster around the nurses' station, for mindless gossip about celebrities whom no one in the real world gives a toss about. And Monday nights are almost always quiet.

When a pale-faced police constable nips out for a bathroom break, Brian slips past her, like a leaf carried on the breath of the wind.

A student nurse in her dove-grey uniform is writing notes on a piece of paper pinned to a clipboard, and doesn't look up as he walks by. He stifles a cough. Staff are used to frequent comings and goings, and they make it their business to know exactly who is doing the coming and going, but he is in uniform, and anyone curious enough to shoot him a second glance will just assume the team of domestics assigned to the PICU is short-staffed and that he has been sent to ease the burden.

The lights have been dimmed, save for the three fluorescent strips that remain on, day or night. The curtains are pulled around three of the six bays. He hears the soft murmur of one mother telling her unresponsive son a story, and the wheezing breath of another child, but most of the kitty cats are sleeping. Time has a habit of bleeding into itself in the hospital, and the divisions between seconds and minutes and hours, between night and day even, become indistinguishable.

His skin is greasy, unwashed, and when he reaches around to scratch his back, his shoulder blade feels as sharp and hard as flint.

Brian checks his watch. A surreptitious glance at the whiteboard by the nurses' station tells him that the next round of medical checks is due at 12.30 a.m., so he has an opening, but he needs to act quickly.

He refastens a press-stud on the bottom of his uniform and slips on one of a pair of white latex gloves. Its powdery feel makes him shiver. He fits the head of his squeegee to his pole, and pushes it towards the bed in the far corner of the ward.

The curtains, blue and pleated, are half-pulled, giving the illusion of privacy but not delivering it. He is so close he can read the label on them. TREATED WITH FANTEX ANTIMICROBIAL BIOCIDAL PROTECTION. He thinks of the girl, hidden away. Protecting oneself is very important.

Police tape surrounds the bed.

It is quiet now, the children asleep, but he is overwhelmed by sensation. The rattle of machinery, the beep of the alarms, the buzz of the intercom, and the smell of stale air mingled with alcohol scrub. He is alert, watchful.

He puts down his yellow triangle—CAUTION – WET FLOOR—and begins to methodically wipe, moving closer to the bed. He isn't supposed to be here, and he half-expects to find himself quizzed by one of the nurses as to why he is cleaning so late. But he remembers the maxim of his father: *Present yourself with confidence, and you can pull almost anything off.* So he squares his shoulders and carries on wiping, as if it is the most natural thing in the world.

When he is close enough, he glances over his shoulder. The nurses are still talking, their backs to him. The curtains around the other beds remain pulled. No sign of the police officer. He bends, fumbles in his cleaning cart for the cardboard box, and amongst the clean pajamas and Roald Dahl books in the locker by the side of the boy's empty bed, he places the set of rabbit bones.

He shoulders his holdall, and pushes his way through the double doors, straight into the boy's father.

He ducks his head, turns his face away. He does not think the man has seen him.

Brian walks briskly down the corridor, risks a look

behind him as he turns the corner, clashes shoulders with one of those dole scroungers whom Karen Bitch-face has just hired.

"Merry Christmas to you, too, mate," mutters a male voice.

Christmas is a month away, you stupid fuck, he wants to shout. But now is not the time to draw attention to himself. He takes a deep breath, steps into the lift. Nerves are making him sloppy. And he is close. So close.

The small, stuffy room on the ground floor of the Royal Southern Hospital is deserted.

In six hours' time, stained uniforms will be hastily removed and shoved into backpacks; boots, wooly hats, and bicycle helmets pulled free from battered lockers. The end of a night shift. Time to sleep.

In six hours' time, he will be lost amid the general hubbub of shouted farewells and the clanging of metal doors as employees of the hospital, mostly domestics and orderlies, ready themselves to leave.

But not now. Now it is midshift, and there is barely a soul about.

Condensation collects on the tall sash windows and drips in globules from the ceiling. Frozen air seeps through the cracks in the brickwork and hits the rising wall of heat from cranked-up radiators. A weak moon is climbing.

Brian is dog-tired, but he cannot rest yet.

"Never look back," his father said once, in a rare moment of reflection. They'd been on a beach in a dingy seaside town he'd never been to before, a few miles' drive from their camper. He couldn't remember the name of the place now, just the feeling of being there. Could still hear the synthetic symphony of the arcade machines, the *clunk* of the coin drop, the waterfall of coins hitting metal, the smell of them on his hands.

"What do you mean, Dad?" He had finished his doughnut, savoring its greasy warmth, and was licking the sugar from his lips. Then groped in the paper bag for another.

"Regrets ain't worth it. You do what you do. Never look back."

And he never has. Because even as he curses this place, there is something about it that anchors him. If anyone ever asks him why he is still working, he winks and says it's because of the nurses. But the truth is, for all the crap thrown his way, being pressed up against brand-new life, bearing witness to the very start of it, renews him.

But it is time to move on, to find somewhere new. The police are close, he thinks again.

The shithouse for cripples stinks of piss. Shreds of toilet paper litter the floor. Avoiding the moat around the toilet bowl, he discharges his stream into the turd-colored water. He removes the soft cotton trousers, and pulls his top over his head. Unzipping his bag, he shoves his uniform into the top of the pillowcase holding the confidential medical notes of a handful of patients with varying degrees of bone deformity.

EIGHTY

12.38 a.m.

Brian Howley was wrong. Erdman had seen him. Or, at least, he had seen the familiar greying hair, the cadaverous frame.

By the time his body had caught up with his brain, the double doors to the PICU were already closing behind him, and Erdman turned, slammed the heel of his hand onto the EXIT button.

"Come on," he muttered. "Come *on.*"

The doors swung open with maddening slowness, and he squeezed his body through the tightest of gaps. His shoes slapped on the hospital floor. He reached the corner, had no idea whether to go left or to carry on running. Scanned the corridors, but they were empty.

The man's a cleaner.

At this hospital.

Jakey was right under his nose.

Just like my brother.

Ignoring the fading ache from his week-old injuries, Erdman bolted down seven flights of stairs, to the main reception area. Scanned the drunks, and the victims of domestic fights, and the walking wounded. Caught a flash of hair in the hospital security lights.

He ran outside, towards the car park.

An ambulance screamed into a bay at the front of the hospital, obscuring Erdman's view. He dodged behind it, looking, all the time, for the stranger who was haunting his life. His lungs hurt, every inhalation a reproach.

A small white car was driving up to the ticket barrier.

A white car with a familiar driver. Not a grey van at all. Erdman guessed that was parked in a garage somewhere, away from prying eyes.

He strained for a glimpse of the license plate, for a clue to share with the police. Except Erdman didn't know much about makes and models and engine sizes. *What can you tell us about his vehicle, Mr. Frith? Um, the paint was sort of rusty, and there might have been a scratch down one side, but it was kinda dark so it was hard to tell.*

He glimpsed the red blur of taillights turning right. Erdman ran to his own car, dropped his keys on the tarmac. By the time he started the engine, the car had driven off.

"Fuck," he said, knocking his fist against the door.

The wind was lifting, sending clouds scudding across the sky. He imagined the darkness tightening around him. His son's life could hang on the decisions he made in this moment.

He pressed down on the accelerator.

Erdman caught up with him at the traffic lights in

Rushey Green, slid as low as he dared in his seat. What the fuck was he doing? He wasn't a hero. He had no phone, no means of contacting the police. But he couldn't let that white car disappear.

Let the follower become the followed.

EIGHTY-ONE

12.59 a.m.

The trees were stripped down to their rafters, and a bitter wind exhaled across the sloping landscape of the park. The dark had settled in for the night, turning bushes into indistinct smudges. A moon was rising in the cloudless sky.

From where she was standing, Fitzroy could just make out the office blocks of Canary Wharf, rising from the ground like monoliths. A plume of steam curled up from One Canada Square, once the tallest building in the City and now surpassed by the Shard. The traffic of the A2 was a distant hum. Even the march of the seasons could not dent Greenwich Park's beauty.

She had gone straight from the hospital to the Major Incident Room, but had sat there, feeling pissed off and useless, wondering where the hell Mr. Frith was, and mulling over the woman's words.

"It's probably nothing," Karen Matthews had said when she'd found Fitzroy in the hospital car park, "but I wondered if you knew about the house."

"The house?"

"Yeah, I'd forgotten all about it, but I was sitting in my office, thinking about Brian and how little I knew about him, when I remembered something that happened last year."

"Go on."

Karen's face had been illuminated in a whitewash of light from a passing car's headlights. "He didn't turn up to work for three weeks. No explanation, no phone call. Nothing.

"In the end, I went to see him. Looked bloody awful, he did. Turned out his father had died. Well, he looked so crushed, I felt sorry for him. I knew his wife was ill, so I offered to help him clean out his father's place, said I could send a team from the hospital, if he wanted. On the quiet, mind."

Karen's face tightened. "He starting shouting at me, said it was none of my business, that the house was his now, and he would clean it out in his own"—her nose wrinkled in distaste—"*cunting* time." She had tutted. "He hardly spoke to me for months after that."

His father's house.

A perfect place to hide things that needed to stay hidden.

Using Howley's date of birth from his personnel file at the hospital, Fitzroy had scrolled through the database containing birth records and found his father's name. From there, it had been easy to trace an address for Marshall Howley on the electoral roll. Being Fitzroy, she also ran a credit check through Experian, searching for Brian Howley's previous addresses.

There was only one. They matched.

Her instincts sang to her, the orchestra in her synapses striking up its overture. She had to rule it out. For her own peace of mind, if nothing else.

Telling no one, she had slipped out of the office five minutes later.

Fitzroy began to run again. It was so dark she could barely see anything, except the soft explosions of her breath hitting the air.

She should call it in. She should. But The Boss had made his feelings clear, and he would pull her off the job. Karen was right, it was probably nothing. If she was quick, she could check it out, and still be back in time to interrogate Howley.

Her coat was damp and heavy, her skin chilled by the wind's cruelty. She thought she sensed movement behind her and turned sharply, but all she could see was the moon's glow as it seeped between the gauze of the trees, illuminating branches shaped like capillaries.

She gazed into the distance, across the sprawling lights of the City.

No one would judge her if she walked away now. She could start a new life. As a florist. Or a librarian.

Clara might already be dead. Grace undoubtedly was, too. And Jakey? His illness would kill him, even if this collector of bones did not.

Why should she risk her career a second time by acting without sanction?

Why should she risk her life?

But she already knew the answer.

Because the judgment of others did not matter. She would judge herself. Because she wanted a life free from the burdens of conscience. Because it wasn't about her at all. It was about giving a young boy and a young girl the chance to survive. Families, the chance to rebuild.

She listened to the whine of the wind, and she shivered.

EIGHTY-TWO

1.01 a.m.

Brian lets himself into his home and breathes in the smell of his other life: furniture polish, disinfectant, and overcooked mince.

He knows immediately that she is at rest; the house is waiting for *him*, he can sense it, and it relaxes now that he is back, creaking and shifting a welcome. But he must not get too comfortable. It is almost time. No getting away from it, no shirking of responsibility.

It is his duty.

His hip aches, and he wobbles slightly as he pulls off his shoes and throws them against the wall. He limps down the hall to the kitchen, where he dumps his holdall on the imitation marble worktop.

Arthritis, perhaps. Or the strain of the last few days. He isn't sure. All he wants is a long, deep bath to ease his bones, to wash away the grime of this longest of days from his tired body, but he knows that isn't possible. Not yet.

Truth be told, he is worried.

That nasty business with Marilyn and the rabbit

skeleton has unsettled him. Reminded him of his fragility. Of his vulnerability.

And he saw the police at the hospital on his way into work, walked right past Karen Bitchface Matthews in the car park, spilling her guts to that plod bitch Fitzroy.

He does not know when they are coming. Only that they will.

He should leave, he thinks. There is nothing to keep him here. He could box up his collection and never look back.

But first, he must move the boy.

Or kill him.

To plunge in the knife.

To unveil the beauty beneath his skin.

His brain is tired, but he needs to think. He floods his garden with light, goes outside to attend to his rabbits. He spends time cleaning the hutch, refilling their water bottles, laying down fresh straw.

When he is finished, the house is still in darkness. He goes into the kitchen and warms a can of soup in the pan, and carries it into her room.

The elastic of her faded eye mask is stretched so tightly across her forehead that a lip of flesh curls over its edges. Her skin is pale. Beneath the mask her eyes are open, but they no longer see. Marilyn will never see anything again.

He sits on the chair and spoons soup into her mouth. It trickles back out again, and he mops at it with a napkin.

"Now, now, my love. You need to keep your strength up."

She does not answer.

He walks back down the long corridor of years they

have spent together. How they loved to talk, to laugh. It was a lifetime ago.

Winter 1974. He sees her in that hospital bed, her eyes alight with hope when he stops by to chat, pain not yet leaving its mark on her face. Juniper Ward, it was called then.

He sees her on their wedding day. A bride in a homemade lace gown, and a bouquet of red and white chrysanthemums.

He sees her laughing up at him, the wheelchair not diminishing her beauty, but magnifying it.

He sees her sadness at never becoming a mother.

He sees her bending under the weight of the scoliosis, like a sapling in the wind.

He sees her now.

Her eyes are open, and they have not changed.

"I love you," he says, and brushes his thumb across her cool, dry cheek. Together, they slip into the worn slippers of silence.

He finishes the soup and washes his bowl. Even though it is late, he cannot relax. Thick curtains keep out the night pressing up against the window, but his ears strain continually for a knock at the door.

Eventually, he climbs into her bed. Her body is cold, and even the warmth of his arms is not enough to chase death away. He shuts his eyes. He will rest for an hour before the toil of the night begins.

The dog next door is barking and his bladder is sending urgent signals to his brain, but he is reluctant to leave his wife, although he knows he must. The forecasted gale has arrived, and with it sleety rain that thrums hard against the roof. He hasn't got 'round to fixing that leak, and soon it will drip into the spare room. He should get up and find a bucket.

It had been raining like this the night his mother had vanished. He was ten. Sylvie. Silver Girl. He still remembers the feel of her warm hand; her yellow boots splashing in the puddles; her smile bright under her rain hat, like a sunflower in a storm. And the hole of her absence burned into the backdrop of his life.

"She's gone." His father's voice had been brusque, unflinching. "S'up to me to make a man of you now."

That night, he'd assisted his father in the cutting room for the first time.

Brian is concentrating very hard on ignoring another, more insistent pull. It pokes at him, forcing him to take notice. He sighs and swings his legs out of bed, carefully, so as not to disturb her. The blood rushes from his head, and a fizz of stars sashay around his brain. He closes his eyes and waits for the sensation to pass.

The house is freezing. She doesn't like the heating on overnight. It makes her knees swell and her legs kick restlessly at the covers. He shuts the door quietly behind him.

The light on the top of the fridge casts a greenish tinge over the kitchen as he runs a glass of water from the tap and leans against the sink to drink. He thinks about making a sandwich. Or putting on the fire in the sitting room and reading what is now yesterday's paper. Delaying tactics. He does not want to leave her behind. But he can see there is no other choice. Time is pressing on. Sacrifices must be made.

The clothes are hanging neatly in a plastic bag on a

hanger in his study. Working quickly because he is cold, he strips off his pajama bottoms and pulls on black trousers that hang loosely around his waist. A white shirt. Black pin-striped trousers. A pair of black shoes with a pointed toe. A chain around his neck. His holdall, and the smell of death in his nostrils.

As he slips out of the room, he catches his pale reflection in the glass. The Bone Collector stares back at him.

"Good-bye," he whispers. "Good-bye."

EIGHTY-THREE

2.41 a.m.

Erdman almost missed him. If it hadn't been for the dog barking, he would have still been asleep, under the old blanket that Lilith insisted they kept in the trunk of their car.

He was cold and uncomfortable, and the most sensible course of action would have been to drive to the nearest police station and tell them everything he knew.

But Erdman had never had much time for sensible, and some instinct had told him to wait. That if this was the man who had taken his son and Clara Foyle, that if there was a chance they were still alive, he would not be holding them in this poky bungalow with its postage-stamp garden, and neighbors crowding in on either side, and no sign at all of a garage or a grey van.

No, Erdman would watch and wait, and choose his moment to confront the man with care, even if it meant staying here all night.

He did not want to scare him off before he had found his son.

Erdman stretched, bumped his knee on the steering wheel, and wished he was wearing a thicker jacket. The moon hung over his car, sharing her light. Frost was furring the ground. And he saw a flicker of movement from the corner of his eye.

His heart began a blast beat in his chest.

The man was walking briskly down the opposite side of the street, a bag in his hand. Erdman slipped from his car and into the night.

EIGHTY-FOUR

2.44 a.m.

The unmarked vans slid slowly into place. An operation involving armed officers took several hours to authorize and prepare, and The Boss knew that this was their one chance, their opportunity. In a nutshell, they couldn't afford to fuck it up.

Of course, he could have handed it over to the night shift. But, as on every one of the ten nights since the first child had disappeared, he'd found himself unable to relinquish his command. Sleeping, warm and safe, in his own bed just didn't feel right until the missing victims had been found, and so he'd been surviving, like Fitzroy, on a few snatched hours here and there.

Fitzroy.

One of his very best officers, gave the Job everything. And yet she seemed intent on screwing up her career. He'd gone out on a limb last year, speaking up for her. She had narrowly escaped an assault charge, and then that scumbag had gone to the papers.

He knew why she had done it. The guy was a registered pedophile living a couple of streets from Grace

Rodríguez's home, who had admitted to walking his dog in Oxleas Woods on the day she had vanished, and there was not a soul to vouch for him.

She had put two and two together, and made five.

She was lucky to have kept her job, but he didn't feel ready to put her out in the field again. Not until he was sure she could be trusted.

The officers in his van were talking in low, strained voices. The air zinged with tension. He checked his stopwatch. He was getting nervous, wasn't sure if he had been right to suggest they wait as long as they had. But he preferred to hit a suspect when they were unguarded, at their most vulnerable. Even so, he'd decided to bring the raid forward by an hour. It was almost time.

With a bit of luck, Brian Howley would be fast asleep, enjoying his night off. With four vans and a phalanx of officers, he wouldn't stand a bloody chance.

The Boss had no way of knowing that his target had slipped out his back door just seven minutes earlier, and was, at that moment, only two streets away from his father's house.

The Boss checked his watch again, and this time, he gave the signal.

EIGHTY-FIVE

2.46 a.m.

A suit and tie is the perfect way to dress. With polished black shoes. A bow tie is too much; sneakers and jeans too scruffy. But a black pin-striped suit, with a dark tie and a crisp white shirt, gives off the correct air of authority, of control. It practically begs for respect.

He has chosen with care. It is important to look his best. A curious contradiction, but the way he dresses makes him both stand out and slip under the radar.

Sleet needles his face, but he barely notices. He shivers, not at the cold, but at the prospect of what awaits. He does not see the father a few steps behind him, walking in the shadows.

The air smells of sulphur from the fireworks unleashed by those scumbag teenagers who hang around the park like dog turds. Bonfire Night has long passed, but they seem to gain some kind of sadistic pleasure from letting them off anyway.

He wonders what they would do if he showed them the scalpel secreted in his jacket.

Tonight, he will finally begin the unveiling of the boy's skeleton. Perhaps a little hydrogen peroxide to whiten the bones.

And then. His collection will be a glorious sight to behold.

He thinks of his wife, and sadness spears him.

She was twenty-seven when they met. Those eyes, that gleam of a grin. The wards had been bigger then; the matron's standards stricter, more exacting. Two months after the general election when old Wilson had won by a nose. When London was a city looking over its shoulder. When bombings and strikes and decaying morality were the workaday fabric of life.

The ward had been sleeping. Until she had asked him his name. He had spun around, surprised out of silence.

"Brian," he had said.

"Hello, Brian."

Her smile was as crooked as her spine.

It had started there, and it had never ended.

But his collection is all he has left now.

He hurries on, through the discarded wrappers and cigarette butts, through the gaping night skies. It is so close he can almost taste it, the balm that will soothe the dreams as cracked as his lips.

EIGHTY-SIX

2.47 a.m.

If Fitzroy didn't get some sleep soon, she would grind to a halt, like an inferior Duracell Bunny whose cymbals gradually slowed down and stopped clashing altogether. She'd been awake for too many hours to count, and her eyes were gritty and bloodshot. By rights, that famous adrenaline buzz should have kicked in by now. Dead or alive, she was desperate to find them all: Clara, Jakey, and Grace.

PC Angela Carpenter had filed an alert as soon as she'd come back to her post and noticed the hospital locker slightly ajar.

Another rabbit skeleton had been found, amongst the boy's pajamas and books. The macabre and the mundane. Another quotation. *"Can these bones live?"* The words made her shiver.

It was the confirmation that Fitzroy needed, the line connecting all the dots. Brian Howley had motive and opportunity.

And he was taunting them right under their noses.

No bodies had been recovered yet, but she knew it was only a matter of time. A serial killer was harvesting children with bone deformities; she just couldn't officially say so yet.

Professional desire usually sharpened her brain, but not tonight. Her body felt heavy, plaited together with fatigue, desperation, and hope.

They would be raiding Howley's home within the hour. And she, Fitzroy, would be waiting at the station to interview him, just as soon as she had satisfied the *ting* that was telling her to check on his father's address. It was probably a dead end and The Boss would be none the wiser, but she couldn't have stayed at the station twiddling her thumbs and doing nothing while she knew the operation was underway. That was the thing about dead ends: there was no way out once you started down them.

As she navigated the short distance along the road, Fitzroy stared at the shop fronts that blurred and wavered in the rain. She couldn't wipe the image of Jakey Frith from her mind. The nub of his shoulder blades, protruding like unformed angel wings. He was only a baby.

Death was cruel like that, brutalizing life's ordinariness. One day it was all packed lunches and swimming lessons and playdates, and then, just like that, it was over. A scooter. A reversing car. A killer. And *bang*. No more hot, sticky hands to hold. No more kisses to lavish. No more clatter and clutter. No more noise except the roar of silence, day after day, week after week, long after the well-wishers had returned to their own families and a new kind of half life had begun.

She thought of her own wound, how it had scabbed over but how the scar was vivid still.

The pain of loss could consume you, if you let it. For some unfortunate souls, once it held you under, it never let you back up for air. All these years later, she could breathe again. But it had been a close call.

She should have protected Jakey, and guilt lay across her like a crown of thorns.

The streets were quiet. A weak moon was trying its best to cut through the damson skies, but it soon gave up, and let the clouds subsume it.

Still she kept walking, past the late-night kebab shops and the doorways inhabited by the dispossessed.

Her feet hurt, and she was very, very cold, but she preferred to avoid the bureaucracy of signing out a pool car, the questions and the sympathetic glances. She sat on a bench outside Saint Mary's the Virgin, the church near High Street, and watched the cars flash by.

Her thoughts touched on Nina, and her new nephew, Max. On David, and the deadweight of their marriage. On the lonely, lost souls of Clara and Jakey. On another night like this.

The ground was uneven, strewn with twigs and clods of mud, and she stumbled along, deeper into the murk.

Fitzroy had not wanted her to come, it was much too dark, but Conchita Rodríguez had insisted. She owed it to her daughter, she said.

They pressed on, into the dark tangle of trees. The autumn leaves had fallen, leaving them naked and exposed, but the moonlight was too weak to penetrate the branches.

Fitzroy's flashlight bobbed as she walked. Mrs. Rodríguez did not speak.

At last, they reached the white tent, the police tape strung around the trees like a grim festival bunting.

The wind was rising, and had blown away the clouds obscuring the moon. In a shaft of silver beneath the lonely branches of a wild serviceberry tree, Mrs. Rodríguez had gazed upon the place where her daughter had faced darkness, and collapsed, in supplication, on the damp, decaying earth.

Fitzroy rose to her feet again.

The heels of her shoes squeaked against frost-tinged pavements. She visualized herself as a heat-seeking camera, searing through the red bricks of the Victorian terrace houses that choked this part of the capital.

She patroled the streets until her feet were a mess of blisters, and then, all of a sudden, there it was.

The house was unprepossessing, ordinary, anonymous. She loitered by an alleyway opposite. In between the whip of the wind and the distant rumble of traffic from the A21, she focused her mind.

She was just deciding how best to proceed, whether to break a window or scale the fence and look for a back door, when she noticed a slight figure scurrying up the garden path.

She shrank back against the wall. At first it seemed he hadn't seen her, but then the hand holding a set of keys dropped to his side, and he turned away from the house, scanning the nighttime street. He took a step towards her and paused, and Fitzroy, whose legs had turned to water, exhaled, not in relief, but as a way of expelling the fear that had built up inside her like a geyser ready to blow.

His eyes were black, and unflinching, and when they met hers, she glimpsed in them a knowledge of unspeakable horrors. She tried to turn away, to run from this dark man who walked in step with death, but his gaze mocked her, and she found herself unable to break away.

He moved across the street towards her, and the skies above her sulked, and the wind stopped, and it seemed as if the night would swallow her up.

Fitzroy let out a cry, and stumbled into the alley, looking for a cut-through, a way out, but it was bricked up and lined with overflowing rubbish bins, and so she pressed herself against the damp roughness. And then he was there, his sour breath in her face, a scalpel in the spokes of his hand.

His voice was soft and courteous, conversational. "Detective Sergeant Etta Fitzroy, a pleasure to meet you at last."

She didn't answer. Couldn't.

His eyes watched her.

"Did you know that as Grace lay dying, she cried out for her father, and she barely mentioned her mother at all?"

Fitzroy had known fear before, but this was a visceral dread that turned her stomach inside out and made her heart clench. This man, the *texture* of him. He wore Grace's death like a badge of honor.

"I'm going to go now," she said. "Let me pass, and I'll walk away, and I won't look back."

He cocked his head, appraising. "I don't think that is going to be possible."

In that fragment of time, when knowledge became

understanding, Fitzroy saw that her future was already decided.

The man twirled and spun the scalpel with such speed that it became impossible to distinguish the dull flatness of the blade from the monochrome November night. Like an archer, he drew back his weapon and brought it up in a graceful arc. It slid precisely into Fitzroy's chest, between the seventh true rib and the eighth false rib.

Her mouth opened to scream, but all that emerged was a sort of strangled grunt. She staggered against a bin, and something wet and rotten leaked onto her skirt, and she fell forward, the pavement skinning her knees.

He loomed above her, his blade raised high, triumphal but determined. He slashed at her arms, tearing through the fabric of her coat, and fire blossomed inside her. Fitzroy opened her mouth to scream again, to scream until her throat was raw, to scream until he disappeared into the dove-colored shadows.

But then a simple thought presented itself to her, and it was so bold, so different from the course of action that she ought to take, that she knew at once it was right.

She immediately went limp, holding her breath. The scalpel hovered uncertainly above her, and then he lowered it, and in the pallid moonshine, he hoisted her body over his shoulder and carried her into his father's house.

When Fitzroy opened her eyes, her cheek was squashed flat against the wooden floor and a dank smell was filling her nostrils.

She pressed her face against its cool hardness. It calmed her, lying there in the dark. Her side was badly bruised, but her armored vest had protected her from the bite of the blade. Faring less well was her arm, which was wet and sticky and hurt like hell. Her mobile and radio were gone. She stared at a spot of mildew on the wall and forced the pain away.

The room was small and rectangular-shaped. The walls were made of brick, as exposed as the human skeletons that were arranged around her in a semicircle. She gaped at them. Their bodies, stripped down to the bone, were suspended from the ceiling by metal poles screwed into their skulls.

But her ruse had worked. Her hands were untied and she was lying on her side in a room with a heavy door. Butterfly wings brushed her insides.

It was freezing, and she rubbed the goose bumps on her upper arms. The gesture pulled at her wound and made her wince. Blood had puddled on the floor beside her, and it smelled like the coins she had collected in a whiskey bottle as a child.

Science had as yet found no way to quantify fear, and neither had Fitzroy. Some insisted the body's blood ran cold; others, that the human heart sped up until it burst from the chest. Fitzroy thought neither of those was quite right. For her, fear was the prickle of anticipation, the cool wash of sweat in the hollow between her shoulder blades, the *knowing* that evil was at work.

She wondered whether she was looking at Grace Rodríguez's bones.

Fitzroy drew in a breath, tried to steady her nerves, to think clearly. She was in a room in a house of the dead, and no one knew where she was.

But a little voice inside told her that Clara was probably here. Jakey, too.

She just didn't know whether they were alive.

Fitzroy forced herself onto her knees, crawled painfully towards the door. She had to try to find them, to find some means of escape.

But her strength was fading, the adrenaline that had kept her going trickling away to nothing, and she could hear the rasp of her own breathing. She needed to get to a hospital. The wound on her wrist had clotted, but the effort of moving had reopened it, and she was losing blood again.

She pushed against the door, but it was locked.

Fitzroy's face was now so pale that it was as if she was frozen in the glare of the moon. She lay down on the floor, just for a little while.

"I need to move," she murmured. "It's not safe."

But there was nowhere to move to. Nowhere to go.

Silly girl.

Fitzroy was a rat in a trap.

EIGHTY-SEVEN

3.03 a.m.

Erdman heard a scream; he was sure of it. A woman's scream. Like she was in pain or something. He hesitated, ducked behind a parked car, and watched.

"F-u-ck."

Under the orange glare of the streetlight, he could see the man carrying a woman into the house. A woman with the same coils of hair as DS Fitzroy.

Erdman knew he had two choices: to knock on the door of one these sleeping houses, to find a phone, call the police, and spend precious minutes waiting and explaining, letting someone else make the decisions and take control.

Or he could do what he had never done before.

What his heart was telling him to do.

He was here, right *now*, and he could do something useful. He could help Fitzroy and find his son.

Erdman ran around the side of the house, looking for a way in. Found a garage door, its paint peeling. He twisted the handle, felt it loosen and lift. The noise was like the crash of drums, and it stilled him. He pulled it down slowly behind him.

It was dark inside the garage, and Erdman had to put his hands in front of him to feel his way. Connected with shiny metal. A van.

He knew, even without light, that this was the van the police had been looking for.

He crouched in the darkness, waiting. But the house stayed silent, watching for his next move.

A minute passed. Then two. Erdman grazed his hands along the wall. Cinder blocks. A shelf. The smooth surface of an internal door.

EIGHTY-EIGHT

3.07 a.m.

Lilith was huddled beneath a duvet that held the fading imprint of Jakey's smell.

The tip of her nose was cold, and she could see the clouds of her breath. The boiler was acting up again, but she didn't know how to fix it. Erdman usually took care of that, but she had been asleep for many, many hours and hadn't seen him since breakfast. He had gone out, she knew that much. She had heard the door slam. And now his side of the sheet was smooth, untouched. He'd probably gone to bed with the whiskey bottle again.

She should do something about it, but she couldn't find the energy to move. She couldn't find the energy to do anything except lie there, and remember the life she'd once had. A life she had railed against, and would now sacrifice anything to live again for one more day.

She fingered the photograph in her hand, the one she took to bed and to the bathroom, the one she carried in her robe pocket. The one beginning to soften and fray at the edges.

"I'm sorry. I'm sorry I didn't look after you." A tear leaked down her nose. Then another.

"I miss you," she said, in a voice as broken as glass.

Six years ago, they had brought him home from the hospital. A tiny scrap whose life was now their responsibility.

She remembered that first walk, that fear of everything: the cars thundering along the road, the shouts of workmen disturbing his sleep, the rain on his upturned nose.

How Erdman had held up a hand to stop the traffic so his wife could push the carriage to safety.

A father's smile of pride and joy.

And then Jakey had woken up and screamed all the way up the hill, his cries getting louder and louder. Lilith had panicked. What if he was crying because he was in pain? Because this terrible disease was already laying claim to his body?

She had scooped him up and run into their house, tears sliding down her own cheeks.

And, because she didn't know what else to do, she had unbuttoned her top and lifted him to her, and he had stopped crying.

Erdman had stared at her then, as if she were some kind of deity.

"He's perfect," he said. "You both are."

And he had been right. In spite of everything, her son was perfect.

But now he was gone.

For Lilith, this newly discovered state of childlessness was not just the tumbling into a bottomless hole. It was much more mundane than that.

It was in the scuffed school shoes in the hall cupboard, the missing place setting at the table, the rooms empty from one echoing hour to the next.

I can't do this anymore.

The air was stale with Lilith's grief; her sweaty, unwashed body; the greasy tangle of her hair.

As the moon sagged in the sky, she dragged herself to the bathroom, pulling Jakey's duvet around her shoulders like a cape. The shadows were contours of grey and black.

He's not coming home. He's never coming home.

Despair, as heavy and black as tar, was sticking to her, pulling her downwards.

She filled her glass with water from the sink. The sink where Jakey had brushed his teeth and washed his shining face. The smell of chlorine was in her nostrils.

If he was coming home, the police would have found him by now.

But he's not.

He's dead.

I cannot hear them say it.

The police.

I cannot hear them say those words.

I will not.

Those words.

Dead.

No.

I will not.

Jakey's waiting for me.

The dark.

He's scared of the dark.

He wants me.

He wants his mummy.

That bleak certainty settled over Lilith like floating

fragments of ash. She shuffled back to the bedroom, her fingers closing around the bottle of sleeping pills on her nightstand.

She thought of Erdman, and the sorrow that would split him apart.

She thought of Jakey, by some miracle, rescued from captivity, only to discover that his mother was dead.

She thought how shock and grief and the sheer horror of it all would hold them both hostage, not just for a few days, but a lifetime.

She thought of seeing Jakey's smile again.

And hope, that sneaking, unwelcome intruder, inveigled its way in.

EIGHTY-NINE

3.16 a.m.

Someone was shaking her, and it took Fitzroy a couple of moments to realize that those violent tremors of movement belonged to her own body. She was shivering and she was in trouble, but at least she was alive.

She rolled onto her side, and something wet seeped down the sleeve of her blouse. She lay still, then forced herself to sit up. Black dots flashed in the air around her head. She counted to seventy before she opened her eyes.

The room was in darkness, the shutters fastened against the moon. A house of sleeping secrets. But Fitzroy knew better. Beneath its quiet façade, the dead were waiting for her. The dead and—please, God—the living.

She had to find them and get out.

She rolled onto her stomach and up to her knees. Placing her palms against the wall, she cranked herself upwards. And then she heard it. A footfall on the stairs. The distinctive *click* of a lock mechanism disengaging.

A whisper.

"Detective Sergeant Fitzroy?"

The door swung in and there was Erdman Frith, slipping an arm around her waist, helping her to stand.

She didn't bother with questions.

Outside the room was a narrow landing, and to the right, a staircase. She stopped to listen for Howley, her heart jumping in her chest, but the house was silent, on pause. Painfully, she eased herself down the steps. They found themselves in a downstairs hallway, with three doors leading off of it. They were all shut. Blood leaked from her wound onto the floor.

"I have to find Jakey," said Erdman.

"Yes," she said. "But we need to get help first."

She tried to get some sense of their bearings, looked around for a telephone, her stolen radio. But all she could see were glass and bones. She stumbled forward, saw a heavy door ahead. Fitzroy could tell a lot about someone from the state of their front door. This one was windowless and the paint was chipped. But it didn't matter. It led to the world outside.

"Let's go," she said, low and urgent.

When Erdman raised his hand to silence her, she thought it was a challenge, but desperation was streaking across his face. From somewhere, the unmistakable sound of footsteps climbing the stairs.

"Hide," she hissed.

Erdman pushed her towards a thick curtain pinned to paneling on the wall before disappearing into the shadows. She crouched down, pressed her cheek against the fabric, risked a look into darkness.

She saw a man, all shadow and bone, rise out of a cellar, cross the hallway, mount the same staircase that she and Erdman had just climbed down.

Silvery light seeped through gaps in the blinds, illuminating the glass cases with their unhappy cargo.

Fitzroy let her eyelids drift down so she did not have to witness the stripped-down bones of those who had suffered, not once, but twice. But not before she glimpsed something in the shadows, just above her.

In the center of the hall, on a raised plinth, stood a cabinet, positioned so that its panes of glass reflected the rise of the moon.

Inside was the hunched, but unmistakable form of a child. Its skeleton was warped, wrapped in sheets and ribbons of extraneous bone. A child imprisoned in life and in death. A child turned to stone.

Ting.

The letter *C* was engraved on a metal plaque. And next to this case was an empty one, waiting to be filled.

Erdman's twin, Carlton Frith. And a space just big enough for Jakey.

NINETY

3.19 a.m.

Brian limps back up the cellar stairs of his father's house. His hip is making a fuss again, but he is too busy thinking about what he will do to Jakey Frith to pay it much heed.

Are the cops waiting outside? He can hear a car with its engine idling, but it's from up the road, he is almost sure of it. When he'd knifed that pig bitch, he'd taken her phone, her Airwave radio.

Slowly, he climbs the main staircase, to the top of the house.

The door to Room One is open.

He steps in, puts a foot in a sticky, viscous puddle. Blood. Lots of it. So, where is she? Brian casts around for some clue to Fitzroy's whereabouts.

A bloody handprint on the door confirms his worst imaginings.

Cautiously, Brian steps back into the corridor, peers over the balcony. The hallway of his museum is in darkness, apart from the wash of moonlight on the bones of the boy. But he can tell it is empty by the way the air echoes.

So, where the fuck is she?

He lingers in the corridor, half-expects the police to hammer on the front door. But there is no sound at all, just the voice of his father, urging him on. And the usual quiet buzzing from the socket on the wall.

If that pig bitch has escaped, she will have to be found.

He starts back down the stairs.

And then he hears it. A gentle *tap-tap-tapping*. His fingers find his mouth, and he gnaws at the torn skin, his eyes searching for the source of the sound.

The sound of bone knocking against bone.

He lifts his eyes upwards, at the pride of his collection. The boy's skeleton is swaying, his forearm swinging against the twisted curve of his torso in a grotesque rendition of someone walking.

Just the wind in this drafty old house.

Except the skeleton is in a locked glass case.

Unless someone had just knocked into it.

Someone like that pig bitch, Fitzroy.

Brian pauses, suddenly uncertain. He wants to hunt her down, to kill her. But he is no longer safe here. He should get moving.

Then, when he is sure he isn't being watched, he will pack up the family's museum and his colonies, and he will run. Find a new ossuary in which to hide his collection, a new hunting ground.

But first, the boy. He must move him now, and then he will harvest the bones.

The first time Brian had seen this house, he had

fallen in love with it. He had been six. The previous owner had led them up a curving staircase, and into an airy room with a projector. "*My cinema room,*" Mr. Thomas had told them proudly. All soundproofed. He had unhooked a hidden cupboard door, and slid out a bank of twelve seats.

His mother, Sylvie, had insisted it must go, every last 1930s original, each with its own pivoting back and plush purple velvet. A crying shame, but she wanted to convert the space into a nursery and playroom. So, his father had ripped out the seats, spent his evenings stripping wallpaper, sanding floors, and painting everything white. Built a false wall to house all of Junior's toys. She used to go up there sometimes, gazing out over rooftops shiny with rain. But the baby never came. After that, she never went up there at all.

Brian moves stiffly back up the stairs, towards the boy, towards Room Three.

He is careful to avoid the creaks. He doesn't want to startle him. Last time, he had cried when he heard him coming. He touches the child's bent arm. Tears are already leaking from the boy's lacrimal caruncle. Almost like he knows what he, the Bone Collector, is planning.

He fixes on the shiny reflection of his eyes in the darkness.

"All right?"

The boy jerks his head mutely, a tiny, insubstantial thing, shrinking into himself until he is almost invisible. His skin is pale from lack of sunlight. Brian examines his own arms. They are the same. White and skinny.

"It's time to go."

His face lights up. "Are you taking me to my home?"

Brian smiles then, nods. "Yes, Jakey. I'm taking you home."

"Yesss." He chews on a strand of dirty hair, eyes him warily. "Now?"

"Yes. But you must be quiet. If you make even the tiniest noise, I'm afraid I won't be able to take you to Mummy. Is that clear?"

He might as well have tapped the boy on the forehead and set him bobbing.

"I will, I will, I will."

"Good. Have you got everything?"

It amuses him, to offer this simple courtesy, as if the boy is a houseguest preparing to leave.

He looks uncertain. "My blanket from the hospital—"

"Don't worry about that, son." Dissolved in acid three days ago, in the cutting room in the cellar, but he need not know minor details like that.

The boy peers up at him from under his lashes, his beautiful bones visible through the thin cotton of his pajamas. The image of them stripped of their skin excites him.

"Let's wrap this around you," he says, and places an old blanket across his shoulders.

The boy stands quietly, awaiting further instruction. Unsure, yes, but Brian smells excitement emanating from him, just like he can smell his fear. Pheromones. He likes that word, likes the feel of it on his tongue.

"Remember what I said about being quiet," he warns, and carries him down the stairs.

He stands there for a moment, listening hard to the silence. Most of the neighbors will be asleep, but there is bound to be the odd insomniac. *Don't get sloppy, Brian*. Even the car with the idling engine has gone quiet.

He opens the side door to the garage, and as quietly as possible, slides back the doors of the van. He winces at the scrape of metal on metal, then jerks his head.

"Get in."

The boy turns to him, his eyes telling him that he absolutely does not want to climb into that dark, cramped place, but his mouth won't move.

"Get in or you won't see Mummy."

The boy makes a small sound, but he clumsily places his knee onto the van's bumper and hauls himself in. With the full weight of his body, Brian shoves hard, and Jakey lurches forward, gouging his forehead on the metal point of a toolbox. He begins to wail, his siren-like cries growing louder and louder. Brian wrenches the doors shut, muffling the sound.

He scans the street through a small window in the main garage door. Still quiet, but at number twenty-eight, a light is now pressing against a frosted-glass upstairs window. He gets into the van and starts the engine. The boy is crying, but the thrum of the engine drowns him out.

He climbs out of the van again, to shut the internal door leading into his father's house.

Brian has watched with interest the newspaper headlines, the unstitching of the families under the world's gaze, the growing agitation of the police. The hysteria over three missing children had heightened his enjoyment.

But this is the climax, the moment he has spent most of his life waiting for.

He had longed for the twin brothers to be reunited.

But this will be better.

Uncle and nephew.

Almost as good as father and son.

And then something catches his eye.

NINETY-ONE

3.22 a.m.

Fitzroy had been lying in an alcove, hidden behind a curtain. After Erdman had pushed her to safety, she had crawled farther into the gap, some instinct for self-preservation propelling her onwards. After Howley passed, she had crawled out again. Dragged herself up the wall until she was standing.

Her blood still marked the floor; the boy skeleton, bones twisted in silent censure, stood still encased in glass.

Then she had heard Howley's footsteps moving above her head.

She hoped Erdman had the sense to stay hidden.

Fitzroy's breath had come fast and ragged. She'd inhaled, used the brief silence to listen to the darkness. Perhaps she should make a run for it. Every nerve ending, every instinct she possessed, was shrieking at her to get out. If Howley found out that she was still alive, he would kill her. But that would mean abandoning the children. And Erdman. She wasn't about to do that.

She had slipped from behind the curtain, headed towards the cellar door. Down the steps, she had gone, to a vision of hell, pungent with death and putrefaction. The rotting-meat smell that pervaded the house was much stronger here, and she'd gagged and stepped backwards, tripping over something that clattered like dry bones. She could hear a clicking sound. Saw bottles of embalming fluid. Tools of torture. A child's purse.

Vomit had coated the back of her throat.

A want so intense filled her up. She would find Jakey and Clara. She must. But where had he hidden them?

Fitzroy was paralyzed by indecision. But indecision was the province of the weak, the enemy of action. It snatched time. It stole lives. And yet. A slowing down was sometimes needed, a sense of measure, of caution.

Memory pulled at her.

After taking Grace's mother on her lonely pilgrimage to the woods, she had guided Conchita Rodríguez, shell-shocked and dull-eyed, to a bench inside the station.

"Stay there," she had whispered to the older woman. "I'll be back."

Fitzroy had pounded up the stairs, ignoring the startled looks from her colleagues, to search the computer for an address.

Once she had dropped Mrs. Rodríguez home, waited for her friend to arrive, she had parked her car farther up the road, and run the couple of streets to his flat.

He had been walking up the path, his back to her, and she had pulled out her old baton, from her days as a uniform, and hit him, hard, across the back of his neck.

The man had folded to the grass, his eyelids fluttering.

For Fitzroy, it was not enough. She stood over him, hitting his arms, his stomach, anything she could reach, and there was a purity to it that cleansed her.

Only when a neighbor had come running into the garden did she stop.

And so it had begun.

The investigation, the media frenzy, the bitter taste of failure.

A mother still searching for her daughter's body, for a chance to say good-bye.

Tonight, she would seek vengeance of a different kind. On the floor was a boning knife, and she picked it up.

Fitzroy climbed slowly back up the cellar steps, holding the blade in front of her. She listened for the sound of his footsteps. Was he still upstairs? Or had he slipped back down while she was searching his underground charnel house? A lightbulb flickered.

Then a voice.

"There was a little girl,

"Who had a little curl,

"Right in the middle of her forehead.

"When she was good,

"She was very, very good.

"And when she was bad,

"She was horrid."

Brian Howley's voice was a singsong taunt as he watched her from the shadow of a side door, a claw hammer dangling from his hand.

"Is this going to take long?" His grin was sly. "It's just that the Bone Collector is in the middle of something."

The Bone Collector. So her theory had been right.

Blood smeared his face, like a scar, and he was limping towards her, his cheeks hollower than usual, as if the flesh was being suctioned from the inside. His skin looked desiccated, as if a gentle tap would be enough to send him flaking to the floor in a pile of dust and dead cells.

The Bone Collector's black eyes were a mesmerizing pool, drawing Fitzroy in like a fish on a hook. There was something familiar in them, but a darkness, too, a shadow in his challenging stare, and that was enough to shake her loose from their hypnotic pull, and remember the task she had set for herself.

"Where are they?" she said.

A buzzing sound. A loud *pop*. A shower of sparks.

The smell of smoke.

The Bone Collector's nostrils flared as he sniffed at the air. A thin arm reached for her, and as his fingers closed over her wrist, a drenching cold unsteadied her. She fought against the urge to sit down. If she did that now, all would be lost. She forced herself to concentrate on the idea of warmth. Long-ago summer holidays in France. The heat of the sun on her skin, the shadow of Mont Blanc. No, don't think of the mountain in all its snowcapped majesty. Forget the cool dip of the valley and the creeping chill of night. Think of the midday burn, the sear of its rays on her face, the clouds of dry dust churned up by passing cars. Think of the forests on fire.

Fire. The word flickered in her mind.

And in the corner of the room, flames began to lick the staircase, grabbing hold of its spindles, rapidly traveling the length of the bannister, catching the varnished wood. Up and up they rose, until the paint on the ceiling began to blacken and split.

The Bone Collector tightened his grip.

Then he lifted his hammer and hit her in the mouth with as much force as he could muster. He enjoyed the soft, wet sound it made.

Fitzroy crumpled, a concertina, her front teeth scattering the ground like leaves.

Behind him, Erdman slipped from his hiding place beneath the stairs.

The fire was spreading rapidly now, catching the mahogany cabinets and the wooden panels at the foot of the staircase, licking the cellar door.

The Bone Collector lunged towards his collection, but the heat forced him back.

He let out a cry of anguish.

The wall of heat was beginning to singe the fine hairs on Fitzroy's face. The heat and smoke would overcome her if the pain in the bloody pulp of her mouth did not. She struggled to sit, eyes signaling at Erdman to go back to his hiding place, to stay away from this killer, this thief of bones.

But Erdman was not looking at the detective. He was looking at the glass case containing the skeleton marked *C*.

The Bone Collector followed her eyes. Turned. Smiled.

"Oh," he said. "A family reunion."

Erdman murmured a promise of freedom to the brother he had loved and longed for all of his life, and shoved as hard as he could.

A scraping sound, the sound of glass dragging against the surface of wood.

Then the display case was tipping.

Falling.

Splinters of glass showered the boy's distorted bones like stars.

"Now, why did you have to go and do that?" said the Bone Collector, and took a step towards him.

The blood in Erdman's veins pumped faster and faster until he thought his heart might stop.

As the man drew closer, and Erdman breathed in his stink, a coldness took root inside him. He had smelled it before, when Lilith had thrown away some out-of-date chicken, but forgotten to empty the trash. The country had enjoyed an unexpected heat wave, and when they came back from their holiday, the kitchen reeked of spoiled meat. It had taken days to get rid of the smell.

Erdman couldn't speak, couldn't seem to form the shapes of the letters in his mouth.

The Bone Collector raised the hammer in his hand.

Erdman lunged, and felt, through the shards of glass and the rising wall of heat, for the twisted skeleton of Carlton Frith. For the briefest of moments, he cradled his brother and then held him high above his head.

"Where is my son?"

The Bone Collector laughed.

Erdman threw the young boy's remains into the flames.

"No!" shouted the Bone Collector, scrabbling towards the heap of bones, which had landed in the center of the blaze.

He dropped his hammer and reached into the fire, dark eyes flashing with fury.

Erdman ran towards Fitzroy, half-dragged her away

from the spreading blaze. Her eyes were closed. The Bone Collector looked back towards the cellar and grinned.

Through the cracks in the door, a cavalcade of undulating blackness swarmed the hallway, driven out by the heat warming up the bricks of the house.

Erdman recoiled as the sea of beetles advanced towards them, thousands of tiny pincers seeking out dead or decaying flesh, the amplification of their movement creating a low-level hum.

They were pouring in now, carpeting the floor, three or four bodies deep. This veil of darkness pressed down on him, paralyzing him.

The Bone Collector lifted a shiny shoe and stamped on Fitzroy's abdomen, and now the fire was inside her as well as out. She fell forward, her face in a mass of insects, crawling inside the mess of her nose, her ears, seeking their own escape from the rising heat.

Erdman grabbed her wrists, dragged her from the beetles, flicking their tiny black bodies from her face, from his own arms.

"I have to find Jakey," he shouted above the roar of the flames. And then he started back towards the staircase, towards the certainty of his own death.

A piece of burning wood fell from the ceiling and struck the Bone Collector's shoulder. He slapped at the collar of his jacket, at the hair at the nape of his neck, his arms as frantic as a hummingbird's wings.

It was enough.

On her knees, Fitzroy tried to crawl back towards Erdman, through the beetles and the intensifying heat. Her jaw was almost certainly broken, but even that was not as painful as the knowledge that his victims might still be inside, that even now their young bodies might be burning, and there was nothing to be done. That if she had told The Boss she was coming here, lives might have been saved.

Her heart hurt at the desecration of the evidence that would help them identify the lost and the missing through the years. The bodies stolen from the hospital's Chapel of Rest. Grace Rodríguez.

But another, quieter voice calmed her.

For the victims, strung up and displayed to fuel the Bone Collector's sick appetites, this was a cremation, of sorts. An honorable farewell.

In the distance, Fitzroy heard the drone of a fire engine, the blare of sirens. A sense of déjà vu washed over her. She lay down on the floor, blistering heat at her heels.

Behind her, the door to the garage slammed.

Then the sound of boots kicking against the front door, the tantalizing smell of fresh air and rain and freedom, and The Boss was helping her to her feet, and she was coughing, and saying Erdman's name over and over.

And all the while, burning rain fell upon the House of the Dead.

NINETY-TWO

3.31 a.m.

He wants to stay and watch the detective burn, fear spreading across her features like a port-wine stain. But he has no choice. He must leave.

Fuck. His hands are marked with blisters, but he ignores the pain. Smoke is in his throat, and he coughs. *Fuck.* In a few minutes, his father's house will be destroyed. His precious collection, gone.

A black hole opens up inside him, and then he's around the back of the van, sliding open the doors. The boy is lying prostrate on the floor, and he pulls out his scalpel. The boy's eyes watch him, but the Bone Collector knows this is not the moment. That will come later. A dirty rag will do for now, and he places it in the boy's mouth, ties the ends together so the gag bites into his cheeks.

His pajamas have slid down, and he sees the white glare of his backside. He yanks them up. It isn't right, an old man like him, looking at a young boy's bottom.

The boy is still, but he is listening. Brian can see it in his heaving shoulders, the rise and fall of his chest.

"Can. You. Hear. Me?" he says. The boy doesn't reply. *Kids, eh? What can you do?*

But they must leave before the police find them and the whole place comes down.

His fingers are slippery with sweat, and he wipes them on his trousers. Hears the boy mumble something.

"What's that?" he says. "What did you say?"

The cold in the garage is making his hip burn, and his burns sting. He pulls out the gag, puts his ear close to the boy's mouth.

His breath is a white whisper. "I want my mummy."

The flat of his hand stings the boy's cheek.

He shoves the gag back in, damp with spittle and fear, and limps back around to the front of the van.

The sounds of his own panting fill his ears, and he pauses, drawing in deep lungfuls of air. He is fired up, alert, the adrenaline doing its job, but his body isn't as young as it once was.

The noise of his breathing recedes, and that's when he hears it. The unmistakable sound of footsteps scuffing the garage's concrete floor.

Brian freezes, holds his breath, but the sound of his own blood pumping around his head is too loud, and he lets it go with a *whoosh*.

There it is again. He spins around, his fingers closing around the scalpel in his jacket pocket, heart beating faster now.

During his sixty-seven years on this earth, Brian has seen many things. The ruined bodies of the corpses he has stolen, the shadows of death at the edges of his life. His father trained him to see it all, to feel his way around the jagged contours of other people's truths and insert himself into their stories without becoming a suspect.

He hasn't seen this, though.

In a patch of moonlight leaking through the square of the garage window is Erdman Frith. In his hand is the Bone Collector's hammer.

In an ordinary London street, on a lonely November night, Brian sees his past and future collide.

It is something he has always feared, and he senses its inevitability, as surely as darkness follows dusk.

A gust of wind sends the moon back behind her clouds. When he looks again, Erdman is gone.

Then he feels an explosion of pain at the back of his head.

He staggers against the van, raises a disbelieving hand to the wound, hears the distant cry of voices, moving closer and closer. There's smoke in his nostrils, the bob of a flashlight outside the garage, like a will-o'-the wisp. There is no point in running.

His fingers close around the scalpel in his pocket.

When the father comes at him again, he will be ready.

NINETY-THREE

3.33 a.m.

Erdman had never hit a man before. But he had heard a child's cry that sounded just like his son. Jakey was in that van, and he had to get to him, before the smoke curling under the door filled up the garage and the house collapsed around them.

He had swung the hammer wildly, and it had somehow connected. But the Bone Collector was not lying on the floor. He was moving back towards the doors of the van. To Jakey.

Panic pressed down on him. He raised the hammer again, and the man turned and smiled. Just like before.

A flower of pain opened up in Erdman's chest.

He dropped the hammer, fell to his knees. Blood blossomed on the concrete floor beneath him, a violent and beautiful vermilion.

Erdman saw the faces of his mother and father, of Jakey and Lilith. And a face just like his own. Everyone he had loved. Three he had lost.

The air around him seemed to flicker. No, just the walls of the garage moving. No, just the world ending.

He wondered if they were waiting for him on the other side, if the ghosts who had haunted the edges of his life would welcome him in death. He wondered if his own death would still their voices at last. Bring him peace.

But he didn't want to die. His family needed him. He needed them.

He tried to call his son's name, but his eyes were growing heavier now, his body's responses slowing, running down.

For so many years, he'd felt useless, a complete disappointment. First to his mother, and then to Lilith, and, heartbreakingly, to Jakey. Hopeless in the face of the illness consuming his son. Scared of hurting him when he played with him. Unable to reach his wife, whose pain and grief, he understood with sudden clarity, had forced her to withdraw rather than lean on a man she couldn't depend on.

But he didn't want to be that man anymore.

Jakey-boy. My champ. Daddy's coming.

Erdman struggled to his feet.

NINETY-FOUR

3.35 a.m.

The Bone Collector opens the van doors again.

He hunkers down on the damp mattress next to the boy, inhales the smell of his fear. His gag has slipped, and he is making a keening sound. He lifts his pajama top, steps cool fingers down the crooked cage of his ribs, strokes the ridge of his collarbone. The scalpel is in his other hand.

If he kills him now, the boy will be quiet.

"It's okay," he soothes. "It will be over soon."

The boy is watching the blade, senses the shift of air in the stillness. Then the Bone Collector feels a blast of pain in the back of his head, and the scalpel falls.

Fast-moving grey patches appear from nowhere, barking furiously, and police dogs surround him and the boy is crying, and the Bone Collector is being dragged outside into the street, the smoky night. Three officers—bloody animals, they are—shove him roughly and circle his wrists with metal, and there is DS Fitzroy, coming at him through the darkness, her face mangled and smudged with soot.

She can barely speak through her broken teeth, her ruined mouth.

"Where's Clara Foyle, you sick fuck?"

Her voice is not raised, but he can read the fury in her body: the defiant square of her shoulders, the flinty stare, the blood-flecked spittle flying from her lips.

He shrugs.

"Fucker," she says and shoves him hard in the chest. He loses his balance, stumbles backwards against the glinting metal of a police car. She raises her fist, connects with his nose. Gristle against bone.

He takes it all.

Chambers catches her arm, looks behind him. "What are you doing? The Boss'll see."

The Bone Collector is aware, on the periphery of his vision, of police officers clustering around Erdman Frith, of a voice in the radio calling for another ambulance. He hears the boy's sobs, and the soothing voice of a woman, the hiss of water, the subduing of fire. Feels the bite of steel around his wrists, and a sly kick in his ribs. Someone is setting up lights, and the white glare makes him squint.

He cannot bear to look at the ruin of his father's house.

Fitzroy is pacing the pavement. He watches her stride halfway towards the boy, and then back towards him, a bruise already darkening on her jaw, teeth loose and broken.

"Why, dear God, did you do it?"

He ponders her question, and settles on the truth. The evidence is everywhere. It won't take them long to discover the charred remains of his cutting room, the smoldering collection of bones. His eyes darken, reflecting the cold, bruised skies above.

"I'll answer your question, if you answer one of mine."

She shakes her head, disgust written in her features, but he knows that she will take the bait, that she cannot help herself. He folds chained hands in front of him and waits.

Eventually she nods, even though it looks like it costs her a great deal.

"How did you find me?"

Fitzroy narrows her eyes, looks down her nose at him. "Thanks to your little trick with the rabbit skeletons, your notes from John Hunter, we discovered your fascination with the Hunterian Museum.

"And one of the victims' family members recognized you, you smug little shit. And we realized that you worked at the hospital, that that was how you were finding and choosing your victims.

"So we raided your house. Except you weren't there. Because you were at your father's place. When one of your colleagues mentioned he had bequeathed you his house, it seemed the obvious place to look."

He nodded then, slowly. Karen, the fucking nosy bitch. There was no point in denials; they knew everything.

"We found your wife." She spat the words at him. "Did you kill her, too?"

Sadness spreads through him. "No," he says. "I did not."

"We've got a search warrant for your house, Mr. Howley. My officers are there as we speak. Now, answer my question. Why?"

He contemplates her words and looks thoughtful, as if considering the most precise way to put it.

"I was looking after them."

"What do you mean?"

"The bones. I was protecting them. A curator, if you like. Caring for my family's collection. It's my job, you see. My duty."

She gives a disgusted snort. "Thank you, Mr. Howley. Very fucking illuminating."

"I took care of them." He pauses. "I honored them."

"Where's Clara Foyle?"

He smiles. He can keep secrets, too.

Fitzroy's look is coolly appraising. She decides to tell him the rest.

"When the raid on your house was unsuccessful, the team headed back to the station. When they couldn't get hold of me, my colleagues searched my desk and found my notes. Your father's address." She smiles back. "They got here in time to watch it burn."

He pushes his face into hers, his breath on her cheeks, accusation in his eyes. "You did that."

She steps back, surprised. "The fire? No, that was nothing to do with me. But how old is the wiring in your father's house, Mr. Howley?" She laughs. "It's a bloody fire hazard."

She shoves him towards the police car, its lights transforming the houses into a kaleidoscope of electric blue. Fitzroy opens the door, pushes him into the backseat, and turns to go.

"Fitzroy!" he calls after her. She stops walking, but she doesn't turn around.

"I'm sorry for your loss."

That is all it takes. She spins on her heels towards him, anger and confusion blazing across her features, but there is something in his smirk that stops her in her tracks.

"Losing a baby is always *so* sad."

He permits himself a benign smile, and then he is driven away.

NINETY-FIVE

3.42 a.m.

Jakey blinked at the lights. To him, they were brighter than sunshine, and a woman with blood on her face was coming towards him, her fingers outstretched.

"It's okay, Jakey," the woman said. "You're safe now. My name is Etta, and I'm going to take you to Mummy and Daddy."

She reached for Jakey's hand, but the boy shrank away. His mother always told him not to go with strangers, and he wasn't going to make the same mistake again, especially not with someone who looked as scary as she did.

He glanced sideways, searching for Ol' Bloody Bones, scanning the faces of the men and women with their shiny flashlights that floated up and down in the darkness, but he couldn't see him. Although his movements were restricted, he had just enough flexibility to slide his hands into his lap, and turn his face into his shoulder. He shut his eyes.

"You're safe now," the woman called Etta said

again, crouching beside him on the damp pavement. "I promise."

Daddy had promised to keep him safe.

Through the cold night air, and the strangeness, and the smoke that hung over everything, Jakey imagined he heard his father's voice.

"Champ?"

Then he was there, his daddy, with his familiar smile, and a white bandage on his chest, and he was pushing past the woman, and crying, and wrapping his arms around him so tightly he couldn't breathe.

"DaddymydaddyIknewyouwouldcome."

His daddy had made him a promise. And this time he had kept it. His daddy had kept him safe. Jakey rested his head on his father's shoulder. The woman with blood on her face had smiley eyes, he noticed. She was watching them and she held out a carton of juice. Slowly, Jakey reached out his hand, and grabbed hold of his future.

NINETY-SIX

4.01 a.m.

DC Alun Chambers was thinking about the meal he would cook for his wife as a way of apologizing for all the hours he had worked on this case that had transfixed a nation. He was thinking about his children, whom he'd barely seen in the last ten days, and the way they always ran to their mother when they were hurt. He was thinking about the soft welcome of his bed.

His eyes lifted to the rearview mirror, to the suspect in the back. Brian Howley's head was bowed, his carved-out face in shadow. Chambers usually made some effort to chat with those in his custody. They were only people, after all. But for once, he didn't feel like talking.

Hell's teeth, he was exhausted. There was an ache in his temples that would only ease with sleep. Once he'd dropped Howley at the station for questioning, perhaps The Boss would stand him down.

His thoughts wandered to DS Fitzroy. He liked her. She was an enigma to him, but she was a good officer.

She deserved to shake off the tarnish of her mistakes, even if she hadn't learned yet to control her temper.

The city streets were beginning to awaken. He saw a cleaner hurrying along with an old vacuum in one hand, a cigarette dangling from her lips; a taxi driver lounging against his car outside the cab office. He followed the progress of a bum waving a tall can of something, Special Brew, probably. Perhaps he'd nip back when he'd got rid of Howley, try to find the man a shelter. It was too cold to be sleeping on the streets.

He deserved help, not scum like Howley, who would still get a roof over his head and food in his belly, in spite of everything he'd done.

DC Chambers's head was full of plans and ideas and random musings, and his eyes were tired, and it was winter dark.

Which was why he didn't see the fox dart into the road.

It froze for a moment, its eyes lit by the glare of the headlamps, and even at that moment, DC Chambers was still thinking.

Except this time it was, *Fuck.*

What happened next played out in a blur of image and sensation.

The police car swerved.

Chambers felt the seat belt pull against his shoulder.

The *thud* as the vehicle clipped the traffic lights at the pedestrian crossing.

A shout of warning from Howley.

The smudge of a red truck rushing at them.

A massive impact.

A roar of noise.

Nothing.

NINETY-SEVEN

Two months later

Some days, when she managed to drag herself from the tangle of sheets, Lilith was certain that someone was watching her. She might be in the bath, or gazing blankly at the television, or lying in Jakey's bed, burrowed into his warm little body, and all of a sudden, the tiny hairs on her arms would stand erect, and she would know that whoever it might be was out there again.

Some days there was warmth in the presence, and it softened the raw edges of her fear, enfolded her in its benevolence, made her feel lighter. Some days the sense of threat was so overwhelming, she would close all the curtains and crawl beneath the covers until she was certain it was gone, and even then she would be too frightened to move until the creeping pearliness of a late January morning filled her bedroom, and she could hear her neighbors leaving for work.

Some—poets, singers, Alyson fucking Carruthers—talked about the absence of a loved one as an *ache*.

Never was one word so insipidly inadequate. An

ache was what you felt when your tooth hurt, or from dancing in high heels, or from standing in one position for too long. The abduction of Jakey hadn't left an ache; it had left a gaping, bloodied crater.

But it would heal.

Jakey was alive. Her beautiful boy was alive. That was reason enough to keep the shadows at bay.

On that strange and terrible night, when she was lost and Jakey was found, Lilith had thought about swallowing every one of those pills.

But Erdman had refused to give up.

He had saved their son.

They had not warned her about the raid, the police. Lilith had been dozing in bed when Belinda Chong had hammered on the door at 4.57 a.m. She had jerked awake, that intrusive, alien sound dousing her in a sweat of adrenaline. The family liaison officer's face had been pale in the security light, the sheen of tears in her eyes.

For a frozen moment, Lilith could not breathe.

And then Belinda had lit up the silence between them with three simple words.

"We've got Jakey."

A sort of light-headedness overtook her, and her legs began to shake, and her knees had buckled, and Belinda was helping to do up the button of her jeans because her own hands were trembling too much, and then they were racing towards the dawn to get to the hospital.

There he was.

Her boy.

Her baby.

She had laughed and wept and kissed every part of his face until he squirmed away from her.

Then she had brushed her fingers across Erdman's cheek, and the two of them had stood, heads touching, and she had made a promise to herself to remember the purity of that moment for the rest of her life.

A few hours after Brian Howley's arrest (the media were dubbing him the Butcher of Bromley, but she couldn't bear to accord him the almost-mythical status of a serial killer, and she had refused to listen to the stories or look at the pictures), Fitzroy had come from her own hospital bed to see them.

Jakey was asleep. They were discharging him shortly. He was still weak from the pneumonia, from a lack of food, but they'd hooked him up to an IV line, and packed up a white paper bag with heavy-duty painkillers and antibiotics. The doctors were reluctant, but Lilith had insisted. Even though a fresh-faced PC was stationed outside his room, she didn't trust hospitals anymore.

The detective looked washed out, and she was wearing a loose T-shirt that made her look younger, gave her an air of vulnerability.

Her jaw was puffed up; some of her teeth were broken or missing. She would need surgery, she told them, to wire it shut as soon as the swelling had gone down. She was having trouble speaking.

After this brief exchange of greetings, Erdman had fetched plastic cups of tea, and Lilith had sat holding hands with him while Fitzroy had set hers down, untasted, with the sort of deliberate gesture that warned them the conversation was about to turn serious.

"He had a secret museum at his father's house, and

a makeshift laboratory in the cellar. Human bones, that sort of thing." Her voice was thick, hesitant.

Lilith bowed her head. Hearing confirmation spilling out of Fitzroy's mouth, well, it was a shock. She wanted to pretend that Jakey's abduction had been a surreal dream.

Fitzroy was talking again, so she forced herself to focus.

"Howley had an obsession with unusual or misshapen bones, and so did his father, it would seem. Marshall Howley only died recently, but early indications suggest he must have been in on it. Some of the remains that survived the fire appear to have been in situ for many, many years. We now believe that Howley—and probably his father—were responsible for the theft of Carlton's body." She reached for Lilith's hand, squeezed it. "And that Jakey was deliberately targeted because of his condition.

"As the hospital has probably told you, we haven't been able to ascertain how he abducted your son from the hospital. Extra CCTV cameras were installed in the hospital after a couple of bodies went missing from the Chapel of Rest last year. The Royal Southern managed to keep it quiet at the time and they paid off the families, but we now think it was probably Howley who took them. We also think Howley disabled the cameras before he took Jakey. They'd been covered with black plastic bags filled with glue. He'd told a passing colleague he was 'bagging' them for repairs."

"And my brother?" said Erdman.

"We're still running tests on DNA samples, but we do expect to confirm that it was Carlton's remains at Marshall Howley's property. We'll process the samples as quickly as possible, try to get you and your family some closure, but as you'll appreciate, there's a lot to get through."

Fitzroy took a sip of her tea and winced.

"He was using his job at the hospital as a way to find victims, both for his collection and as a means of making money. He would locate potential targets—we believe he became aware of your husband and son during your visit to the ER and realized the family connection—then used medical records to obtain addresses. He was also selling body parts to laboratories. We think he helped himself to a few bodies over the years. When we raided his home address, we also found a ledger that seems to suggest he was bribing a funeral director, whom we arrested a couple of hours ago. There was a piece of clothing, too, that may have belonged to Grace Rodríguez."

The pain in Fitzroy's jaw, in her heart, was making it difficult to speak, but she was determined to share what she knew with this family who had suffered so much.

"We assume Howley was planning to kill Jakey, and either sell his bones, or keep them for his museum. Thank God we got to him in time. But . . ." The detective suddenly found the pattern on her coat interesting.

"But, what?"

"I'll be honest with you, Mr. and Mrs. Frith, because I know that's all you've ever asked from us." She took another, cautious sip of tea. "I'm concerned for the safety of your son."

"In what way?" Erdman's face was pale.

Fitzroy had the grace to look embarrassed. She

pressed her knuckles to the tender length of her jawbone.

"Tell us," he insisted. "We'd like to know."

"In case Howley tries to finish what he started. When I arrested him, he was babbling some crap about protecting his bones, his collection. It's just rubbish, nonsense, the kind of self-justifying bullshit we sometimes get from suspects. Obviously, he needs a psychiatric evaluation."

"Is he going to get it?"

Fitzroy's face had shut down then, and she set her cup on Jakey's overbed table with exaggerated care.

"That's partly why I've come to see you both." She took a deep breath. "Belinda told you what happened last night?"

Erdman gave a tight nod.

"Well, the situation hasn't changed. As you know, Brian Howley never arrived at the police station. DC Chambers, the officer bringing him in, was badly injured in the accident, but there was no sign of Howley. Somehow he managed to free himself and simply walk away. By the time the paramedics arrived, he'd disappeared. We're looking for him, but he's still out there. Somewhere.

"We're watching his house. Both houses. We *will* find him, but until we do, I'd like to discuss the possibility of bringing Jakey into protective custody."

Howley was out there.

The bastard who had taken Erdman's brother, who had abducted her son, was still out there.

But go into protective custody? Remove Jakey from his home, his school, everything he knew? Her instinct was to refuse. Jakey had endured enough disruption. He needed stability, familiarity.

"Have you found Clara Foyle?" she asked, a deliberate diversionary tactic.

Fitzroy looked away then, wouldn't meet her eye. She pretended to stir her tea, even though Lilith knew she didn't take sugar.

"Believe me, Mrs. Frith, I won't stop looking until I do." Lilith believed her. The conviction in her eyes was impossible to feign.

The detective's face had taken on a grey-greenish pallor. "Excuse me, may I use Jakey's bathroom?"

Lilith tried not to listen to the sounds of retching and wondered if she should go in and check on her. Erdman raised his eyebrows. A few moments later, the toilet flushed and Fitzroy emerged.

"Sorry about that," she said, wiping her mouth gently with a tissue. "Must have been something I ate."

That was two months ago, and they hadn't had much to do with the police since then. The Frith family hadn't gone into protective custody. Erdman and Lilith had decided to live their lives the way they wanted to. To allow Jakey to live his. A panic button had been installed. A marked car had sat outside for a few nights, and there'd been the odd phone call, to make sure they were okay. Erdman had wanted them to move, talked endlessly about the possibility of a house by the sea, a fresh start. Of renting out their own house, selling Shirley's. But Lilith was content to wait. Nothing seemed to matter except spending time with Erdman and Jakey.

Until the package arrived.

It was a typical morning, or rather, typical of the

mornings that belong to those trying to rebuild their lives.

Jakey and his parents had eaten breakfast and talked about Carlton, and the little boy had insisted again that Clara was still alive, that she had helped him to survive in the Dark Place. The counselor said it was his coping mechanism.

Erdman's eyes had darkened, and Lilith had cuddled Jakey on her lap, and after a while, he had wriggled free and gone to play with his cars. Lilith had stroked Erdman's hair, and he had smiled down at her, then he had left to collect the surprise.

A short while later, the postman knocked on the door, and before she could gather herself to articulate a sentence, he deposited a package in her hands with a cheery, "There you go," and thrust a stylus pen at her for a signature.

"I haven't ordered anything," she protested.

He frowned, checked the notes on his docket. "Mrs. Lilith Frith, number two-two-seven Granville Terrace?"

"Well, yes, that's me, but I'm not expect—"

"Must be a present, then," he interrupted. "Enjoy."

She shut the door slowly, turning the box over in her hands. There was no return address, nothing at all.

Helping herself to a vegetable knife from the block on the worktop, Lilith made herself comfortable at the kitchen table and slit open the package.

A large white envelope fell out.

She lifted the flap, carefully removed its contents. She stared at it. A minute. Two minutes. It couldn't be. It must be a mistake.

She shoved it back inside the envelope.

Her fingers found their way to her mouth, and she bit down, splitting the nail. A deadening sense of shock settled over her. She slid her hand back into the envelope again and pulled out the monochrome X-ray of a twisted rib cage.

At first, she had thought it was part of Jakey's medical notes, forwarded by the police or doctors at the Royal Southern. But then she had realized. It was time- and date-stamped 24 November 2012.

Jakey had not been at the hospital that day.

He had been with Brian Howley.

Hands trembling, she pulled out another piece of paper. The loops and whorls of his writing marked out the flat, white expanse.

And you shall live.

Fear propelled her to the bookcase, and she pulled down her Bible, a battered relic from school. There it was. Another quotation from Ezekiel.

Was it a threat? Or a valediction?

She shivered, suddenly aware that the central heating hadn't come on and a thin January snow was falling. Under the kitchen spotlights, the black-and-white transparency glinted coldly.

She shut the curtains and locked all the doors and windows, and once or twice, she muttered a prayer.

She had never believed in ghosts.

But the bogeyman was real.

By the time Erdman arrived home an hour later, Lilith had hidden the X-ray at the back of her underwear drawer. There was no need to stir up old feelings. She would give it to Fitzroy, and the detective could decide what had to be done, and she would tell Erdman that she had changed her mind, that she did want that fresh start by the sea after all.

"Did you get it?" she said.

He was grinning as he opened up his jacket and showed her what was hidden inside. She smiled back at him, saw her own love for her family mirrored in his eyes.

"Jakey," she called up the stairs. "Can you come down here for a moment, please?"

"I've already finished my reading book."

"We've got something to show you."

As their son made his way downstairs, Lilith and Erdman shared a conspiratorial glance. A swell of gratitude crested inside her at this chance to remake her marriage, to try to be a different kind of mother to her son.

Jakey limped into the sitting room. His face was pinched and wary, the legacy of a time that would take him years to forget.

"What did you want me for, Mummy?"

Erdman moved towards their son, who had endured so much, who reminded them every day that hiding from life was no life at all.

He unzipped his coat and lifted the squirming puppy into Jakey's arms.

NINETY-EIGHT

Miles Foyle loaded the last of his suitcases into the back of the car.

Amy watched him do it. Now that the moment had come, she could not bear to watch him leave, but she did not know how to say that. Neither of them knew how to speak to each other these days.

"Drive safely," she said.

"I will," he said.

"When will you be back?"

"I don't know."

Miles patted his pockets. Felt for his passport, his wallet. His face was thinner now, unshaven. Fresh lines scarred his forehead and the delicate skin around his eyes. A colleague would be running his private GP practice while he took an extended leave of absence.

"Eleanor will miss you."

"She can come and stay for a bit when I'm settled. But I need to get away from London. I can't be here anymore." He bowed his head, fiddled with the strap of his watch. "I see her on every corner, Amy. I hear her in every child's voice." He lifted his eyes to meet hers, and she saw the anguish within. It reflected her own. His voice cracked. "I wasn't there. I wasn't there when she needed her daddy the most, and this place reminds me of that every single day."

Amy understood. God, she understood. But Eleanor was settled in school. She had friends, clubs. It would be cruel to uproot her now, when so much of her young life had already been ripped to shreds, a swatch of cloth caught on barbed wire.

"Is Gina coming out?" Her voice was light, casual. She was tired of arguments, of the weight of sadness that never seemed to lessen.

"I haven't spoken to Gina in weeks," he said carefully.

"Oh."

Amy tried to smile, but then tears were spilling down her cheeks, and they clung to each other as if that physical act would somehow bridge the crevice that had widened into a canyon in the days and weeks after Clara's disappearance.

"Will you be back for the memorial?"

"Of course."

"Detective Fitzroy has promised to come."

"That's good of her."

"Yes."

If he didn't get going soon, Miles would miss his flight.

"Will you be okay?" he said.

"I don't know."

"I can stay. If you want me to, I'll stay."

"I don't know."

Miles placed his arms gently around his wife, and felt her thin body shake. She wasn't wearing any makeup that morning and her nails were plain, unvarnished. He liked her better this way.

"I'll be back, I promise."

Her lips twisted into a smile, and she swiped at her nose with the tissue in her pocket. She carried them everywhere these days. Grief ambushed her in the most unlikely of places.

He opened the driver's-side door, started the engine. Amy hadn't seen this car before. He'd rented it, she guessed. He'd leave it behind at the airport. Just like he was leaving her behind. Disappointment settled on her like stone.

He wound down the window.

"You can come, too, if you like. With Eleanor. Sit on the beach. Eat nice food. Swim a bit." He held out his hand. "Forget for a while."

She reached out to touch his fingertips. "Sounds like a plan."

NINETY-NINE

Fitzroy stretched out her toes, luxuriating in the warmth and space of the bed. For once, she was on a rest day with no particular place to be, no pressing need to do anything except putter about at home. She ran her hand over the curve of her stomach.

She couldn't get used to sleeping alone.

In the still of the Sunday-morning city, she could just make out the faint beginnings of birdsong, and the shape of the Howley case file on her nightstand.

A thin wail rose from the crib in the spare room.

Fitzroy smiled into the darkness, and padded across the flat, bent over the crib, and picked up her nephew.

"'Morning, Max," she whispered. "It's a bit early to be waking up." He nestled his head into the crook of her shoulder, and she inhaled his sweet, sleepy smell.

Nina and Patrick were celebrating their wedding anniversary this weekend, and she had offered to babysit.

"Are you sure?" Her younger sister had looked wary, their relationship still feeling its way back to life. When Fitzroy had said that she was, Nina had flung her arms around her, and laughingly, she'd returned her hug.

David was not there. He had moved out a few weeks ago. A temporary arrangement, they'd agreed. So they could both sort out how they felt. But she still didn't know the answer to that.

Fitzroy carried her nephew back into her bedroom, to the tall window that stared out at the lights on the horizon.

He was out there. And she would find him. She would find Clara, too. She would never stop looking.

In the police interviews after his abduction, she had coaxed from Jakey his whispered conversations with Clara, the two sets of footsteps he had heard crossing the room next door.

So close. They had been so close.

The team had thrown everything into the search, thousands of hours, hundreds and hundreds of officers, but Howley and Clara were gone—not forgotten, not yet—but already fading like a painful memory.

Until Mrs. Frith's call last week.

News of the X-ray had unsettled Fitzroy. Was it a line in the sand? Or a warning?

Whatever his motive, it stirred in her a recollection of that day when they had found Jakey cowering in the back of the van, and she had realized that life, with all its fragilities and inconsistencies, was a gift.

After Chambers had driven off with Howley, Fitzroy had begged The Boss to let her back into that house. About to refuse, to tell her that it would be irresponsible and unprofessional and dangerous, he had seen the need tearing her features apart, and had changed his mind.

But it was nothing more than a smoldering ruin, a collapsing roof, too hot and too treacherous for anyone to enter.

So The Boss had driven her to the hospital instead.

"You did well tonight," he said, a meager compensation.

Alone, she'd returned a couple of days later, when the ash was still warm, to watch specially trained fire officers sift through the wreckage of so many lives.

Grace was dead. She watched them bring out her remains from an upstairs room in Marshall Howley's house. The skeleton's cervical ribs had been consistent with the teenager's hospital records.

But the intensity of the heat had destroyed most of the museum downstairs. There was no sign of Clara.

Not even when they searched and searched until night swallowed day, and Fitzroy dropped to her knees and joined them, scrabbling through the soot and debris, tears tracking down her filthy cheeks.

All that was left of his collection were a handful of bone splinters and a pile of dust, and Fitzroy's own memories of loss.

With trembling hands and a fractured heart, she had gone back to the silence of the flat, and picked up the phone to call her sister.

Now, with the arrival of Jakey's X-ray, he was taunting her again.

But she was coming for him.

Max's head grew heavy on her shoulder, his breath deep and even. His eyelids fluttered, and he made a whimpering sound in his sleep. She wondered where

Clara was, whether she was warm, whether he was hurting her.

Whether she was dead.

Her heart swooped and soared with the joy and fear of it all.

ONE HUNDRED

A weak February sun warmed Erdman's bones. It had been a long time since he'd felt able to tackle the garden, but here he was, cutting back roses, and pruning the hawthorn. Tidying up in readiness for the tenants, who were due to move in next week.

The song thrush had returned, there were piles of crushed shells on the patio, and its pretty voice cheered him.

The police still hadn't found Carlton's body. They had warned him it was unlikely they ever would. Traces of his DNA, yes. But the fire had been devastating, caused by a combination of faulty wiring and too much varnished wood, and by the time the fire crews had arrived, it was too late to salvage much of anything at all.

Over the weeks that had followed, he'd discovered his own way of handling grief. He had allowed himself to forgive his mother.

She had loved her family, and she had tried to protect him by keeping secrets. That knowledge had washed clean the stain of inadequacy he had worn for most of his life.

As for Lilith, last night she had reached for him in a way she hadn't done for as long as he could remember. The memory of her warm mouth made him weak.

Erdman dug his fork into the half-frozen earth, slipped off his old gardening coat, and hung it over the handle. He was thirsty. In the kitchen, he leaned against the worktop, now covered with boxes half-filled with crockery, and downed a cold Coke from a can.

"Champ?" he called. "Where are you?"

But Jakey didn't answer.

Not surprisingly, he had been quieter, more withdrawn, since the events of November, but Erdman and Lilith had promised themselves that they would not let *him* steal anything more from their son. From their family.

Christmas had been difficult. A simple meal and a few gifts for Jakey. The joy they had felt at the return of their son was tempered by the knowledge that Clara Foyle was still missing, and the fear that their son's ordeal had marked him in ways they could not see. But they had found a way through it by shutting out the world's media and focusing their energies on their boy.

Every night, after school, they played games together. On the weekends, they went to the cinema and chased a ball around the park, and Lilith had bought him a special helmet and protective pads so he could ride his bike. This time next week, they would be living by the sea in a lovely old house Erdman and Lilith had chosen together.

And if Jakey cried out in his dreams, and slept in their bed every night, so be it.

Slowly, he was coming back to himself.

Erdman found Jakey by the sitting room window, his puppy at his feet.

"Do you want a sandwich, champ? Or you can come and help me in the garden, if you like. I've got some weeding with your name on it."

His son looked up at him with haunted eyes.

"Are you okay, champ? What is it?"

For a long time, the boy didn't answer, but Erdman saw that his mouth was trembling, that he was folding in on himself, trying to make himself smaller, hidden. The counselor had warned them that this would happen, that the trauma of his ordeal would discolor the ordinary, that the shadows would always be there, threatening to block out the sun.

"Jakey?"

The boy turned his gaze back to the street outside. It was empty, just a few parked cars and a woman wheeling a bike.

"He's back, Daddy. I saw him. Ol' Bloody Bones is back."

ONE HUNDRED AND ONE

Finding somewhere to live was easy enough. No one wants to rent a drafty beach house in the middle of February, especially not one battered by winds sweeping in from the estuary.

The isolation suits him.

He sits in a chair by the window. A jagged flare of lightning illuminates the bay. Then the rain comes.

In the background, the radio rumbles on. A meteor has crash-landed in Chelyabinsk, Russia. That Paralympian with prosthetic legs has shot dead his girlfriend. And the police have still not found him.

Or her.

He swallows down his mug of tea. The dregs are cold, but he does not notice. He has paid his rent for six months. There's an option to buy, his new landlord said in his e-mail. If he likes living here.

He knows he will.

This house has three bedrooms. A boarded-up attic. A small garden for his rabbits.

He watches the waves crash against the harbor wall,

and feels at peace for the first time in weeks. His wife, he thinks, would have hated it. He misses her still.

The local newspaper is spread across the table. He turns the pages, pauses, intently reads a story. After fishing in the drawer for a pencil, he jots down a name. A street.

He writes a letter.

Later that day, he moves the mahogany display cabinets he bought at an antiques street market from the garage to the hallway. They are tall and narrow. They have glass doors.

He tries not to remember what he has lost.

He pictures the boy with the skewed skeleton, the Frith family house in the city with its FOR RENT sign, the ease with which he had pried their forwarding address from a temp at the professional cleaning firm, brought in to scrub away the history of its inhabitants along with the dust. He will bide his time, he thinks. Not yet.

Not yet.

As for the girl with the hands, the defeated eyes, her future is not yet decided. But there is no rush.

She is safe for now, undiscovered.

It is almost time, he thinks, to begin again.

A few days later, he leaves the house.

His hair is longer, much darker. A pair of wire-rimmed spectacles distract from his black eyes, a beard disguises his jaw, the hollows of his face. He wears a loosely fitting white shirt, soft faded jeans. He has put on some weight.

He follows the coastal path, gazes at the frothing sea. When the wind blows, he tastes salt in his mouth. It is fitting that he finds himself here, walking in the boot prints of his ancestor.

He walks through the Old Town until he finds the house he is looking for, squashed up against its neighbors. The window frames are painted white, the bricks an ugly contrast of brown and black.

He knocks on the door.

A young woman answers. She is twenty-five. She is wearing a dress patterned with floral sprigs and thick black tights. Her face is collapsing, her underdeveloped facial bones unable to support the muscles and tissues of her adult self. Her chin is small; her eyes slant downwards. Her blond hair hangs over malformed ears. Something about her reminds him of his wife.

He feels a joyous knocking in his chest.

"You came," she says, and a smile lights her face. "I couldn't believe it when I got your letter. Thank you." She dips her head shyly. "No one has ever asked to draw me before. I'm not your average"—she laughs—"model."

He cocks his head, smiles back. Runs his tongue along his teeth.

"The imperfection is the beauty," he says.

The young woman colors, and her fingers flutter to her face. The man is tall, and his presence seems to fill the door frame. He scuffs the sole of one of his shiny black shoes on the porch step.

Back and forth.

Back and forth.

He seems awkward, perhaps a little shy. It is endearing. She smiles up at him, encouraging. Before silence can stretch between them, she holds open the door, and the Bone Collector follows her in.

ACKNOWLEDGMENTS

There was once a girl who dreamed of becoming an author. Those dreams would have stayed that way were it not for those who have become a part of my own book of life.

Thank you to the incomparable Trisha Jackson from Pan Macmillan, who championed *Rattle* from the very beginning. It's been a joy working with you. Shout-outs must also go to Natasha Harding, Claire Gatzen, Anne O'Brien, and the fabulous Pan Mac publicity team.

Much love to my agent, Sophie Lambert, for her sharp eye, brilliant ideas, and unrivaled ability to tease from me a story worth telling. Your faith and friendship are valued.

To all the team at Conville & Walsh, especially Jake Smith-Bosanquet, Alexandra McNicoll, and Carrie Plitt, your skills really do help pay the bills.

I owe a great debt to all those who suffer from fibrodysplasia ossificans progressiva. Your stories inspired the character of Jakey Frith. Particular thanks must go to Chris Bedford-Gay, his son Oliver, and the charity FOP Friends; and to Nancy Sando, a founder of the nonprofit organization IFOPA, whose positivity and spirit taught me that this disease need not mean a life sentence. Jakey's condition was accelerated for the purposes of storytelling. Any mistakes concerning his disease process are my own.

Florin Feneru, Identification and Advisory Officer at the Natural History Museum, your knowledge and patience should be applauded. Very loudly. Again, any errors are mine.

Thank you to my lovely friends, who have asked enthusiastic questions and shared in my moments of excitement; to my writing buddies; to Richard Skinner and the Faber Academy crew.

I owe a very large drink to Keith Loakman, for letting me borrow the Bank; to Tracie Couper, for her amusing workplace anecdotes (her magazine is nothing like *Psychic Weekly*, by the way); and to Cherry Anthony, my very first reader.

Mum and Dad, I'm so grateful for your unconditional love, your unstinting enthusiasm, and all the unpaid childcare; Steve and Cein, see, you can finally read it now; thank you to Pops2, my most vocal champion; and to Steve Bliss, the copper in the family. Any inaccuracies concerning police work are my fault, not his.

Thank *you*, reader, for buying this book. Writers are nothing without their readers. I hope the eagle-eyed amongst you will forgive me the liberties taken in altering the names of a few of Blackheath's beautiful streets.

Every story has its heroes, and these are mine.

My Isaac and Alice, who never complain about the weekends I spend in front of the computer, the untidy house, the half-empty fridge. You are a continual source of joy.

Lastly, Jason: Who makes me fall in love again every day. Who provides endless cups of tea and tissues. Who saves my words (and my sanity) when I nod off over the laptop. Who is full of ideas and encouragement, and is always in my corner, spurring me on.

So, this one's for you, lovely boy. You believed in me before I dared to believe in myself.

Connect with
Us